SHENG KEYI

Northern Girls

Life Goes On

Translated from the Chinese by Shelly Bryant

CHINA LIBRARY

PENGUIN BOOKS

UK | USA | Canada | Ireland | Australia
India | New Zealand | South Africa | China

Penguin Books is part of the Penguin Random House group of companies
whose addresses can be found at global.penguinrandomhouse.com.

Penguin
Random House
PENGUIN BOOKS CHINA

This paperback edition published by Penguin Group (Australia)
in association with Penguin (Beijing) Ltd, 2015

1 3 5 7 9 10 8 6 4 2

Text copyright © Sheng Keyi, 2004
Translation copyright © Shelly Bryant, 2012

Originally published in Chinese as *Bei Mei* by Changjiang Literature and Art Press

The moral right of the author has been asserted.

Cover design by Di Suo © Penguin Group (Australia)
Text design by Steffan Leyshon-Jones © Penguin Group (Australia)
Illustration by Rania Ho © Penguin Group (Australia)
Printed and bound in China by South China Printing Company

National Library of Australia
Cataloguing-in-Publication data:

Sheng, Keyi.
Northern Girls: life goes on/Sheng Keyi
9780670076161 (paperback)
Women--China--Fiction.
Women internal migrants--China--Fiction.

895.16

penguin.com.cn

A Note on Chinese Usage and Names

In Chinese, a person's given name always follows their surname. Therefore, the protagonist of *Northern Girls*, Qian Xiaohong, has the surname Qian and the given name Xiaohong. Depending on the occasion and the familiarity between people, given names can be shortened to a repetition of the final syllable, such as Honghong for Xiaohong.

In southern China, it is common for people to refer to one another by combining the sound *Ah* with the final syllable in their name, for example, *Ah* Hong. Whilst pinyin, the standard Romanisation method for Chinese characters, has been used throughout this novel, the word *Ah* has been written as such to avoid confusion with the word 'a'.

Northern Girls

Northern Girls

Sheng Keyi was born in southern China's Hunan Province. After working in Shenzhen for many years, she moved to Beijing where she now lives. *Northern Girls*, first published in 2004, established her at the forefront of the 'post-70s' group of writers in China, tackling themes of urbanisation, social upheaval and gender issues. She is an award-winning author of several novels such as *Death Fugue* and collections of short stories including *Fields of White* which was published as a Penguin Special.

ONE

I

Her. Right there. That's Qian Xiaohong, from Hunan province.

A little over a metre and a half tall, sporting short black hair with just a hint of a curl, her round-faced look is pretty much that of a model citizen, good and decent. She's just the sort of girl a guy wouldn't mind taking home to meet his parents. However, her breasts – through no fault of her own – are much too large for civilised, polite society. Such breasts could not help but invite the same suspicion and groundless gossip normally saved for young widows.

Xiaohong's breasts, to put it bluntly, are gorgeous! Even observed through clothing, it's easy to imagine their consistency. To touch them must be heavenly. To simply gaze upon them is to fall under their seductive power. The problem is that same unavoidable difficulty that always arises in tight-knit communities. When everyone is cast from the same mould, the person who stands out for any reason at all is sure to be seen as something of a maverick. And so, Xiaohong's full figure has always made her just a little too striking in the eyes of those around her.

Xiaohong's mother died of cirrhosis of the liver at a young age. Her chest was as flat as could be so it's clear the child gained nothing by inheritance. From then on, Xiaohong was brought up in the shelter of her paternal grandmother's bosom.

Her grandmother, a widow for fifty years, passed away at the age of eighty. She was the only one who knew the secret behind Xiaohong's well-endowed physique, but she went to the grave without ever breathing a word of it.

Ever since Xiaohong was in year five of school, rumours had surrounded her. There was always a stinging word hissed in her direction, ever a pointing finger trailing in her wake. All the other girls in the village dutifully hunched forward, guarding their chests under loose-fitting clothing, doing all they could to prevent their breasts from giving the slightest impression of sluttiness. Only Xiaohong allowed her twin bulging mounds to appear as openly and ominously as storm clouds descending upon an unsuspecting city. It was a rare gift she had, the way she carried that pair, and no one could deny that it required courage for her to do so.

At the ripe old age of thirteen, Xiaohong lost all interest in her studies. As soon as she finished middle school, she dropped out, preferring to take life easy and hang around the village.

Her father's work regularly took him away from home for weeks at a time. When he was back, Xiaohong would run and sit on his lap like a little girl, cuddling up to him, cheek to cheek. The villagers would look at them askance. Clearly the affection between father and daughter made them uncomfortable. He worked as a contractor and, with his earnings, built a two-storey house with suites on each floor. Both the interior and the exterior of the house had a more cosmopolitan air than anything in the city. Xiaohong chose for herself a room on the upper floor with a private staircase running up the outer wall.

Noticing that her family seemed to have a little money, some guys had hopes of becoming Xiaohong's man. It was often said that her earliest involvement with the opposite sex came when she was in primary school, first hooking up with boys from the secondary school, and later moving on to the young men of the village. She brought them home, each leaving his impression on her bed. Some claimed that, during the summer months, she sometimes did it while out enjoying the cool evening breeze. She was even known to go at it in broad daylight inside the large culvert at the power plant. Such was Xiaohong's reputation, and it rolled over the village in waves.

Xiaohong's only sibling was a sister eight years older than her. When she was ten, Xiaohong, her sister and their grandmother used to all squeeze into one room, the two girls sharing a bed. After her engagement, Xiaohong's sister, assuming that the younger girl would be none the wiser, often welcomed her fiancé to join them in the crowded bed.

Xiaohong and her brother-in-law got along well, very well indeed.

While village tittle-tattle was not always to be believed, spine-tingling tales about the activities of Xiaohong and her brother-in-law ran rampant on the village grapevine, and the odds were that they were true, too. Things finally came to a head in the year following her grandmother's death, when Xiaohong turned sixteen. That spring, the fields were wild. Oilseed rape plants spread out to the horizon, rippling like golden waves in the breeze. One day, she was about a mile outside of the village, working in the fields with her sister and brother-in-law.

'I'm so thirsty,' she said, and turned with a swing of her hips to head for home.

The way her rump swayed as she retreated was all that was needed to turn her brother-in-law's insides to jelly. As the poets say, spring – when the bees are dancing and the sun caresses your skin – is the time for mating. So who could blame the girl's brother-in-law for wanting to sleep wrapped in the arms of a good woman? On most nights, his wife would lie beneath him just like the third-of-an-acre plot he worked all day, quietly letting him plough her as he had the soil – and just as unmoving in response to his touch. With this in mind, the poor man suddenly lost the will to continue his work. He twisted his body this way and that, contorting himself in the oddest manner, frowning intensely. After a few moments of letting it brew, he finally succeeded in emitting a loud fart.

'Oh, my stomach!' He shouted, 'I think I've got the runs!' The urgent expression he wore made it seem he was in a desperate state.

'Ever notice how frequently lazy folks have to find a toilet?' his wife said. 'Go on. Looks like you'd better hurry.'

He set off at a trot.

The diligent woman kept at her work, placing each sprout neatly in its own hole and the pepper seeds in rows as orderly and pleasing as a well-embroidered fabric. When she'd finished, she looked over her handiwork with a maternal eye and smiled in contentment, her face as brown as the petals of a wilting flower. She was now in need of a little water herself, and the other two still hadn't returned. The wind blew over her solitary figure, her dusty drab overalls covered in mud. With her feet immersed in the loose soil, she looked exceptionally short. After a while, she climbed the ridge. Bringing her right hand to her forehead, she sheltered her squinting eyes and looked towards the family home lying in the distance. The tiled walls her father had built glistened like gold in the sunlight, as if thousands of precious jewels flashed before her, but there was no sign of her sister or her husband.

Beginning to have some misgivings, she slapped her hands together to remove the clods of soil, left the patch of land she had been working, and made her way home dejectedly. She went to the outside toilet, but her husband was not there. Could he have gone to the kitchen to get some water? No one was there either. In her heart, she began to feel a sense of dread, some vague notion of what must be going on.

She climbed the outer stairs to Xiaohong's bedroom, one hand clutching her chest, the other braced against the wall. She opened her mouth wide to breathe, feeling a little dizzy in the bright afternoon sun.

The door, unlatched, was open about an inch.

'*Feng Ge*, you need to get dressed and go. She's going to start suspecting something.'

'She's too blind to ever notice.'

'But what if she *does*?'

'She won't.'

'What if you knocked me up this time?'

'You bear it, I'll raise it.'

Legs trembling, Xiaohong's sister kicked the door open with a bang and stood there, the doorway framing her shape. With the sun behind her, she cast a long shadow that fell across the room and onto the bed, drawing a line between the two faces that lay there.

A bee flew past her, buzzing into the room. Dust motes danced in the long rays of the sun.

All was deathly silent.

Without a hint of embarrassment, Xiaohong slowly sat up and began to dress herself. At first, she'd been afraid of hurting her sister, but now that they were face to face, she felt relief, as if a cairn of stones had tumbled to the floor. Saying nothing, she finished dressing, simply turning her back to the door as she waited for her sister's tirade to begin.

Her brother-in-law stood up, his naked body quivering all over, as if he had just completed the most exquisite act of his life. His wife stood there muttering, her face puckered in anger, wrinkly as a bitter gourd. She gazed breathlessly at his naked body. A sudden *whoosh* escaped her lips before she covered her face and ran. Rushing down the stairs, she came to an abrupt halt, feeling that things were the wrong way round. She thought, Isn't that little bitch the one who should be ashamed? Why isn't that bastard running away? I didn't do a fucking thing wrong! Why am I the one fleeing?

With that thought, she let it fly, her voice crashing through the house with her wailing and weeping.

'You bastard! You shameless hussy! What a cheap, rotten pair! Don't you even give a fuck about our reputation?'

She raised her voice higher and higher, as if in hope that the whole neighbourhood would come to support her cause. And sure enough, no sooner had the cries of condemnation been raised than they all crawled out from their little holes, coming from all directions, like ants scurrying over a disturbed mound. They rushed madly to the scene, and gathered in a mass at the foot of the stairs.

II

'You'd better disappear from this place for a while. I'll handle your sister.' The way he spoke, it seemed as if her brother-in-law already had his wife well under control.

'And you? Don't you need to slink off somewhere and hide?' she asked bitterly.

'Nah. You gotta start thinking about marriage. Me, I'm a guy. So it makes no difference to me. No big deal,' he said, flippantly.

Xiaohong swallowed the words she wanted to say, thinking it best to keep her thoughts to herself.

The next day, she set out for the county guesthouse to see if she could get a job as a receptionist.

Upon arrival, she saw that the guesthouse was a three-storey building with plaster peeling off the outer walls. The road in front of it and the boundary walls were all of a uniform bare concrete, clearly neglected since the day they had been built. Xiaohong put what had happened in the village out of her mind, telling herself, It isn't really incest when it's with a brother-in-law. Men with their son's wives, women with their husband's brothers – it's not like any of it is exactly rare. At first, she was afraid she would end up pregnant with her brother-in-law's baby, but then her 'Aunt Flo' came right on schedule, signalling another turn in the cycle of life.

Amongst the staff at the guesthouse, Xiaohong's curvaceous figure was as eye-catching as ever. She carried herself with a measure of pertness, her tail wagging as she walked like a bitch in heat. The sight of those swaying hips inspired a lustful admiration in a good many of the guesthouse's male patrons, who would call the reception desk and try to strike up a little banter with her. She was gracious enough to entertain their attentions, giving the odd coquettish giggle as if someone had tickled her under the arm.

Once, Xiaohong was chatting away with a fellow from the northeastern region of China when he said, 'Why don't you pop in later and I'll let you taste some special delicacies from the north?'

When her shift ended at midnight, she went to his room. He opened the door and, as she squeezed past him into the small quarters, he poked her in the side and said, 'What a tiny waist!' Tickled, she twisted away from him. Her two grand peaks pressed flat up against the wall, only to bounce back into the fullness of their proper shape when he had closed the door. There was a musty smell in the cramped room, which had yellowing walls and a grungy quilt thrown across the narrow bed. Beside it was a nightstand topped with an ashtray holding a single smouldering cigarette butt. White smoke rose up from it in a wispy trail. Xiaohong's acquiescence to the handsome northern guy's skilful exploration of her body seemed to fill him with an even larger measure of courage. Apparently having never seen such voluptuousness, he pressed his hand to her breast with great fervour, as if wanting to confirm that what he held was indeed the real thing. His hands moved over her body at a giddying pace. He needed both hands to do justice to a single breast, squeezing it like a balloon between his palms. As he entertained himself in this way, Xiaohong's moans in response tickled his eardrums like the hum of a mosquito. Suddenly remembering something, she pulled back. With a flick of her eyelashes, she asked, 'Where are those northern delicacies you promised?'

He leaned in close and murmured, 'I'm right here.'

She smirked in response.

He boldly moved his hand to her lower parts, but again she pulled away.

'You playing hard to get?' he asked with a laugh.

'It's that time of the month,' she replied. 'I can't do it.'

Shrugging in obvious disbelief, he said, 'I'll pay you.'

'See for yourself,' she said, crudely raising her skirt and lowering her underwear.

Seeing the spot of blood, the northern guy said, 'Never mind that. I don't care if things get a little messy. That should prove just how much I like you.'

She thought about her hometown and the taboos she'd inherited in regard to the female cycle: don't look, don't touch. Ignoring those rules, everyone back home said, would bring a person the worst sorts of misfortune. City folk were certainly different.

She turned her most charming smile on him and, noticing how pleasant-looking he was, said, 'You look like a teacher.'

'I am,' he replied, 'Secondary school.'

She bit her lower lip then asked, 'You aren't married?'

'I am,' he said again. 'This is all *because* I'm married.'

Xiaohong didn't see any logic to such a relationship.

'It's only after marriage that you can have an affair. Your mind can't stray if you don't already have a wife. But, I guess you wouldn't understand,' the northern guy said.

'No, why would I?' she retorted. 'I'm going to clean up.'

She went into the washroom and freshened up, enjoying the cool of the water as it splashed against her skin. When she had finished, she still felt a bit uncertain about going any further with the northern man. In the end, persuaded by her own body, she went at it with gusto. Gasping, the man showed equal enthusiasm, flipping her body first one way, then the other, like a fish twitching back and forth at the end of a line.

When they were done, he asked, 'How much?'

Dumbfounded, she replied, 'Huh? How much what?'

The guy froze for a second, his surprise seemingly even greater than her own. 'Why... money.'

'For what?' she asked.

'For hooking!' he answered.

III

Cars passed back and forth, kicking up billows of dust, interrupted by long buses crunching their way along the gravelly road. Xiaohong wore a blue tank top and short skirt, exposing nearly as much flesh as an innocent nappy-clad infant. She stood beneath the sign at the bus stop cracking sunflower seeds, utterly bored as she watched the flow of traffic. Many things passed through her mind – like the first time she'd been with a boy and the whole mess with her brother-in-law. Standing there, it was as if all her random musings were being crushed beneath the passing tyres, drifting away on clouds of dust.

Xiaohong's cleavage was a deep gulley, forming an axis down the length of her body, a straight line flowing downward from the tip of her nose to the space where her thighs branched out to either side. It was to that critical spot that the imagination flowed, as all rivers flow to the sea, their natural destination. Everyone at the bus stop, both men and women, took note of her bust line, and it set their minds wandering. The women, filled with a mixture of reluctant admiration and envy, stuck their noses in the air indignantly. The men felt their bodies begin to stir, their minds coming to life to entertain all sorts of obscene fantasies.

The bus rambled in like an old drunkard. As it pulled over, the eyes of all the passengers fell onto the bus stop through the window – or, to put it more accurately, onto Xiaohong's cleavage. In a place this small, it took guts to show off so much skin. The men waiting for the bus, cursing their luck at its arrival, took one last long look at the girl, and then one by one climbed aboard. Xiaohong hummed the lyrics of a popular tune, her feet casually tapping the ground as she sauntered over to the bus queue.

She squinted to protect her eyes as the wind kicked up another round of dust. When she opened them, all she saw was a puff of smoke from the back end of the bus as it puttered away. She stomped her foot and cursed, her chest heaving.

'Xiaohong! Xiaohong!' The female voice calling her name was coming from the end of a long shadow. Xiaohong spied a fluffy head of hair like a spruced-up bird's nest, great bobbing silver earrings and scarlet lips spread in a wide smile.

'Yang Chunhua!' she shouted. Chunhua, the girl who had shared a desk with Xiaohong at school, stood before her, dressed like a whore without being the least bit sexy.

'What you been doing?' Chunhua asked, eyes aimed straight at Xiaohong's chest.

'Just working at the county guesthouse.'

'Making good money?'

'One-fifty.'

'Working for peanuts! You ought to find a job at my friend's company.' With that, Chunhua clucked her tongue and led Xiaohong off by the hand.

They walked a short distance to an area with lots of restaurants and entertainment – not exactly prosperous, but lively enough. The narrow uneven streets were lined by posters bearing patriotic slogans, dust-covered leaves dangled from branch ends, and betel nuts were being chomped between the teeth of passersby. Everywhere you looked life bubbled, like a pot of water at full boil. As the girls made their way along the streets, Chunhua clung tightly to Xiaohong's hand as if afraid she'd fly away.

Walking through a wide shuttered gate and past a row of counters to reach the office, the girls saw several men chatting on a black sofa, engulfed in a cloud of cigarette smoke. A girl at a desk pecked away at the keys of a calculator. Chunhua called, 'Hi boss. This is my old classmate. Whaddya think?' Xiaohong was startled by the falsetto of Chunhua's voice.

The boss, a man named Mr Tan, stood up. He was forty-ish, balding, not too tall, and a little too broad. Sweeping his eyes over Xiaohong's most prominent features, he smiled and waved to her with the hand holding his cigarette.

'What's your name?' he asked.

'Oh, she's *Qian*, as in the character for money; *Xiao*, as in small; *Hong*, as in red,' Chunhua replied for her, moving to sit next to a young man who quickly wrapped an arm around her waist. Xiaohong offered Mr Tan a bright smile.

'Good. You can start tomorrow.' He didn't waste any time on the formalities.

That evening, Mr Tan got a private room at the Springtime Restaurant and hosted a business dinner. Guests of honour were the Red Flag Chemical Plant manager, Mr Liu, a department store manager, Mr Zhang, and the import-export company representative, Mr Li. Xiaohong toasted them all on behalf of Mr Tan. Mr Liu, face as flushed as a suckling pig served at a New Year's feast, kept his eyes glued to the curve of Xiaohong's bust, much to her irritation. Xiaohong, not schooled in the art of refusing a drink, swallowed glass after glass without spilling a drop. She had never drunk alcohol before and she soon began to feel light-headed, as if she had been sitting in a classroom on a hot summer afternoon with the chirp of cicadas lulling her into a state of numbness. She felt drowsy. The men, all with bloodshot eyes by now, each took it in turn to toast Mr Tan. Xiaohong, knowing the dinner was far from over, made her way to the washroom, first clearing her bowels, then vomiting, before heading back to the table to start all over again. Cup after cup they drank, moving from 120-proof white spirit to sorghum spirit, from sorghum spirit to red wine, and from red wine to draft beer. She felt like her stomach was a gutter. When the guests were at their jolliest, Xiaohong accepted one final grand toast in honour of Mr Tan. Chunhua sat looking on the whole while in astonishment.

The next day Mr Tan, bald head even shinier, said, 'After grinding away for so long, we've finally broken through. And the money is going to be good! Red Flag is a big enterprise, and getting in with them is no small matter. We oughta be able to make do for a year or so now. Come here. There's something I want to show you.'

When he opened the warehouse, Xiaohong saw a heap of scrap metal.

'Valves. The copper in each one is worth hundreds of *yuan*,' Mr Tan said.

It was as if Mr Tan had brought her into a treasure trove, making her feel in equal measures flattered and overwhelmed. She hardly knew what to do with herself. What contribution had she made to the company that Mr Tan should hold her in such high regard?

'Drinking always brings out a person's true character. I can tell you're a straight, trustworthy girl. And I'm always a good judge of people,' Mr Tan said, as if he'd read her mind.

After a moment, he added, 'Tomorrow, I want you to start sleeping in the warehouse. There's a small room there with a bed, blanket and television.'

'You're the boss!' It was the first time Xiaohong had ever sucked up to anyone.

'You catch on fast,' he said, pleased.

*

Within a few days, Xiaohong had figured out that Chunhua was virtually a concubine. Her lover was Mr Tan's counterpart, also engaged in the scrap metal business. His name was Ma Xun, but everyone in his office called him 'Boss'. In fact, Xiaohong noticed that everyone around here loved to be called 'Boss'. Even if a man ran nothing more than a small betel nut stall, his customers would shout, 'Hey, Boss!' in greeting, much to his pleasure – and theirs, since it usually resulted in discounted betel nuts. Mr Tan told her that he and Mr Ma were bound as tightly as brothers. Chunhua had originally worked for him, and had made a good impression at business dinners, but when Mr Ma wanted to pry her from his grasp, Mr Tan had given her up with an open-handed generosity. 'Wasn't it better like that?', he asked through yellowy smoke-stained teeth.

Just after she received her first month's salary of 400 *yuan,* she was invited over to Chunhua's for a round of mah-jong. The two girls planned to relax together and renew their old friendship. They only played for small stakes, not more than a couple of *mao* a game. Luck was with Xiaohong and she picked up twenty or thirty *yuan* during the course of the evening. Mr Ma sat across from Chunhua, and chatted to Xiaohong about her work. He was as content losing a hand as winning. Xiaohong spoke candidly of her gratitude to Chunhua, saying she had earned 400 *yuan* this first month. Mr Ma nodded and said, 'Not bad. Keep it up.'

Chunhua glanced at Mr Ma and he winked at her. Xiaohong noticed and wondered what they were up to. Figuring that the pair didn't want to talk about it in front of others, she pretended she hadn't noticed. After a moment, she felt something tap against her under the table.

'Something on your mind, Chunhua?' she finally asked, unable to stand it anymore.

Chunhua, with a conspiratorial smile, said, 'There's a simple way we can make a lot of money, but I don't know if you're up for it.'

'What would I have to do?'

'You've got a key to Mr Tan's warehouse, right?'

'Yeah.'

'Well, you know how much the stuff in there is worth?'

'Yeah, I know.'

'Mr Tan's got a great big inventory and he wouldn't notice if it was down by just a little each month. I know where you can get a lot of money for that scrap on the streets. You bring it to us and we'll help you sell it. We'll split the money sixty-forty, or seventy-thirty, or whatever. After a few months, we leave town. Whaddya think?'

Lost for words, Xiaohong thought to herself, So that's how 'tightly bound' Mr Ma is to Mr Tan, huh? Aloud, she only said in a sedate tone, 'Let me think it over.'

Actually, she had already considered the possibility before, going so far as to attempt to smuggle out a few metal pipes worth 500 *yuan* or so. Having walked a short distance with them hidden under her blouse, she felt the metal suddenly get very hot. The streets had been empty that night, willow branches swaying along the side of the road, their rhythm driving her own heartbeat to an even higher tempo. She felt like a thief.

Xiaohong, are you so greedy for a few extra *yuan*? she berated herself, her curses stirring her to such an extent that she felt she was hovering above the street. Thus, she had turned around and walked back to the warehouse, putting everything back where it belonged.

She didn't discuss the plan further with Chunhua. She felt caught between two loyalties. On the one hand, she had a boss who trusted her, and on the other she had a friend who had served as her benefactor. If she didn't go along with the plan, Chunhua would suspect she had told on them. But if she did go along with it, not only would she be letting Mr Tan down, but if things didn't go right, they could get caught. It seemed Chunhua thought of her as a mouse and had purposely released her into Mr Tan's granary. But, Xiaohong thought, While I might have stolen glances and a few hearts, I never stole anything for money! Moved by her own decency, she thought, I'm actually kind of virtuous.

Later that night, Xiaohong lay on her bed in the guard room, staring all night at the glimmer of the white walls. She finally came to a lamentable resolution: she would resign. She remembered seeing a restaurant near the bus stop that was hiring and thought it worth having a look.

The next day, she went to Mr Tan and told him of her decision. He sat, as always, with a cigarette clasped between his fingers.

'Xiaohong,' he said, 'if you're unhappy with something, feel free to tell me. Don't leave in a temper.'

Waving her hands, she quickly said, 'No, no, it's nothing like that. You've been very good to me, Boss. The work is good. How could I be unhappy with anything?' She was embarrassed and a little breathless. One of the buttons popped off the front of her blouse and dropped to the floor, rolling under Mr Tan's desk. Her blouse was obviously too tight, or her breasts too unwilling to be bound by the conventions of the world around her. Xiaohong didn't even notice.

As she turned to leave, Mr Tan tried another tactic, hoping to change her mind. 'I'll give you another 300 *yuan*.'

Xiaohong wasn't interested. 'Why would you offer me money?'

'Consider it a bonus,' he replied.

'I don't want it. I didn't do anything to deserve it.'

'What is it you want, then? Do you think the 300 *yuan* will be some sort of black mark against you? Or that refusing it will make you noble?'

'I just don't deserve it. Mr Tan, don't you ever worry about backstabbers?'

'Sure. It's a big jungle, so it's no surprise if you meet all sorts of beasts.' Mr Tan didn't even bother to try to hide his own experience in this area.

'You've been around a lot longer than I have. I'm sure you know much more than I do about the way such betrayals go.' Xiaohong was trying her best to at least drop him a hint.

'You don't need to worry about me. Trust me, Xiaohong,' he said, beginning to chuckle, 'I know all about it.'

'You know? What the hell do you mean *you know?*'

'Let me tell you something, Xiaohong. That whole scheme with Chunhua was all my idea. Let me formally apologise to you. I have no reservations about your loyalty now.'

So that's how it was. As the offense of it began to sink in, Xiaohong said evenly, 'But Mr Tan, the problem is, I don't trust *you* anymore. Best of luck to you.'

IV

'You're hiring, right?'

Xiaohong had stormed out of Mr Tan's place and hoofed her way over to the Contentment House Diner. The manager, a woman in her thirties, glanced up, displaying a face plastered with makeup – liner-blackened eyes, mascara-curled lashes, lips painted pig-blood red – and earrings dangling almost to her shoulders with hoops as big as the hand-grips on a bus. Xiaohong felt that all it would take was a smile on that face and the whole façade would crumble, tumbling to the ground in a dusty heap.

The manager inspected Xiaohong, eyes running a couple of times up and down her length. She smiled faintly as her gaze came to rest on the girl's breasts and asked, 'Why don't ya come and tell me about your experience?'

'What experience?' The testy tone of the question caught Xiaohong off guard.

'I mean your work background, of course. You didn't think I was asking about experience in the bedroom, did ya?' The woman reached over and turned up the radio by her side.

Xiaohong knew all about what went on in bed, and even knew that the correct terminology for it was 'lovemaking'. She didn't get what the hell all that had to do with her getting a job. Obviously, this woman was just toying with her.

Just then an unkempt man emerged from a back room, mumbling, 'You an applicant?'

'Yeah,' she answered huffily, 'and I got plenty of experience at work, and in the bedroom, too!'

'Girl, you've got spirit,' he said, a little stunned. 'How old're you?'

'Who cares?' the manager butted in, with a pronounced roll of the eyes. 'I say she's not cut out for work here.'

'I'm sixteen, and I've got plenty of *fucking* experience,' Xiaohong retorted. She could tell the older woman felt threatened by her. Young as she was, she'd learned a thing or two about the female psyche, and she could see clearly enough how other women felt about her.

'Sixteen, hm? Well, you're no child, are ya? You done restaurant work before?' He was obviously attracted to her.

'Shut up and get out!' The manager put on a stern face and started shooing the man out, as if he were a stray chicken that had wandered in from out the back.

Xiaohong was puzzled by the man's comment. Things that attracted men didn't seem to go down so well with women, she thought. Male tastes were forever at odds with what women liked.

The man slouched, his trousers slithering lower over his scrawny backside as he turned to shuffle out from under the manager's onslaught. Lost in thought, Xiaohong nearly gave herself a black eye when she ran into the diner's glass door as she made her own way out.

Back on the sunlit streets, with every step, her foot landed right on the head of her shadow, shortened in the midday glare. Dazed, she nearly stepped into the gutter, barely managing to avoid a lump of rotten watermelon. Its mushy red pulp was spotted with a smattering of black flies that she at first mistook for its seeds. They buzzed about, scattering away from the squishy mound as she stepped over it, only to fly in a circle before settling back down to their putrid meal once again. She averted her eyes, looking up into branches too withered to offer any relief from the heat. Her stomach churned. I'm so bloody thirsty, she thought.

She dug out a coin and bought a banana-flavoured ice lolly. Sucking on it, she began to take note of the posters plastered on the wall beside her, promising miracle cures for sexually transmitted diseases, prostate problems, syphilis symptoms and the like. Nothing that seemed to indicate a demand for her services.

'Hey!' Was that someone calling her, or was she hallucinating in the heat?

'Hey!' he called again, this time beckoning her to come over. The man with not enough backside to hold up his trousers had followed her, now slouching so much that he almost looked like a hunchback.

'Why don't ya see if my friend has work at his place?' he said, in a suggestive tone that let her know what he hoped the night had in store.

Xiaohong took one more merciless drag on the ice lolly, leaving only a tiny sliver of ice, which she withdrew just long enough to say, 'Lead the way.'

She continued to relish the remnants of the ice lolly in the way she'd done since childhood, sometimes sucking on it vigorously, sometimes slowly licking its length. The man looked straight ahead, his Adam's apple bobbing frantically up and down.

'You thirsty?' she asked. 'I'll get you an ice lolly.'

'No thanks. Let's just get to my friend's place and I'll get some tea,' he said. 'And, uh, when we get there, just say you're my niece, alright?'

She stole a glance at him, nibbled at the wooden lolly stick and gave a sly giggle.

'Look. We're here.' He pointed. 'The City Hair Salon.'

She was taken aback. She'd expected to see a restaurant. The entrance was pretty large and there were shadows of people moving about behind the shop's frosted glass face. Red letters on the door proclaimed:

Help Wanted — Shampoo Girl — 16–20 yrs old — No experience necessary

*

'Let me see your hands.'

Xiaohong obediently spread out her fingers.

'Very sensual. Clip your nails,' the boss said upon examining her hands. 'You'll need a day of training.'

He was a twenty-something, long-haired androgynous sort: from the front he looked neither male nor female, from the back he could pass for either. Xiaohong secretly wondered what lay behind that image.

Including herself, there were four shampoo girls and a man to train them. Xiaohong began the third stage of her career with a sense of pride. Within an hour, the girls had all warmed to each other. Within a fortnight, the male customers had all warmed to Xiaohong, each dragging out his visit, waiting his turn until she was free.

She was a natural shampoo girl. A customer would settle into her chair, keeping his head at just the right angle, aligned perfectly against her ample bosom. He would sit, scalp covered in bubbles, chatting to her. After a rinse would come a fifteen-minute massage, throughout which he would lean back, cushioning his head upon her chest. Seeing the customers comfortable pleased the boss, who would quietly reward Xiaohong, reaffirming her sense of self-worth and confidence in her ability.

Xiaohong got along especially well with her bunkmate Li Sijiang, a simple, honest girl. She was as pure and beautiful as a mountain spring, with an unspoiled sweetness. Sijiang was a year younger than Xiaohong and had a face as fresh as apple pie.

One night, Sijiang said, 'You don't have to sell yourself like some porn queen.'

'Oh, come on! It's not like I sleep with people for money.' Xiaohong smiled, 'You still a virgin?'

Sijiang didn't respond. Xiaohong got out of bed, turned off the light, and climbed into the younger girl's bunk.

'Come on. Don't keep secrets!' she prodded. 'Tell me all about it. And don't leave out the juicy stuff.'

'This, uh... well, once...' Sijiang suddenly developed a stammer that made it sound like she had a mouthful of shredded radish.

Xiaohong moved closer. 'Here,' she said, snuggling up to Sijiang, 'feel my boobs.'

Sijiang's hand didn't move to accept the invitation, so Xiaohong grabbed it and brought it to her own chest. The hand lay there lifeless for a moment, then hesitatingly it moved to the curve of the breast.

'It's really big,' Sijiang whispered. 'Don't they get kind of heavy?' She asked, with just a touch of awe. 'Here, feel mine. They're like oranges.'

Xiaohong reached out her hand. It really was like the difference between oranges and melons.

'I guess I should give my brother-in-law credit for that,' Xiaohong said, giggling. 'Ever since I was ten, that bastard couldn't keep his hands off me. With all the touching and rubbing and kneading he did every chance he got, I guess they grew into it. It was when I was fourteen that he really *did* me, though.'

She started to cry.

'That bastard. What a piece of shit.'

V

The scrawny fellow who couldn't fill out his trousers came a couple of times to have Xiaohong wash his hair. As soon as the plaster-faced woman heard, she put a stop to it, applying layers of jealousy in an attempt to seal him to her.

After completing their probation period, Xiaohong and Sijiang came up with a buddy system, or what the locals called 'all for one and one for all'. Unexpectedly, it was Sijiang's pretty face that caused them real trouble. She caught the eye of a young man working in his girlfriend's shop next to the salon. His future was bright, thanks to his business-savvy girlfriend, a burly woman who knew exactly how to manage him. He used to sneak over to the worker's quarters at the salon to see Sijiang, and the two of them liked to go to the movies. Until his girlfriend found out. She stormed in, all flab and provocation, pointing a finger of her overworked hand at Xiaohong and shouting, 'You slut!'

She didn't really know which shampoo girl she was looking for, but a glance at the rack on Xiaohong was all the evidence she needed. Xiaohong just shook her head, not quite sure what to say. Finally she shrugged and asked, 'When your bull starts nibbling in your neighbour's garden, do you blame the bull or the neighbour?'

The woman, too choked with rage to speak, looked ready to pull the girl's hair out. Xiaohong wondered if she had gone a bit too far.

'Sijiang,' she said later when they were talking about the incident, 'he's got no balls. He's totally under that woman's thumb! And here he is playing both of you, hedging his bets, but he's not even worthy of hooking himself to either of you.' Xiaohong remembered the northern man back at that hotel, and how he'd said he'd give her money for 'hooking'. She figured it meant being paid for making love or something like that.

'But he said he likes me, not his girlfriend,' Sijiang said, utterly confused.

'He's toying with you. Us women, we're too easily flattered. This guy is just one big prostate problem!' Xiaohong didn't quite know what a prostate was or what sort of problems it caused. She only knew that, what with the sorts of cures advertised on all the posters along the roadside, it must be something serious and something that nearly all men suffered from. She had her own way of thinking, and gradually her influence over Sijiang grew to the point that the girl adopted her ideas on any and every subject.

One day while entertaining a customer, Sijiang blurted out, 'You got any trouble with your prostate?' The man didn't quite catch what she had said, thinking she had asked him to sit up straight. Before she could repeat herself, Xiaohong smacked the back of her head, and so she swallowed the question.

All the same, they were thirsty for more information on the subject so they spent their after-work hours scouring posters on poles along the street outside the salon. They focused on those with headings like, *Good news for prostate patients*. Some were only half exposed, while others had so many layers of glue on top that it was impossible to make anything out. When they finally caught sight of one nearly-intact sheet, they were able to put together enough of what they had seen to figure out where the prostate was located.

Sijiang shook her head, 'A man's thingy sure is complicated.'

VI

Winter came suddenly, but nothing seemed to dampen the spirits of the two girls. On cold days, their feet were stuck inside shoes that didn't quite manage to keep them warm, and their fingers, constantly immersed in water as they kept at the hair-washing trade, suffered even more. Each day passed without incident, and Xiaohong began to grow restless. It was as bad as letting one's sex life fall into a mind-numbing routine, without change of position, pattern or partner. She was bored sick. Even the nice things began to seem like chaff to her. She continued to chat up customers as she scrubbed their scalps, all the while staring out of the window in boredom. Watching the people walking along the street, she felt they all knew what they were doing in life.

'Why not go to Shenzhen? It's Hong Kong's nearest neighbour, so wages there are about ten times what they are here,' said one of her regulars, Li Mazi.

'I've seen that place on TV. All I know is that the sky is always blue, the buildings are tall, people work like cows and the men have lots of wives. I don't know if they need shampoo girls, though,' she said, languorously.

'Sure they do. Plenty of hair to wash there too. And not just on the head. The local girls are ugly. If someone like you or Sijiang were to go, your stock would be sky high, for sure,' Li Mazi said proudly, adding that he would be willing to help them make the journey to Shenzhen if they wanted to go.

His words lit a fire under Xiaohong, making her huge breasts heave with enthusiasm, leaping like rabbits trying to escape from the confines of her blouse. As she began to get a clearer idea of the situation, she saw an image of Shenzhen before her eyes, a romantic city that seemed to have risen right out of the lines of a poem, its streets filled with dignified men. When she had finished washing Li Mazi's hair, she stretched and began to think how good it would be to see the world. The main problem, she thought, was not one of money. She had already saved enough to make it work. What she needed was a companion. She pulled Sijiang aside to talk it over.

'How far is it?' Sijiang asked.

'By train, it's an overnight journey.'

'How much is the ticket?'

'About 80 *yuan*, I think.'

'Where will we go when we get there?'

'Li Mazi said he'd arrange it for us.'

'Let me think about it.'

'What's to think about? If you don't want to go, I'll go by myself. And don't you go accusing me of abandoning you once I'm gone!'

When the end of the month came and Sijiang was still hesitant, Xiaohong lost her patience. She said hotly, 'Sijiang, it's a good thing you aren't in labour. You're taking forever.'

But her friend remained undecided, wavering back and forth between the two options.

That night in the dorm, Xiaohong settled on a plan.

'Hey Sijiang, tomorrow morning can you tell the boss I've quit? Then at night, I'm going to meet Li Mazi at the train station. You just keep washing, and who knows, maybe one day you'll be the shampoo queen.'

Her final words pushed Sijiang into action. Her fresh, round face reddened. She said, 'I'm coming with you!'

Two

I

'What on earth does he do in Shenzhen?' Sijiang asked.

'Whatever the hell he does, it's none of our business. We're just there to wash hair. We've got enough to worry about, what with sprucing everyone up, adding colour, long hair, short hair, massaging scalps of every shape and size, applying a bit of acupressure here and there. With all we've got on our plates, it's scary enough to think about how we're gonna keep our own heads above water,' Xiaohong answered heatedly. Sijiang thought she was sounding more pompous by the minute.

As the train clanked noisily along, the passengers dozed, each drifting off into his or her own dreams. In sudden excitement, Xiaohong elbowed Sijiang in the ribs and said, 'Hey, tell me what you think we'll be like when we come back from Shenzhen five years from now.'

Sijiang opened the eyes set so delicately in her apple-shaped face, turned a bewildered gaze on Xiaohong, and then closed her eyes again.

'God! Wake up, will you? Can't you just stay awake for a while?' said Xiaohong, poking Sijiang a couple more times.

'*I'm* awake,' Li Mazi said, leaning closer to her. The light from the window flickered over his form as the train sped along. Xiaohong felt he was getting a little too friendly.

'Oh! We're moving so fast. I think I'm going to be sick.'

Xiaohong covered her mouth and ran to the washroom.

*

'We get off here!' called Li Mazi.

'What? We're there?' Xiaohong was startled out of her sleep. Looking out of the window, she saw the words Guangzhou Station, and turned away to go back to sleep.

'Let's go!' Mazi shook Xiaohong.

'It's still dark. Where are we?' Sijiang said, wiping a bit of drool from her chin and looking out of the window. The light fell on a crowd of people carrying bags big and small, parents with children in tow.

'Come on! We've got to change trains here at Guangzhou!'

'Oh. Huh? Hey! Where's my wallet? Crap! I can't find my wallet!' Sijiang, fully awake now, was feeling all of her pockets frantically. Finding each one empty as she felt it, she let out a cry of distress.

'Can't be! Look carefully. Where did you put it?' said Li Mazi.

'Right here,' Sijiang said, raising the corner of her shirt and showing him the front pocket of her trousers. Li Mazi, reaching over to pat it, found that it was empty, just as she had said.

'Five hundred *yuan*! I can't believe this!' Sijiang sobbed, her tiny eyes turning into two narrow slits as she cried. To add insult to injury, all the other passengers in the carriage struggled to hide their knowing smirks, turning to look stoically out of the windows.

Xiaohong felt her friend needed a shock, like a bucket of cold water splashed in the face. 'How could you just sleep like a pig? You think this is your own house? Your own room? Your own bed? Do you know why there are criminals? Because people like you create opportunities for them to take advantage of! If you aren't on guard, it's like you don't even mind. It's practically an invitation!' She knew that if she comforted Sijiang, she would cry even more. She may not have had much of an education, but she knew how to take measure of the people around her.

As disembarking passengers took their luggage from the overhead compartment, a bag hit Sijiang on the head. She resisted the urge to cry out, though the tears still dribbled down her face as she stumbled off the train.

It was hot. They staggered along the platform, peeling off layers of coats and sweaters as they went. Sijiang touched all of her pockets again, suddenly feeling that her clothes were very outdated.

'Don't fret. We're here now. It's alright,' said Li Mazi.

'Hey, Sijiang, he's right, y'know. Just keep moving forward. Here.' Xiaohong gave her two hundred *yuan*. As soon as the money was pressed into her palm, Sijiang started crying again, her young face displaying a whole host of emotions.

'Alright. Let's get on the train to Shenzhen now. And stop speaking in our hometown dialect. Here it's just plain ol' Mandarin.' Li Mazi had spent a lot of time outside of Hunan and spoke Mandarin fluently. Xiaohong and Sijiang, on the other hand, were constantly tickled by their own attempts when they first started. Later, they just found it bewildering. Everything flowed fine in the Hunan dialect but when it came to Mandarin, they were tongue-tied. The words just got stuck. They were afraid no one would understand them, except Li Mazi. Xiaohong, recalling her primary school lessons word by word, played teacher, with Sijiang her only student.

'*You. Are. Li. Si. Jiang. I. Am. Qian. Xiao. Hong. He. Is. Li. Ma. Zi. We. Are. In Guangdong.* Wah! Look at all them banana trees! They're covered in fruit!' The last observation came out in a sudden burst of flowing Hunanese. Sijiang doubled over with laughter. Li Mazi put a finger to his lips, reminding them that there were other people on the train. Xiaohong glanced around and noticed a manual labourer sitting nearby, openly laughing at her through his leering, lecherous expression. She turned away, silently cursing him.

Sijiang began to feel her pockets again, top and bottom, inside and out, not missing a single one.

'Hey Honghong, when we've made a bit of money, I want to buy a whole load of beautiful clothes. What we've got on now screams 'country bumpkin'. You think we'll get laughed at in Shenzhen?' Sijiang moved a little closer to Xiaohong as she spoke.

'We've got to wash tons of scalps first but then there'll be plenty of new clothes, plenty of good food and plenty of men to choose from too,' Xiaohong drawled, chattering idly.

'Hey, come on! I keep telling you to use Mandarin,' interrupted Li Mazi, his eyes springing open from his nap.

'Alright, if we have to. *We. Will. Soon. Be. In. Bea-U-ti-ful. Shenzhen. Si. Jiang. You. Happy? I'm. Hoppy. I'm. Not. Even. Nervous. I'm. Easy,*' said Xiaohong. And so they made their journey, brushing up on their language skills as they went. Whatever they saw they called it by its Mandarin name, Li Mazi giving guidance when they were wrong. By the time they reached Shenzhen, the two girls' tongues were completely tied in knots. Li Mazi said, 'Keep practising. It'll get smoother as you go along.'

I I

The rickety bus rolled along, pulling over at each stop as it went. The young fellow collecting tickets stood up for the whole journey, welcoming those coming aboard and bidding farewell to those alighting. He had a small black bag clasped between his thighs and one hand pressed over it, making it look as if he were touching himself in a less than appropriate manner. When Xiaohong saw him, she fought to suppress her smile.

Seeing the girl's response, Li Mazi pontificated, 'For a man, money is a lifeline'.

'And a woman's lifeline is...?'

'A woman's lifeline is her man.'

'Oh God! A woman's lifeline is also money! You think a woman should rely on some guy? No way!' she said unequivocally. To herself, she thought, Looking at the desperation of that guy who couldn't fill out his trousers, or that under-the-thumb man who was so keen on Sijiang, you'd think it was men who counted on women for survival, not the other way around.

'To get money, women always have to go through men. You'll understand before long,' Li Mazi retorted haughtily.

'So, whoever holds the money is in control?' Sijiang said, as if feeling her way through a fog.

With a surprised gasp, Li Mazi said, 'That is profound.'

'Sijiang is right. It is a simple matter,' Xiaohong said, speaking rapidly in their hometown dialect.

'Passengers going to Magang get off here,' called the conductor. The bus spat out the three passengers and pulled away in a cloud of black smoke that choked them half to death.

'Where the hell are we?' The two girls were perplexed. The air here was rotten, filled with a yellow dust turned up by the tyres of passing cars as they came off the flyover and onto the open road. The buildings were arranged in a random, disorderly fashion. Sijiang stuck close to Xiaohong, who felt she was drifting about in an odd place.

'This is the outskirts of Shenzhen. We're only a short distance away from Magang town centre here,' Li Mazi pointed vaguely in the direction they'd been travelling in. The landscape seemed to be made up of patches of mist, fog and various shades of grey. There was no sign of the skyscrapers they'd heard so much about. Four legs suddenly felt heavy with exhaustion and disappointment as they trudged along behind Li Mazi through the town to a desolate wasteland. Eventually, they saw a white sign with red lettering, Waste Collection Station.

'You're a rubbish collector?' Sijiang asked, deflated.

'No. It's a recycling station,' Li Mazi replied indignantly. 'I just help the boss out a bit. Don't look down your noses at this place or at my boss. He makes a lot of money at this.'

Xiaohong mused to herself, I've heard of a rag and bone man saving up enough to build a small house but I never imagined a rubbish collector could amass a fortune. Sijiang was hungry and discouraged, though not nearly as disappointed as Xiaohong, who said loudly, 'What the hell kind of backwater joint have you brought us to? Hey Sijiang, let's have a look around first, then we'll talk about what to do next.'

And so the three of them proceeded down the dirt road towards the waste collection station, in single file, carrying their variously sized baggage. They passed a European-style building, then a small square, then, on rounding a bend, came upon a makeshift shack.

III

'I've told you before. No overnight guests! I'd have to pay a fine if I let anyone stay.' A rough-featured man with a square head was lecturing Li Mazi in Mandarin that had a heavy Cantonese accent, his arms and legs waving in a furious display of anger. Li Mazi, deftly avoiding the flailing limbs, kept calling him 'Mr Zhuang' and 'Boss' which seemed to appease the man to some degree. Mr Zhuang's face visibly brightened when he saw the two girls enter the room behind Li Mazi, only to become tainted by a lecherous cloud.

'Well, Li Mazi, we really *do* need you here. There's lots of work piled up waiting for you.'

'Mr Zhuang, Boss, these girls are from my hometown.' At the boss's softened tone, Li Mazi spoke with a little more confidence.

'Oh! In that case, welcome, then! Must've been a rough trip. Why don't you take them in to get some rest?'

The workers' quarters were situated in a low, humid building, accommodating three or four people to a room. Inside each room was a basin, a big window, and a smattering of colourful plastic bags. Li Mazi, being a manager, had a private room equipped with a bed and a desk, leaving a narrow space in which a person could walk from one end of the room to the other.

'Li, I asked the canteen to cook up something a little extra, seeing as you've travelled so far. Not an easy trip.' Xiaohong and Sijiang just wanted to flop on the crowded bed, but were prevented by Mr Zhuang's intrusion.

'Thanks a lot, Mr Zhuang. We've given you a lot of trouble,' Xiaohong said.

'Mr Zhuang is a good man. You'll see that all the more as you get to know him,' Li Mazi said, obviously trying to gain a few brownie points with the boss. Mr Zhuang laughed and made a little small talk.

Before turning to leave, he added, 'If there's anything you need, just ask Li Mazi. Or you can come and find me, if you like.' The girls nodded in unison, then gave a slight bow as the boss left the room.

Li Mazi laughed and said, 'The boss is always like that. No male visitors can stay overnight, but then he's so friendly towards any female guests. Everyone knows it. That's the advantage of your sex.'

'Advantage? What a load of crap. He's just horny and has got his big eyes on us. You really think he'll be able to restrain himself for long?' Xiaohong turned slowly round and round, looking about the room.

'Just so you know, Xiaohong, if you offend him, I lose my livelihood.'

'Hmph. So Sijiang, I guess it's up to you to hook up with him then.' Xiaohong took a gulp of water. Sijiang, thinking her friend really did mean her to sleep with Mr Zhuang, turned bright red and squirmed visibly.

*

Li Mazi's bed was as hard as a rock. After they'd had something to eat and taken a short nap, the girls got up and found themselves aching all over.

'You sleep alright?' Li Mazi asked, coming into the room with a pleased look on his face.

'Alright? You must be kidding! I'm sore from head to toe.' Xiaohong retorted, stretching her sore muscles. 'The boss give you a raise or something? What're you so happy about?'

'I don't know whether it's good or bad, but it looks like we're all in this together, so we'll have to see what we can do to pull through it. Mr Zhuang knows this guy who owns a hair salon. He's not really looking for workers, but he can arrange for one of you to work for him. There's this one thing, though. He wanted me to ask...'

'Well? Ask what?'

'...whether you two are virgins?'

'Virgins? What's that got to do with anything?'

'Xiaohong, you don't understand how things are. A lot of farmers around here are rich and they have certain tastes. If a guy can get a virgin and, you know, deflower her, he'll pay a whole whack for it.'

'Li Mazi, what the hell have you got us into? We didn't come all the way here to be prostitutes!' Xiaohong shook, her breasts standing up in rage. Sijiang held her back.

'Settle down, Xiaohong. It's not like anyone's gonna rape you. It's up to you whether or not you do it,' Li Mazi said, trying to placate her.

'Anyway, your bed strong enough for three people?' Xiaohong asked Li Mazi, a bit on edge. 'We'd look pretty ridiculous if it collapsed in the middle of the night.'

Lifting the sheet, he said, 'See for yourself.'

'God! Bricks! No wonder it's so hard. I guess if anyone tries to attack us during the night, we won't have any problems defending ourselves,' Xiaohong said with a snigger.

'Who's going to attack us in our sleep?' As soon as the words were out of her mouth, Sijiang blushed at her gullibility. She said to Xiaohong, 'You sleep in the middle. I'll squeeze over against the wall. OK? Alright, then. That's settled.'

'And you,' Xiaohong turned to Li Mazi and said sharply, 'you better keep to your side of the bed and keep still.'

'I won't even breathe. Good thing it's still cool. If it were June, we'd melt.'

Xiaohong crawled under the blanket and lay on her back. Li Mazi dozed off, leaving a gap between himself and Xiaohong. She felt cramped in the tight space. Wanting to turn to lie on her side, she considered whether she'd prefer her oversized breasts to face Li Mazi's smelly feet or Sijiang's back. She settled on the warmth of the other girl's back. She spent the whole night drowning in a concoction of Sijiang's body odour and Li Mazi's own indescribable flavour.

The next morning, Mr Zhuang offered to arrange for one of the girls to go to work in the salon. Sijiang didn't want to go, nor did she want Xiaohong to leave her alone. No matter what, she said, they had to stick together. Since Mr Zhuang's offer was not going to work, they decided to manage their own job search, so off they went into town.

'Hey Sijiang, you hear this chatter around us? Sounds funny, doesn't it?'

'I don't understand a word of it.'

'Then we learn! There's nothing that can't be learned.'

The two girls, hand-in-hand, walked into the Magang Market and tried their best to twist their tongues enough to make themselves understood by the locals. 'Excuse me. Are you looking for shampoo girls?'

'You got any experience?'

'Yes.'

'You got a temporary residence card? No? Let me see your ID card, then.'

'ID card?'

'Yeah.'

'We don't have any ID cards.'

'Maybe a family planning card, then?'

'Nope. We just got here.'

'Not licensed to work around here? You better watch yourselves, then, if they come checking for papers. If you get picked up, you'll be spending some time in the slammer!'

IV

'Mr Zhuang's invited you both to karaoke tonight,' Li Mazi said excitedly, his eyes lowered in an obscure expression.

'Carry-o-pee? What in the world is that? Never heard of it,' Xiaohong said.

'Yeah. Carry what? And aren't you coming with us?' Sijiang had always enjoyed gatherings with large groups.

'It's just singing. Kind of like a talent show. You know, holding a microphone while you sing your heart out.'

'Li Mazi, I doubt it's so simple. I think what Mr Zhuang really wants is a chance to get his hands on Sijiang.'

'Me? Hardly. It's your boobs the boss is always staring at, you know.'

'You both have plenty of assets to your credit. Anyway, it's on a boat. There'll be lots of food, lots of drinking and lots of singing. Whatever you do, just don't provoke him. Oh, I almost forgot. You find any job leads?'

Xiaohong answered, 'We need a bit of help before we can do anything. We've got to get temporary residence cards.'

'Hmm. We'll need to ask Mr Zhuang. Tonight while you're singing, when he gets a little tipsy, that's the time to ask him about it. Make sure you do it then.'

'Alright, I'll try. What a hassle!'

On Li Mazi's advice, the two girls dressed in their best clothes and put on some makeup, and then went to join in the karaoke session, carrying themselves uneasily. Sijiang was especially nervous. She was holding a scarf in her hands, constantly twisting it into knots then unwinding it again.

'You two beautiful young ladies are here!' Mr Zhuang's smile was as shady as the dim lights inside the private karaoke room that he had reserved.

'Let me introduce you. This here is the mayor. He takes care of a lot of business for me,' Mr Zhuang went on, enraptured.

A man in his fifties, looking like a humble farmer, was sitting on the sofa. His face was as dark as a well worn wok. He smiled woodenly at the girls, without quite daring to look them in the eye. He kept his head hunched down close to his chest, enveloped in a thick cloud of cigarette smoke.

Xiaohong thought to herself, If this mayor is so capable when it comes to taking care of Mr Zhuang's business, surely he's up to securing a couple of temporary residence cards. Sitting down close to the man, she made sure to keep his wine glass full and his cigarette lit for the rest of the evening. The mayor focused on drinking and smoking, not uttering a word.

'Here, have a little more,' Mr Zhuang said to Sijiang as they were finishing their supper, having showered his most gallant attentions on her throughout the meal.

'I've already had plenty to eat, and don't think I could hold another drink,' said Xiaohong, answering for her friend before turning to the mayor. 'How about we sing a duet?' He nodded and they left the table to sit on the sofa. The waitress turned on the speakers, which emitted a deafening sound as the TV screen displayed a bikini-clad girl running across a sandy beach. Mr Zhuang shifted in his chair, his thigh pressing up against Sijiang. In a panic, she tried desperately to respond appropriately to his attentions, as she looked for a way to wriggle away from his looming form.

'Mr Zhuang, why don't you two join us over here?' Xiaohong called out, offering her friend an escape route.

'You sing first. Go ahead.' Mr Zhuang turned towards her, his face as red as the Taoist deity Lord Guan's.

The mayor was some singer. Throughout his soul-stirring rendition of a classic pop song, he strained breathlessly as his voice cracked trying to reach the high notes. His off-key tune was a perfect match for his lack of rhythm. He belted out the whole song practically all in one breath, except for the notes he missed out, which was about one out of every five.

'That was touching,' Xiaohong said, applauding. She poured him some tea and lit a cigarette for him. After a moment, Mr Zhuang and Sijiang came over to sit with them on the sofa. Xiaohong felt that the way had been paved, and the time was ripe for her to approach the mayor. When Mr Zhuang started to sing an old favourite, she made her move.

'Wow! Mr Zhuang is a good singer. Mr Mayor, you two must practise singing all the time.' She bawled into the mayor's ear loud enough to be heard over the music's blare.

The mayor nodded and said, 'The boss does sing well.'

Xiaohong thought, Well, at least he doesn't have any delusions about his own abilities. She continued to blindly heap praise on the two men, buying a little more time.

The mayor then pointed at Xiaohong and said, 'Big waves.'

Confused, she asked, 'What waves?'

'These. Your boobs,' he said, rubbing his hands along his own chest. 'Anyone ever surf those waves?'

In the Hunan dialect, waving meant kissing, but what was kissing to a letch like the mayor? Hoping to learn something from the man, she put on a coquettish smile and said, 'I wouldn't know anything about that.'

'Well, your waves are big, so I'm sure someone's surfed them,' he said, sounding like a farmer discussing something as innocuous as his crops.

It crossed Xiaohong's mind that this was a whole new style of discourse for her. She hadn't been careful, and things had gotten out of hand before she even had a chance to bring up her own business. Once the talk turned toward her bust, it was hard to do an about face. Anxiously, she said, 'Mr Mayor, I just arrived here and I've got a little problem. I wonder if you might be able to help.'

'People come every day, and every day people leave. It's a very mobile population,' he said, his speech a little slurred. He wore an expression as enigmatic as Buddha's.

'I heard they check papers here?'

'Sometimes they check, sometimes they don't.'

'Mr Mayor, can you help us get temporary residence cards?'

'Are you a virgin?'

'Who? Me?' Xiaohong gasped in astonishment.

'I only help virgins.'

V

Li Mazi lounged, legs splayed and eyes roving over his magazine. His briefs swayed in the breeze from the window where he had hung them up to dry, drawing the eye to a large hole in the crotch. Seeing Sijiang enter the room, he sat up hastily.

'Ah, your cheeks are all rosy. You have a good time?'

Looking like she'd been caught with her hand in the cookie jar, she kept her gaze turned toward his legs.

'I thought you'd be back late,' Li Mazi smiled sheepishly.

'So, everything arranged, Xiaohong?' he asked, turning away from Sijiang.

'Arranged my arse. That fat fucking pig,' she said in a choked tone.

'Hey, not so loud. What did the boss have to say?'

'I spoke to the mayor directly.'

'Now you've done it. Look, I know Mr Zhuang is a randy old guy, but he's not all bad.' Li Mazi flung the magazine away from him, feeling a twinge of pity for the two girls.

'A stream's twists and turns all eventually lead to the sea, and Mr Zhuang is just one twist in the stream,' said Xiaohong. 'I thought we could take a shortcut and get right to the ocean. How was I to know the bloody mayor only cared about popping a girl's cherry? Even if I *were* a virgin, I would never take this route to get what I want. And to think, I wasted some of my best moves on him tonight.'

'But, Xiaohong, if the mayor said he won't help you, there's no point going to Mr Zhuang now,' Li Mazi said, shaking his head.

Sijiang's face was flushed and her eyes glassy with the after-effects of alcohol. She had been fidgeting ever since she came through the door. She stood, she sat, she stood, and then she sat again.

'Relax. Why don't we sleep on it and we'll figure something out in the morning,' Li Mazi said.

Sijiang had caught the term 'slammer' earlier in the day and was worried that they were in real trouble. She couldn't have been more startled if she'd heard the word 'brothel'.

'Something on your mind, Sijiang?' Xiaohong asked.

'I... I,' stammered Sijiang, her watery eyes shot back and forth between Xiaohong and Li Mazi. She grew even redder.

'Never mind. Don't worry,' said Xiaohong. 'You stay here for a couple more days, and I'll go out and see what I can do. If I don't come back, then you'll know something's happened. We didn't travel all this way just to run into a dead end now. If we find that we really have reached the end of the line here, then I guess we'll just say we've had our fun, and it's run its course.' Xiaohong was determined to finish what she had begun.

'But Xiaohong, you don't understand. That Mr Zhuang, he kept grabbing my hand. I barely managed to fend him off.'

'OK, so let him feel you up, then. Who knows, maybe if he gets off on it, he'll help us with our problem after all. It's not like you're a virgin. Surely your hand's seen worse action than that.'

'Xiaohong, I... I *am* a virgin.'

'What the hell? That night, didn't you say...?'

'I lied. I was afraid you'd laugh at me, being so green at this age.'

Xiaohong replied, 'Sijiang, that's the most ridiculous thing I've ever heard.'

'Honghong, I'm thinking I'll get the mayor's help with our temporary residence cards,' Sijiang finally blurted out the idea she'd been mulling over.

'Huh? You? Do it with that fat pig? You might as well do Li Mazi!'

Li Mazi spluttered, surprised and a little hurt. Impulsively, he said, 'Xiaohong, why don't you play the hooker then? I'm sure you could bring in a whole truckload of such 'fat pigs'!'

The argument continued heatedly, but no resolution was found. Xiaohong had spoken thoughtlessly and didn't realise she had hit a nerve with the other two. Li Mazi's kindness towards Li Sijiang had planted a seed of affection inside her, and she'd quietly nurtured it ever since.

'There's no bridge that can't be crossed.' And with that, Xiaohong flopped onto the bed, bum out and face to the wall, and fell straight to sleep. Sijiang looked at Li Mazi. Li Mazi looked at Sijiang. Then they both looked at the empty half of the bed beside them. Sijiang's apple-shaped face turned pink from ear to ear, and then proceeded to run through all the shades of red. The thoughts that raced through her mind were evident in the change from one hue to another. Li Mazi could see that she was touched by his attentions, but he felt things were moving a little too fast. He didn't grab her hand and pull her to the bed, feeling such a crass act would be incompatible with the fondness shared between them. Li Mazi had originally brought the two girls with him in order to please Mr Zhuang, thinking that if one of them became his boss's little secret, his own position would be secure, at least for a time. He had a further plan, which involved him starting at Mr Zhuang's toy factory, where he would become the manager of a couple of hundred female employees. He'd be perfect for the job, he thought, keeping tabs on all those beautiful girls. He'd be the envy of everyone he knew. He had hand-picked Xiaohong upon seeing her coquettish charms, never suspecting she had such a hot-blooded, independent streak in her. She was quite a handful, and Sijiang was clearly under her thumb. He was sure the loss of Sijiang's virginity would have to get Xiaohong's stamp of approval before it could get her own thumbs up.

So, dare he make a move? It'd be a whole lot easier when the pair had both run out of money. Problem was he had no idea how much money Xiaohong had brought with her. He picked up the tattered magazine and flipped through the pages. Sijiang lounged on the bed, her posture clearly indicating that she was not really asleep. There was no evidence of that lack of self-consciousness that marks the face of one in a deep slumber. She was vigilant – looking not the least bit like the girl who had slept like the dead on the train just a few days earlier.

Xiaohong woke up in the middle of the night, noting that the gap beside her had grown. She felt movement under the quilt, eager and intense. She immediately knew what was up. Shit! That Li Mazi! Give him the slightest advantage and here he starts in on Sijiang. It's always the innocent-looking ones you have to worry most about. She felt torn between fury and discomfort. Needing to pee, she wanted to head to the washroom. On the other hand, she didn't dare move until all was quiet. Finally she turned, heaving her two mounds out of the bed. After relieving herself, she returned to the bed. She didn't sleep a wink for the rest of the night.

VI

Xiaohong got up early, washed her face, put on a bit of makeup and headed into the town. She passed a group of men and women, labourers sporting identical blue uniforms with red letters emblazoned across the shirt pocket, looking like a brigade of committed revolutionaries. Each of them chewed on a bit of a steamed or fried bun, or a biscuit. Like tides, they moved in steady waves through the iron gates of the factory and disappeared. Xiaohong rattled the gate, peering inside.

'Who you looking for?' the security guard asked sternly. He was very smartly dressed.

'Huh? Oh, I'm not looking for anyone. But, um, do you know if they're hiring here?'

'How old are you?'

'Seventeen.'

'Where you from?'

'Hunan.'

'How long you been here?'

'A while.'

'Where you staying?'

'With a friend from back home.'

'What can you do?'

'Anything anyone else can.'

'We aren't hiring.'

'Not hiring? Then what're you asking so many questions for?' Xiaohong was on fire. She had answered everything honestly and all the while this security guard was just toying with her. She had almost spilled everything about what had happened the previous evening. She felt like forgetting all about temporary residence cards and laying into this git, and letting the police just come and pick her up there and then. Instead, she checked her temper and glared at the guard, shooting daggers at him from beneath her eyebrows. Her meaning was clear enough: 'You just wait and see.'

The guard was suddenly stricken with fear. What if this girl was in league with some local gang? The boss went to great lengths to avoid trouble. He tried to placate Xiaohong. Tittering, he asked, 'You really just got here?'

Xiaohong closed her eyes for a couple of seconds. When she opened them, she continued to glare at the guard, but it wasn't clear whether it was a look of blame or contempt. It was like she was peering through the dark, searching for some intelligence in his words.

'Come on, sweetheart, don't be mad. I'm just a working stiff myself. If the boss catches me talking to you too long, I'll be sacked. Why don't you head over to Fu'an county? They're hiring at the Lucky Duck Handbag Factory, or so I hear from some friends from my hometown. It's just a few miles away. There's a direct bus from here.' The security guard pointed to the bus stop. When she looked in the direction he pointed, Xiaohong realised it was the same spot where the bus had dropped them off a few days before.

As she left, she turned back to offer the guard a nod and a smile, but he didn't seem to notice.

It was sunny. A hand selling tickets hung out of the bus window near the rear door, thumping against the side of the vehicle. When she had boarded, the bus, adapting to the slow pace of traffic, puttered along for a while before turning onto a wider avenue where it finally picked up a little speed. Xiaohong, uncertain exactly how long she had been sitting on the bus, watched as passengers got on and off. The driver had an unsteady foot on the accelerator, making Xiaohong feel like her insides were rolling about. She hadn't had anything for breakfast, and the previous night's feasting and drinking had long since been digested amidst the roar of the karaoke session. She dry-heaved and the taste of bile filled her mouth. She gave a little belch. The other passengers sat looking at the passing scenery, dozing or smoking. The bus clanked along, burning diesel and releasing black smoke on either side as it went.

'Fu'an county stop,' called the ticket collector.

Xiaohong's face had turned an odd shade of green by the time the bus stopped.

'This is Shenzhen?'

'Course it is.'

Xiaohong wasn't quite ready to get off.

'You'll have to buy another ticket if you want to continue your journey.'

'How much?'

'Two *kuai*.'

'What?'

'Two *kuai*. Two *yuan*,' said the ticket collector, switching to more formal language and holding up two fingers. Xiaohong dug out the money.

After a short distance, the ticket collector announced, 'Check point. Everyone off. The bus will wait for you over there.'

'Check point? What're they checking?' Xiaohong was confused again.

'You gotta have a border permit to go into Shenzhen. You got yours?'

Xiaohong shook her head blankly.

'If you don't have a border permit, you'll have to get off the bus and go back.' With that, the ticket collector snapped the door shut and as soon as she had stepped off, the bus began inching its way into the lane marked Buses Only.

'Shit!' Xiaohong looked towards Shenzhen, turned on her heel and made her way back.

Stopping to ask for directions along the way, Xiaohong became more confused. Finding the Lucky Duck Handbag Factory was like finding a prostate problem or syphilis lurking in an otherwise healthy population – always there, but hard to locate. Reading the advertisements posted all over the telephone poles and signs along the roadside, she began to feel that the world was a chaotic place, and wondered if there was any disease that could not be found here.

'Where you going, Miss?' A motorcyclist, face shielded by a black helmet, pulled up in front of Xiaohong.

'The Lucky Duck Handbag Factory. You know it?'

'Oh, of course, I know where that is. Come on, I'll give you a lift.' Xiaohong, feeling like an ant that had dropped inside a kettle with no obvious way out, was so relieved she nearly cried when she heard his words. The motorcycle turned here and there, manoeuvring through the streets at a dizzying pace.

'Here we are.'

'Thank you. Thank you so much,' she said, turning to leave.

'Hey! You haven't paid yet!' the man's face was stern.

'Huh? I need to pay?'

'Of course! Ten *kuai*.'

'What? Ten *yuan*? That's daylight robbery!'

'That's the standard price. Hurry up about it. Unless you wanna find a spot for some wave-action. I could overlook ten *kuai* then.' The reckless motorcyclist cast a meaningful look at Xiaohong's full breasts.

'Son of a bitch! You thief! Why did I even bother to get up so early today, just to put up with *this*?' In her anger, she reverted back to her hometown dialect, allowing her to add a little salt to her cursing. All the same, she dug out the money, then turned angrily to the gate of the Lucky Duck Handbag Factory. The iron gate was surrounded by hundreds of people, row upon row of them. The sea of black heads shimmered before Xiaohong's eyes.

'They hiring?'

'Yep.'

'Heard they only want thirty people.'

'Huh?'

'Now, we're all just queuing up for the privilege of filling in the application.'

'Then what?'

'Then we wait till we hear from them.'

Xiaohong whiled away her time chatting to those around her.

When it came to lunchtime, no one budged. Xiaohong, not daring to vacate her place in the queue, waited until the sun was nearing the horizon. Only then was she invited to part with another two *yuan* for the right to fill in applications for herself and Sijiang, choosing a random date to use as her friend's birthday on the form. The results would be announced in a week. In seven days, applicants should come to the factory gate to receive the news. You'd think they were applying for the CEO's post, she thought.

By the time she got back to Li Mazi's quarters, it was dark. The window in the little shack was lit, making a pitiful sight. It seemed to stand in lament for the loss of something that fell just outside the reach of its glow – perhaps the dampened hopes of the two girls, who had relied on Li Mazi's good manners in suppressing any natural urges. How many days had he spent with Sijiang before moving in on her? And her a virgin! The hymen – that insignificant piece of flesh – what did it matter? And all along Li Mazi, the prick, was just waiting to poke through that little membrane. What was it about that tiny piece of flesh that made all the men so greedy for it? Xiaohong thought of that cheap bastard Li Mazi getting his hands on Sijiang's 'lifeline' and felt a surge of hatred on her friend's behalf.

VII

Sijiang was not in the shack. Li Mazi leaned against the bed in a daze, dark rings beneath his eyes, making him look like one of those great national treasures, the panda. Clearly the previous night's activity had taken its toll on him. Upon seeing Xiaohong enter the room, he rolled his eyes until the whites were visible, rubbing his face and brushing his clothes in an attempt to tidy up his appearance.

'Sijiang? She go out for a walk? Come on, there's no need to be so secretive!' Xiaohong asked hastily, not even attempting to hide her contempt.

'She... she went to see Mr Zhuang,' he answered haltingly.

'What the hell does that old goat want with her? Aren't you worried?' Xiaohong thought he was just trying to cover his embarrassment over what had happened the night before.

'What've I got to worry about? Sijiang's business has got nothing to do with me,' Li Mazi drawled.

'What the hell? Nothing to do with you? Didn't you have a go at her last night? What sort of an inhumane beast are you?'

'If I were inhumane, I'd have done her from the start! Sleeping here with two half-dressed girls, I'd have to be mad not to be tempted! But don't worry – I didn't even try to get inside her pants. Just ask Sijiang.'

'Oh!' It suddenly began to dawn on Xiaohong. 'You mean you were just trying to help, you know... initiate her?'

'Xiaohong, if you keep on like this, you're going to drive me crazy.

Say whatever you want. Oh, I'll freely admit that I spent the whole night fantasising about the pair of you. I'm not a very educated man, though I at least tried to *act* like a gentleman. But come on...'

Xiaohong sighed, 'I never meant to bring you this kind of trouble.'

'I blame myself. But be honest, with a living guy lying beside you, didn't your mind begin to wander just a little?'

Xiaohong, laughing unconvincingly, replied, 'I guess you'd best ask Sijiang. She was the one sleeping closer to you.'

'If *you* don't have anything to say, there's certainly no point asking *her*,' Li Mazi said, in frustration.

'What you two talking about?' Sijiang's voice entered the room first, and she shuffled in behind it.

Li Mazi picked up his magazine and rummaged through its pages, as if in a trance. Xiaohong giggled.

'Where in the world did you go?'

Sijiang reached into her pocket and pulled out a pair of green cards.

'What's that? Temporary residence cards?' Xiaohong scanned the bronze lettering a couple of times. The third time, her eyes suddenly grew rounder, nearly popping out of her head.

'Um...' Sijiang hesitated, her fresh-as-an-apple face serene, like an infant putting on her socks for the first time. The task accomplished, she had a new-found confidence and her eyes looked just a little less lost. Li Mazi took the documents and read over them with a wooden expression before handing them back to Sijiang.

'Mr Zhuang did it for you?' Xiaohong hoped she was wrong.

'I went to Mr Zhuang, and he took me to see the mayor. The mayor's the one who got it done.'

'Done? The mayor got things done? Sijiang, you... you.... What have *you* done?' A fire leapt into Xiaohong's eyes. 'Why didn't you talk to me about it first? Didn't we always say we'd find a way?'

'Honghong, I saw a lot of people get picked up on the streets today.

What's virginity anyway? I don't feel I've lost anything at all. And from tomorrow on, we're both free.'

Xiaohong couldn't quite see the link between 'virginity' and 'freedom'. She had a vague feeling that it was a paradox, but then, the results were undeniable. Virginity seems to be of tremendous significance to everything except 'true love', she thought.

At night, noisy, boisterous laughter filled the neighbourhood. Inside the shack, there was only the sound of three people breathing, each silently pondering the loss of Sijiang's virginity. Xiaohong was filled with regret, Li Mazi with remorse. Only Sijiang showed nothing. Li Mazi's sorrow seemed to reach another, more personal level, as if he couldn't help wondering how satisfying it must have been to break Sijiang's hymen – though he realised, of course, that the pleasure of it was nothing compared to the value of a temporary residence card. Xiaohong regretted that it had come down to Sijiang selling her virginity.

Light from the bare bulb lit Sijiang's bowed head, shining on the bit of white scalp where her hair parted, her face hidden from view. Tears dropped onto her leather shoe, washing away the grey dust and exposing a patch of black. She pulled her foot closer to her body, leaving the tears to drop silently onto the floor. She shifted her hips from time to time, trying to find a comfortable position. Xiaohong, understanding Sijiang's discomfort, got up and carried the red plastic bucket out to get some water, her chest thrust proudly forward, held even higher than usual. Her slippers beat a furious path along the concrete away from the room, then slapped their way back, accompanied by the slosh of water in the pail. Li Mazi said, 'Want to boil it?' Xiaohong exhaled heavily. He took out a gadget, dropped the brass coil into the water, and plugged the other end into the wall socket. Tiny bubbles started to rise from the coil.

'Sijiang, wait for the water to heat up then you can bathe. If it's not enough, we'll boil more.'

'One bucket definitely won't be enough. I'll go and get some more and bring it right back.' Upon saying this, Li Mazi left, his footsteps sounding like he had been walking for days on end.

'Um, Sijiang, when you did it, did he use protection?' Xiaohong moved in close to Sijiang and sat down with her beneath the bare bulb, the shadows of their heads resting side by side on the floor.

'What protection? How the hell would I know?'

'What I mean is, a condom, you know?'

Sijiang shook her head, looking at the shadow on the ground.

'OK. Well, when was the last time you had your period?'

'It's been eight or nine days, I guess.'

'Bad timing. Didn't that pig at least ask?'

'No. What's so bad about the timing?' Sijiang was getting anxious, her red eyes opening wide.

'Think about how pigs breed. Once the sow's in season, next thing you know her belly's full of little piglets.'

'Huh?' Sijiang straightened up, her hand searching her torso, feeling first her liver, then her stomach, as if afraid she had a litter of piglets inside her.

'Don't worry. That old fellow's probably shooting blanks anyway. Don't fret. What's done is done.'

'Yeah,' Sijiang answered, though her mind was obviously weighed down by it all. 'Here, let me return this to you. He gave me three thousand *yuan*.' Sijiang opened the inner pocket of her jacket and pulled out a wad of notes. Peeling off a couple, she handed them to Xiaohong.

'I've got money. You hang onto that,' Xiaohong said, pushing it away.

'What the hell, Xiaohong? You think it's dirty?'

'Dirty? No, that's got to be the tidiest money I've ever seen.'

'Then why won't you take it?'

'I told you. I have money. If I run out, then I'll ask you for it.'

'Alright. Honghong, I want to make some money, learn hairdressing and open my own salon. I don't want to be a shampoo girl. Or, how about we go in together? We could open the grandest salon in the city!' Sijiang tucked the money back into her pocket.

'Sounds great! Then we'd be our own bosses. We could hire a few shampoo girls. And no matter what we did, no one would dare mess with us then!'

They talked on, giggling, their heads leaning close together. Li Mazi came into the room, water in hand, and looked blankly at the scene. Sijiang clammed up as soon as he entered, casting a glance in his direction. Xiaohong got up and, grabbing another pail, put on her slippers and went down the corridor.

VIII

It was afternoon, and Xiaohong was alone in the shack poring over Li Mazi's frayed magazine, a cheap pirated copy, the cover of which displayed a seductive woman. Li Mazi was nearly thirty. If he needed to rely on these things for consolation, who was she to stop him? Actually, he was to be pitied. Whenever he went back to his hometown, he seemed to be such a big shot, everyone envying his success, but who knew whether his life was really all that comfortable? Perhaps if he had stayed put, he'd have a wife and kids and wouldn't have to depend on these cover girls for company. As Xiaohong was pondering this, Mr Zhuang came in.

'Ah Hong, what you doing here all alone?'

Xiaohong, her mind spinning with the effort of deciphering his heavily-accented speech, said, 'Mr Zhuang! Have a seat.' He plopped his posterior onto the bed, right up against her.

'Li Mazi and Sijiang popped out to buy a few things. They should be back any minute.' She just wanted to prevent him from trying to get too friendly. In fact, the pair had just stepped out.

'Are you settling in OK, Ah Hong? Anything I can do? So young and so far away from home, it can't be easy,' he said mildly.

'I'm very appreciative, Mr Zhuang. We've troubled you for several days already. We'll leave as soon as we can,' she said, sparks flying in her mind like a freshly struck match.

'You misunderstand me, Ah Hong. I didn't mean that at all,' he said with a wink and an air of deception. He bumped his hip against her, a gesture loaded with obvious meaning.

She understood well enough, thinking, This forty- or fifty-year-old man is here trying to trick a little girl. If he knew I could see right through him, he'd be humiliated. But Li Mazi still works here and, after all, when we needed a place to stay, he did help us. Pretending not to know what Mr Zhuang was up to and making no attempt to avoid him, she said, 'Mr Zhuang, you really are a good man.'

He beamed and moved a bit closer. He stretched out his right hand and put it on her right shoulder. With his left hand, he held out two fifty *yuan* notes. 'Ah Hong, take this and use it. If you have any problems, come and find me.'

Xiaohong cursed to herself, This guy is even more disgusting than the mayor. And he expects me to sleep with him? I'm not going to end up hooked on his bait.

'This... Mr Zhuang...' Xiaohong said, deliberately seeming a little tempted.

'Ah Hong, take it.' He tried to press it into her hand. He was not a big man and his arms were too short. With his right arm wrapped around her, he had hoped to pull her into an embrace, but he could not reach all the way around her. Pretending not to understand his intentions, she hesitatingly took the two notes from him. She said a few nice words to him, and deliberately stood up to put the money into her wallet, trying desperately to find a way out of this entanglement.

Suddenly, she gasped, 'Mr Zhuang! I've got diarrhoea. You sit, I'll be right back.'

He looked at her askance. Ignoring his stare, she unwound a long length of toilet paper and ran off to the washroom.

By the time she returned from the fetid toilet, he was gone. Li Mazi was there smoking, and Sijiang was washing an apple. Xiaohong sat on the bed, pulled the blanket up over her mouth and laughed. The other two looked at each other in confusion.

'What a pain! Without anything in the bowels, I can't believe I spent so long squatting over the toilet.' She told them what had happened, offering a few choice insights in conclusion.

'Honghong, you really have a way of seeing right through people,' Sijiang said, handing her the apple.

'Hey Sijiang, pack your things. We're leaving in the morning.' And with a loud crunch, she took a big bite out of the apple.

'What? Tomorrow?'

'Yep. If we don't get out of here, Mr Zhuang is going to start docking Li Mazi's wages.'

THREE

I

'Hey, Sijiang, look! Dorm beds, ten *yuan* a night.' After craning her neck and looking in all directions, Xiaohong finally came across some cheap accommodation.

'Where? Where?' Sijiang's small eyes were locked in a sort of tunnel vision.

'There, the Spring Hotel,' Xiaohong pointed toward a humble sign, under which was a forked path. On the sign, carefully drawn in red ink, was an arced line that pointed straight ahead, topped with a tiny arrow. It was a sleek, slippery marking of the path, standing erect like a living thing.

'Sijiang, what does that remind you of?' Xiaohong said, bursting into laughter.

Sijiang looked at the arrow, scratched her chest and pondered a moment, 'It just looks like an arrow. What you laughing at?'

Xiaohong tweaked her friend's nose and, not wanting to make her feel bad, decided not to say, Doesn't it remind you of the mayor's thingy?

'You two ladies looking for a room? Come on. Follow me,' a woman, looking young and pretty, said to them with a smile. At a second glance, they thought she seemed a little wilted, her age indiscernible. She wore dark red lipstick and her eyes had been outlined with two thin black marks. It took a moment for Xiaohong to realise that the eyeliner had been tattooed on.

'It is ten *yuan* a night?'

'Yeah, definitely. Not a penny more.'

'Alright, we'll have a look.' Holding hands, the two girls followed the woman's large rump around a few bends to a very quiet back street, through a dark, narrow passage, and clacked their way up a wooden staircase to the second floor.

'It's like our old place, with bunk beds and everything. How many people per room?'

'Five. Two per room costs thirty a night. Which one you wanna stay in?'

'Five to a room,' Sijiang rushed to put her bag on one of the beds, as if afraid someone was competing with her for a place.

Once their money had been collected, the owner wiggled her well-rounded hips as she made her way out the door.

'Well, it's got a strong perfume smell,' said Sijiang, wrinkling up her nose. The room was messy, but too dimly lit to really see how dirty it was.

'They've still got mosquito nets up. That's weird.'

'The mosquitoes are even worse in winter than other times of the year. Stay here long enough and you'll see for yourself,' a female voice said in their hometown dialect.

Xiaohong stared at Sijiang. 'Did you say that?'

'You mean it wasn't you?'

They were both bewildered.

'Eh. It was me.' A head popped out from under the mosquito net on one of the upper bunks, a pair of bleary eyes looking out from a pretty face.

Such an angel! But what kind of girl would be hiding in bed asleep in the middle of the day? Xiaohong thought, wearing an expression of surprise mingled with scepticism. Sijiang looked even more perplexed.

'I said it. So, what are the two of you doing here? Take my advice and go back home,' the pretty girl said lazily, and retreated behind the mosquito net. The two girls stood where they were, confused.

'Hey! I'm sleeping! Keep it down, will ya?' another girl said in a muffled voice.

Xiaohong's stomach started rumbling. She stretched out her upper body, gave an exaggerated shrug, and whispered, 'Hey Sijiang, at least it's not expensive. Let's give it a try and see how it goes. We'll have a look around the area while we wait for news from the Lucky Duck Handbag Factory. Maybe we'll even meet some guys who want to hang out for a couple of days and buy us dinner.'

After going out for some fried noodles, they returned to the dorm and found the other girls sleeping soundly. The leisurely lifestyle was apparently contagious. When Xiaohong and Sijiang lay down on their bunks to daydream, they, too, ended up sleeping until dinner time.

When the three other women in the room got up, they took the cups and bowls beside their beds and, rattling them, flip-flopped about the room. A thick smell of perfume filled the quarters. Sijiang, with a nose like a dog's, was sensitive to the heavy smell and sneezed several times. The three women in their fine-quality sleepwear were all very good-looking. They twisted their bodies lazily inside their pyjamas, showing off their supple forms. When they'd finished washing, they sent out for dinner.

'You two eat yet?' the first girl to speak – let's just call her Li – directed the question towards Xiaohong.

'We're not hungry. We had a snack,' Xiaohong waved her off, while Sijiang stared unblinkingly at Li's pretty clothes and pretty face. They ate hurriedly and without expression, as if merely going through the motions. The second girl, Lu, cleared the dishes and took out the rubbish when they had finished. The third, Liu, opened a small handbag and removed three bottles, laying them on the table. They placed three stools in front of the table and dropped three derrières onto them. Xiaohong and Sijiang stared at the backs of these graceful figures. The mirror reflected the entire room. Sijiang sat with her feet dangling off the bed, the mosquito net covering half of her shape. Xiaohong leaned against the bed, gazing at the three girls in the mirror. Each clutched a small hand mirror, inspecting first the right cheek, then the left, using it like a magnifying glass. They lightly touched here, carefully pinched there, applying this and that to their faces, then tapped the skin lightly.

'Fuck. Last night, my damned rich uncle and his dirty mouth... it made me want to puke.' Li applied the tweezers to her eyebrows, bit by bit, like a chicken pecking at grains of rice.

'His Hong Kong dollars aren't bad, though. You score a bull yet?' Lu bared her teeth, using her fingernail to pick at a spot as she hissed.

'A bull? Without going to bed, you think a rich uncle's going to part with a bull?' Liu said, who was stouter than the other two. She teased her short hair to stir a little life into it.

'Hey, you two girls, what the hell you doing, so young and here on your own? It's hard to get out once you start working in this line. I suggest you both go back home,' Li said, using her fingertip to pick something out of a little bottle and apply it to her half-opened eyes as she swept a glance over Xiaohong and Sijiang.

A bull? And what the hell line of work is this? Xiaohong thought to herself.

'Oh well. Why don't you both wash and get made up? You can come to the Sea Pearl Hotel with us tonight and sing,' Li said.

'We don't have any makeup.' Sijiang looked enviously at the newly-constructed faces. She had always wanted to experience such a makeover.

'You can sit here. I'm done. I'll get dressed now,' the short-haired Liu got up and stripped naked. She displayed her bare chest proudly, looking first for her bra, then her panties, searching through a row of underclothing hanging on a line stretched across the room, her large breasts jiggling as she moved. Sijiang, unused to seeing other women's naked bodies, stared right at her. She found that all the essential parts were the same as her own, but not identical. As she looked, her face burned with embarrassment, and she couldn't help but take a second look at such an attractive physique. Feeling dwarfed, she forgot to close her mouth, which was gaping in astonishment.

'Go on then,' Xiaohong said, nudging her. Sijiang clamped her mouth shut and her throat issued a little gurgling sound. She walked to the table. Seeing the bottles that covered it, she was stupefied.

'Apply this first. You got any other clothes?' Li asked, handing Sijiang a bottle of toner.

'Some, in my luggage. Wow, your eyes are so dark, and your lashes are really long. And your skin is so fair,' Sijiang said, enviously.

'Here. Do the foundation, then a little powder.' Li, seemingly used to hearing such praise, pushed the case of powder toward Sijiang and continued, 'The lights are dim at night, so you need plenty of makeup if you don't want to look pale as a ghost.'

Sijiang nodded and rushed to put a layer of powder on her face. Looking at the mirror, she added an additional layer.

'Hey Sijiang, don't overdo it,' Xiaohong stood to one side, stifling a laugh. Just at that moment, she noticed several dark red scars on the inner part of Li's arm. Obviously, they were cigarette burns. She looked at Li in surprise, but only received an indifferent smile in return.

'Working in this line, there's no place for any real feelings. Showing true emotion is a sign you're finished,' Li said, placing a white pearl earring on her left earlobe.

There it was again, 'this line'. What exactly was 'this line'? Xiaohong wanted to ask, but thought better of it.

Lu, her fingers bent back at an awkward angle, applied a heavy coat of varnish to each nail, the brush licking at them like a cat. Finishing the job, she held them to her lips and blew gently. The sharp claws looked like a ready defence against any attacker.

Liu, facing the mirror, put on her bra. Twisting her arms behind her to close the clasps, she entrusted the care of her breasts to the garment. She turned sideways as if posing, then said to Xiaohong, 'Why aren't you getting ready?'

'I only need ten minutes to get made up,' Xiaohong gazed at Liu's bust to see the effect. The embroidered, lacy bra gave her chest a boost and Xiaohong suspected it was not a cheap piece of clothing.

'Nice bra. Expensive?'

'Embry brand. It cost me a hundred.'

'Wow, that's pretty steep,' Sijiang said, startled.

'These briefs, fifty-eight. Oh well, at least it's not cold.' Liu wiggled her hips. Both cheeks were exposed, with a small strip of cloth cutting up the median line between them, converging with another string around her waist.

'Ha, that's ridiculous. You may as well wear nothing!' Xiaohong said, talking straight, even to a stranger.

'It's sexy, don't you know? My rich uncle loves it that way, and so do the young guys!' Liu took a long, admiring look at her buttocks then turned around to put on her jacket. Sijiang, her makeover finished, showed off the results of Li's basic operation. Her tiny eyes looked considerably bigger, her skin a powdery white with a rosy tint to the cheeks. Her hair was let down and combed out. When she looked in the mirror at her apple-shaped face, her eyes filled with excitement.

'Oh yeah, I forgot to ask – are you two virgins?' Li's expression was serious.

'I was, once upon a time,' Xiaohong said, giggling.

'Then it'll be easier. Go and get dressed.' Sijiang grabbed her crumpled jacket. Li looked at it and said, 'Don't wear that. I'll find something for you.' She turned and asked Xiaohong, 'And you?'

She just shrugged. 'Me? I'll just wear what I've got on.'

11

Sea Pearl Night Club flashed on and off, first green then red. Seen from a distance, it dazzled like an elegant woman walking at the end of a long country road, but upon drawing nearer, it was clear just how thin the layer of glitz really was. Everything around it was desolation and construction work, making one wonder what the owner had seen in the location. Xiaohong was awed by the grandeur of the place and suddenly felt shabby standing beside it. She regretted not dressing better for the occasion. Seeing Sijiang in her white jacket pulled snug around the waist, she thought the younger girl looked like a star.

'You look like you could party all night. I mean it,' she said, fingering the fine fabric appreciatively.

Her friend, obviously aware she was just stating the facts, pouted and said, 'When we make a little money, I want to buy tons of nice clothes.' Sijiang was always saying this sort of thing, as if she were afraid she would forget why she had left home.

'Come on you two! People've been asking and we told them we had some new girls,' Li called back to them over her shoulder. 'You don't need to pay the cover charge.'

When the waitress opened the heavy wooden door, the powerful beat of the music flooded over them, startling Sijiang. She clung to Xiaohong's hand. Shadows flickered in the strobe light as it played over the crowd. Sijiang, spooked by the quick switches between starkly lit images and sudden darkness – making everyone look like ghosts – was too disoriented to make out any faces. She could only see flashes of teeth and the whites of strange eyes, unable to tell who anyone was.

'Hang on a while,' Li shouted to them. 'There'll soon be people looking for a little company while they sing. There'll be plenty of chances to pick up some cash then.'

'Don't we have to pay to sing?' Xiaohong asked.

'Pay? The guests should pay you to sing!' Li retorted.

Xiaohong had put her foot in it again. Ever since meeting Li, she had committed too many blunders and been confronted with too many ominous sounding terms. Like, what did she mean by 'bull' or 'this line', and now 'guests'? They not only didn't have to pay to sing, but they would get paid for it. Was this some kind of scam? Her eyes scanned the crowd as it grew, seats gradually filling up. Groups of girls scattered, each gravitating to a different table. Some were invited to sit with the men, whose arms quickly snaked intimately around their bodies. Some couples made their way to the dance floor, embracing each other feverishly and swaying to their own rhythms.

Sijiang's palms were sweaty. She shivered.

'You cold?' Xiaohong asked.

'No. I'm just scared some guy's going to ask me to dance and I don't know how to.'

'You call that dancing? Looks to me like they're just groping each other.'

A man came over and led Li and Lu away. Li turned back and said to Xiaohong, 'When you finish singing for your guests, remember to get a tip.'

So that's what she meant by 'guests'.

Before long, Liu was led away as well. Sijiang clung even more fiercely to Xiaohong. 'Let's sing together, OK? I don't want to split up.'

'Yeah. I know.'

It wasn't long before a tall guy approached and politely asked, 'You ladies waiting for someone?'

The two girls shook their heads and followed him to a private room.

Inside, a short-legged man sat on the sofa, one leg dangling over the arm, singing a drunken raucous tune. The tall guy nudged Sijiang toward him.

'Dude,' Shorty said in Cantonese, 'you got a good eye. Keeping Big Tits for yourself, huh? How about you let me at her when you've had your fun?'

'You beauties understand Cantonese?' the tall guy asked, fingering a strip of long whiskers growing out of a mole on his chin.

'Not a word,' Xiaohong answered, eyes glued to the black strands of hair.

'It's your first time here?'

'How'd you know?'

'Because I've never seen you before. How long have you been in Shenzhen?'

'Just a coupla days,' popped out of Sijiang's mouth before Xiaohong could answer.

'Come and pick a song to sing for us.' The tall guy handed the song list to her, lit a cigarette, and started chatting with Shorty. Sijiang sang the 1980s Taiwanese hit *Innocence*, while Xiaohong searched frantically for some familiar tune to sing.

After a while, the tall guy put out his cigarette and asked, 'Hey beautiful, how about some tea?'

'Yeah. Tea and a late night snack,' Shorty chimed in, pulling at his waistband.

'Tea? They serve tea in places like this?'

'I didn't mean here. Let's go out for dim sum and a drink.'

'Go out? Where d'you have in mind?'

'Not far. Come on, it'll be fun!'

The girls followed them to a van in a dark corner of the car park. They piled into the vehicle, and Shorty squinted through the windscreen as he drove, trying to find his way through a series of twists and turns in the unlit streets. After several minutes of driving through the darkness in silence, he came to a sudden stop in a deserted area.

'Where are we? What are you doing?' Xiaohong said, voice pinched in anxiety. It was beginning to dawn on her that they had been misled.

'What are we doing? You can't see for yourself? We'll save money on the room and give you two a little extra. Win-win, right?' The tall guy laughed cruelly, voice quivering with desire. Unable to wait any longer, he pushed Xiaohong from the van and banged the door shut. Shorty grabbed Sijiang and held her tight.

'Just cooperate, you fucking bitch, and you won't get hurt,' the tall guy forced Xiaohong up against the back of the vehicle.

'Don't! I'll scream!' she said, struggling against him.

'Scream your fucking heart out. It won't do any good.'

She looked around. There was no light anywhere.

'Please,' her voice cracked, 'just let us go. We don't want any tips.'

She struggled to get away, but he was strong. He pressed himself more violently against her, kneeing her hard in the groin.

'Bitch! Don't try and tell me you're not a hooker!'

He pinned her to the vehicle, his knee pressed firmly between her legs. He dug his fingers into the flesh under her arms. She couldn't move. He freed one hand to yank her pants down, renewing in her the will to fight back.

'Keep struggling and I'll stab you.' Her resistance seemed only to serve as further stimulation. It was like he had lost all reason, roaring at her viciously. The two were at a stalemate against the van when it shuddered with a few random shocks before settling into a steady rhythmic rocking – up and down, up and down. The movement invigorated him further, and he rammed himself as hard as he could against her. She lost the power to resist, or even to cry out. Dizzy, she fell limp. The tall guy let her go, ready to proceed now that he had her where he wanted her.

Her mind sprang back to life. She shook her head at the thought of being raped and, maybe, killed. If only she could find a shred of humanity in this guy, maybe she would still get out of this alive. So, shaking and crying, she started to beg.

'Please, mister, let me go. I'm begging you.' She fell to her knees in front of him.

'Yeah, let her go!' Suddenly, the van door flew open, 'Take me instead!' She saw a flash of white from Sijiang's jacket, and heard an inhuman cry escape from her throat.

III

The tail lights of the weaving van stood out blood red against the black night as it drove away. Faced with the kneeling figure of Xiaohong, her tormentor had finally come to his senses. He backed towards the vehicle with an awkward crab-like gait, climbed aboard, and tossed Sijiang out into the dark wasteland. Xiaohong collapsed, feeling a sharp pain where she had been kneed, as if her genitals had been sliced open with a blade. Sijiang stood silently looking on, then fell to the ground and crawled over to her friend.

'Sijiang, you... you alright?'

'I, I, I didn't want to... he had a knife. He made me take my clothes off. He... held the knife while he did it and held it when he was finished.'

So, the shocks Xiaohong had felt from the van were Sijiang's initial resistance. The rhythm that followed was Shorty going at her.

'Same here, Sijiang. I had no strength. My legs were weak. I was so afraid he was going to kill me.'

'Honghong, let's go back. Look at those lights. I think it's the hotel,' Sijiang said, as she wiped the tears from her face.

'Yeah. Let's go.' Xiaohong stood up and shook her arms. 'It's so near. How come I couldn't see it just now? I was scared, so scared I couldn't even scream. Damn, that bastard's fingers hurt! Fuck him! You know that ticklish spot under the arm? Is that an acupuncture point or something? He dug his fingers in there with so much force I thought I'd pass out. How can a person grip hard enough to make it feel like that?'

'I don't know.'

'Hey Sijiang. After he did it, did he pay you?'

'Yeah. He gave me a note. I don't know how much it is.'

'At least you got something.'

'Honghong, look. What's that black shape?'

'Where? Don't scare me. Let's just hurry. It looks like we've hit the main road.'

'Let's not be so trusting in the future, OK? We barely got out with our lives tonight.' They grasped each other's hands a little more tightly. Their voices trembled.

*

'What's this? You two go back to a guest's room or what? It's three a.m.,' a pyjama-clad, makeup-less Li hissed at the pale image reflected in the mirror in front of her when the two girls finally walked into the room.

'Where are the others?' Xiaohong asked.

'Not back yet. They went to spend the night with customers. What the hell you two been up to?'

'Fucking nearly raped, and just about killed too.'

Xiaohong sat on the edge of the bed. She suddenly realised just how sore her crotch was, right in the spot the tall guy had pinned her with his knee.

'Then you got lucky. A few days ago, a couple of women were found in the woods, raped and murdered,' Li said casually, flicking the ash from the end of her cigarette on top of the pile of butts already filling the ashtray. 'I forgot to tell you, you need to use the rooms at the night club for your customers. Didn't figure you'd need one on your first night. Where'd you go? Both with the same guy? Did you get a bull?'

'What the hell are you talking about? We thought we were going for dim sum and tea, but instead we were manhandled to some godforsaken place. They said we were hookers. I said I wasn't a hooker, and I just wanted my tips for singing. And so the bastard forced himself on me. He just about poked his knee right through me,' Xiaohong said heatedly, chest heaving.

'You two aren't in this line of work? Then what do you expect to do here?' Li shook her head in disgust, stabbing out her cigarette. 'You'd better get out of here now, then. The longer you go on, the harder it is to turn back.'

'I don't know anything about that. I just know there was a woman who offered us a place to stay, and it was cheap, so we thought we'd give it a try.'

'That fat-arsed woman? She's the *Madame*. She drags you into this line, and whatever money you make, she gets a cut.'

'If you don't stay on here, what else can you do?' Sijiang, trying to unravel the knot, stared at Li in consternation.

'If you don't go through her, you'll never have work. The guests here are considered pretty generous. Sing with them a while, let them feel you up, and you make a few hundred or so. Every now and then, you'll catch a bull.'

'What in the world's a bull?' Xiaohong couldn't contain the question any longer.

'A thousand Hong Kong dollar note. But they only come along once in a while. Only if you find a really rich, really generous customer that really likes you.'

'A thousand?' Sijiang took out the note Shorty had tossed her and found it was red and unfamiliar. She waved it at Li. 'So what's this?'

'Hong Kong note. Hundred bucks,' she answered with barely a glance.

'What use is Hong Kong money?' Sijiang looked puzzled.

'Hong Kong money gets a good exchange rate. So hooking up with a Hongkie is a good thing.'

'You could make a few thousand a month like that?'

'Roughly.'

'Wow.' Sijiang was like a student, with the light beginning to dawn.

'But going on like that, won't you get spoiled with use... you know, down there?' Xiaohong asked.

'Of course you can't do it every day. Three, four times a week or so. And always with a rubber. There was this one girl, she wanted to make money to send back home for a sick relative to get some medical treatment. She'd do two or three guys a night. It only took two months and she was wasted, her body ruined and riddled with disease. She left to get it treated, but never came back. I have no idea what happened to her.' Li sighed, suddenly seeming like an old woman.

'You're so pretty. Why do you hoo— work in this line?' Xiaohong stopped herself just in time. She was trying to learn the lingo – substituting 'this line' instead of 'hook' – afraid of saying something taboo. 'This line' made it sound like a legitimate profession.

'You wouldn't understand.' Li cast a glance at Xiaohong, letting the girl know she didn't care for anyone's understanding.

A moment later they heard the clacking of high heels running. Lu burst into the room, clothes hanging open, underclothes in disarray, hair in a wild mess and wheezing like an asthmatic.

'Fuck! Raided! So damn dangerous! So sudden. The hotel manager didn't even have any warning.' She reached for a plastic cup and gulped down the contents.

Li gave a sharp laugh. 'A raid? Then looks like you getting away has cost the cops another two grand. Fuck them! As soon as they're out of uniform they're some of our best customers. Then when they're not here looking for company, they trap us. How are we supposed to get by if they keep making our guests antsy? I haven't seen Liu yet. She must have been hauled in.'

Lu's face fell in dismay. Li rallied and continued, 'Fuck! Fucking bastards! Is everything just about money? Arrested and fined, fines paid and then arrested again. Two grand a pop! It's a fucking cash cow. Did you see the john get picked up? Those damned cops, if they're not going to let us do our job, they might as well cut the balls off all the men in town!'

She ranted on, then lit a cigarette. Opening her handbag, she took out a wallet. She was silent for a moment, then said, 'Not enough. We need another six hundred. We'll wait till morning and see if Liu comes back. If not, we'll have to go to try and bail her out.'

IV

'Xiaohong, how about going back home? This place is so chaotic.' The bed squeaked, shaking under Sijiang's weight as she crawled onto Xiaohong's bunk, seeking some solace. Her voice quivered. With the noise from the nearby factories, the nights were restless and uncanny. The five girls staying in the room, with the exception of Li, had all had a difficult night. Unfazed, Li simply continued filling the ashtray with more butts, and the room with more smoke.

'What a shitty night!' Xiaohong stretched her arms, then put her right hand over her genitals again, saying, 'Oh, that hurts! Go back home, hm?'

'Yeah. I plan to.'

'Plan? You plan to go back now. It's like letting that guy do you for nothing. You think you're going to take your three thousand *yuan* back home and open up your dream shop? You really want to use the three thousand you've made over these few days for that?' Xiaohong said in irritation, trying to keep her voice down. Lu was tossing and turning on her bed. Li napped a while, then got up again to light another cigarette. She took a long drag, exhaled, paused a moment, then took another drag and exhaled again. With Li smoking like that, Sijiang kept choking. Hardly able to speak, she gazed through the mosquito net at the red tip of the cigarette. Someone kept sniffing, as if she had a cold, but they couldn't tell if it was Li or Lu. Whoever it was, she stealthily unwound a length of toilet paper, as if trying not to let anyone know.

'Well then, what do you have in mind?'

'Tomorrow, let's go to the hair salons around here and see if anyone's hiring. We keep expectations low – we just need to earn enough to fill our bellies so we don't starve. Things will turn around for us,' Xiaohong said through clenched teeth. Sijiang sighed softly and put her hand on her belly.

'Honghong, if I've… you know, got one in the oven now, you think I should go through with it or not?'

'If you have it, it'd be a little pig. That freak!' she said, taking another dig at the mayor.

'You're right. OK, I can't have it.'

'Then just go to the hospital and get rid of it.'

'An abortion? Won't it hurt?'

'It hurts like hell. Once, my brother-in-law took me for an abortion. It hurt so bad I broke out in a sweat and fainted. The doctor gave me a shot in the arm and then I didn't know a thing. God, they let an intern practise on me! It took forever. I can still see those stainless steel scissors and forceps in my mind. It's enough to scare anyone.'

'How'd they do it? They cut the stomach?'

'Nah. They go in from down there, then cut out that little piece of meat, slice by slice.'

'Ugh!' Sijiang clicked her tongue against her teeth, then let out a long, frightened wail.

'So Sijiang, that's why you've got to use a condom. And always calculate your cycle and make sure it's safe.'

The pillow shook a couple of times as Sijiang silently shook her head.

'You get what I mean, don't you?'

The pillow shook again. 'I don't get it.'

So, Xiaohong taught her a formula, even though she couldn't remember where she'd learned it herself. When Sijiang couldn't follow the explanation, Xiaohong pinched her. 'You've got to remember. A week before and a week after your period comes, you're safe.'

'Oh,' Sijiang said. 'How come you know all these things?'

'If I want to understand, I just understand.' There was a note of frustration in her voice. 'I'm tired. Let's get some sleep.'

Sijiang felt Xiaohong's well-endowed chest turn toward her and press against her side, warm and soft like the hot water bottle she'd always slept with during the winter back home. Giving in to the urge, she put her hand to her own breasts. They no longer seemed like oranges, but more like dry, empty orange peels. Without knowing why, she slipped her hand into Xiaohong's shirt. When she'd done it before, back in their hometown, it was Xiaohong who had grabbed her hand. Why she wanted to do it this time, she didn't really understand. She just knew it was something she wanted very much. Xiaohong shifted her position slightly, allowing Sijiang easier access. In the darkness, she couldn't tell if her friend had purposely twisted to cooperate with her act, or if it was a sleeper's random movement. The mound of flesh she held was smooth and sagging in its idle state, both strong and pliant. Xiaohong turned drowsily, rolling the other breast onto Sijiang's hand. Sijiang squeezed the melon-sized breast. In her sleep, Xiaohong moved her hand to her injured genitals, softly moaning in pain.

V

In the industrial area on the outskirts of Shenzhen, people went to and from work each day like a column of ants, no one giving much thought to how they all fit together. There were billiards halls everywhere, where games cost two *mao*. The pavement outside the shops was filled with plastic chairs and tables, and piled with empty cola and soya milk bottles, peanut shells and food scraps. Colourful barber's poles rotated outside a salon, with numerous towels drying in the sun – the very picture of a thriving enterprise.

'Hey Sijiang, look, The 007 Salon's recruiting shampoo girls.' Just after ten in the morning, the pair had set out to scour the streets, not letting anything slip past their attention. It had not been easy to locate this red flyer.

'Boss, we've come to apply,' Xiaohong said, with a bright smile, looking the manager right in the eye.

'Where are you from, young lady?' asked the short-haired, middle-aged woman, intrigued.

'We're from Hunan. We worked in a salon there.' Xiaohong thought the boss looked pretty straightforward and honest.

'Do you know how to wash faces?' The woman's gold earrings flashed. Her lips pursed and then relaxed, as if she were trying to keep hold of all the teeth in her mouth. It made her look like a gorilla.

Thinking this might be another one of those weird code words they used here, Xiaohong answered reluctantly, 'We wash our faces every day.'

The woman grinned broadly, exposing both teeth and gums in a way that was even more unsightly than a face in mourning. She said, 'I meant facials. You wash the customer's face for ten minutes or so, using cleanser, like this, and like this.' She used her hands to demonstrate on her own face.

'That's easy,' Xiaohong said. 'I'll wash her face and she can wash mine. Then we'll know how to do it.'

'You'll start work at nine in the morning and finish at two in the morning. Four hundred *kuai* a month, with room and board.' The woman closed her lips over her teeth. It seemed she was stifling a laugh. Xiaohong and Sijiang glanced at one another, trying hard to hide their pleasure. Eyes opened wide in delight, they practically flew back to the Spring Hotel.

When they arrived, they found that Liu had been bailed out. It seemed like everything was back to normal and that their mishap was over. There was still plenty of laughter, though perhaps mixed with more pointed barbs than before. Xiaohong and Sijiang expressed their thanks and bade farewell to Li, Lu and Liu. Dragging their worn-out luggage, they made their way straight to The 007 Salon.

Four

I

Privately, Xiaohong and Sijiang called their new boss the Ape. Her husband was called Zhan Shibang and the salon took its name from him, since Zhan Shibang sounded a bit like James Bond. Husband and wife, both of Hakka descent, were relatively easygoing. They had a daughter at secondary school about the same age as Xiaohong and Sijiang. They also had a five-year-old son, doubtless the result of a casual night's whimsy.

'Ah Qing, Ah Ling, here are a couple of new girls. I want you all to get on with each other, OK?' The Ape waved her simian arms. When she had finished her introduction, she picked up a shopping basket in her two large, working-class hands and headed to the market.

'The boss is a good person,' said Ah Qing, a girl from Guangdong with a fair-skinned face covered in acne. She spoke with a long, lazy drawl. Ah Ling was twenty-two or twenty-three and a real beauty. Since she knew how to cut hair, her salary was much higher than that of a shampoo girl and she thought of herself as in a whole different league from them. Her smile was always a little strained. She had a regular customer, an older Taiwanese man, who often came to see her. Every salon had a massage room and The 007 Salon was no different. The man did not care who washed his hair, but he only wanted Ah Ling to do the massage. When the time came, the pair would slip off into the massage room, not emerging until much later.

'That Taiwanese guy is loaded. He wants Ah Ling to be at his beck and call, but doesn't want to keep her on a retainer, if you know what I mean. What an old miser! Working in Taiwanese factories never has as good benefits as getting in with a Hong Kong company,' Ah Qing said, her pimples dancing all over her face as she spoke. It was her dream to one day find a sugar daddy of her own.

The salon was not very busy. Whenever a scalp came through the door, one of the girls would scrub it, wash the face and add on a massage, all at a leisurely pace without having to worry about anyone sitting in a queue rushing them.

'How long you been away from home?' Xiaohong asked Ah Qing, who seemed like an old hand at this business.

'Two years,' she said after a pause.

'Two years?'

'Yeah. I can cut hair too, but my technique isn't as good as Ah Ling's.'

'Ah Qing, what a pretty name,' Sijiang said in a sing-song voice.

Ah Qing laughed, her teeth looking like rice that had been washed clean.

'Ah Hong, Ah Jiang,' as Xiaohong and Sijiang had become known, in keeping with local custom, 'there's a lot to learn. You'll pick it up as you go. Anyway, I've got no real interest in working in a salon, but it's better than working in a factory. That's exhausting. The dorms are bad, the food is terrible and the wages are even worse,' Ah Qing whined.

'Can you teach us to do facials?' suggested Sijiang.

Ah Qing looked at the two girls in the mirror and patted the seat in front of her. 'Come on then. Who wants a seat?'

Sijiang sat down. Ah Qing wrapped a dry towel around her neck and another tightly around her hair. She squeezed facial products out of tubes and set to work applying them to Sijiang's face, with Xiaohong as an eager spectator.

A man entered, interrupting them. His face was as dark as a chestnut. He carried a helmet in his hand and wore faded jeans that were almost completely white.

'Ah Qing, how about a facial? Oh! Two new girls, huh?' he said.

'Hey Bud, you want a wash? This is Ah Hong, and this is Ah Jiang. Which one you want?' Ah Qing obviously knew him well and she spoke as if she were the *mama-san* at a brothel.

'Either one'll do.' Bud sat in the chair and held out a comb, offering it to whoever would like to give him a hair-wash and facial.

'Ah Jiang, go ahead. You'll be fine. This is Bud Kun. He's a nice guy.'

Bud really was nice. Sijiang stood behind him. He quietly looked at her in the mirror, closed his eyes, and tilted his head to one side. Sijiang, copying Ah Qing's earlier actions, wrapped a towel around him and began applying the scrub cleanser. Bud's face was like a toad's, covered in pimples. Sijiang cringed as she touched it.

'Bud, you still out catching bad guys day and night?' Ah Qing asked, leaning against another stool.

'Yep. Thieves and robbers, they're everywhere. Everyone's looking for something extra to take home for the Spring Festival.' He couldn't open his mouth all the way, and his words came out muffled.

'Bud, what do you do?' Sijiang asked.

'Village security.'

'This is a village? With all the factories and tall buildings? How can it be a village without any fields?'

'There are still fields, but with villagers these days getting so many benefits from the government to build factories, who wants to farm the land anymore?' Sijiang stared at him. She suddenly felt the lump under her fingertips was less repulsive – maybe even a little endearing. Her fingers began to move with more confidence, taking great care over her work. When Bud finally left, his face was no longer the same dull chestnut that had come in earlier.

That night, the two girls slept in the salon's massage room, with its one small window and set of bunk beds. The air was stagnant and stale.

'Hey Honghong, what's that smell?' Sijiang was always sensitive to odour.

'Sijiang, I think you must have been a dog in a previous life. The air is pretty bad, well... I think it's semen.'

II

Ah Ling gasped in the massage room, a deep-throated hum like a woman in the throes of ecstasy sounding on and off at irregular intervals. The human expressions of pleasure and pain are often interchangeable, like when tears of joy flow or a nervous laugh escapes. Xiaohong saw no contradiction here. Joy often has a hint of sorrow buried within it, and even a series of horrifying events can transform into happiness.

From the sounds emanating from the massage room, one could guess that the old Taiwanese guy was giving his best effort, despite the helpless embarrassment he must have felt. It was unlikely he knew much about what went on in a young woman's mind and he certainly had no clue about how to manage her sexual needs. No matter how long he spent with her, panting unevenly, he never seemed able to bring her any satisfaction. Ah Ling hoped the old man would give her money to open a coffee shop and offer an escape from salon life. He always dressed in brilliant colours that reflected well on The 007 Salon, though his manner of speaking betrayed some stinginess.

Whenever he came to the salon, Ah Qing would smile like a thief and say, 'He's just an old cat gnawing on a hunk of fish. He can't even finish the task. Just the smell of it, and he's already full!'

'Gross. With those age spots all over, it must be horrible to do it with him!' Xiaohong giggled as she combed her newly-dyed blonde hair.

'Sijiang, don't get cleanser in Bud's eyes,' Ah Qing warned. Sijiang had been assigned to wash Bud's face on a regular basis and the two had become quite friendly. When he was free, he would take her for a spin on his motorcycle or out for a snack. Sijiang, having grown used to cradling his head against her chest, no longer blushed when she washed Bud's face. The more experience she gained, the chattier she became. She was as comfortable scrubbing as he was lounging against her, and the time she spent giving him facials grew longer with each of his visits.

A perceptive girl, Ah Qing was good at discerning what ought to be said and what ought not. When she chose not to speak, as she seemed to do more often in recent days, she wore a lonely expression, like fallen leaves floating on water.

One day, after his facial, Bud suddenly said, 'There've been lots of crooks to catch lately. I'm aching all over. How about a massage?' Ah Qing turned away as Sijiang followed him into the massage room. Xiaohong, having just finished washing a customer's hair, caught sight of an embarrassed look on Ah Qing's face as she went into the washroom.

'Ah Jiang, how many siblings do you have?' Bud asked when they were in the massage room.

'I've got two sisters. I'm the oldest.'

He lay down on his stomach and Sijiang, not quite knowing how to go about giving him a massage, proceeded on a chaotic program of pinching and prodding at his back. He didn't seem to mind, concentrating instead on chatting idly with her. When she'd finished with his back, he rolled over. For a moment, Sijiang couldn't decide where to begin. Bud took her hand and said, 'Ah Jiang, I really like you.'

Having never heard words like these from a man before, Sijiang felt her apple-shaped face begin to burn. Her lips moved to form the words 'I like you too', but just as the words were ready to burst forth, they inexplicably pulled back before she could release them.

'Ah Jiang, you like me too, right?'

She nodded vigorously.

She took hold of his arm just above the elbow and started massaging. He looked at her and said, 'My leg's a little sore.'

She moved to his thigh and began her massage on the outside, working her way inward as she went. Pulling himself up and propping himself on an elbow, Bud asked, 'Ah Jiang, are you a virgin?'

She hesitated, an unhappy expression coming over her face.

'Never mind, I'm just asking. Don't be mad. It doesn't matter a bit whether you are a virgin or not. I thought... I just wondered if you'd massage this part,' he said earnestly. His jeans looked like they were inflated. Exhaling, he opened his zip, caught her hand and pushed it inside his trousers.

III

The fellow whose head was currently in Xiaohong's hands had been to the salon several times before. He worked at the neighbouring factory. He wore an employee ID card on his chest that read 'Project Supervisor: Si Daling'. In his mid-twenties and quite good-looking, he loved to come in and chat with Xiaohong. She always called him Supervisor, since that was what his badge said. When she'd finished washing and drying his hair, she'd massage his scalp using so little force that it was more like caressing than massaging. He always kept his head forward, avoiding the natural cushion of Xiaohong's breasts, which made his neck look tense. 'Relax, lean back a little,' she said. Upon leaning back, his head touched her chest and he immediately closed his eyes, a seemingly automatic response.

'Si isn't a common family name. Is it your real name?'

'Yeah. I only ever knew one other Si at college. We were especially close, sharing the same surname.'

'You're such a nerd. Are all college boys like you?' Xiaohong's hand was working on his neck. She felt the skin turn hot and his pulse increase. The Supervisor said nothing. Taking a deep breath, he opened his eyes and looked straight ahead at the mirror's reflection of a pair of eyes staring at him with a flirtatious smile.

Avoiding her gaze, he said, 'Why don't you come and work in the plant? Girls who work in salons pick up lots of bad habits.'

The pair continued to chat. When they'd finished, Si said, 'Would you like to come to my factory and have a look round?'

The shop was not busy. Ah Qing was arranging towels and clearing up some scattered hairpins. Sijiang had not come out of the massage room. Xiaohong said to Ah Qing, 'I'm going out for a while. I'll be back soon.'

Situated on a huge lawn, the factory looked like one big garden. They went into the dormitory and climbed to the third floor. 'Here it is,' Si said.

'You live here alone?'

'Yes. It's a bit messy. You like to read? I've got lots of books.'

Xiaohong went to the bookshelf to have a look. She picked up a book on appreciating Tang poetry. Flipping the pages, she finally found the starting point. Fortunately, Si was busy pouring tea and didn't notice her unfamiliarity.

'You like Tang poetry?'

'Yeah.' Though she had, in fact, read some of Li Bai's poetry describing the moonlight falling into a bedroom, she regretted her affirmative answer as soon as she'd given it. 'Hey, Supervisor, where are you from?' she asked, fearing Si would start talking about classical poetry if she didn't quickly change the subject.

'Zhejiang. After I left college, I came south to Shenzhen on my own. It's a tough city. Ah Hong, have a seat.'

She sat on the edge of the bed and Si sat down next to her. Both were antsy in their movements, obviously feeling the awkwardness of the situation.

'You want to see my photo album?'

'Of course!'

He pulled out a large album. It was huge. He placed one side on his right leg, the other on Xiaohong's left thigh, each bearing half the weight of the oversized album. Neither his right arm nor her left moved. They sat as still as if they were soldiers standing at attention, waiting for Cupid to descend upon them. They drew their heads together over the album, Xiaohong's fringe brushing against Si's nose as his breath blew softly against it.

'You're so handsome. None of these guys are as good-looking as you.' Their hearts leapt to their throats, making their breathing heavier. The chemistry in the air was dizzying, making them lose all sense of space. Xiaohong struggled to find something funny to say, just to prove she was not getting carried away.

The fingers of his right hand sought those of her left. One, two, three, four, five – step by step, it moved nearer until it pressed upon her left hand. She moved her hand a little and he responded more forcefully. The left hand gave in and the right hand caressed it softly. The album sat on the thighs, with no free hand to turn the pages. The left ear felt hot breath flowing over it, then a tongue tickling it before it was overcome wholly, lost in a tide of lips, mouth and tongue. Her mouth turned to meet the coming flood. There was half a second's pause and they surrendered to the deluge in a frenzied pleasure.

'I don't want to mislead you. I'm sorry. I got caught up in the moment.' The lips released her gently and the tide receded.

'You should find a better job,' Si said, casting his gaze upon her ample bosom.

IV

A woman's life is never easy. All of the ladies employed by The 007 Salon were unwell. It was not physical, but more of a mental issue. They had all changed during their time at the salon. Ah Ling was thinking of how she could overcome the old man's stubbornness, breaking down the barrier securely established between them and moving things on to a new level. She was determined to go out and find an easier way to make a living. Ah Qing was so distracted that whenever she washed hair, shampoo dropped onto the customer's body, but no one knew what was bothering her. Sijiang suddenly seemed like a full-grown woman, her gestures taking on a new charm. Meanwhile, Xiaohong was busy learning to appreciate Tang poetry and, though Si came by less frequently, her mind was forever dwelling on the moment that had passed between them that day in his room. Educated people were different, more easily upset over small matters. Even after all the men she had been with, she'd never felt so intoxicated before. Could it be love?

It was only upon hearing that Si wanted her to find a better job that Xiaohong realised that she had completely forgotten about the Lucky Duck Handbag Factory. Even if she went now, it would be too late. Flinging the book away, she said, 'Hey Sijiang, come and give me a massage!'

Sijiang was eating some sour plums that Bud had left for her, sucking and chewing on them, her teeth and tongue at war inside her mouth until every trace of flesh had been scraped off the stone and there was no flavour left. She would spit out the pit and pop another plum into her mouth, as if eating the plums was a sign of her loyalty to Bud, though it might have been that the flavour simply helped her to savour her own affections for him. She stood behind Xiaohong, her hands aimlessly kneading away without any rhythm or pattern. Xiaohong's head touched Sijiang's chest and she cried out in surprise, 'Hey Sijiang!

Have you filled out? That's some improvement. Is that what comes from constantly munching on those plums?'

Recently, Sijiang had begun spending the whole night with Bud.

Sijiang nudged Xiaohong, her eyes narrowed. 'What've you been up to these past few days always reading that book? Did Mr Supervisor assign homework or something? What the hell's so great about Tang poetry? And whoever heard of a book that you have to start reading from the back? Ah Qing, you ever seen anything like this before?' she asked, looking at Ah Qing's reflection in the mirror. Ah Qing grinned, her pimples coming to life, but said nothing.

'Hey, some poems are quite interesting. How about I recite a few for you?'

'Whatever,' Sijiang spat out her plum stone in dismay. 'Why don't you just save your recital for your beloved Mr Supervisor?'

'Ha! Who cares about him? He's a college boy and I'm a shampoo girl. You think I'd be stupid enough to go falling for him?' Xiaohong was scolding herself, but it sounded like her disdain was aimed at Si and that he was no better than a vagrant. In her left ear, though, there was always the sound of a warm surging tide, with a constant breeze leaving her left cheek a little paralysed.

V

Mr Zhan was a typical, jaded, middle-aged man. Short and stout, with sharp features and tiny eyes, he wore his long hair combed back and his face devoid of expression. One day, he decided to take everyone to pray at the local Phoenix Mountain upon which sat a temple where supplicants could burn incense and seek guidance in life. It was said that the pious would receive whatever they asked for. Mr Zhan divided the employees into two groups to make the journey. Sijiang and Xiaohong were in the first group.

Phoenix Mountain was not very high. After a short forty-minute climb to the top, Mr Zhan went about burning incense, praying to Buddha and seeking insight from the fortune-tellers there. He wore a very pious expression throughout his visit. Sijiang burned an incense stick but, too embarrassed to kneel, turned and walked away. Xiaohong, with a faint smile, turned her bulging bust to face the sun.

'Ah Hong, come and make a wish,' Mr Zhan said, waving her toward the censer.

'Wish? What would I wish for?'

'Money, love, marriage, health – whatever you want, just ask for it.'

Xiaohong, heart leaping, turned her back to the sun and went into the temple. On the ground was a red mat for kneeling. Of course, it was fine not to kneel too. But then, without kneeling, how would she show her piety? And without demonstrating piety, how could she hope to see her request granted? Xiaohong's mind turned to the Supervisor. Remembering his breezy touch, her cheek numbed to all other sensations and she dropped to her knees on the mat. This was the second time she'd ever knelt. The first had been when that tall bastard had tried to force himself on her. Now, facing this Buddha, where such supplication was acceptable, Xiaohong suddenly felt that the act of kneeling was like offering to put her head into someone else's hands. She closed her eyes and remained on her knees for about ten seconds, three columns of smoke from the incense she held rising into the air. She kowtowed three times, inserted the incense into the burner and stood up gloomily.

'What'd you pray for then?' Sijiang asked, giggling.

'She can't tell you. If she does, it might not be granted,' interrupted Mr Zhan.

Xiaohong made a face. 'It's a secret. I'm not telling.'

They continued their ascent up the hill. The incline was not steep, making their trek more like a stroll than a climb.

'Ah Jiang, Ah Hong, there's something you should know.' The mountain was tranquil, the air occasionally filled with birds flushed from their hiding places as the group walked by. Mr Zhan's slicked back hair, blown by the wind, took on a chaotic look.

'What is it, Boss?'

'Ah Qing's been down lately. It's because she likes Bud.'

'Oh, I noticed she was depressed, but wasn't sure why. She's a bit mysterious.' Xiaohong picked up a fallen branch and waved it about casually. She tried to recall Ah Qing's face, but couldn't get past the layer of acne. Sijiang, surprised, stood motionless, looking as if she had done something wrong.

'Ah Jiang, I'm not blaming you. Bud likes you. But before you came along, he was always very nice to Ah Qing.'

'Mr Zhan, I like Ah Qing. No wonder she's been walking around like she's in a trance,' Sijiang said. 'How could I have missed it?' A touch of sadness mingled with relief crept into her voice.

'You go on ahead. I'll catch you up,' she said, plopping down onto a stone step.

Xiaohong and Mr Zhan walked on ahead, passing several caves as they climbed the steep steps to the pavilion on the peak. The east side of the hill was shrouded in the smoke from the temple's offerings. Through the haze, Xiaohong caught sight of the temple's brilliant orange tiles and red pillars. The surrounding area was filled with neighbouring peaks, clouds rolling across them like a herd of galloping horses.

'It's so beautiful here and the air is so clear,' she sighed, her gaze sweeping over the scenery.

Mr Zhan walked over, hands clasped behind his back. He casually leaned closer and said 'Ah Hong, are you settling in to life at the salon?'

'It's not bad. Do you have any complaints?'

'Nah, you're doing fine. But I've been thinking...' Mr Zhan began cautiously, his eyes falling numerous times onto Xiaohong's bust, his thin trousers flapping in the wind.

'Go on, Mr Zhan. I promise it'll stay between us.' He wore a brazen expression, reminding Xiaohong of the recycling station owner, Mr Zhuang. Either these two looked a lot alike, or it was just that men, once they reached a certain age, liked playing their little tricks when they had a pretty young girl for an audience. Who did they think they were fooling, anyway? Xiaohong saw it clearly enough. The boss's eyes might only make their way to her cleavage once in a while, but that occasional glance was enough to reveal his most secret desires.

'I'm thinking I'd like to open a shop in another industrial park. You know, selling food and all the daily necessities. A place like that can be a gold mine.'

'Oh, a gold mine. Then what're you waiting for?'

'Well, I was also thinking that I don't have anyone to run it. Would you be interested?'

'Eh? Mr Zhan, are you joking? Me? The boss? Aren't you afraid I'd run away with your money?'

'If you like, you can take it all.' His voice quivered excitedly, like a randy rooster leaping onto the back of an unsuspecting hen.

'Now you're really making me laugh. I'd better watch out or Mrs Zhan's gonna murder me.'

Mr Zhan seemed to think things were looking promising. Taking the liberty of pinching Xiaohong on the backside, he said, 'Nice and tight. Sexy.'

Xiaohong, while not quite managing to hide the irritation on her face, still kept her temper in check and pretended to consider his idea.

'If Mrs Zhan knew your plans, you wouldn't get in trouble with her?'

'Trouble? I gave her that salon, and the income from it isn't half bad. She's got no hold over me.'

Xiaohong eagerly looked for Sijiang's arrival. No sooner had she thought of her friend than she began to wonder, might Sijiang have planned all of this with Mr Zhan? If he'd already been bold enough to start pinching her backside, she could only imagine what was next. One misstep now and she would offend the boss, leaving her to pack up and head out yet again.

Just then, Sijiang's head appeared as she ascended the last steps. 'That climb wore me out! How's the view?'

VI

Bud still asked Ah Qing to wash his hair and give him a massage from time to time. Cherishing the opportunity to do so, she expended a lot of energy on each of his visits. Ah Qing was very quiet, rarely smiling wide enough to expose her teeth. Her acne extended across her whole face, leaving hardly any area on either cheek that was not occupied. Nothing seemed to make her despair. As long as Bud still wanted her to serve him now and again, why should she despair? When she took his head in her hands, she was happy, her pleasure running as deep as sorrow.

After Sijiang had finished eating all her plums her mouth still continued in its habitual motion. As she watched Ah Qing rub back and forth on Bud's scalp, she couldn't be sure where his heart really lay.

Business at the salon had been slow recently. When Bud left, only Xiaohong, Sijiang and Ah Qing remained in the salon, each doing her own thing. Ah Ling, finally overcoming the old man, had got her wish of becoming a small business owner. Her departure had quite an impact on the other girls. Ah Qing was especially affected, and experienced frequent mood swings. Though Ah Qing had ridiculed the old man, there was no denying that Ah Ling was now indeed her own boss. Of course, if she married Bud, she could count herself as an even greater success than Ah Ling. Sijiang was thinking the same as Ah Qing, but who knew what was going on in Bud's mind?

Si, on the other hand, never showed his face around the salon, and Xiaohong knew he was avoiding her. She'd gone to look for him once at the factory, but had not been permitted past the gate. The guard had a sharp eye, but of course Xiaohong knew that if she really worked at it, she would manage to get him to bend the rules for her. But then, she wondered in frustration, what would she say once she finally got to see Si? She browsed through the Tang poetry each day, thinking of him as she did so. This sort of food for the soul left one hanging in limbo. She felt half-dead. After enduring many days like this, Xiaohong decided to let the Supervisor fade from her mind. This only led to her falling more deeply in love with Tang poetry, a source of great amusement for Sijiang.

Sijiang did not sleep at the salon. Only Xiaohong knew that she spent her nights with Bud. Xiaohong popped round to their place a few times, one of many cheap rental houses constructed of sheet metal. In summer, it felt like a sauna. While it did not smell of semen, it was surrounded by the overflow from the neighbourhood's sewage. It was a messy community, with vagrants ambling about during the day. There was no furniture in the house except one bed for sleeping and another upon which they piled their clothes. There was just enough space for two people to move about between the four walls. It pleased Xiaohong that Sijiang was settling into her little nest.

VII

One afternoon, Ah Qing was having a nap while Xiaohong and Sijiang chatted, sharing a bag of peanuts. Just then, two men in dark glasses came in.

'Gentlemen, you want a wash?' Xiaohong asked, getting up and greeting them with a big smile.

'Come with us to the village security office.' They did not remove their glasses from their immobile faces.

'Why? I've got my temporary residence card.' Having done nothing wrong, Xiaohong was not afraid.

'Enough talk. Get on.' They practically dragged her to a Yamaha motorcycle. With Xiaohong squashed in the middle between the two men, they took off in a puff of smoke. Sijiang stood for a long time like a block of wood, stunned. She could not understand why Xiaohong had been singled out, leaving her behind.

The Yamaha drove for about ten minutes before dropping Xiaohong at a courtyard and roaring off. It was crowded with all sorts of people – men and women, glamorous and plain, beautiful and ugly, anxious and unconcerned, nervous and relaxed. Those are more than just words that people use. They are the things one notices about others, formulating judgements based on the way they dress or look. Xiaohong's eyes wandered over the courtyard and fell on a village security sign. She recognised it then as Bud's workplace, and her heart leapt. All she had to do was go to the office and find Bud.

Just as she was thinking this, the iron gate opened and a vehicle pulling a trailer rumbled in. Less than ten minutes later, everyone had been herded into the trailer and the door slammed shut. It was pitch black inside.

Being arrested for no reason was bad enough. Now, on top of that, it was dark, and she had no idea where the vehicle was going as it rattled along. The passengers were all resigned to silence. Xiaohong's breasts were flattened against her body, making it difficult to breathe. There was a window about the size of a small wash basin that let in a little air, but it didn't get far into the carriage before it was absorbed by those standing closest to the window. Having inhaled it, they generously released it again, filtered now through their own garlic-scented breath so that the smell of cheap dumplings circulated throughout the trailer.

Feeling oppressed, Xiaohong resisted the urge to vomit, since she had no space to release it anyway. If she could get a small circle that was free of people, she'd gladly puke up all that she could.

After travelling for about twenty minutes, they stopped and the door opened with a *whoosh*. Everyone leapt quickly down from the trailer to discover it was no paradise that they had arrived in. It was a larger courtyard than the previous one, with even more people squatting or sitting on the ground, creating an open line of sight. It was different from the village security yard. This was obviously the home of some strict bureaucracy. Heavily armed police with batons dangling at their waist paced up and down, their boots clicking along the concrete. When the sound of whipping came from a shed, panic shot through the crowd. Some poor terrified soul tried to climb the wall. As the old saying goes, even dogs will climb a wall in an emergency. He was dragged down and given a good kicking by a group of officers in leather boots, while everyone else looked on. It was clearly a case of slaughtering the chicken in order to send a message to the monkey. Xiaohong watched in utter bewilderment.

There were some small shacks behind a locked iron railing. Several people stood inside eyeing those in the yard, desperate for freedom. To them, freedom was simply the chance of joining the crowd in the larger compound. Xiaohong looked at herself, standing there in the middle of all this. Sijiang would find Bud and surely he would know this place, wouldn't he? The concrete ground was cold and hard. Xiaohong had just stood up to stretch her aching legs and rub her sore backside when the shouted order came, 'Get down!'

A pair of boots walked towards her and she was faced with an energetic-looking fellow. 'Please sit down.' The officer looked at her with an expression of regret, speaking calmly.

'Mr Policeman, I'm not sure why I'm here. What do I need to do?'

Xiaohong, sensitive to the guard's change of tone, pounced on the opportunity. She looked at him sadly.

'You'll need to get your friends to bring three hundred *kuai* to bail you out. Tomorrow morning, everyone will be moved to the detention centre at Zhangmutou. It's a good forty kilometres from here.' His skin was almost as black as his boots and his expression was that of a consummate professional.

'Eh? I shouldn't be here. I've got a temporary residence card. I'm innocent, really!' Xiaohong said, her eyes beginning to tear.

'Hey, Dachang!' someone shouted from the interrogation room. With a hurried glance at Xiaohong, the officer turned and walked crisply towards the shed.

'Bloody hell! What is going on?' Xiaohong cursed to herself as she kept a careful eye on the courtyard gate. She waited so long she thought there might be a change of season coming, but still there was no sign of Bud and Sijiang. It grew dark and rain began to fall like bombs from an enemy plane. Caught unawares by the sudden downpour, only a small portion of the crowd managed to stay dry, huddling together for shelter like a coop full of chickens. Xiaohong's stomach churned as she shifted her weight, first to her right leg, then to her left, changing her position partly to fight off the effects of the concrete on her tired feet and partly to pass the time. Just then, she saw the officer who had ordered her to squat sitting on some steps. It looked like he was recording something in a report. After hesitating for a long time, she finally went over and stood in front of him.

'So, what's your situation?' Obviously, he'd already noticed her. He was very young, with an air of boyish shyness still about him. Xiaohong told him her whole story from beginning to end. He nodded, his pen scratching the page as he took some notes. 'Wow,' he said, and handed the note to her:

Bail paid. Please release. Officer in charge: Zhu Dachang

Her eyes reddened and she wanted to cry.

'Can you give me your phone number?' She swallowed hard, and her voice came out with a gurgling sound.

Zhu Dachang hesitated for a second then scribbled down his phone number.

Xiaohong received it with both hands, fiercely nodded her thanks, then went out of the iron gates and into the gathering dusk.

VIII

The night was brightly lit by street lights and the glare of neon. Xiaohong stood on the road and suddenly felt lost in these unfamiliar surroundings. Despite her absolute exhaustion, she forced her resisting legs into action. Asking passersby for directions, she walked all the way back to the salon, thinking over everything that had happened. How could they just pick me up without even questioning me? Why wasn't Sijiang picked up as well? It couldn't be Mr Zhan sending me a warning, since he didn't get what he was after, could it? Questions buzzed through her head as she dragged herself along, fighting off the gnawing uncertainties, asking for directions every now and then. About two hours later, she found herself back at The 007 Salon, where she gorged herself on food.

The Ape's cooking had never seemed quite so delicious before. Even the boiled chicken, its joints still a little bloody, hit the spot, though usually the mere sight of it was enough to turn her stomach. Had she spent much longer in that courtyard, even a meal of human flesh served up on a platter would have suited her just fine. Nervously, Sijiang watched her eat. When half the bowl of soup had disappeared into her stomach, Xiaohong noticed the look of guilt on her friend's face.

'Honghong, I tried to find Bud, but he's gone to Guangzhou and won't be back until tomorrow. I was going to come and get you then.'

Finally finding the energy to complain, Xiaohong put down her bowl and chopsticks and said, 'Tomorrow? I'd have been done for by then. They're sending everyone to Zhangmutou tomorrow!'

'So how'd you get out?' Sijiang was just about shocked speechless.

'I met a cop inside, my sister's classmate. He helped,' she said, casting a glance at the Ape. 'Auntie, your cooking is delicious!' she said, turning to the older lady, whose face was inscrutable, her mouth never quite managing to conceal its overlarge set of teeth.

Xiaohong suddenly felt very lonely. Her eyes reddened as she thought, Sijiang's got Bud and the Ape has The 007 Salon. If I'd really had to wait till tomorrow, relying on others, who knows what sort of torture I'd be facing now? Fortunately, to her credit, even in her darkest moments, she still had a bit of pride. Not a single tear dropped from her eyes.

That night, when the salon closed and everything had been tidied away, the Ape came to Xiaohong for a little talk.

'Ah Hong, you know I'm running a small business here. We've never had any trouble before.' As she spoke, she paid no attention to her teeth, allowing them to protrude from her mouth every which way.

Xiaohong kept her cool, understanding the Ape's meaning, but not knowing what sort of strange trouble was brewing. After consideration, she said, 'Auntie, I have no idea how something like this could've happened.'

Ignoring her, the Ape went on with her own concerns, 'I'm running a legitimate business here. When people see you picked up from The 007 Salon and hauled in, it damages our reputation.'

Xiaohong cursed silently. What a load of shit, she thought. The whole place smells of semen! Absorbing the blow, she sat silently through the Ape's hypocritical speech, waiting for her to finish.

'Ah Hong, it seems The 007 Salon won't be able to keep you.' The Ape's deflated lips finally managed to spit out her main point.

Can't fucking keep me? As if I'd want to stay! She resisted the urge to voice her thoughts. Choked with rage, she stood up and turned her angry face to the wall and her silent back to the Ape. She couldn't lay into the woman, since she hadn't collected her wages yet. If she showed her feelings, she would lose out, and it would have no effect on this fucking bitch anyway!

'Auntie, it's not Ah Hong's fault. She's the victim here!' Sijiang said, seeming mildly deranged.

Ah Qing had sat throughout the exchange, saying nothing as she toyed with a comb. Suddenly, as if dragging her voice up out of a pit, she said, 'The boss has plenty of troubles of her own!'

'Yeah, that's right,' the Ape latched on to Ah Qing's words. 'Ah Hong, you've done your job well. I'm also in a difficult position here.'

Xiaohong turned around. The Ape had thought she was crying, and so was surprised to see the smile on her face as she said, 'Ma'am, thank you very much for taking such good care of me these few days – your delicious cooking, and the way we ate together like one big family... it was really heart warming.'

'Ah Hong, about this month's wages – you've been here eighteen days, so that's two hundred and fifty.' The Ape exhaled, once again exposing a smile that looked like mourning.

Two fifty! That's funny. I've got no idea how the old Ape came up with that figure. But I do know I deserve every penny of it, Xiaohong thought as she neatly accepted the money from the boss's hand.

The Ape turned away, a sinister smile on her face.

IX

'Honghong, the boss says you went out that one afternoon, and there in broad daylight you were well, you know... hooking. She says that's why you were picked up.'

'Hooking in broad daylight? Because of the time I went to Si Daling's factory? If I'd really got it on with the Supervisor, I'd have been the first to admit to it when I was dragged over to Zhangmutou!' Furiously, she dumped the contents of her luggage on the bed in Sijiang's little shack.

'Yeah. Mr Si is different from us.' But Sijiang was at a loss to say in which respect they differed.

'He's got more status, but if we work harder, we can be like him. You with me on that?'

Sijiang gave an apprehensive nod.

'Hey, didn't you say that the cop you met was your sister's classmate?'

'I lied so the Ape wouldn't ask more questions. His name is Zhu Dachang.'

Staring at the piece of paper with the scribbled down number, Xiaohong said, 'I'll still have a chance to thank him.'

'He gave you his number? Ooh, I think someone likes you...'

Xiaohong chuckled and said, 'Sijiang, you've got a twisted mind. Bud has corrupted you. Hey – how's his kung fu?'

'What kung fu?'

'You know, his 'wrestling' skills.'

Tittering, Sijiang said, 'I'm not telling you that. Tomorrow, I'm going to tell Bud that I won't be working at The 007 Salon anymore either. You and me, we're going to keep up a united front.'

'Sijiang, don't be so impulsive. If you think you should carry on there, then do.'

'Honghong, let me tell you a secret. When I do massages, if I massage the guy's privates, they slip me an extra fifty, or sometimes a hundred. The boss knows nothing about it.' Sijiang's shadow loomed along the wall.

'You've got a bright future, Sijiang. For a little extra work, you make a hundred and fifty, just like that.'

'You don't understand. I always think of it as playing with a dog. You know how it is when a male dog's all randy? These men, they're exactly the same. Only difference is they don't sit there panting with their tongues hanging out. Ah Qing's even more skilful, in case you didn't know. She's got all sorts of tricks up her sleeve!' Sijiang licked her cracked, dry lips.

'Who says I didn't know? The Supervisor told me not to keep working in a salon. He told me all about the things that go on there. By the way, if you see him, will you ask him to leave a phone number for me?'

✳

'Heard what happened to you yesterday.' When Bud and Sijiang got back, Xiaohong had just got up. 'I asked around at the village security office and it seems like it's a complicated issue. Do you have any kind of relationship going on with Zhan Shibang?'

Xiaohong jumped as if someone had stepped on her tail. 'Fuck no! I don't have any kind of relationship with him at all! How can those people be so disgusting? What did they say?'

'Well, don't pursue the matter any further,' he warned. 'It's Mrs Zhan who's on the attack.'

'Bud, that day we climbed Phoenix Mountain, you know how I turned down Mr Zhan's offer to open a shop for me to run? Did you tell anyone about that? I only told you and Sijiang,' Xiaohong glanced at her friend.

'Ah!' Sijiang said ruefully. 'I told Ah Qing. She must have told the boss. No wonder she's been acting so spiteful!'

'Nevermind. It could be a blessing in disguise. Something good will come out of it. Something was bound to happen eventually. I never wanted to work in a salon anyway, no matter how bad things got. This all just makes everything easier.'

'Honghong, I'm going to quit too. It's almost the Spring Festival. I got a letter from my mother, and I really must go home for it this year.'

'You earned a little money and now you wanna go back and show off, huh? But Sijiang, I don't want to go back.'

'My mother's worried. She said girls come over here and pick up all sorts of bad habits. Have I picked any up?'

'How would I know? Ask Bud! If he says you're alright, then you're alright.'

Bud laughed, showing an uneven row of teeth. She noticed that the blemishes on his face had disappeared, leaving his skin smoother than before. Or, maybe she had just got used to it.

Xiaohong looked at Bud's innocent face then looked at Sijiang. She thought to herself, What a perfect match!

FIVE

I

The paper was crumpled, the phone number written there having long since been committed to memory. Still, Xiaohong was reluctant to discard it. Should she call Zhu Dachang or not? Would he be willing to help her one more time? Would it even be him answering the phone?

Don't be so bloody irritating! She scolded herself. He gave you the number, at least give him a call.

'Hello. I'm looking for Zhu Dachang.'

'This is Zhu Dachang. May I ask who's speaking?'

'I'm... eh? Are you really Zhu Dachang?'

'Yeah.'

'I... I'm... last night...'

'Oh, it's you. I only thought of it after you left, but I should've asked if you had money for the bus.'

'Oh...' Xiaohong's eyes reddened and she said in a choked voice, 'I... walked home. It was a long way.'

'I'm really sorry. I overlooked it. Where are you now?'

'I'm... at a friend's rented room. I resigned from the salon yesterday.'

'It's better. You don't want to work in a salon.'

'Yeah...' she was touched and her tears began to flow.

'Hey! Are you crying?'

'No, I'm not crying.'

'Give me your address. I'll come over.' She told him. He was familiar with the area. 'Wait there for me. I'll be there in twenty minutes.'

Hearing these simple words from Dachang, a warm feeling flowed
over her. She really wanted to cry on his shoulder. Putting down the
phone, it was the first time she had felt truly isolated. Her beloved grandmother was gone, her only sister considered her an enemy,
her brother-in-law was coldly indifferent and her father engaged himself
in other projects and other women that kept him away from home. No
one had the time to listen to her or look after her. She began to feel
that her former self had done many absurd things. Though she had
hurt her sister badly, bringing disgrace on the whole family, she had
maintained a sense of self-righteousness through it all. Only now did
she begin to feel some remorse and sorrow over what she had done.

Dachang, though he was a stranger, acted like a friend. Through
a simple act of kindness, he showed a depth of concern. She'd never
expected to meet such a good person.

She quickly finished tidying up the room, putting away all the underclothes she'd hung out to dry. She tossed them into a basket and
stashed it out of sight, then hurried to put on her favourite blouse,
wash her face and put on a touch of makeup. When she finished, she
turned to the mirror to try out which expression was most appropriate
to greet him with. She settled on a pouting smile, finding it the most
natural. But when he came in, she had no smile of any kind for him.
Instead, her eyes turned red, the corners of her mouth turned down
and a sob escaped from her.

'What happened? Come on, tell me,' Dachang said anxiously. He
wore civilian clothes, a brown jacket over light-blue jeans. Having ex-
changed his boots for a pair of trainers, he looked more like a normal guy.

'It's nothing. Really, it's fine.' Xiaohong wiped her tears and
put on a smile.

'Missing home? It's not easy being on your own far away from home. I know.'

Xiaohong shook her head, then nodded, at a loss to stop the tears. She tried to calm herself.

'Your friend rented this place?'

'Yeah. She lives here with her boyfriend.'

'Then you're the third wheel?' he teased. She laughed. 'Come on. I'll take you for a nice meal.'

His motorcycle bore a police licence plate. As Xiaohong climbed onto the bike, she immediately felt she would attract a lot of envy.

The bike drove past Dachang's work place, the very spot where Xiaohong had spent half a day locked up. They drove on for a while then stopped in front of a Western-style café. Newly opened, the café was overrun with baskets of fresh flowers, the ground covered with little red scraps of paper from the firecrackers set off at the grand opening celebrations. The table was small, and their thighs bumped underneath it. Xiaohong did not move away, nor did Dachang. Actually, there was nowhere to move to. It was as if the table had been designed for lovers, pressing them closer together by narrowing the distance between them.

'I usually have the Indonesian fried rice. It's not bad. You might like the seafood rice.'

Xiaohong flipped through the menu, looking over the strange-sounding names, unable to work out what connection any of them had with rice. The waitress rattled a bunch of objects. Xiaohong knew that they were called knives, forks and spoons, but couldn't remember which was which.

'Zhu Da... er, *Zhu Ge*,' she began awkwardly, finally settling on Big Brother Zhu. 'This is my first time eating foreign food. How do I use these things?' Zhu demonstrated how to use the cutlery.

'OK, I get it. Anyway, it's still filling the stomach, just with different tools that's all.'

The light was not very bright. A male singer's voice came through the speakers, his uncanny vibrato gave Xiaohong goose bumps. 'So what's your next step?' Dachang asked. His hair was short and wavy, and he had a wide forehead.

'I'm thinking of finding factory work. Do you think you'd be able to help at all?' As soon as she spoke, she was afraid he would reject her. She waited nervously for his answer.

'Shouldn't be a problem. I've got a room near here. You can stay there for a few days if you want. Of course, I won't be there.'

'That's perfect. Then I won't have to be the third wheel,' Xiaohong said, giggling.

II

As Xiaohong got ready to leave, Sijiang cried bitterly. 'Sijiang, what're you crying about? It's not like I'm dying. I'll still come and see you when I'm free!' Xiaohong stuffed all her clothes into her bag, suddenly feeling a little sad.

'Honghong, this is for you. You love wearing it,' Sijiang said, taking a beige knee-length jacket from its hanger. Xiaohong tried to refuse, but Sijiang stuffed it into her luggage.

'Now, you take care of yourself. You've got to think things through, you know?'

'Sure.'

'And what're Bud's plans? Have you met his family yet?'

Sijiang shook her head. 'He never talks about his family.'

'Well, no matter what, just make sure he helps you find a job in a factory so you can make a better living. Then you can scrape by while you two take your time talking about your future.'

Sijiang nodded, feeling like her heart was breaking.

'Sijiang, we can only depend on ourselves. You know what I mean? You don't need to be afraid of others. There's nothing at all to be afraid of. You just have to be bold, and don't be taken in by anyone. Don't let other people get the better of you.'

Sijiang listened, nodding in agreement. Abruptly she said, 'I have a feeling we'll be together again.'

Xiaohong laughed. 'Of course we will! Who knows what will happen in the future. Look at these past few days – things have changed so much. The things in this bag have been packed and unpacked so many times. God only knows what tomorrow holds.'

They were both silent for a while. Sijiang sighed. Xiaohong sighed too, then lifted her luggage and parted ways with Li Sijiang.

III

Zhu Dachang's room was on the fourth floor of a building next door to the police station. It was a single room with an en suite bathroom. There was a mattress, and the room was well-lit. It was in a completely different league from Sijiang's little metal shack.

'With cops living on either side, there's nothing to fear at night. You just get settled in, and tomorrow I'll get in touch with the factories. You'd better be prepared, because whether it's twelve- or eight-hour shifts, it's going to be tough,' Dachang said, with a stern expression.

'I'm not here for a holiday,' Xiaohong answered. 'I'm not afraid of hard work. I'm just afraid there's no work to do.'

Dachang smiled.

He must be around twenty-seven or twenty-eight, Xiaohong speculated, but didn't have the nerve to ask.

Dachang stayed for a little while then said, 'I've got to go to work. You can sleep or read if you want.' He pointed to the mattress.

Xiaohong picked up a book and flipped through it. 'It's so thick!' she said.

'You ought to read *Human Weakness*. I think it would be good for you.'

That one didn't look too thick, so she reckoned she could finish it. After he left, Xiaohong lay on the mattress thumbing through the book. But how could she read it? Her mind kept turning to Dachang, wondering why he was being so good to her. Did he have some ulterior motive? If so, why had he not acted on it? She continued to flip through the book as she contemplated, eventually drifting off to sleep.

'Hungry? I've got spicy chicken or pan-fried pork. Which one you want?' Before dark, Dachang was back, carrying two takeout boxes.

'Hey! That spicy chicken smells good!' Xiaohong said, licking her lips.

'Yeah, you can't just eat instant noodles the whole time. Give it a couple of weeks, and I bet just the sight of the packets will make you want to puke.'

'*Zhu Ge*, those instant noodles are enough for me, nice and crispy. I've already had a pack.' She pointed to the box marked *Dr Kang*.

'Huh? You ate it dry? How did you manage to choke it down? And without adding any seasoning!'

'I don't know. I opened it, saw it sitting there dry and so ate it dry,' she said, attempting to defend herself.

'Whatever suits you. You can finish the whole box, if you want.' Dachang shook his head and smiled. 'I checked around at the factories. I think the conditions at the toy factory are a little better than the others. Tomorrow or the day after, you can report to work. It may take a few more days to get a bed for you, so you can stay here in the meantime. You brought your ID card, right?'

'I don't have an ID card.'

'How old are you?'

'Seventeen.'

'Without an ID card, you think anyone's going to give you a job?'

'But I haven't done anything wrong!'

'Who knows what you have or haven't done?'

'If I had an ID card, would it prove I'm no thief?'

'Look, without an ID card, there's no way anyone will employ you. So, tomorrow I'll help you get a temporary ID card. Tell me your date of birth.'

When they had finished dinner, Dachang took her for a ride on his bike. They wound through the industrial area and across a residential neighbourhood to a muddy beach. They stopped there for a while, standing amidst waist-high grass, the wind whipping around them.

'Don't go out alone at night. It's a bit of a chaotic neighbourhood, so you've got to be careful,' Dachang said, as she stood facing the sea.

'OK. I don't think I'd want to anyway.' Xiaohong told him about the time she had been tricked into going to that deserted place in the middle of the night and been treated like a prostitute. She concluded her story with, 'Things would've been better if I'd known you then.'

'If someone really wants to do something like that, knowing me isn't any use. What could I have done? In the end, you've just got to remember what I'm telling you. Don't go out alone at night.'

By the time they got back, it was rather late.

'I start my shift at twelve. If you don't mind, I'll just stay here and read for a while,' Dachang said, glancing at his watch.

'Of course, it's your place. You can do whatever you want. Look, I'm going to read too.' She said, before adding, 'Eh? *Zhu Ge*, how do you read this word?'

He came over, scanned the sentence, 'There's a dictionary next to the mattress. It's a teacher with infinite knowledge.' Looking exhausted, he yawned.

'*Zhu Ge*, you're tired. Relax for a while.' Xiaohong budged over on the mattress, making more space for him. He leaned back and continued reading. Xiaohong read too, struggling against her own sleepiness. After a while, her eyes began to close, and her head drooped onto Dachang's shoulder. The weight on his upper arm grew uncomfortable, but he found it too inconvenient to move. Gradually shifting so that Xiaohong's head lay in a more level position, he extracted himself and tried to move away, only to find that something had hooked onto his sleeve. Turning back, he saw that it was Xiaohong's fingers. Her eyes were closed, as if she were caught up in a dream. He pondered for a moment, then reached up and turned off the light. The street lamps outside filled the room with an orange glow.

Dachang, half-lying on the bed, felt his body getting stiff. His right arm was trapped beneath Xiaohong's left shoulder, her right hand draped across his chest, pressing against his pounding heart. He closed his eyes, afraid to move.

Xiaohong had liked him from the beginning and had always wanted to express her appreciation. Was hooking her finger onto his sleeve an expression of affection or gratitude? She couldn't be sure herself. She lay quietly, listening to the sound of time slipping away. There was no movement from Dachang. She stretched her body, burying her head into his chest, listening to the drumming of his heart. He inched his way down the bed a little bit at a time. By the time half an hour had passed, he was finally lying flat. Even as he struggled to resist, he steadily lost ground, pledging himself ever more firmly to the bed. Their heads touched, though they tried their best to leave some space between their bodies. Which of them drew closer to the other's face? It was really hard to say. The whole process was slow as clockwork, making it impossible to tell which movement inspired the other. Dachang's face was hot, and his breath was laboured and feverish. His rising temperature made him seem ready to explode. He remained motionless, Xiaohong caressing him as she lay draped across his body. His patience amazed her. Had his body not offered irrefutable evidence to the contrary, she would have suspected he was suffering from impotence.

'Your whole body is hot, but your mouth is cold. How do you do that?' Through the layers of clothing, Xiaohong pressed against him. He smiled in embarrassment and said he didn't know. He was passive alongside her manipulations, keeping his eyes closed the whole time, as if that would help him avoid temptation. Her bust, to him, was like a mound of warm, wet sand. When she pressed it against him, it was like the rise and fall of the tides, the ebb and flow in the wash of his red-blooded desire. His face burned. Xiaohong stripped off his jacket and his shirt. He reached out his hand then stopped. When she slid her hand into his trousers, he trembled and stretched out his hand, leaving it suspended in the dim light, looking like the distress signal of a drowning man. He sighed deeply.

'You don't like me, do you?' Xiaohong poked at the hand hanging there, feeling a little abashed. Seeing the signs of emotional distress, she looked down at her breasts. They seemed almost vulnerable. Dachang let out a little wordless groan, then patted her back and said, 'You are a good girl, and I don't want to hurt you. I don't want to hurt anyone. If I did this, wouldn't it make me a complete lowlife?'

'When you ignore me, that hurts me.'

'Xiaohong. Ah Hong, you will understand one day. I am a Hakka man.'

'What does being Hakka have to do with anything?'

'What I mean is, well, I'm from the area around the Guangdong Mei District. And I'm going to be married soon.'

'Oh, you're afraid you'll hurt *her*.' Xiaohong pulled back, hand and body, like the tide receding from the shore.

'At first, I was a secondary school teacher. I only put on a cop's uniform when I came here. She came over not long ago. She's a school teacher.' He stood up, looking at his watch. 'It's nearly time for my shift. I've got to go.'

He stood unevenly, straightening his uniform and cap. Looking at Xiaohong, he said, 'You get some rest.'

The closing of the door erased any trace of Zhu Dachang.

IV

The following morning, someone knocked on the door. Xiaohong opened it to find a man about the same age as Dachang, dressed in the drab hues of autumn.

'Eh? Dachang isn't here?' The man glanced around, his mouth slightly opened in a look of innocent surprise.

'Um... I'm a friend of his. I'm just staying here for a few days,' she said, leaning languidly against the door frame. She knew this guy lived next door and that he was also a cop. Reckoning that knowing one more cop would just create another avenue that might prove useful in the future, she retreated into the room and said, 'Have a seat.'

He came in, his professional eye making a sweep of the room, then said, 'Seat? I don't see any seats in here.'

'Sit on the bed,' she replied, pointing to the mattress.

His eyes roved here and there, always coming back to settle on Xiaohong's breasts.

'Isn't that a generous offer on our first meeting?' he asked.

'I'm sorry. There aren't any chairs,' she replied, pretending not to understand what he meant.

'Huh. Never mind, I don't need to sit. I'm Zhu Dachang's colleague,

Ma Xiaoming.' He took out a pack of *Triple-5* cigarettes and lit up.

'Oh, *Ma Ge*, are you here to take care of me?' Xiaohong smiled. Ma searched for something to say, obviously hoping to get to know her a little more intimately.

'You mean Dachang taking care of you isn't enough?' He wore an ambiguous expression, as unclear as water dumped into a roadside gutter. After a moment, he added '*Ma Ge* will take good care of you. What you feel like eating? I'll go and get something.'

'Anything's fine. Whatever you buy, I'm sure it'll be good.' Xiaohong fanned the pages of the book, creating a noisy stir. Ma was very thin, like a pole with clothes dangling from it. She suddenly imagined what he would look like in the act of making love, and thought his body might just snap like a twig if things got wild. She couldn't keep back a giggle as she pictured it.

'When you laugh, you sound like a Hunan girl,' he said, the way he stood on his scrawny legs making him look like a comic figure.

Xiaohong thought, Dachang must have told him about my situation and so he's purposely come knocking on my door. Though she had always been a little in awe of police officers, she was not in the least bit stirred by her visitor. He was just another cop.

With another giggle, she said, '*Ma Ge*, you're so smart! I *am* from Hunan!'

V

A few days later, in the evening, it rained cats and dogs. The downpour and the floods were in furious conversation, their exchange carried back and forth on the whipping winds. When the rain had stopped for a while, Xiaohong heard the ground groaning with the sound of overflowing waters that continued to bubble through the drains. The rain was like a sentient thing in its onslaught against the breadth of the earth's bosom. The further it spread out, the more the ground seemed bound to give way under it, as if its weight would open a great gaping chasm.

Xiaohong leaned on the edge of the window sill, watching the waters cleanse the streets, like tears washing over an eye. She suddenly thought of her home and her brother-in-law, and felt that those things were like a ravaging storm. She'd come so far and yet they whipped back at her, like the winds blowing in the night. The rain was too heavy, the leaves bruised by the convulsive shake of the wind and the shine of the neon lights was like the sudden flash of a set of white fangs. Cars ran through puddles, the water splashing arrogantly onto a nearby pedestrian, who screeched like a bird in alarm.

When the storm passed, the night was pale and still.

Restless, Xiaohong used her finger to take measure of the various books in the room. 'So thick. Who wants to read that?'

She lay on the bed, bored, staring at the ceiling till she thought her eyes would fall out. She thought of the suggestiveness of Mr Zhuang. She remembered Lu's face. The tall guy and Shorty. The Ape and her protruding teeth. The way Mr Zhan's trousers had blown in the wind. Li Sijiang and Bud in bed. Ah Qing's pimply face. Zhu Dachang's overheated flesh. Ma Xiaoming's unbelievably thin frame.

Tap-tap-tap.

She hopped off the bed, flopping like a fish out of water. It was just Ma with a plastic bag dangling from his fingertips as he stood trembling.

His eyes squinted over a mouth opened in a wide grin.

'I bet you must be bored to tears. Look: beer, peanuts, phoenix claws and fried noodles.' He brought the plastic bag in, rustling it in front of her nose, offering her a whiff.

'You're so sweet, Ma!' she slapped him on the back, liking the prospect of some food and a drink.

Xiaohong chomped away on a phoenix claw – a grand name for a chicken's foot – chewing and spitting out the bones.

'If you eat in such an unladylike way, you're never going to get married! Of course, *I* don't mind. Here. Bottom's up!' Ma, lips bulging as if he were gargling mouthwash, took a toothpick and began to pick at his teeth.

'Ugh. This beer is bitter.' She wiped her mouth. Basic needs met and belly full, her spirits rose as the night wore on.

'How have your first couple of days at work been?' Ma stood up, looking a little plumper now, but still grinning like a cartoon character.

Xiaohong laughed and said, 'You don't need to think. Just go through the motions each day. A robot could do it.'

'Is it tiring?' He looked at her warmly.

'Not tiring exactly, but we're not allowed to talk. It's like walking on eggshells the whole day.' She took off her shoes and settled back on the bed.

'If you talk, you'll be distracted. If you're distracted, you'll get less work done. What boss wouldn't like for his employees to go at it with gusto for him?' Ma settled a hip onto the mattress and sat facing Xiaohong. She giggled.

'What're you laughing at?' he asked innocently.

'Go at... what?'

'What do you mean?'

'Aw, come on. I'm just teasing.'

He thought for a minute, then broke out into another cartoonish grin, and said mischievously, 'You're young, but you're very naughty, aren't you?'

'Who says I'm naughty? I just say whatever comes to mind.'

Ma, feeling his eyes grow a little dim, wondered if it was the effect of the three cans of beer. After the can she had drank, Xiaohong actually felt more sober than normal. She could see he had something in mind, but then Ma wasn't Dachang, and she felt no desire for him.

'What's that book you got there?' he asked, pointing to the volume lying beside her. Seeing him stretch across her and take the book, she quickly picked it up and handed it to him.

'It's Dachang's. I don't know what it is.'

He took it and flipped through the pages, back to front, then front to back. He squinted at her and said, 'Zhu Dachang, has he mounted you?'

Mount? What sort of dirty talk was this? There was far too much colourful language to pick up here. It was the first time she'd heard the term.

'He did you, didn't he?' he said, changing to a more familiar phrase.

'Don't talk nonsense. *Zhu Ge* has a girlfriend. He wouldn't go fooling around behind her back.'

'So what if he has a girlfriend? If he wants to mess around, he'll mess around.'

'I don't know about people like you, but I know *Zhu Ge* hasn't done anything to me. He's a gentleman.'

'Being a gentleman just means he does it in secret. Gentlemen know how to do *everything*, and do it just right. If you say he hasn't done it with you, I find that hard to believe.'

'For God's sake. Let's drop it. I'm tired of it. If I say he hasn't, then he hasn't.'

'Hasn't slept with you and yet he helps you find a job? Lets you stay here?' His eyes narrowed.

'Well, if you want to say it like that, you brought beer, phoenix claws and peanuts over. Does that mean you've got something up your sleeve?' she said heatedly. Only when it was too late did she feel that this was like opening the door for him. Hoping to remedy the situation, she quickly added, 'I don't think you're that kind of guy!'

But Ma didn't miss an opportunity. Eyes bleary from the beer, he said, 'You're absolutely right! I do have an ulterior motive. I think you're sexy!' He seemed unable to control himself. He grabbed her and pressed himself onto her, pinning her to the bed with his bony body. He was strong and, though she struggled, she couldn't move. As he pawed at her, it brought to mind the claws they'd just consumed. She was unable to do anything.

Breathing heavily, he said, 'Don't move. Please. That's it... that's it...' He pressed against her. Though he did not undress, he thrust his pelvis repeatedly against hers, madly, as if he had never seen a woman before. In less than two minutes, he let out an odd sound.

And then he went limp.

VI

In the end, which was weaker, a man's cock or his will? Ma was just like a pig in the dog days of summer, wallowing in a puddle of sewage for the sake of cooling its overheated body.

Xiaohong did not feel any sense of loss, nor did she feel that Ma was a bad fellow. Compared to those creepy men who, when aboard a public bus, liked to rub their privates up against a woman as the vehicle bounced along on its route, he was at least honest, doing things openly. Those creeps on the bus took advantage of the crowded conditions which made random collisions of body parts inevitable. But if a woman dared to glare at one of them, he would respond with an innocent look, as if denying that anything had happened at all. Ma, on the other hand, even as he was thrusting frantically, had looked at her with miserable eyes, so he at least acknowledged his own weakness.

Ma was ridiculous and pathetic. Her maternal instinct sparked just enough pity in Xiaohong to make her willing to tolerate his performance.

Her work at the factory was neither very tiring nor very demanding, and it was a way to make a living. Other than her toilet breaks, it was almost like her backside was glued to the stool where she sat working. Twenty or thirty people worked on the assembly line, all girls around her age. Her line manager, from Guangdong, was taller than average, with a round, pale face. Her features were long and angular, her chest flat and her voice coarse. She didn't work on the line, but just stood with her hands behind her back watching everyone. From time to time, she would take a more active managerial role, her high heels *clack-clack-clacking* as she walked up and down, supervising. In tribute to her flat chest, Xiaohong and the rest secretly called her Runway. One of Xiaohong's colleagues, Ah Jun, was a girl from Guangxi and a member of an ethnic minority group. She was shorter than Xiaohong and had hair so long that it brushed against her buttocks when she walked. Her plaits were her only really striking feature. Her speech was as sharp as a knife and she was always ready to help others. Xiaohong hit it off with her very well.

'The manager originally came from the assembly line. Most importantly, if you want to move up you've got to be extremely good-looking and secondly you have to be willing to make some sacrifices. Look at her. She's so flat-chested! Your prospects are much brighter than hers.' A knowing smile appeared on Ah Jun's skinny face.

'Wouldn't I love for that to be true? That slut!' Xiaohong said in frustration.

'Runway only worked on the assembly line for two months, did you know?'

'Quiet! She's coming!'

Ah Jun immediately fell silent, suddenly appearing intently focused on her work. Her eyes were round, as if in surprise.

Feeling the pounding footsteps stop behind her, Xiaohong caught a whiff of perfume. She looked over her shoulder and saw Runway's haggard eyes staring at something. Following the line manager's gaze, she noticed that the big boss was talking to the foreman.

*

At the roadside food stalls outside the factory, one *kuai* could buy a meal that would leave anyone stuffed. During her hour-long lunch break, this was the only place to eat. Xiaohong ate, drank a cup of lukewarm water and looked at her watch. She had twenty minutes before she needed to clock in again.

'Ah Jun, I think Runway likes the foreman. Today, I saw her eyes lingering so long on his figure that I thought they'd fall out!' She couldn't help herself. She wanted to find out whatever information she could gather about Runway.

'You've got a sharp eye!'

'It's not that hard to see.'

'Well, Runway got the line manager's post based on the foreman's recommendation. But of course, things aren't quite so simple.' Ah Jun was still stubbornly munching on a phoenix claw.

'How complicated can it be?'

'You're new here, so of course you don't know. The so-called line manager is whoever's next in line to sleep her way to the next level. Just like Runway, the previous girl who held the post moved right up the line. She's a secretary in the office now, which meant everyone in line behind her got bumped up too,' Ah Jun said, disgusted – and perhaps a little disappointed that she'd been passed over. She'd been on the assembly line for over a year and had never been promoted.

Hearing her friend's explanation, Xiaohong laughed and said, 'Someday I'll move up the line and then I'll pull you right along with me. I'll turn the whole line on its head.'

'When're you going to move into the factory dorm?'

'Maybe in a few days. The supervisor said there's no bed ready for me yet, so I'll stay at my friend's place for now.'

'That cop?'

'Yeah.'

'He likes you, huh?'

'No.'

'I think he does.'

'I told you, he doesn't.'

'He's very nice to you.'

'He's got a girlfriend.'

'So what, I'm sure you can take over that role. You met her?'

'No.'

'Who knows? Maybe she's really ugly.'

'However ugly she is, she's still a teacher.'

'He mounted you yet?'

'Mounted? You mean you say that too? Bit trashy, no?'

'Trashy? That's the most civilised way I know to say it. You're so old-fashioned!'

'Shit! I can't keep up with all this slang. Hey, Ah Jun, you speak Cantonese?'

'Of course. We speak it in my hometown. I'll start by teaching you some swear words!'

VII

After making arrangements for her to work in the factory, Dachang didn't come back to his quarters to see Xiaohong, nor did he ask her how long she would be staying. Ma Xiaoming, on the other hand, was always in close proximity, often dropping in for no reason, drifting in and out at leisure.

After the first time he'd had his fun with her, he tried to have another go at it, but since he had not been drinking this time, he was a little more sensible. When Xiaohong gave him a polite refusal, he did not resort to begging as he had before. In his frustration, he took on an especially cartoonish look. He said, 'It's already happened once, so why turn me down now?'

Xiaohong felt it a very strange thing to say, as if what had happened once before gave him licence to do as he pleased with her any time he wanted. She replied, 'It didn't mean anything. We are just friends.'

'Don't you have any sense of decency?' He was really upset.

'How am I not decent?' Her face fell in humiliation.

'You worked in a salon! And, you were hauled in! Who do you think you're fooling?'

'Fuck off! You're so bloody irritating!' As she turned up the intensity, she switched to her hometown dialect.

'Well! You little slut!' Ma turned to Cantonese, fury making each of them switch to a different dialect. It was like a donkey braying at a horse, who then snorted in retort. Neither understanding what the other said, all the venom in their cursing was wasted. Disappointed, Ma turned and stormed bitterly out of the room.

Xiaohong sat alone, chest heaving in anger. She continued to mutter curses. Venting her resentment, she kicked furiously at the wall, regretting any shred of sympathy she had felt for him. She should have used her all-too-decent hand to slap him right across his lecherous face. It certainly didn't pay to be nice to people.

Cooling down, she picked up a book, hoping it would lull her to sleep. After she had dozed off for a while, there was a knock at the door.

'Dachang?' She felt a burst of joy. Opening the door, she was startled to see a strange woman standing there, eyes like ice and not a trace of friendliness in her expression.

Before Xiaohong could speak, the woman marched right in. She spent a full ten seconds staring at Xiaohong's breasts, then proceeded to inspect the four corners of the room, like a police officer carrying out an investigation of a crime scene.

'You. Who are you?' Though she had an idea, Xiaohong hoped to buy a little time with her question.

'Who am *I*? You mean Dachang didn't tell you? Just like he didn't tell me who *you* are?' The woman had dark skin. Her expression was so awe-inspiring that it caused Xiaohong to stumble over her attempt at using Mandarin.

'You... you've got it all wrong. I'll be moving to the factory dorm soon. *Zhu Ge* and me, we're just friends.' She didn't know what she could say to make the woman understand.

'Just friends? You take me for an idiot? If not for Ma, I'd still be in the dark!' The woman said angrily, hands on her hips.

Ma? What did Ma say? That scumbag! What a bastard! Xiaohong wanted to haul Ma into the room and give him a few good slaps before making him clear up this mess.

'Don't act innocent with me. I know you're a trashy little thing. I can see what you are, you slut!' The woman was like a beast cornering its prey. Even as she changed her position, her hands stayed firmly on her hips. Her eyes swept once more over the room.

'Hey! Have a little respect! You're supposed to be a teacher. You don't need to resort to such foul language.' Xiaohong, barely able to stand anymore, took on the look of a cornered badger.

'What's being a teacher got to do with it? You think a teacher can't swear as well as a cheap thing like you?' The woman's stance was uncompromising.

Xiaohong suddenly realised that there was something wrong with the woman. The more you entertained her, the more energetic she became. The more charged her arguments, the more self-righteous she became.

Burning with anger, Xiaohong lifted her head proudly, stuck out her chest and smiled contemptuously. 'What is it you want? I'm sleeping with Dachang. So what? Fuck off!' And with that, she slapped her hands on her hips.

Shocked to hear this, the woman's face changed. Plopping herself down on the bed, she began to whimper softly.

VIII

Though Xiaohong had added nothing new to her luggage, it seemed heavier than ever as she carried it to work before dawn the next morning. Leaving was like a sudden blast of cold wind in the face, blowing a feeling of uncertainty into her mind. She stretched then shrugged violently, feeling depressed and cold. The curtains were drawn over the window of Dachang's room, which was shrouded in darkness. All that separated the warmth of the room from the chill she felt was a thin layer of glass. Xiaohong exhaled heavily but she did not cry. Spitting on the ground, she said to herself, 'A window of opportunity will open somewhere.'

After tossing her luggage into the guard room, she ate a bowl of noodles at a stall near the factory. She had just clocked in when her stomach began to gurgle. Feeling a little discomfort, she went to the washroom. She made ten more trips to the toilet during her shift, making a bee line there so many times that the flat-chested line manager came to her with a warning. 'According to the rules, you're allowed three toilet breaks per shift. It's obvious you're just being lazy.' Runway took a condescending tone, as if she were some VIP and she spoke without an ounce of sympathy.

Ah Jun spoke up for Xiaohong. 'Ma'am, she's got diarrhoea. See how horrible she looks!'

'Diarrhoea? If everyone gets diarrhoea like her, who's going to keep up production?' Runway turned on Ah Jun, raising her voice a little.

People always mistook Ah Jun for a gentle person. Xiaohong wondered where she had really come from. Runway didn't quite dare to be too fierce.

'You think I *want* to have diarrhoea? You think it feels good? How can you be so cold? Didn't you come out from the assembly line yourself? How can a worker so quickly become an accomplice of the capitalists?' It took great effort to retaliate in this way. Her body was spent from the day of illness, and she could barely lift a hand. She hardly had sufficient strength to run to the toilet. Finishing her spiel, she could only lie on the work bench.

Runway had not expected this outburst from Xiaohong. Recovering from the initial shock, she said, 'I'll report this situation to the director!' She turned, her rump swaying as she marched to the office.

'Ah Hong, you need to get some medicine.' Touching her forehead, Ah Jun let out a cry, 'You've got a fever.'

'Have I?' Xiaohong felt her own head.

'Maybe you just haven't quite adapted to the water here yet. What'd you eat this morning?'

'A bowl of noodles from the stall next door.'

'How could you eat there? It's filthy!' Ah Jun's eyes enlarged to occupy her whole face. Xiaohong didn't have energy even to shake her head in response, much less to speak.

Just then, Runway came back.

'Ma'am, Ah Hong's got a high fever. Feel it,' Ah Jun said anxiously.

'Fine. Ah Jun, take her to the hospital. Go straight there and come straight back. Xiaohong, you take half-day sick leave. Go on!' Runway jotted down a few notes on Xiaohong's work card.

'Ma'am, can you arrange a bed in the dorm for me? I don't have a place to stay. I've put my luggage in the guard house.'

'Seems there might be a free bed. Go and see a doctor first, and we'll see what we can do when you get back.'

Not wanting to go to the hospital, Xiaohong stopped at a nearby shop and picked up some medicine, then went back to Ah Jun's bed in the dorm to rest. The diarrhoea stopped but the fever had not yet subsided. She fell into a fitful sleep. Her whole body was so hot she was afraid the quilt would burst into flames. She was dizzy, feeling like her system was an irrigation ditch through which waters rapidly rolled. Just as she finally fell into a deeper sleep, through the haze she felt someone pushing her. 'Ah Hong... Ah Hong, someone's here to see you.'

Groggily, she opened her eyes to see Ah Jun's grinning face.

'Hey, Ah Hong! It's me!' Suddenly a head leaned in so close that Xiaohong could only see a dark shadow.

'Me! Li Sijiang! I came to see you after work.' Seeing the familiar smile on that apple-shaped face, Xiaohong felt a flood of affection.

'So, Sijiang, you worked out how to get here, huh?'

'Bud gave me a lift. I wanted to see your workplace. No fever now,' Sijiang said, feeling her forehead.

'Where is Bud? Why didn't he come in?'

'He's outside waiting for me. For a while there, I was afraid I wouldn't find you. Lucky for me I bumped into her,' Sijiang said, pointing to Ah Jun and giving her a big grin. Ah Jun pulled a chair over to the bed and invited Sijiang to sit down.

'She's been really nice to me. I felt like I wanted to die today!' As she spoke, Xiaohong got up from the bed. 'How the hell are you? How is your new job in the factory?'

'Life in the factory... from morning to night, you stand until your legs are wobbly, without anywhere to sit your arse down even for a minute.'

'Ha! Sijiang, all I do all day is sit until I think my arse is glued to the chair! Bloody hell, it's unfair!'

'Xiaohong, are you alright?' Runway came in, bringing the smell of perfume into the cramped quarters.

'Yeah, I'm much better, Ma'am. Is my bed ready?'

'Yes. Next door, upper bunk. Tomorrow you report for your shift as per usual.' Runway finished her account and left. She never talked unnecessarily to the assembly line workers, as if attempting to maintain the dignity of her post.

'Phew! What is that crap?' Xiaohong spat through the heavy fragrance lingering in the room, provoking peals of laughter from Sijiang and Ah Jun.

After Sijiang left, Ah Jun went with Xiaohong to buy a quilt, pillow and wash basin. Ah Jun bargained for her, making the shopkeeper unhappy to see his prices slashed. Still, profit was profit, and he had no choice but to sell. After spending just a little money, she had everything she needed. They walked back to the dorm, both girls wobbling under the weight as they lugged their burdens along.

When they returned, Xiaohong saw a familiar motorcycle parked outside the dorm. Hearing someone call her name, she turned round to see Zhu Dachang standing there casually, a strange smile on his face. She hesitated a moment, wrinkling her nose and trying not to cry. She wanted to smile but didn't manage to.

'Put your things down and I'll take you both for dinner,' he said.

Ah Jun shook her head several times. 'You two go ahead, I've got a friend from my hometown coming over. I need to wait for him.' She smirked at Xiaohong.

'I'll take you for pork chops.' He liked to say, 'I'll take you'. It had a warm, companionable sound to it. Xiaohong swallowed, warmth filling her heart.

'I'm sorry you were treated so badly,' he said to her, obviously embarrassed by what had happened. 'She's often jealous for no good reason.'

'Don't talk like that. I've caused you trouble. I never meant to.' She hadn't really stopped to think about how angry that woman might be or the suffering it could cause Dachang.

'Well, I told her there was nothing between the two of us, but she said she'd die before she'd believe that. According to her, you admitted it, so why should I try to hide it? She forced me into saying I'd been to bed with you before she'd finally give it up. Women! Unbelievable!' he shook his head.

'You mean I'm unbelievable? Anyway, both of us gave the same answer. So, does this mean it's over for the two of you?' God, what kind of game is this? Have I got myself into trouble now? She thought and stood up straight, her eyes opened wide, glancing at him from beneath her lashes.

'Actually, it's really nothing to do with you. She's always believed every rumour she's ever heard about me. I don't know if I can stand her anymore. It'll never end. Even though I admitted it, she was still sceptical. Anyway, let's forget it. How about we go and try those pork chops?'

'I'm sorry. I don't think so.'

'Silly girl. You just work hard, then, and call me if you need anything.'

IX

Xiaohong found that the beige jacket she'd hung up was missing. Ah Jun had reminded her not to leave it out. Still, it had to be washed and hung out to dry. She was too lazy to make a complaint. She knew how things worked here and knew that anything of even a little value could grow wings and fly off into someone else's embrace.

Her work became even more tedious, an unending line of monotony. She counted it off on her fingers. Twenty days she'd been at it, twenty days on end. Other than the half-day of sick leave, every day was the same and she went through it all in that robotic fashion. Clock in at eight a.m., clock out at eight p.m., without any margin of error. Back to the dorm, eight beds to a room. People were always coming and going, each individual's smell mixing with the rest. Only the odour coming from the shared toilet was stronger, becoming especially offensive when a queue of women waited to clear their systems. The tap water was always cold but they had so little time for washing their faces that it didn't matter much. When they did have time for a quick spit bath, they just had to grin and bear it. Factory regulations allowed a fan in the summer and a small space heater in the winter. It was lucky that winters this far south were mild, making it easy to bear. Frostbite and flu, at least, were not major problems. Each day when they came back, they'd dillydally through their cleaning up. At ten-thirty, it was lights out, and they went to bed. They slept till morning, then got up and queued for the toilet. After washing, dressing and running a comb through their hair, they were herded back into their cage on the factory floor where they repeated the previous day's routine.

There was about a fortnight left until the Spring Festival holiday. People began to stir, all decked out in festive colours. Clothes and food were plentiful, ready for holiday-makers to purchase in preparation for their celebrations. She went shopping in the evening with Ah Jun, who bought a little of this and a little of that, getting ready to make a trip home for the holiday.

'Ah Jun, how long's it been since you went home?' she asked. Ah Jun seemed to want to buy the whole market and take everything back home. Xiaohong wondered where this strong desire to purchase so many things came from.

'Two years! My parents are looking forward to me being home. I want to get some more clothes for my brother and sister.'

'You're the oldest?'

'Yeah. They're still at school.'

'Ah Jun, you work so hard. Why don't you buy some clothes for yourself?'

'I'm in the factory all day every day. I only need my uniform.'

'You're so generous. If my sister was like you, I'd be so happy I could die. But remember to get something for yourself.'

When they went for fast food, Ah Jun always bought the cheapest meal, such as tofu or radish. She'd simply say, 'That's what I like to eat.' But Xiaohong didn't believe it for a minute. How could she like that bland stuff?

Looking at her friend's face, Xiaohong saw those eyes light up when they talked about her family and felt a twinge of sadness.

It was crowded. People were exchanging money everywhere, peeling notes off fat wads of cash, each stack as thick as a roll of toilet paper. They took in a note, handed out a note, everyone seemingly willing to spend every last penny. Workers happily parted with their money. Ah Jun joined the ranks, buying so much that the two of them could hardly carry it all home. Accompanying Ah Jun had its rewards. Halfway home, a small slip of red paper pasted on a wall caught Xiaohong's eye. She leaned in closer and saw a job advertisement:

Qianshan Hotel — hiring two front desk attendants

The paste was still wet, so obviously it had not been there long. Without a word, Xiaohong tore off the address.

'What are you tearing that off for?' Ah Jun asked in surprise.

'Do you know where the Qianshan Hotel is?'

'Hm. I suppose it must be in Qianshan Town. About three or four miles from here.'

'I'm going to apply tomorrow. You tell Runway that I'm sick to my stomach and went to the hospital. Remember to take leave for me so I don't lose my hard-earned money!' Xiaohong put it all so simply, it was as if she'd been planning it for days. Ah Jun was a little dumbfounded.

Six

I

When it came to dressing, Xiaohong had a certain flair. She would mix and match, trying on this blouse with that skirt, and in this way came up with new outfits to remain fashionable. With a dark blue jacket over stone-washed jeans and a simple pair of flats, hair let down and parted on the side, and clothes pressed neatly so as to emphasise her full bust, she decided she made a very good impression. Having squeezed her way onto the bus and jostled along for about ten minutes, she reached Qianshan Town. As soon as she alighted, she saw the sign for the Qianshan Hotel in faded gold letters. A few vehicles were lined up in front of the hotel. It looked pretty quiet. The façade was glass and Xiaohong almost crashed right into it. Flustered, she pushed open the door, feeling a flush of embarrassment. The clothes that had made her feel so satisfied just a little earlier now seemed tawdry and tacky. The wall beside the reception desk was hung with several flashy clocks. The time displayed on each clock was that of a different location, with the names of various cities written on cards under their respective time-pieces. A pretty girl in a dark blue jacket sat smiling at the counter.

'Hello, Miss. Is there anything I can help you with?' she said. She had long hair, almond-shaped eyes and skin so fair and delicate it almost seemed you could see right through to the blood vessels beneath.

'Oh. Um, I'd like to speak to the manager. Which floor is his office on?' Xiaohong thought the girl, her uniform and her smile very attractive, even though her teeth were not very white.

'May I ask what it is concerning?' a lady standing nearby, slightly older than the girl, asked.

'Well, I'm here about the desk attendant's job.'

'Oh?' The older woman turned to the almond-eyed girl and asked, 'We're hiring?'

'I think so. I'll call and ask the manager.' The girl punched the buttons on the phone. 'Hello, Mr Pan? There's a girl here to apply for the desk attendant's post... Mm-hm... Mm-hm... OK.'

Putting down the phone, the almond-eyed girl smiled at Xiaohong and said, 'The manager's office is 509. Go on up. The lift is next to the stairs.'

'Thank you, both.' Xiaohong smiled happily. She already liked this place.

The carpet was old, its red weave soon to be completely threadbare with age. Walking on it, there was no echo of footsteps, making it seem as if the people floated over the ground like spirits. She knocked on the door of the manager's office and heard a muffled response, 'Come in!'

When she wrenched open the heavy door, she was met with a suite so luxurious it stopped her in her tracks.

'Mr Pan, hello! I'm here to apply.' She had already finished speaking by the time she finally located the manager's figure in the vast room.

'Please have a seat. I'll be with you shortly,' Mr Pan said, not even bothering to look up at her from his perch behind the desk.

Xiaohong sat on a sofa, her eyes making a quick tour of the room. She thought to herself, Wow! Stylish, very stylish! The chandelier hanging from the ceiling was made up of numerous small bulbs, layer upon layer, lighting the room brightly. Trophies glistened inside a trophy case, a couple of them even larger than the giant pickle jar in the kitchen back home. There were also rows of books, and a painting hung on the wall. The manager's oversized desk was as big as a bed.

The manager looked to be in his early thirties. He wore a white shirt and dark blue tie, looking very presentable. He gestured to Xiaohong, motioning her to sit in front of the desk so they could talk. He looked her over with a quick glance, then stopped for a second look, like someone who suddenly remembers something he left behind just as he's about to step out of a room.

'You're very busy. I'm sorry to bother you.' She sat across from the manager, a strained smile on her face. Mr Pan looked like a cultured man, a cut above fellows like Mr Zhuang, Mr Zhan and even the mayor. It seemed there was something in the air that affected Xiaohong, making her unconsciously slip out of her casual, Bohemian manner of speech.

'Where are you working now?' Pan smiled gently, cheeks bulging as if each had a cube of sugar tucked into it.

'At the Rising Star Toy Factory. I'm from Hunan, eighteen-years-old.' She gave the falsified age reflected on her temporary identity card, smiling the whole time she spoke.

Looking satisfied, Mr Pan handed her a form, saying, 'Fill this in first.'

The application form was thorough, including a section for educational qualifications. Xiaohong wrote 'secondary school' in the little box then filled in the rest with more accurate information. When she'd finished, she passed it to Mr Pan with both hands, respectfully. He smiled as he glanced at it, saying, 'Very impressive.'

Hearing the manager's praise was a sudden pleasant surprise. She replied, 'Just point the way, and I'll do my best!'

'When can you start?'

'Tomorrow.'

Mr Pan called the front desk and said, 'Huang Xing? Come to my office for a moment.'

Almost immediately the almond-eyed girl came in, obviously quite at ease in the manager's presence. 'Mr Pan, is there anything you need?'

'Ah Xing, your new partner, Qian Xiaohong. She'll be working with you. Make arrangements for her to bunk in with you and Zhang Weimei.'

'No problem, Sir,' Ah Xing replied in Cantonese. Xiaohong had not expected things to go so smoothly. Tomorrow she would be in a pretty little uniform like Ah Xing's. She had to contain herself to keep from jumping up and down with excitement.

11

Leaving the Qianshan Hotel, Xiaohong rushed back to the toy factory. The first thing she did was share her good news with Ah Jun. Had it not been for Ah Jun, she would never have seen the job ad and would have had to continue to put up with Runway's showing off.

As soon as she sat down beside Ah Jun, the girl whispered, 'Ah Hong, Runway is furious. I think she's reported you to the big boss.' She continued anxiously, 'How did it go?'

Xiaohong winked. 'Ah Jun, I just want to do well. Look around – do you really want to stick around in this lousy place?'

Hearing this, Ah Jun became a little melancholy. 'What makes you think it's so easy to just get up and go whenever you want?'

'Don't be silly. If you don't try, how will you know? I bet you've never even set out to look for something better, have you?'

Ah Jun just shook her head.

Just then, Runway came in and stood behind Xiaohong. Coldly, she said, 'The director wants to see you in his office.'

'Huh? What's the big deal? Didn't I get Ah Jun to request time off for me? Why did you report me to the director? Who do you think you are? What are you trying to prove? You think you're any better than the rest of us? You think you're so high-class now you can turn on us?'

The manager had assumed Xiaohong would mumble some sort of explanation, humbly begging to be excused. She never imagined the girl could be so spiteful. All the workers on the assembly line stopped what they were doing to watch Runway's reaction.

'What are you staring at? Back to work, all of you! Don't think I won't dock your pay.' Choked with anger, she swallowed and let out a fierce cry to punctuate the statement. The workers turned obediently back to their tasks. Xiaohong cast a contemptuous glance at Runway's flat chest then turned and swaggered into the office.

'Are you familiar with our factory regulations?' The director's face was barely visible over the top of his imposing desk.

'Yes. I've read the manual several times.'

'Then, can you tell me where you were in violation today?'

'I'm not sure. I had a stomach ache and went to the hospital. I asked someone to help me apply for time off from Runway.'

'What?'

'Um. I mean, I asked someone to help me apply for leave from the line manager.'

'Do you have some evidence of your hospital visit?'

'No, I forgot to ask for a doctor's note.'

'I see. According to regulation, you'll be docked fifty *yuan* for being absent without approval.'

'What? You're docking me fifty *yuan*?' she was furious, 'Doesn't matter anyway. I resign right now!'

'Well, that's up to you.' The response was cold.

'I've made up my mind. I quit!'

'OK. Ask the line manager to come in, please.'

'I won't. You can go and get her yourself.' She sat down, her chest knocking against the front of the desk. Taken aback, the director stood up, went to the door and waved. A moment later, Runway came in.

'She's resigned. Take her to Finance and settle her account there,' the director said.

'The first month's wages are a deposit, which she only receives after completing six months of work. She's got no account to settle,' the line manager replied.

'So for these twenty days I've worked here, I get nothing? That's just evil! You're a bunch of blood-suckers!' Xiaohong stood up, boiling.

'It's factory regulation. It's all clearly written in the manual. You said yourself that you've read it,' the director said.

'If everyone is like you, resigning after just twenty days of work, what happens to production?' Runway said, not unreasonably.

'You're just a bunch of blood-suckers!' Seeing that she was just wasting her breath, she added a feisty 'Fuck you!' and turned to go. As she rushed out of the office, she bumped into Ah Jun. Turning up her nose, she walked straight past her.

Xiaohong called Dachang from a nearby pay phone. When she told him she had resigned from the toy factory, he was not at all surprised. 'You should do whatever suits you,' he said. 'I knew you wouldn't stay with a factory for very long. It's a soulless place to work, and there's no freedom.'

'Are you two still doing OK?' she asked cautiously.

'We're fine. You got a lot of stuff to move? I'll come and help you.'

'Yeah, that would be good. I'll wait for you at the dorm.'

He was there before long. Reaching into the cargo box attached to the back of his motorcycle, he drew out an object heavy as a brick. 'This is for you.'

'What is it?'

'It's the *Ci Hai*. You know, an encyclopaedia.'

'God, it's heavy. I can hardly lift it.' Xiaohong took it in both hands. She'd never seen such a huge book before. When she looked at the back cover, she was startled by what she saw on the price tag. 'Ninety-eight *yuan*? Oh my God! That's expensive!'

Dachang replied, 'As long as you use it, it's not too much. If you want to improve your working opportunities and if you want to live a little more comfortably in Shenzhen, you've got to study hard. And not just the *Ci Hai*.'

'Yeah, OK.' Her head was spinning.

'My sister's the same age as you. She's studying Chinese at Zhongshan University. What I'm trying to tell you is that education can change your destiny.'

Opening the *Ci Hai,* she saw words so densely packed it looked like a swarm of mosquitoes had landed on the page. 'My God! How many years will it take me to read this?'

Dachang laughed. 'You'll never finish it, not in a million years. It's a reference book. It'll teach you everything you ever want to know. It is very useful.'

'OK, I see. Let's go now.' She carefully tucked the book into her bag.

'Xiaohong, you're on your own here. I want you to take care of yourself. Working at a hotel, it's easy to pick up bad habits as well.' He put on his helmet, making his head seem abnormally large.

'*Zhu Ge*, I'll always remember what you've said.' Her eyes were reddening.

'You're very clever and you're young. I really believe you can make a difference.'

What difference can I make? she wondered, climbing onto the back of the motorcycle as she mulled over his words. Can I be the big boss of a company? Will I make loads of money? Become famous?

Confused, she felt she'd fallen into a fog. She wanted desperately to see through it, to catch sight of the landscape lying in the distance. All she knew, though, was what was right before her eyes – the Qianshan Hotel. Nothing was more real to her than its beautiful setting and the pretty uniform she would wear there.

III

The Qianshan Hotel was a fifteen minute walk from Li Sijiang's house. Taking a leisurely tour of the neighbourhood, Xiaohong went to see her friend.

'Sijiang.' As soon as she reached the door, she began calling out.

'Who's there?' Sijiang opened the door with a crash. 'Honghong! You found your way here?' Her apple-shaped face looked a little withered and her tiny eyes were lifeless.

'Ha! Of course I did.' Xiaohong went through the door, a big grin on her face. Sijiang's underclothes were hung up all over the place drying. Just as Xiaohong prepared to give her friend a good ribbing about it, she saw Bud lying on the bed amidst a heap of laundry. 'Hey Bud!' she greeted him with a hearty laugh.

Bud, barely managing a smile, said, 'Have a seat. Try some peanuts.' He pointed to a chair as he offered her a bag of nuts.

'Alright. Sijiang, you don't like those plums anymore?' she teased. Sijiang looked anxious, and Bud's face was inexplicably downcast. Xiaohong noticed that his nose was flat, and Sijiang seemed a little pale. Obviously something was bothering the pair of them.

'Hey, I'm not disturbing you am I? I just wanted to drop in and let you know, I'm not working at the factory anymore.'

'How come? Where will you go?'

'The Qianshan Hotel. It's not far from here.'

'That's great. When I'm off, I'll drop in to see you there.' Her voice was listless, like that of a dying hen.

'You alright, Sijiang? Why do you look so down?'

The corners of Sijiang's mouth sagged. She tried not to cry, but the tears began to run down her face.

'Bud, what's going on? What's wrong with her?' Xiaohong turned to Bud, knowing this must have something to do with him.

He stammered for a long while, as if unsure where to begin. Finally, he exhaled and said, 'She's gonna have a baby!'

'What did you say?'

'Sijiang's pregnant.'

'Honghong, what am I going to do? I, oh...' her words were lost in a flood of tears.

'*Aiyah*! What're you going to do? You're going to get married and have the kid!' Xiaohong yelled.

'But... he... he's... he's got a wife and kid already! Oh...!'

'Don't cry, Sijiang. Bud, you really got a wife?' Xiaohong asked suspiciously.

He nodded.

'How could you do this to her? Don't you have a conscience?'

'I, I didn't *mean* to get her pregnant. She's the one who suggested I go bareback! She said it was during her safe time and now here we are.' Bud obviously felt himself a victim in all this.

Xiaohong partially blamed herself. When it came to the rhythm method, she'd been Sijiang's mentor. This was on her head.

'Sijiang, what were you thinking? I told you, the safe time isn't ever a hundred per cent safe.'

Sijiang recited the theory like a lesson beginning to end, coming to the tearful conclusion,

'What do you think you need to do, Bud?' Xiaohong turned to the so-called man of the house.

His flat nose twitched and his eyes were downcast. 'There's no other option. We've gotta abort it.'

IV

At the workers' quarters of the Qianshan Hotel, each of the room's three occupants had her own bed. Near the window was a writing desk that they shared. The three beds surrounded the window, forming an empty square in the centre. Draped over the mosquito nets on the outside of the beds were curtains, offering a little privacy in the sleeping areas. Hanging from Ah Xing's bed were some stuffed toys.

As she helped Xiaohong get settled in, Ah Xing said, 'Tomorrow you can get a curtain to hang around your bunk.' She was quite tall and slender. When she gestured with her hand, it almost seemed her whole body twisted with the movement. Her face was pale, with hardly a hint of colour, making Xiaohong wonder if the skin might break under even the lightest touch.

After staring for a while, Xiaohong could not contain herself anymore. She asked, 'Ah Xing, how come your skin is so beautiful? Aren't you Cantonese?'

Ah Xing smiled. 'What do you mean? You think only you Hunan girls can be good-looking?'

Hearing this, Xiaohong lightened up a little. 'I didn't mean that. But the good-looking girls from Guangdong never look Cantonese.'

Perhaps she was used to hearing people praise her looks. For whatever reason, Ah Xing was obviously not affected.

'How old are you, Ah Xing?'

'Nineteen.'

'I'm eighteen. What about Wu Ying? Doesn't she live here?'

'She's twenty-five. She's got a three-year-old kid and her husband is a supervisor in a factory. They all rent a flat somewhere.' Pointing to the other bunk, she said, 'She's from Chaozhou. Her name's Zhang Weimei. You'll work the early shift with her tomorrow.'

Xiaohong looked at the posters on the wall next to the third bed, a huge picture of a Hong Kong pop singer's face staring back at her.

'OK, what time do I start?'

'Eight. The canteen is on the first floor. If you get up a little after seven and grab some breakfast, you should be right on time. Oh yeah, try on your uniform. I thought you'd wear a small.'

Xiaohong took out the uniform and tried it on. It was a dark blue skirt and matching waistcoat over a white blouse with a bow at the collar. When she put on her high-heeled shoes, Ah Xing said, 'Hey, not bad! See for yourself.'

Xiaohong stood in front of the mirror. 'Hm. The shoes aren't quite right. I'll have to buy another pair.'

Ah Xing laughed. 'Let me tell you a bedtime story... once upon a time, there was a man who bought some elegant new pyjamas. When he got home, he found that his slippers didn't go with the pyjamas, so he bought a new pair. After a couple of days, he decided that the carpet in his house was rather old, so he changed that too. And then, he finally realised that the whole house was even more worn, so he decided to upgrade to a new place as well. You see all the hassle a new pair of pyjamas can cause?'

Xiaohong chuckled and said, 'What? You mean he didn't trade his wife in too? Anyway, I just want to buy a new pair of shoes. These are old. They may give the whole outfit a bad name.' She turned back and forth in front of the mirror, as if seeing herself for the first time.

'Ah Xing, you think I look alright?'

Ah Xing smiled at her and said, 'Xiaohong, didn't you hear me praise you just now? You look great and you know it.'

'I'm too short. If I was as tall as you, it'd be just right.'

'Napoleon wasn't tall and he did alright for himself.'

Xiaohong looked blank at the reference.

'Na-po-le-on. I'll tell you about him later. I want to listen to my programme now.' She turned on the radio. A woman's voice spoke seductively, asking to dedicate a song to her ex-boyfriend.

'That's cool. How do you request a song?' Xiaohong asked as she took off her uniform.

'Just call the station. There's a hotline. We called once. It took about a month before we finally got through. It was a lot of fun.'

Listening to Ah Xing, she felt her new colleague sounded pretty cultured, like someone who had some education.

V

Zhang Weimei had a rather depressing countenance. When she laughed, her already prominent cheekbones rose even higher. Her eyes were not very large, but were cunning like a rat's. New pimples constantly appeared on her skin, creating a rather mind-boggling pattern. Not too short, her figure did provide a small amount of compensation. Unfortunately, she had wide hip bones, covered with plenty of flesh, making her look like a much older woman when seen from behind. At the same time, she wore her hair in a short, girlish style. She was a bundle of contradictions and the conflict between them was intense.

All of this, however, did no damage to Zhang Weimei's healthy sense of self-esteem. When Xiaohong greeted her in the morning, she glanced up without any show of feeling, nor did she have anything to say. At the reception desk, there was a small mirror hanging on the wall. When she was free, she would look at it and dab at her lipstick or poke at the corner of her eye. On the lobby's left side, there was a Western café. The Chinese restaurant was on the second floor, and the rooms occupied the third through ninth storeys. Weimei had been working here for some time and was familiar with everyone who came in and out. Xiaohong just followed her lead, smiling all day until she felt her face would freeze in that expression.

'Any vacancies?' A fat man with dark skin came into the lobby, a girl following in his wake.

'Sorry, can you speak Mandarin?' He had used Cantonese and Xiaohong hadn't understood.

'Bugger off! Where do you come from, anyway? I've been talking like this for decades! Where do you get off asking me to change now?' His voice was thick and he stared at her with cloudy eyes. Xiaohong had no clue how to engage in this battle.

Finally, Weimei turned from the mirror, scrunched up her cheeks in a big grin and said, 'Don't be angry, sir. She's new. How many rooms do you need?'

'One.'

'You can register here.'

'I don't wanna mess with the hassle of registering. Here's my ID card. You fill in the forms for me.'

Weimei took the ID card and the registration forms and pushed them across to Xiaohong.

'Excuse me, sir, how many nights will you be staying?' Xiaohong asked.

'How long you think I wanna stay here? A short while will do. I don't wanna talk to you.' He turned to Weimei and said, 'I'll take an hour.'

'For an hour, it's the same price as the half-day rate,' she replied. 'That'll be a two hundred *yuan* deposit.'

The man pulled out a bulging wallet, dropped the notes onto the counter, took his completed registration slip and turned to walk off. He shoved his wallet into his back pocket, creating a large, round lump.

Weimei's straight hair covered half her face. Xiaohong looked into the mirror at the reflected image and saw two yellow specks fly out from between the other girl's fingers and stick to its surface. A bright red spot of blood appeared on the reflection. Weimei took a tissue and dabbed at the bleeding spot, then scrunched up her face at Xiaohong, as if sharing the credit for her victory over the pimple. The warmth of the smile caught Xiaohong by surprise. Her chest heaved, a fitting response to the rare smile on Weimei's face.

'Your face is so clean. I have a problem with my glands.' Weimei sought a suitable explanation for her chronic acne.

'You shouldn't pick them.'

She'd never had a problem with acne herself, and so was a little uncertain about how to handle it. All the same, she continued, 'From what I know, there is one way. Get the used bubble wrap from Visitation One birth control pills. Fill it with water then apply the water to your face. That'll take care of all your spots.'

Weimei felt a shock run up the length of her body. Clearly she had all her feelers out, searching for any way to get rid of her acne. Those little spots had been a big source of trouble in her life. She quickly picked up a pen, asking, 'What's that? What's that? Say it again and I'll write it down.'

'Visitation One.' Xiaohong repeated the secret remedy.

'Visitation One. Sounds like the name of a satellite.' Weimei scribbled busily, her mousy eyes scanning the page as she wrote.

Now that they had begun to get a general feel for one another, Weimei really warmed to Xiaohong. A short while later, the curt Cantonese man came to check out, the fire in him now visibly cooled. He even tried to be nice to Xiaohong, using funny, broken Mandarin. His young companion walked into the lobby as if she had simply made a quick trip to the ladies' room. It was as if nothing had happened. She went out of the door, turned right and disappeared. When the man turned, Xiaohong stared at his back pocket, noticing that the bulge of his wallet was substantially smaller now.

VI

Xiaohong felt one could get bored with this sort of work, as it involved little beyond registration procedures and note-taking, reviewing ID cards and filling in public security forms. The more pleasant duties involved the cheerful, energetic work of flirting with customers. One of the perks was observing the men and women who came into the hotel and then passing on juicy tales about their private business.

Xiaohong enjoyed her job. Of course, she made sure to maintain a professional smile, even when she was in a mood more fit for smashing everything in sight, remembering what had happened to her first month's salary at the factory. To put it plainly, she felt that the job was to sell smiles. And, garbed in her professional wear, at least she could sell them with some dignity.

As the Spring Festival holiday approached, hotel discipline was relaxed. With people all over the country scattering back to their hometowns, only a few remained behind, stuck here where they endured the boredom.

But Weimei didn't have time to be bored. Having gotten rid of her spots, she would now search through her hair, seeking out split ends, teasing each one out and snipping it off, one at a time.

With Weimei's narcissistic preoccupations, naturally it was pretty boring to work with her. Xiaohong preferred to work on the desk with Ah Xing or Wu Ying. Ah Xing had a pleasant personality, and Wu Ying a well-developed sense of humour. The most important thing was that each had a congenial temperament. It was a nice change, like running in the sun over fields of grass.

But even as she was busy making new friends, she didn't forget the old. Sijiang's situation troubled her. She covered half a shift for Weimei in order to arrange a full day off for herself. She got ready to go with Sijiang to the hospital to get rid of the 'Happy Bastard', as Sijiang called it. Sijiang's look and her walk seemed like that of a woman in the final month of her pregnancy, ready to give birth at any time. Her face no longer looked like a fresh, juicy apple. Not only had the circle of her face shrunk, but the skin was drying up as well. The Happy Bastard simply caused too much physical trouble and was not worth the torment Sijiang was enduring.

Xiaohong knew the psychological pressure was too much for Sijiang. A length of meat and a pair of steel pincers entering the body were two entirely different things and the horror Sijiang felt of the forceps was something for which Xiaohong had complete sympathy. As they walked to the hospital, she kept saying, 'Sijiang, it's nothing. In a few minutes, it's done, just like that.'

Sijiang felt shackled with a heavy burden, like some heroic martyr marching forward. Her eyes were now pools of deep water, like those of a soap opera character losing her child. The look of desperation made her pale and hollow. Her hastily combed hair, carelessly tied, blew in the breeze, it was like reeds blown recklessly in the chill wind.

'Just a few minutes? In a few minutes, a life can be born, and in just a few bloody minutes a life can end,' Sijiang murmured.

Xiaohong hesitated. Sijiang went on, 'No. Let's go home. I don't want to go to the hospital. It's a life, my little cub.' She stroked her belly, stopping in her tracks. Amidst the hustle and bustle of the passing cars, she spoke softly but Xiaohong heard every word.

'You're going to have it?' Xiaohong asked severely.

'I... I thought...' Sijiang just nodded, a light flashing in her eyes, then fading again.

'Fuck! Sijiang, now is not the time to be maternal. If you give birth to this wild creature, it's all over for you. You'll be ruined! And anyway – look... just look!' Xiaohong pointed to a beggar woman sitting under a bridge holding a child. 'Is that mother great? The child is begging! She just created another life to suffer slowly with her. If she loved that child, she would have destroyed it more quickly!'

Sijiang was shaking. Her small eyes widened, growing brighter. She bit her lower lip with her upper teeth, as if she could bite the answer out from her own flesh.

VII

While Sijiang's answer was still hanging somewhere between her upper teeth and lower lip, they arrived at the entrance to the People's Hospital. The huge red cross drawn on the hospital's white wall was as shocking as the effect of fresh red blood splattered across a white sheet.

Xiaohong practically dragged Sijiang through the hospital door. It was filled with a smell so pungent it could make a healthy person ill.

Sijiang was like an insect without its head, still scurrying along. Her eyes filled with tears. She seemed like some farm animal being led into the slaughterhouse, vaguely aware of some impending disaster, but unable to resist it. Xiaohong took a number and led Sijiang to the second floor obstetrics and gynaecology ward. Overwhelmed, they joined a long queue in the ward. Sijiang gave Xiaohong a bewildered glance, as if she were a lone figure searching for a familiar face amongst the revolutionary ranks. Finding it, her heart was warmed, and her confidence bolstered. She tugged on Xiaohong's sleeve and whispered, 'What do you think they're all here for?'

Xiaohong scanned the crowd. They were all young women in uniform, the name of their factories embroidered on the chest. Some waited alone quietly, others sat with a companion from work, talking softly. Occasionally, one of them looked indifferently at Xiaohong and Sijiang, her face fixed in a gloating expression. Xiaohong nodded and said, 'Looks like they're all like us, so you don't need to worry.'

After helping Sijiang fill in her medical history, the pair found a place to sit. Then Xiaohong smiled and said, 'Hey Sijiang, how many unborn babies you think have been flushed down the hospital's drains and out into the sea?'

Sijiang, with a wooden smile, said, 'Must be nice being a man. Damn them, they don't have to take responsibility for anything!' In her hatred towards Bud, she hated the whole species of which he was a part. He hadn't even come with her to the hospital.

'No kidding. Oh yeah, Sijiang, how much money did Bud give you for your hospital fees?' Sijiang's complaint reminded her to ask about this point.

'Five hundred. He said to take care of the problem first then go home to recover.'

'Fuck him! He really is stingy. I ought to let the little tosser come and see for himself the trouble he's caused. You got to be thicker-skinned and demand more than just five hundred from him. What a bloody cheapskate!'

'Ah Hong, what right do I have to say anything? It's not like he hurt me on purpose.'

'Don't be a fool. Of course you have a right. He did this to you. He knocked you up and he doesn't even plan to marry you!'

'H-he... he didn't mean to. He cares about me.'

'Like hell he does. He cares enough to spice things up in bed with you. Care? That's just what people say when they want to coax you into doing something. If he really cared, he'd give you five thousand!' Xiaohong hissed angrily.

Sijiang glanced around, embarrassed. 'Ah Hong, keep it down.'

'Sijiang, this is what we'll do. Get sorted out today, then tonight go back and ask Bud for the money. I'll even come ask him on your behalf. Five hundred... that's nothing! If you don't nip this in the bud now, it'll only become a bigger problem later.' As she finished saying this, Sijiang's name flashed on the board above the door.

Huddling against Xiaohong's back, she made her way into the ward.

'When was your last period?' a middle-aged doctor in her forties asked without looking up. Her face was so thickly covered with freckles that she was as spotted as a stretch of pavement after a swarm of sparrows had flown over.

Sijiang hesitated, calculating.

'Which of you is Li Sijiang?' The freckled doctor looked up and, taking in both girls with a glance, turned her gaze on Xiaohong.

'She is!' Xiaohong pushed Sijiang in front of her.

'When was your last period?' Her voice sounded like the cold, metallic clamp of the forceps used in this ward. Poor Sijiang counted, whistling softly below her breath as she stood shaking before the doctor.

'It ended thirty-five days ago.' The doctor scribbled something on her notepad, her mouth moving as she wrote, as if she were copying someone else's homework.

'Are you having intercourse with your boyfriend?' she asked in a steely tone.

Sijiang did not answer.

'Yes. She's sleeping with her boyfriend.' Xiaohong spoke on her friend's behalf.

'Any symptoms?' The doctor glanced at Xiaohong, the freckles looking like a row of ants marching across her face.

'Nausea every day, vomiting, no appetite…' Sijiang searched frantically for a way to describe the desperate days of pregnancy she had endured so far. She retched as she spoke. She suddenly wished that someone would just stick a hand into her uterus and pull out the thing inside of it.

'You know it's painful, don't you? If you're afraid of pain, you shouldn't do it rashly.' As far as the doctor was concerned, it was all old hat. In her words was a cold-hearted gloating, as if she had never done it rashly herself.

Fuck! Who does she think she is? Xiaohong cursed, hotly and silently, though she didn't dare say anything out loud, fearing that Sijiang would suffer for any indiscretion.

The doctor handed them a form, then took Sijiang's blood pressure, a urine sample and did a pelvic exam. They lined up to pay, pushing their way through the crowd like a pair of piglets trying to reach a sow's teats, each squeezing her way to a different window. When they'd finally finished, they sat and waited for the test results, fatigue slowly setting in on them.

'Everything's normal. You want to go through with the abortion? Have you ever had one before? It just takes a couple of seconds,' the doctor said, looking over the lab results. Sijiang's apple-shaped face was a picture of confusion. She shook her head then nodded.

'Doctor, she's nodding to your first question, and shaking her head at the second. Wait... I mean to say, she's never had an abortion before, and she wants to have one now.' Xiaohong stammered her way through an explanation.

The doctor aimed a casual look at Xiaohong, as quiet as a mosquito. Xiaohong wanted to catch a good look at the spots on that face but before she could, the doctor's glance had flitted off again.

'We're fully booked today. Come tomorrow morning and we'll do it.' Even speaking as softly as an insect's buzz, her voice was cold and metallic.

As they left the clinic, Sijiang sighed heavily. 'Cats in heat howl the whole night long. Dogs in heat sniff each other's backsides in search of a mate. Why do humans in heat have to go to so much trouble? Ah Hong, if I could just push it out while squatting over the crapper, everything would be alright.' Sijiang couldn't let go of the hope that the whole pregnancy was just a nightmare. She was like a starving person constantly imagining bread or rice. Sijiang was slowly coming to accept the reality of her sad situation. The next day, she would hand her body over to the freckled doctor.

Surprisingly, like a single drop of water in a vast ocean, Bud's flat nose was nowhere to be seen.

VIII

Five hundred *yuan* marked the end of Li Sijiang and Bud Kun. According to Weimei, Bud was considered pretty humane. It was as if, having been tucked away in a village for years, he had come to the city and had to embrace the sudden openness and influx of new things. Once their pockets were filled with a little cash, guys like him always wanted to try out the 'Northern Girls' (as the Cantonese liked to call girls who came to the city from the rural provinces), using them to create a life of leisure, or – you might say – indulgence. Most of the local guys went for the working-class women, pursuing them like male dogs sniffing at every bitch they came across. Affection grew as their ears were scratched. Though the bitch might be alert at first, eventually – whether out of vanity or because she really was flattered – she finally gave in to the male dog's advances. He, having had his way with her, would leave as soon as he was done.

Weimei came to the conclusion that Sijiang was fortunate she hadn't met with some shady character and become a tool for sex, drugs and all manner of illegal activities. They were like leeches, attaching themselves firmly as suction cups to already irritated skin and sucking out the will to live. Hearing her say this, one might be led to believe Weimei had had some encounters with a shady character herself. Surprised, Xiaohong gained a new perspective on Weimei. When she repeated the words to Sijiang, she placed special emphasis on how fortunate the situation was, as if applying salve to Sijiang's wounds.

On their second trip to the hospital, Sijiang was surprisingly brave.

She walked in front of Xiaohong with the ease of one entering the washroom in her own home, as if she had done it countless times before. Her tiny eyes shone and her footsteps were more lively. Sijiang lifted her chin and proudly thrust out her chest as she stood before the freckled doctor. The woman was visibly startled. Sijiang's posture looked like that of someone who had come to settle accounts with the doctor.

'You've decided to go through with the procedure today?' This time, her voice was warmer, more like a set of stainless steel forceps left sitting in the sun. Her freckles began dancing across her face as her mouth pulled itself into a rare smile.

'I'm doing it today. The sooner the better,' Sijiang replied, her apple-shaped face rounder than ever.

'Go and clear your bowels, then go into the operating room across the hall.' The doctor pointed toward a door with her pen.

'Doctor, I'll go with her. She needs me,' Xiaohong said urgently.

She swept her eyes over Xiaohong, but did not say anything. Xiaohong took her silence as consent.

The bloody waste in the operating room renewed Sijiang's fears. Long-held tears began to fall from her eyes. Blood stains were everywhere, like a crimson history written on the metal surfaces and white linens of the operating room. Stainless steel forceps rested on a pan. Sijiang heard their metallic clink. With all of these cold objects, she could not conceive of how each would, in its own way, enter into her warm flesh. She retched, spitting white streams of saliva into a rubbish bin filled with blood-covered refuse. Then the dam broke and she really vomited, emptying the remaining contents of her stomach onto the bloody mound.

'Hey Sijiang, don't be afraid. It'll be over soon.' Xiaohong, patting Sijiang's back, handed her a stack of tissue.

'Don't dawdle. Pants off and lie down.' The doctor, carrying a pan in, urged impatiently. She neatly unfolded the cloth lying inside the pan, and with a series of crisp sounds lined up a set of white scissors and forceps.

'Hurry up! There are a lot of patients waiting for me,' she urged again.

Sijiang was shy about removing her pants, and her white thighs trembled as she climbed onto the operating table. With soulless eyes, she looked innocently at the doctor.

'Lie down. Spread your legs. Knees up!' The woman had already put on a white mask and gloves, leaving only a pair of elusive eyes visible.

Sijiang was numb.

Xiaohong gently helped her spread her thighs, then the doctor bound her legs to the bed and started the procedure in a mechanical way, never displaying the slightest emotion.

Sijiang, grasping for straws, grabbed Xiaohong's hand.

'Hey Sijiang, I'll tell you a joke. Listen, but don't laugh. There was a female worker who bought a new house. She took two weeks off to do the renovations. When the two weeks were up, the renovations weren't done, so she thought she'd extend her time off. When she put in her request with her supervisor, she wrote, she wrote, *Not quite done in the bedroom. Need another two weeks.'*

Sijiang didn't get it. Then, the freckle-faced doctor took the speculum and brought it towards Sijiang's lower body. Sijiang screamed.

'What are you screaming for? I haven't even started!' The doctor sat down between Sijiang's thighs and picked up the cold metal tools.

Xiaohong gripped Sijiang's hand with some force. She felt herself tense up. Tears glistening like crystals flowed down the apple-shaped face and soaked into the dirty sheets.

The doctor, face expressionless, stabbed with her forceps. Sijiang howled. The doctor grasped the metal and wiggled it back and forth. Bleeding like a stuck pig, Sijiang continued to wail, the cries growing gradually weaker. It was like being in a dream, the sounds drifting to her as if from a great distance. She broke out into a cold sweat, lying in a puddle of fluids. Her tiny eyes looked straight up at the ceiling, as if their ferocity could nail Bud to the giant red cross painted on the white wall before her.

IX

The typical Spring Festival weather settled in – a fine misty rain blowing on the wind. To the eye, it was gentle and kind, rich in charm and beauty. When it hit the face, though, it showed itself cold, hard and merciless. In fact, in the North – which, to the locals, meant anywhere north of Guangzhou – this would be considered mild weather, but here, people were shrinking into their coats, muttering, 'It's freezing!' Every time someone came in or out of the lobby, a cold blast of wind would rush in, covering Xiaohong in a layer of goose bumps.

In the afternoon, it was sunny. The hotel, decorated for the season, flashed red and green. *The Wedding March* was playing constantly, its notes hovering over the entire hotel, as if the whole place was filled to overflowing with endless amounts of good cheer. Everyone was as infected with the mood as if it were his or her own wedding day. Or, put another way, it was as if those already married wanted to renew their vows, returning to the first days of new love, while the unmarried would imagine such a union, tasting the sweetness of marriage. In short, it was a wedding celebration.

Zhang Weimei felt it the strongest. From early in the morning, she alternated between enthusiasm and frustration. She constantly turned to the small mirror, as if hoping to see herself in her own wedding gown reflected there. But her boyfriend had said that without a Shenzhen green card, there was no point talking about marriage. They had helped build up Shenzhen society for two years, and there was no good reason for the city to deny them the chance to start their own little family. They would certainly be a law-abiding household, not creating any trouble. Weimei had never really thought about how many couples there were just like them in Shenzhen. They were no better than a pair of ants in a vast colony.

'Is it that hard to get a green card? What do you have to do to get it?' Xiaohong had only been in the city a short time and so was a complete novice when it came to green cards.

'Money! You buy it,' Weimei snapped, as if she were none too pleased to offer Xiaohong enlightenment on the topic. Changing the subject, she said, 'Mr Pan's brother, Pan An, is having his wedding banquet, so there will be plenty of action for you to see.'

Xiaohong took a hard look at Weimei's face, but could see nothing beyond the green card problem there.

'Pan An? Isn't he that tall, slim, quiet fellow?'

Weimei nodded.

Xiaohong had seen Pan An and had heard that he was a member of a triad, but found that difficult to believe. The image of frail, scholarly-looking Pan An carrying a mobile phone as big as a brick could not help but make one think, How could a guy like that be connected with fighting and killing?

'What girl would dare marry him? And, why not choose a more auspicious day to get married?' Xiaohong cackled so hard she could hardly breathe.

'So he's in a triad. What's the big deal? Triad members offer a sense of security. If anyone bullies you, he'll be taken care of in no time.' Weimei said, her expression dreamy. But she seemed to have a clear enough picture of the situation. 'Being a female gangster has a beauty of its own!' These dark ideas made Xiaohong feel Weimei had a mysterious charm about her.

At dusk, the hotel practically swelled. The entrance was covered with a thick layer of firecracker wrappers, like decorations flying from a marital bed as it is being broken in. The banquet guests arrived, their hungry mouths smiling in congratulations. The car park overflowed with shiny cars – a bright red Ferrari, a silver Volvo, a black Mercedes-Benz, a white BMW as dazzling as a bright patch of sky.

A man dressed in jeans emerged from the Ferrari. He lit a cigarette, took a loving walk around his car, then, glancing back at it over his shoulder went into the hotel.

'Jimmy, I haven't seen you for a while. You've got another new car!' Weimei scrunched up her cheeks, greeting the fellow with a rare enthusiasm.

The guy glanced at the dyed blonde hair in front of him, then turned back with a wink and a smile, pointed at Xiaohong and said, 'A new beauty, huh?' He turned back to the reception desk and stared at Xiaohong, blinking. There was an unbridled mischief in his eyes, as if he were looking at some caged animal or a goldfish in a tank. Clearly, he thought himself a hardened veteran with years of experience.

'I thought it was that Hong Kong movie star, Jimmy Lim!' Xiaohong noticed that he had a child's face and she firmly resisted the attentions of that boyish smile.

'No, he's Jimmy *Lim*, I'm Jimmy *Chan*. Everyone says he looks like me.' Jimmy tossed his mobile phone onto the counter. Suddenly he craned his neck, leaning his face in close to Xiaohong's breasts.

'Have a good look,' she said, thrusting out her chest and giving him a better view of her employee name tag.

'Oh, Qian Xiaohong. Tonight, you and me, karaoke. How 'bout it? Think it over and let me know when I come back,' he said, and turned and walked coolly away.

'Hey! You left your phone!' Xiaohong shouted at his retreating figure. He turned back and took it, giving Xiaohong a meaningful look. She was like a fish caught in a net soon to be served up for his dinner.

'He wants to ride your waves. You better be careful. He's into drugs,'

Weimei quickly warned.

Just then, the bride came in amidst a sea of merrymakers. Two glamorously dressed children came in behind her carrying her train. All the voices were lost in the crash of the firecrackers. Each wore a dumb smile, like a bubble floating in the surf. The bride had a pretty face, though her figure was less than perfect. She wore a gown with a red bodice, the waist trimmed with black lace backed with yellow lining. On closer inspection, it was obvious that the bride was not merely plump around the middle, but with that belly, she was pregnant.

'Um... Weimei, her stomach is pretty big.'

'You only just realised that? She's a northern girl from a town in another province. I heard she used to be a supervisor in a hotel in Shenzhen while she was studying at the university. When Pan An and his friends were there one night, he met her and took her home. He wasn't planning to get married but she was determined to have the kid. They were at a stalemate and this is the eventual outcome.'

'Huh?' Xiaohong was startled, thinking suddenly of Sijiang. Had she decided to stay the course, what would've been the outcome for her? At this moment, she must be holed up in her little room, crying all alone. Who knew whether Bud had even been to see her? And he had seemed so gentle on the surface.

The bride stood at the entrance, smiling, shaking hands and greeting guests. Her two arms glittered like a golden Buddha, covered – it was more like she was *bound* – with golden chains, each of her ten fingers sprouting a gold ring, one of them with a huge diamond on it. The elegant costume made a stunning scene. Xiaohong was dazzled. Even the bride's smile seemed to be golden. Weimei was lost in a dreamy state, trying to conceal a sort of hunger. She watched as all the pomp and pageantry was showered on a working-class girl hailing from outside of Shenzhen. It was all more surreal than a dream.

'Xiaohong, a wedding is just a big show. The gold and silver, pearls and stones hanging on the bride is just a way of showing off the family's wealth. Pan An has made a lot of money in Hong Kong and he can use his Hong Kong dollars to buy a diamond ring as easily as you or I could buy a cheap knock-off.'

Xiaohong laughed. 'If a wedding is showing off wealth, then what is marriage? I think at the heart of it, marriage is the same sort of thing. The showing off is just a temporary thing and when it's over, the couple still have to live together quietly.'

Weimei said, 'You talk as if you've been married before. You mean you don't want a scene like this?'

'Of course. I don't want anything as glitzy as this, but I wouldn't mind the feeling of wearing a wedding gown.'

Hearing this, Weimei sniffed a couple of times and fell silent.

Around seven or eight that evening, the wedding ended. Jimmy Chan brought his ever-smiling eyes back downstairs and said, 'Ah Hong, you thought it over yet?'

Faced with his young, good-looking figure, it would be a lie to say Xiaohong's heart did not stir. She could already feel herself growing a little moist. She hadn't given his invitation much of a thought at first, not taking the guy seriously. Men who moved in the underworld never gave an inch and so were not easily deceived. Xiaohong thought a moment then said, 'I'm on duty tonight.'

'When do you get off?'

'Midnight.'

'OK. Then, I'll be here right on twelve to get you!'

His no nonsense approach and his firm tone were irresistible. Xiaohong, at a loss for words, did not know whether to be pleased or anxious.

X

At midnight, Jimmy Chan's Ferrari appeared at the hotel entrance, as punctual as clockwork. He squinted and smiled at Xiaohong, then drove her all the way to the grand entrance of another hotel, where two security guards scurried out to help guide him into an empty parking space before the couple made their way into the hotel's nightclub.

In the karaoke room, Xiaohong saw the groom, Pan An, arms wrapped around a sexy young thing. This was highly out of the ordinary. On his wedding night, here was Pan An, out drinking with his mates and womanising. That wedding banquet that he had been compelled to attend was just an elaborate mating ritual, and now his pregnant bride was tossed into the bridal chamber and left there alone.

It was a jumble of singing and chatting in the smoke-filled, noisy scene. No one cared who came in or out. Xiaohong consumed a couple of apples from the snack tray as she sat for several minutes. Jimmy's hand settled on her ample breast for a moment, he then took her by the hand and led her out of the room.

He did not tell her where they were going and she did not ask. They quickly reached a tacit understanding. The Ferrari practically flew, a flash in the darkness behind two columns of light. They travelled far and fast, like two people shooting for some distant planet, peaking with an inexplicable joy. The car turned into a seaside villa, stopping in the exquisite back garden.

Everything in sight was of the finest quality.

'You take a shower while I have a smoke,' Jimmy said. Xiaohong reached out and embraced him. He touched her breast and she began to moan incessantly.

'Go and shower first,' he said again, squeezing her breast. She obediently went into the washroom. The bathtub was sparkling white. Xiaohong, dawdling, felt an irresistible desire to lose herself emanating from her chest and flowing over her whole body. After she had bathed, she went back into the room and saw Jimmy, half of his body visible above the quilt, toying with a cigarette. He sniffed hard at a piece of white paper then swept his cigarette butt back and forth across the top of it. With all of his strength, he again inhaled deeply then flicked his lighter. After lighting another cigarette, he put his free hand around Xiaohong's neck and swung himself across her. He stroked her breast as the cigarette quietly burned, enjoying both of them as the smoke coiled upwards. When the cigarette had burned down, he extinguished it and moved himself onto Xiaohong's body. Whether from his kisses or from the taste on his lips, Xiaohong began to feel lightheaded.

When they had finished, ten minutes passed as they lay quietly. Xiaohong, not satisfied, reached over and touched Jimmy. He said blankly, 'I don't do the same girl twice. Here. This ring is for you. It's not payment for what we've done. Even if we hadn't done it, I'd still give you the ring. If you have any trouble, you can always come to me. Now, get dressed and I'll drive you home.'

XI

'Ah Hong, hurry! Get up. Wake up.' It was already after six. Xiaohong, tossing and turning, had just got to sleep and, in her dreams, was engaged in an intoxicating embrace with Jimmy Chan, when she was jerked suddenly awake.

'Huh? What's up?' she said impatiently, turning aside.

'Hurry, the police are looking for you,' Ah Xing urged, confusion on her face and in her voice.

'What? Why are the police looking for me?' Hearing the warning was like a cold splash of water in the face. As soon as she heard it,

Xiaohong's heart froze. On the verge of panic, she sat up suddenly.

'I've got no idea. They're waiting for you outside.'

Xiaohong got up and peeped out the bedroom door. Sure enough, two armed officers stood there like wooden posts.

'Hurry up, we're waiting for you!' A cop wearing spectacles accidentally poked Xiaohong's pyjamas, right in the chest. His voice was cold as marble, as if to say, 'We're above such temptations.'

'What's the problem?' Xiaohong gripped the door with her right hand, left hand on her hip. Anyone interfering with another's early morning dreams ought to be a little more polite and respectful. She was quite pragmatic. Her temporary residence card in order and her permit for working at the hotel settled, she was quite the law-abiding citizen. Other than having made love to Jimmy Chan the previous night, she had not been involved in any illegal activity. Surely they wouldn't be bothered about her bedroom adventures. That would be much stricter governance than could possibly be warranted.

'We're investigating a case and we'd like your help. Please come with us.' The burlier officer spoke a little more moderately.

'You need my help, right? Then why are you treating me like a criminal? I'm just an ordinary, innocent citizen,' Xiaohong said with a faint smile. She thought of Zhu Dachang and Ma Xiaoming. Beneath those uniforms lay nothing more than simple men. Knowing this, regardless of their occupation, she didn't feel the same reverence she once did, much less fear. All the same, having just emerged from the warm bed, she inevitably began to tremble, her breath whistling through chattering teeth.

'Bloody hell, it's cold this morning!' She swore in her hometown dialect, then turned and went into the room to change her clothes.

Dawn was breaking slowly, as if suffering from a hangover. The wind was blowing hard as they headed to the main hotel building. Xiaohong hugged her clothes tighter around her, arms crossed. The burly fellow said, 'I'm Liao Zhenghu. I've got some questions for you. Last night at the Qianshan Hotel, one of the guests lost twenty thousand Hong Kong dollars. The whereabouts of all of the hotel's staff will have to be reviewed. Interviews will be held in Mr Pan's office.'

Liao was as compact as a tiger, with a sturdy frame and narrow eyes. He began in a professional tone but once he had brushed against Xiaohong, he turned as smooth as silk. The other officer was a pale, thin Cantonese man. His wan complexion and scrawny shape seemed to have been the result of too much drinking.

In the hotel corridor, they ran into one of the younger employees coming out of the office. She was obviously tense after the cross-examination, her face a shade of bright red. Pretending to relax, she stuck her tongue out at Xiaohong, staying close to the wall to avoid the gaze of the officers. The friction of her clothes against the wall made a soft swishing sound.

'Please be seated.' The manager's desk had been transformed into a judge's bench, and a square, dark face stared at her from behind it. The officer's skin tone brought to her mind the legendary Song Dynasty minister, Justice Bao, making him an even more imposing figure than the hotel manager, Mr Pan. A woman sat to his left, pen in hand, ready to capture Xiaohong's statement. Xiaohong sat across from Officer Bao, in the same spot and manner that she always adopted to make her regular reports to the manager.

'Please give me a truthful account of your movements between eight p.m. last night and four a.m. this morning. And pay attention, I want a truthful statement,' he said, the secretary's pen busily nibbling its way across the page like a silkworm on a mulberry leaf.

'I... yesterday from two in the afternoon until midnight, I was on duty. When I finished my shift at midnight, I went for karaoke with a couple of friends. After singing, I went back to my quarters and went to bed.'

'Where did you go for karaoke, with whom did you go, and what time did you finish? What did you do when you left?'

'I was at the Furama Hotel. There were a lot of people there. I didn't look at my watch when we left. After that, I went home to sleep.'

'From what I know, the Furama Hotel's karaoke lounge closes at one, and when you got back to the dorm, it was nearly three. In those two hours, where did you go?'

'I'd rather not say. But I can tell you, I was not at the Qianshan Hotel.'

'If you don't tell us, we'll have to take you back to the police station for a more careful interrogation.'

'I... I went with my friend to his villa.'

'Who is your friend?'

'I'd rather not say.'

'You have to say, and you'd better tell the truth. It's for your own good.'

'Jimmy Chan.'

'Oh, him. What were you doing with a gangster?'

'Ah Sir, this doesn't seem to be relevant to the case,' Liao interjected.

'Are there signs for recognising gangsters? I couldn't tell.'

'What were the two of you doing?

'I'd rather not say.'

'You have to tell me and I want every detail. I only want to hear the truth so that we can establish your credibility.'

'Well, OK then. Listen carefully. As soon as we went into the house, he kissed me frantically. His mouth tasted of alcohol because he'd been at Pan An's wedding and had several glasses of strong spirit there. We kissed for about twenty minutes, then he told me to shower. He's very handsome and, y'know, I was reluctant to part from him, so we kissed for another five minutes before I went into the bathroom. I stood in front of the mirror while taking my clothes off because, y'know, I like to see my own body. He has this mirror running along one whole wall in the bathroom and I stood looking at my reflection and vainly admired myself for quite a while, but I don't remember exactly how long. Maybe seven or eight minutes. I discovered that my breasts had shrunk a little, probably because it had been a while since they'd been touched by a man. I sat there feeling sad for about a minute then turned on the water heater. The water was really hot. I asked him to come in and help me adjust the water temperature... Do you want me to continue the story like this?'

No one spoke.

'Am I supposed to go on like this?' she asked again.

The men were all lost in their own reveries. Though there were no outward signs of change, doubtless they were each engaged in fantasies of Xiaohong's naked form standing before the long mirror.

'Yes, carry on,' Officer Bao said hoarsely.

'Have you recorded it all?' Xiaohong asked the secretary. She was determined to make these good-for-nothings suffer a little longer. She smiled at Liao, as if he were an undercover operative working for her. He gave her a light-hearted, longing look.

'He came in and helped me adjust the water temperature, then pecked at me all over my body. He was very rough, as if he wanted to crumble me into little pieces. When the bathtub was full, he put me on the floor of the tub and climbed in. The water overflowed badly. He did not enter me right away, but spent some time kissing my breasts. It was even longer than he'd spent kissing my mouth, probably fifteen minutes or so. My chest practically went numb from all the nibbling he did. Afterwards, he applied bathing foam to my body, his fingers rubbing every inch of me. I asked him to do it in the bathtub, but he said he liked the bed, preferring the feel of being under the covers. After about forty minutes, he wrapped me in a towel and threw me onto the bed, thrusting himself against me over and over.

He was in no hurry to enter me. He lay there half naked and lit a cigarette, with me rubbing and playing with him the whole time. He likes this sort of prolonged foreplay. We're alike in that way. About thirty minutes later, he and I really became one. It took about twenty minutes and then we were done. Or, to be more accurate, he was done. I still had a way to go. After we'd rested for fifteen minutes, we went at it vigorously one more time. This time, we did it for a long time and he really took me to the top. We rested for another half hour or so then he drove me home. He said he never spends the night with a woman. The rest, you already know. Now are you clear on everything I did? You can go and find Jimmy Chan, if you need a witness. I don't have his phone number.'

The secretary turned to Officer Bao. 'Ah Sir, I've calculated. There are twenty extra minutes.'

'Well, that's basically what happened. Maybe we didn't make love for quite as long as I thought. This is just an estimate, so there's bound to be a little difference here or there,' Xiaohong said, imitating the officers' tone.

Officer Bao exhaled heavily and asked, 'When was the last time you saw Zhang Weimei?'

'Last night at midnight.'

'Before that, what did you two talk about?'

'I've forgotten. Yesterday, there was a big wedding banquet. I think we talked about marriage and things like that.'

'Uh-huh. If you hear any news of her, contact us immediately. This is the phone number of the police station. You can go. Thank you for your assistance,' Officer Bao said, offering Xiaohong a business card. He started to stand up but then, thinking better of it, handed the card to Liao to pass to her.

And so the interview ended. It was nothing more than a group of guys passing the time playing soldiers. When she got to the dorm,

Xiaohong walked around Weimei's bed. Underneath it was only a pair of broken slippers. The poster had disappeared. As for the twenty thousand, without conclusive evidence, no one could really be certain what had happened. Weimei was nothing more than a suspect. If she really had done it, Xiaohong could only admire her. If she could use the twenty thousand to get married and get her green card, Xiaohong wished her all the best. If the money really had belonged to one of Pan An's Hong Kong connections, how could she have any sympathy for him? If it could be used to set up a home for one little family, giving a couple happiness and stability, it could be considered an anonymous donation to help others, an accumulation of good karma. Those staying at the Qianshan Hotel had too much money entirely, so much so that they were willing to stand there burning it right before your eyes.

Breakfast was plain porridge with a custard-filled bun. Ah Xing had ordered on Xiaohong's behalf.

'Thanks, Ah Xing. I'm starving. Hey, do you know when Weimei left?' Xiaohong lifted the bun and bit half of it off, her cheek bulging.

'I guess I was sound asleep. I don't know if she came back at all. She stays over at her boyfriend's pretty often.' Ah Xing took a small sip of her porridge. 'Hey, you little floozy, who were you with last night?'

'Ah Xing, what do you think? Did she do it?' Xiaohong asked, avoiding the sensitive topic.

'If not her, then who? She's run off now. That's as good as admitting guilt. If she comes back, it's a sure thing the triad thugs will take care of her. Messing with Pan An's associates is suicide! You know, at first, I thought it was you, since you hadn't come back in the middle of the night. I guess now everyone in the hotel knows you spent the night with Jimmy Chan. Well, Xiaohong, from now on, nobody will dare to bother you. Jimmy Chan is a known commodity around here.'

XII

After her convalescence, Li Sijiang looked no different from her earlier self. There was no trace of what she had been through on her bearing. Experienced women need only look at a girl's hips to know whether or not she's been around. What their eyes cannot see is the after-effects of an abortion. So, after a week, Sijiang was once again, in effect, simply a young girl in the pink of health. Of course, the chicken soup and hearty meals Xiaohong bought her each day were not unrelated to her quick recovery. Xiaohong took care of these expenses from her own pocket, the five hundred from Bud having long since been exhausted to settle the hospital fees. Sijiang had a little money but she was not at all willing to spend it on herself, thanks to the thrifty nature she had inherited from her upbringing on the farm. Xiaohong believed that money was there to be used for times of real need and so spending it should not be considered a waste – as if one's self were some worthless thing.

Xiaohong suggested Sijiang leave the factory and work in the hotel, since conditions of the staff quarters there were good. Sijiang was hesitant, still secretly holding out hope that Bud might reappear. Whenever she saw Sijiang like this, Xiaohong could hardly breathe and her blood would begin to boil. 'Sijiang, you can give up thinking that Bud will show up. You need to get a grip and forget all about him. After what you've been through, you can see how insincere he is. Just think of him as a pile of crap. You've passed him through your system and now you've got to wipe yourself clean, pull up your trousers, do up your belt and get on with your life. Move on.'

So, Sijiang, tears streaming down her face, began to pack up her few miserable belongings – some wrinkled, worn clothes, a pair of old-fashioned, dusty shoes, a toothbrush and towel, a washbasin and a cup. She crammed it all into the rough grey canvas bag she had brought with her when they first came to Shenzhen.

She was in bad shape when she finally left the flat, joining forces with Xiaohong at the Qianshan Hotel.

XIII

On the eve of the Spring Festival, Sijiang put on the hotel uniform and began shuffling plates in the café.

The receptionist at the Western-style café was a pretty girl with plaited hair. Her black plaits were long, inspiring envy in many a girl. The plaits hanging down the length of her tall back gave one the impression she was hopelessly conservative. There was a young fellow from the north called Li Xuewen who worked at the Qianshan Town Cinema, and he was the only one who could put a happy, albeit shy, smile on Plait's face. She would become very flexible when he was around, turning back at the most confusing angles to exchange glances with him. Li Xuewen would come to sit at the café several times a week, either with friends or alone, but always when Plaits was on duty.

We must take a moment for a description of Li Xuewen, since he will soon become entangled in the complex affairs of the women in this tale. Actually, Wu Ying, Ah Xing and the other staff at the Qianshan Hotel knew him quite well. Other than the fact that none of them had seen him naked, he really had nothing else that he could call secret. He was 1.8 metres tall. Hailing from Changchun, he was a graduate of the Luxun Academy of Fine Arts. The 28-year-old was a Cancer, he wore glasses and had no distinguishing marks. There was nothing particularly striking or surprising about him. He was quite handsome. When he walked, he was not a very impressive figure, his feet shuffling along as if to polish the floorboards. He looked a bit like an old professor, or a man who'd dropped something and was looking for it on the ground. All the same, he seemed like a solid figure – the kind to give one a sense of security.

It was said that Li Xuewen set up a number of IPOs for the Qianshan area, helping local leaders and distinguished dignitaries get in while it was hot. This alone set him apart from the average worker so, in relative terms, Li Xuewen was in a much more advantageous situation. He was a piece of pie worth having. And while this piece of pie might walk with his head bent looking at the ground, he never missed an opportunity to pursue beauty when he saw it in the girls around him.

Wu Ying had been with the hotel longer than anyone and she knew all about the competitiveness that had existed between the two beauties, Ah Xing and Plaits, from the beginning. Before the two girls had met, each went about with head held high. On meeting, they came together like two aggressive cobras, each seeing herself reflected in the other. If either felt her territory invaded, she was sure to lash out at the other. Then Li Xuewen dropped between them. And so his relationship with Plaits developed at a snail's pace – largely due to Ah Xing.

The strange thing was that Plaits and Sijiang hit it off right away, getting on very well. Perhaps beautiful girls liked having someone like Sijiang around – a leaf to act as background to their flower's bloom. Sijiang actually played the role of leaf quite happily. But her loyalty was pledged to Xiaohong and she always fully reported any news connected to Plaits to her. Xiaohong was on good terms with Ah Xing and would naturally pass the reports on to her. So, when Plaits got squeezed, Sijiang was an unwitting accomplice.

Ah Xing had a soft, gentle look. Though her viciousness never showed on the surface, her actions proved that a schemer lay beneath this veneer of innocence. She was bold and confident. Although Li Xuewen would hold her hand whenever they saw a movie together, sometimes kissing her ear, nothing ever really came of it. Ah Xing was defensive, attributing it to shyness. She was just waiting for him to make his next move. But it was obvious that the attacks Plaits had launched against Ah Xing were a major factor influencing Li Xuewen. Xiaohong felt it was a fair fight, each having an equal shot at happiness. After all, everyone has a right to love and be loved. She encouraged Ah Xing to take the initiative saying that if Plaits and Li Xuewen went to bed together, it would complicate things.

Under Xiaohong's instructions, Sijiang would pay careful attention when Li Xuewen was in the café, taking note of every word and every look that passed between him and Plaits. The girl's plaits seemed to grow darker and shinier every day. One day, Sijiang noticed that their expressions were strange. They seemed distracted, as if they were deliberately avoiding one another, exchanging only furtive glances. But their eyes were continually drawn back to each other.

'Reminds me of that sweet potato dish they eat in the northeast. They say it is so sweet and sticky that it never leaves you. It's too sticky to break off and, even though it's sweet, you never get sick of it.' The description brought the image to Ah Xing's mind, and she took it like a punch in the stomach.

Ah Xing came up with a perfect plan, keeping even Wu Ying and Xiaohong in the dark. She made a sudden announcement that it was her twentieth birthday. She invited Wu Ying, Xiaohong and Sijiang to a small restaurant, where she booked a private room. Of course, she also invited Li Xuewen to join them. Being the only man at the party, he was the star. They sang karaoke before and after dinner, and Ah Xing had had a little too much to drink by then. Tipsy, she suddenly started to cry – the first time she'd ever shed a tear in front of the others. Everyone, including Li Xuewen, was stunned. She was obviously sad about something. 'Time...' she said. 'Three years have passed in the blink of an eye since I finished secondary school. These three years have just been frittered away. If it's not family trouble, then it's money trouble. If it wasn't for all that, I'd be graduating from university now. And my work, my life, my love life... it would all be so different. Why am I fated to be like this? *Why?*'

Ah Xing gave her little speech without pretension. Although she had set out to put on a show for Li Xuewen, actually it had turned into an exposure of her true self.

Sijiang's narrow eyes had turned red. She said, 'Ah Xing, everyone has their ups and downs. I'm worse off than you. I didn't even go to secondary school. On top of that, you're gorgeous! It's only now that I realise that those of us without an education are just here to be trampled on by everyone else.'

'Well, Sijiang, maybe that's not the way to look at it,' Xiaohong said. 'Whether other people trample on you or not has got nothing to do with how educated you are.' Xiaohong was also a little tipsy by now and the presence of a man in the room caused her to take on a sexy, sultry tone. She didn't mean to burst Sijiang's bubble in this way, but she objected to the place she found assigned to her in that line of thinking.

Ah Xing's mood seemed to inspire some sympathy in Li Xuewen, like an almond blossom brings rain. He showed himself to be a gentleman, quietly settling the bill when no one was paying attention. It was impossible to tell whether it was his heart or his body that was stirred but all the same, he took Ah Xing's arm and said, 'That's enough for tonight.'

It was likewise impossible to tell whether Li Xuewen took it upon himself to take Ah Xing back to his dorm, or whether she pushed her way in, but either way, they went to bed together. Afterwards, Ah Xing said without shame that in Li Xuewen's room, she'd got the best birthday present ever. Her first love, first kiss and first time with a man had all come into her life together on that night. Once he takes a girl's virginity, a man with even just a little conscience is tied down. In order to give Ah Xing some confidence, Li Xuewen had plunged into the whirlpool of her life. He would not find it easy to drift away now.

According to Sijiang's reliable reports, Plaits had passed the daylight hours in an uneasy state over the past several days, constantly driven to distraction until her eyes glazed over. At night, as she slept on the lower bunk, Sijiang felt the bed trembling all night long. In the morning, there was always a stack of used tissue beside the bed. Plaits cried silently night after night. Sijiang felt guilty, as if she'd been an accomplice to a crime and felt miserable for days for what she had done to Plaits.

'Sijiang, you know what Li Xuewen said?' asked Plaits. 'He said she was a virgin, so he should behave responsibly towards her. But who's being responsible towards me? Surely it doesn't mean our love should be sacrificed on the altar of her hymen!'

'You two were in love?' Surprised, Sijiang could not quite believe that Plaits and Li Xuewen had been together countless times.

'In love? You need to ask? You think I'd go to bed with a guy I didn't love? I rejected a rich guy's advances, choosing instead to be with him, even though he's like a pauper. Sijiang, I need to get out of here.' A cold look settled into the girl's eyes. Sijiang felt a sudden surge of sympathy for Plaits and a sort of natural contempt for Li Xuewen.

'Don't leave. Get him back. You're prettier than Ah Xing and you two were already together before she came along.' Sijiang was unwilling to lose Plaits, who was her only friend besides Xiaohong. She had to find a way to help the girl.

Plaits shook her head determinedly. 'No way. Even if he comes back to me, I couldn't forgive him. I want to completely disappear from his world. When he thinks of me, I want him to be unable to find a trace of me.'

Plaits really did leave, and she left with tragic flair. After she had gone, her fragrance lingered in the bedroom for several days. Sijiang stood in front of the empty bed, dazed. Plaits left her pager number for Sijiang but when she tried to call it three days later, it had been disconnected.

And so Plaits was like the disconnected pager number, cut out of existence just like that.

XIV

When Wu Ying was in a good mood, she would often bring her three-year-old son, whom everyone called Sparky, to work with her. As soon as he arrived, excitement would boil over at the hotel. Xiaohong was very fond of the adorable little guy. In fact, all the girls at the hotel were fond of him, calling him 'Handsome', and the handsome fellow enjoyed being with the girls. As was customary here, he called all of the unmarried girls *Jie Jie*, or 'Big Sister', and all those who were married, Auntie. With his endless stream of big sisters, a world of happiness was written across his face. But he had a special liking for Xiaohong.

This beautiful, clever child was Wu Ying's only consolation in life, like decent, warm clothes in which to wrap herself. Wu Ying, with a mother's sacrificial heart, gave Sparky all the joy and happiness she could shower on him. But on Wu Ying's face – that face that was once so beautiful – were signs that she had weathered a horrendous storm, turning her features hard and mottled in the process. Her eyes were often red from crying.

After Weimei left, Xiaohong was left partnered with Wu Ying for duty. Xiaohong and Ah Xing both knew all about Wu Ying's situation. Her husband, Yan, had nothing much to commend him, apart from a tall stature. He was ugly, his eyes were set too closely together, his head was angular and he had a sallow complexion. No one could quite imagine how Yan had managed to get such an attractive woman as Wu Ying to marry him. According to Wu Ying herself, Yan had a little substance to him. That was easy enough to comprehend, or how else could he have become a plant manager? Wu Ying had looked for a guy with substance and his appearance was not really that unbearable. If one could only see that substance, surely it wouldn't be so hard to believe they were together.

One thing that was clear, though, was that Wu Ying was not happy. In fact, she was suffering. Ever since Yan had begun an affair with another woman, Wu Ying had been having her affair with loneliness.

One day, Wu Ying slipped Xiaohong six hundred *yuan*, along with a smattering of small notes.

'What are you doing?' Xiaohong blurted out, dumbfounded.

'Dividends. Didn't Weimei used to give them to you?' Wu Ying said, rubbing her eyes. She had never been a selfish person. Xiaohong shook her head. As she did, she caught sight of Weimei's little mirror, which had apparently been left behind. She saw the familiar face reflected back at her, looking especially charming in the warm golden glow of the hotel lighting. Xiaohong hesitated, turned to have a better view of that face, chuckled, then took the little mirror in her hand and turned her head back and forth for a closer inspection.

'Hey! You crazy or something? If you don't want it, I'll take it and buy dinner.'

'Go ahead. Get something nice for Sparky to eat.'

'Ah Hong, you really don't want to know where this money came from?' Xiaohong was fascinated by her own reflection, so Wu Ying snatched the little mirror and, waving the money, lowered her voice.

'Is it stolen?' Xiaohong's eyes opened wide.

'Of course not! You know how we can give the guests discounts? If you collect the full price from the customer, you can count the balance as a bonus. As long as Mr Pan doesn't notice and signs off on the accounts, it's fine. Once every couple of weeks or so. You really haven't ever done that?' Wu Ying handed the money to Xiaohong.

'I haven't seen a single penny! That bitch Weimei pocketed it all herself. Greedy little thing. I asked why she was always opening the cash register drawer when there wasn't any reason to, shuffling the cash around. Six hundred! That's a month's salary! And don't we have to work hard to get it? But then sometimes, it just falls into your lap.'

Xiaohong was really excited, and a new, deeper bond with Wu Ying was born. She hugged Wu Ying tightly, saying, 'When are you bringing Sparky again? I'll give him a big treat!'

'Hey, behave yourselves. You're in public!' Li Xuewen suddenly appeared in front of the counter carrying a couple of fast food containers. His glasses were thick and he squinted through them at the two girls. It was as if he had been on the road for a long time, and now his eyes were unfocused. Ever since he and Ah Xing had got together, he always looked tired. She, on the other hand, enjoyed an expansion of her feminine energies. The two were quite a contrast.

'Ah Xing still sleeping? Can't you stop trying to fatten her up?'

'Yeah, you two really know how to enjoy life, eating Western food every day!'

Xiaohong and Wu Ying each took their shots at Li Xuewen and he swaggered happily on his way. Going out of the front door, he turned back to look at them both and said, 'When are you two free to come to the theatre and sing? We've spent more than a million on new speakers. It certainly gives your confidence a boost to sing there now.'

'You're not afraid Ah Xing will be jealous if you ask Ah Hong to go? I'm old, so I don't have enough energy to sing,' Wu Ying said, laughing.

Xiaohong noticed Li Xuewen's eye flickering as he looked at her, as if he had something stuck in it. She couldn't be sure, but he might even have been winking at her. She giggled and said, 'Xuewen, when Ah Xing puts you out to pasture, you'll know better than to play around.'

XV

In the afternoon, bored to tears, Xiaohong bought a few of Sparky's favourite snacks and went to Wu Ying's house, a rental place down a back alley. If she had never been there, she would never have guessed – and having been, could hardly believe – that a woman as bright as Wu Ying and a child as lovable as Sparky lived in a place like that. How could they come from such darkness, passing each day there? The flat was a place of eternal night lit by a single fluorescent bulb during the day. The ground was uneven and covered in a layer of grime that coated the feet of anyone who stepped on it. The bedroom was so narrow that one could not turn around inside it. The double bed with its black mosquito net took up virtually all the space.

'Wu Ying, you... all three of you sleep here?' Xiaohong hesitatingly asked her direct question.

'His dad basically lives at the factory. It's rare that he comes back.' In her dejection, Wu Ying's face was darker than the dirt in the room.

'Daddy hasn't been home for a long time,' Sparky echoed brightly. Xiaohong picked him up. He said, '*Jie Jie*, come and play every day!' It was clear that his words expressed his mother's sentiments as well as his own.

There was a sound of footsteps outside the door, and Yan's tall form stepped into the house. 'You're all at home?' he said. Sparky shouted, 'Daddy! Daddy!' Yan patted the boy's head and smiled at Xiaohong, who returned the silent greeting.

Yan explained his presence, saying, 'I need to pick something up,' and went into the bedroom. After a brief moment, he said, 'I've got to get back to work.'

In and out in less than ten minutes.

Tears trickled down Wu Ying's face. She turned, smiling sadly, and said, 'Ah Hong, now you've seen everything. He hasn't been home for two weeks. When he does come home, this is how it is.'

The whole house seemed to fill with an even more depressing air and the ceiling seemed to have crept a few inches lower. Xiaohong was uncomfortable. What could she say? How could she comfort Wu Ying? First Sijiang, then Plaits and now Wu Ying. How did women always seem to find themselves in these sorts of circumstances? Xiaohong almost blurted out the word 'divorce' but, guessing that Wu Ying was seven or eight years older than her and was not an unassertive woman, she kept her mouth shut. Wu Ying must surely have her own way of coping.

'Wu Ying, if he really doesn't want this home, the way things are dragging on is bad for you.' Xiaohong looked around the house sympathetically.

'I'm hoping that maybe he'll come home one day. Ah Hong, wait till you are my age, then you'll understand.'

Xiaohong nodded her head thoughtfully.

'There's more to it than you realise, Ah Hong. You can spend the last drops of your youth at the hotel. You'll be sought after while you're in your late teens and early twenties. But after a few years, even a dog won't take a second sniff at you. Learn something. Pick up a skill. Don't be passive like me. The girl living with him is no older than you. He forgot all about this home long ago. He doesn't even care about his son. He spends all his money on that woman. I've seen her. She's a worker from Jiangxi. She's got it pretty rough, too.' In her raging anger, she was becoming a little incoherent, but still she understood and accepted the realities of life. She swallowed noisily, like a dog.

'Xiaohong, I know you'll give me an earful for this, but to tell you the truth, when I was your age, I was as idealistic and proud as you. Even now, I still feel Yan and I are interdependent. A day of marriage is months' worth of bliss, and the ties of kinship cannot be erased.' Wu Ying's tone was coldly desolate.

'I can't stand this! You've lost your confidence, Wu Ying. You're only twenty-five, but you talk like you're an old woman whose sense of romance has long ago dried up. Honestly, I think you should leave him. He should take half the responsibility for raising Sparky and each of you should go out and look for your own happiness. There's no reason for a woman to be locked away in an empty house.'

The light suddenly went out and the house was shrouded in darkness and there was a surge of cold air. Sparky, in Xiaohong's arms, began to cry in his fright, 'Mummy!' Wu Ying groped her way to him.

'Is your electricity cut off?'

'No, the fuse is getting old and the wires are no good. I'll go see what I can do about it in a while.'

'Wu Ying, if you are afraid, who do you call?' Xiaohong asked in the dark.

'If I'm frightened, I call for my son. As long as he's here, I'm not afraid.'

It was bright outside, and filled with the sounds of footsteps and laughter. A skinny ray of light slithered through the door but it did not reach far into the house, nor did it illuminate Wu Ying's tears. Their eyes adjusted to the darkness, allowing them to see each other's shadowy form and face. When they had sat a while in the muted atmosphere, Xiaohong had a proposal. 'Wu Ying, let's go. Let's take Sparky to Li Xuewen's place to sing.'

Wu Ying responded softly, 'You go ahead. I'll stay here and help Sparky with his homework.'

XVI

After Weimei and her poster had run away together, a girl from Chengdu who called herself by the exotic-sounding name Julia

Wilde soon arrived to fill the empty bed, bringing a tantalising new dimension to this small world.

As for Xiaohong, she did not miss Weimei, nor did Ah Xing or Wu Ying. And of course, nor did the girl now sleeping in Weimei's bed, having never met her. Julia Wilde often made vehement complaints about the smell of Weimei's bed. Xiaohong said, 'It's perfume mixed with sweaty feet. The ventilation in the room isn't very good, but there's no need to make a fuss about it.'

Julia was a woman of strong desires and she was not prone to hiding her wealth of sexual experience, constantly telling others the things she had done. She was always willing to make do with any old thing. Before coming to the Qianshan Hotel, she had been working in the service industry in a neighbouring town but the pay here was better.

'You were right to come here. The Qianshan Hotel is a place you'll want to stay. Everyone who works here manages to come across better prospects. Look at Weimei. She made big money and then went on her way. Our own Ah Xing found herself a promising man. Wu Ying has enough with her little Sparky to make us all envious for the rest of our lives. Maybe none of us will ever have a little guy like that.'

Julia smiled broadly. 'What about you? Where's *your* boyfriend?'

'Me? Oh, I'm convinced that he'll be there waiting for me when I make it to the top.'

Julia's sensuality was not just on the surface. One afternoon when Xiaohong knocked off work, she opened the door to her room to see Julia's bed rattling. She could vaguely see Julia through the mosquito net, her hands working her own body. The jittering stopped suddenly. Apparently, it was not quite enough, and the bed began to shake again.

'What're you doing in bed in the middle of the day? Why don't you get up and do something constructive? Playing with yourself is no good for your health!' Xiaohong yelled, turning to face the door.

Julia sighed in exasperation. 'That's it, I'm done. You're so bloody jealous of my pleasure that you had to go and screw the whole thing up! So are you coming in or aren't you?'

Xiaohong, wanting to wash her mind clean of all thoughts of what was going on behind the mosquito net, chuckled. 'Comrade Julia Wilde, you little Jezebel, how long has it been since you've had some?'

Julia poked Xiaohong's side and said, 'You little tart, you expect me to believe you don't do it?'

Xiaohong leaned against Julia. She wasn't sure whether it was the other girl or herself that went limp but it was like two bodies of water flowing comfortably into one another. Julia grasped Xiaohong's breasts and said, 'I just envy you. These things are way more important than a pretty face.'

Xiaohong pinched Julia in return. 'Damn! You're as bad as a hooker! You better not get me turned on!'

Besides playing with herself and, of course, men, Julia most liked playing with her earrings, a pair of jade studs, smooth and cold. They were always there attached to her ears in the daytime. Then at night when she had finished bathing before bedtime, she'd always take them in the palm of her hand and play with them a while. This was the only thing she undertook with any level of seriousness. The jade pieces had been her grandmother's grandmother's, passed down from one generation to the next. No bigger than a pair of soya beans, they were nothing much to look at. But even though they might seem insignificant to others, and even though Xiaohong mocked her every day, she played with those small balls constantly, treating them like treasures.

As if conjured up by their discussion of sex, Julia's boyfriend, a security guard from the hotel's west entrance appeared a few days later. He was a clean-shaven fellow from Sichuan and the two fell into their local dialect, whispering sweet nothings as they cuddled. At night, Julia said, 'Xiaohong, I hope you don't mind. It's a long way for him to travel back. It's better if he just stays here.' She turned to the guard and added, 'Dear, you'll just have to make do with staying here for tonight.'

So he did make do, and he did so often and happily. Sometimes he even made do for two weeks at a time. Julia said he had lost his job and was looking for another one. Xiaohong could not imagine what the fellow was capable of doing. He dressed decently, with a touch of idleness to him, like the sort who might be suitable to be some old woman's kept boy. The beds in the dorm room were unevenly distributed, with Julia and the guard sharing one while Xiaohong took two for herself, but Julia made no suggestions of changing. All she said was, 'Xiaohong, you might want to put cotton wool in your ears at night, or put your headphones on. Just make do, forty minutes at most.'

One couldn't help but admire Julia. Xiaohong picked up the tune where Julia left off. 'You can do whatever you want.'

The worst of it was that Julia's creaky old bed was like her body – sensitive to every touch. It would hum and quiver, picking up its tempo in cadence with the increasing activity of the two on it. As for the cotton wool and the earphones, they were tried but not very true methods for dealing with the problem. They couldn't remove the dark images that spread through the mind like cancer. Xiaohong finally found a perfect solution. She would lie on her bunk and make good use of her own hand. At first, she found the act had grown unfamiliar to her, having been abandoned long ago. However, she did manage to pick up the craft once again, eventually becoming quite skilful at the application of her handiwork. It went on like this for about ten days. But she found that her perfect solution was less than perfect – if she continued like this, she was likely to rub herself raw.

'You little Jezebel, look at how pale and haggard I am,' Xiaohong said, facing her reflection in the mirror.

Julia stepped up behind her and looked. 'Yeah, you need some nourishment from a man.'

'Fuck it, Julia! You just lend me West Gate Guard for a while and you sit there and listen. How about that?'

Julia stuck out her fat tongue and said, 'Ah Hong, I'm really sorry. Just hang on for a couple more days. He starts work at a bar next week. I'll compensate you for your mental anguish then.'

Having had enough of those two, Xiaohong channelled her energy into her work. Her breasts were a little bloated. She was thirsty, even though she was full. Should she look for a man herself? During the five minutes it took her to walk to the Qianshan Hotel, she seriously considered this question. What exactly were her goals?

When the woman on duty reported to Xiaohong that a guy had been in looking for her an hour earlier, she almost believed that she had some sort of psychic powers. But her ego was quickly deflated when she saw that the number was Liao Zhenghu's. She was bored with the police. She could no longer stand the crooked look of civil servants.

When Xiaohong next saw Wu Ying, she noticed a dark shadow around her right eye, as pronounced as a panda's.

'Wu Ying, go home and rest. I can take care of things here.' Xiaohong knew that Wu Ying must be having trouble with Yan but she couldn't imagine what might have happened to prompt the patient, quiet Wu Ying to become involved in any sort of violence.

'Nothing's wrong. Absolutely nothing. I thought about what you said and you're right. Yesterday, I went and told him I want a divorce. He didn't agree to it and we tussled so hard that we even took it onto the street. Ah Hong, we really beat the crap out of each other.'

'Oh Wu Ying, I don't know whether what I said was right or not. I was just thinking out loud. After all, you're the one who has to live with it, whatever happens. I'm so sorry.'

'I stand by it. After beating the crap out of him once, I'll happily keep on doing it until we finalise the divorce.'

'Well, you have my support. Why don't you come and stay in the dorm and save a little rent money?'

'No, he'd come to the hotel looking for me, and I don't want this to become everyone's gossip. I can still afford the rent.'

'Anyway, if you need anything, just let me know. Oh yeah, did you know Ah Xing's pregnant?'

'Yeah. It's not a good time for them to get married, so Li Xuewen went with her to the hospital for an abortion. It seems like there is an epidemic of pregnancies and abortions this year. It's becoming as common as the flu. Be careful, Ah Hong. It's not good for the body.'

Xiaohong sniggered and said, 'Just about every girl will have the flu at some point, and after they've had it they realise how much better it feels to be healthy. Only then do they take better care of themselves. Which reminds me... I have to get in touch with Liao Zhenghu. Maybe there's some erotic potential there.'

Liao picked up the phone and in an official tone asked whether or not there was any word of Zhang Weimei. It was the same old nonsense – if anything happened, let him know immediately. After a few minutes, he called her back and said, 'There were a lot of people in the office just now. It wasn't convenient to talk. I'm calling you from my mobile phone now. I hope you don't mind.'

Xiaohong answered, 'Whatever you say, Ah Sir, I wouldn't dare cross you!'

'Never mind. Up for a cup of tea when you're free?'

Xiaohong laughed. 'Tea's always good. You mean you have to be especially 'up' for that?'

Liao didn't say anything, as if he were flummoxed by her words. There was a dry rasping sound in his throat as he took a deep breath and said, 'How about tonight?'

'I've got nothing better to do, shouldn't be a problem.'

At first, Xiaohong thought of asking Julia along, thinking that the pair of them could surely put Liao into a spin, but Julia was on the night shift. It was obvious the sex-crazed little fiend was nursing other desires and clearly was not interested in such things as tea. She simply said, 'Ah Hong, when you drink tea, you've got to look for a little variety. Don't suppress adult impulses or ignore your natural urges. Remember, it's just human nature!'

Armed with Julia's encouragement – or rather, instigation – she could see right through Liao's motives. So, within a few minutes of meeting him in a teahouse called The Storm Shelter, she looked over all the most important parts and decided that Liao was a man with plenty of physical strength. There was none of the silly nonsense of him wearing his police uniform to take a girl out for tea and this pleased Xiaohong. His sturdy form hid a shy manner. His narrow eyes remained focused on Xiaohong's face, avoiding her chest. This purposeful avoidance made his expression somewhat wooden, like a zombie out of a Hong Kong movie. All the same, Liao was a talkative person, strictly logical and full of all sorts of theories. He seemed to be a guy with a bit of depth. Everything from the surge in shares five years previously to the price of a working girl's virginity, from the time he left college to a life of hard work in Shenzhen, all the way up to his present situation of relative ease – he poured it all out to Xiaohong. Liao finally revealed the hidden anguish that lay behind the whole discourse. Xiaohong came to the vague understanding that he, like her, was suffering from sexual frustration.

'You don't have a girlfriend?' Xiaohong asked.

Liao shook his head. 'In this city, the ratio of females to males is seven to one. All these women walking along the streets and not one of them is mine. It's a bit unfair. I know that young working girls think going to bed with a cop is a thing to be proud of, but I can't let myself be seduced by such things.'

Liao didn't seem to be putting on a show. Or if he was, it was a good one. She said, 'Then don't be seduced. Just pick one of them and settle down with her.' He picked up the fine, tall, slim silver teapot with his large, rough hand, like an eagle catching a small prey.

'This tea is good. You have to sip it a bit at a time,' he said, carefully pouring more tea into Xiaohong's cup. 'You girls definitely don't have it easy. You drift like clouds and the wind could change direction at any time. If you need anything in the future, just call me. A temporary residence card or a border permit or whatever.'

Xiaohong's belly gurgled, too full of fluids. She felt she was going to drown.

'Border card? Oh yeah, that. How do you get one? How much does it cost?'

Liao smiled coyly and said, 'Did I say I wanted your money?'

'Then you want *me*?' She gave him an unruly look.

He replied sternly, 'That's not what I meant. That's a separate matter – and if it happened, I wouldn't refuse.'

XVII

Ah Xing was in bed for nearly two weeks, enjoying the treatment of a woman in post-natal confinement. Li Xuewen already treated her as a prospective wife, bringing her chicken, fish, pigeon, ginseng and, the delicacy, bird's nest. Reversing the normal order of things, he watched her as she ate, nursing her back to tip-top condition. When Ah Xing came back to work, she was in fine shape. She turned the whole unpleasant business into a thing of beauty to which others might aspire.

'Well, each of us lives a different sort of life.' Xiaohong secretly felt that it was not fair on Sijiang, who had been keeping her whereabouts something of a secret lately. Her shifts were not the same as Xiaohong's, so even though they both worked at the Qianshan Hotel, they did not get to spend much time hanging out together. Sijiang gradually came to mix more with the staff at the café.

At first, Xiaohong thought of the *Ci Hai* that Zhu Dachang had given her as a brick that might, at a pinch, serve as a pillow, but later she placed it on the desk, rustling its pages from time to time. Everyone who saw the book was shocked. They would gasp in amazement and say, 'Xiaohong, you're reading such a thick book. You've got quite a promising future.'

As she casually flipped through it, she would unconsciously scan the words and so gradually developed a habit of reading the *Ci Hai*. Julia often said ironically, 'You are so skilled at opening that book. But you'd learn more if you'd go and gain some more experience in the bedroom. Studying is just a load of crap!'

'You really are twisted. Even reading a book can be a shameful act to you. *Aiyah*, what a life! You must have a master's degree in interpersonal relationships, Dr Love!'

'You're wrong. I already have a PhD, I'm an expert on men!' She was very flirtatious and men could always idle away hours at a time just soaking up her presence.

On a breezy, sunny spring day, Xiaohong finally got the chance to go to the park with Sijiang for an afternoon of skating. Sijiang rushed to buy their entry tickets and pay for rental of the skates. In her wallet, mixed in with the *yuan* was a very eye-catching assortment of Hong Kong dollars, which Xiaohong noticed immediately. 'Eh? Sijiang, what you doing with Hong Kong dollars? Who'd you get those from?'

Sijiang stammered, 'It was a little tip from a customer.'

'Such a huge amount and you call it a little tip? No, you've been sneaking around lately. Is there something new going on?'

The skating rink was crowded and the music was loud and intense, accompanied by the rhythmic swish of the skates. Sijiang's reply was lost in the noise and Xiaohong couldn't really be bothered anyway. The two plunged into the joy of gliding over the rink, the wind whistling past their ears. Sijiang grinned and opened her arms wide, sleeves fluttering in the breeze like a flag. It was an otherworldly feeling.

And then she fell.

There were several girls about her age, carrying backpacks as they glided easily, some even carrying ice cream cones as they went. They called to a table of boys, something about a particularly nasty essay they were all working on, adding comments about their English teacher's funny way of talking. They were like a flash of blinding sunlight in Sijiang's eyes.

'Sijiang, look at them. You think we could study while we work?'

'How can we study? Where would we go? And what would we study? I've lost touch with everything I ever learned at school.'

'Don't worry. We can find out about all that. I can ask Liao Zhenghu, or we could go and have a look around for ourselves sometime when we don't have anything else on.'

'They look really happy,' Sijiang said wistfully, gazing after the group of students.

'Kind of regret it now, huh? We should've worked harder at our studies when we had the chance.'

'My family didn't have any money. Thirty *yuan* didn't cover tuition fees, so they were overdue every semester. I couldn't bear to face my classmates and teachers, especially wearing the hand-me-downs that had already been passed along my cousins before they got to me. I wore my cousins' old clothes and worn-out shoes. I looked like a sack of grain that had already been through the mill. I was afraid of how the boys at school would see me when I grew up and wasn't willing to go through that sort of shame anymore.'

'Sijiang, you're still a talented girl.'

A couple of boys slid over to them, hoping for a bit of fun. Xiaohong pulled Sijiang to another part of the rink but the boys followed them, so the two girls left.

When they got outside, Xiaohong paged Liao from a phone booth. She asked him if it was possible for them to study. Liao was on duty nearby. He soon arrived on a motorcycle with a sidecar and whisked the girls away to the Cultural Centre.

There were brochures everywhere for activities such as computer training, arts courses, evening classes, self-study for exam preparation and so many other options that it made their heads spin. They read for a long time, carefully looking over the information, giving serious thought to the practical value of each course. Finally, with Liao's guidance, Xiaohong and Sijiang reached a consensus: self-study for exams. They reasoned that when they had finished these studies, they would have a nationally-recognised diploma, and that the programme fit their needs. Unlike the other courses that put emphasis on a single profession and required a regimented schedule of classes, this course only required an exam twice a year. But when it came to the choice of major, the two girls had divergent opinions. Sijiang was born to deal with money, so wanted to study finance. She felt maths was another good option, since it was easy to pick up. Xiaohong liked to rely more on rote memory, so wanted to choose something that required memorisation and recitation.

Liao said, 'Choose what you like. This is a question that doesn't require agreement. It's like you two both want to fit into one pair of trousers. Both of you want a qualification, so you each need to walk the path that suits you best. Take all of this information away with you, think it over and then decide. Once you pay the tuition fees, it's not that easy to change courses.'

The next day, they went back with their fees and registered. They took their time to do everything properly, while Liao's sturdy frame stood by. He smiled coyly and said, 'You two have some sense of the crisis that can come to those without education and knowledge, and you realise how important studies are. That's already half the battle. Put your youthful energy into work and studying, and life will repay you in kind. I can't wait to see you two in a few years.' He sounded like a teacher, talking a lot of general nonsense. But his preaching did not bother the two girls. They smiled, looking like a pair of mature women, and likewise turned their eyes towards a bright future.

XVIII

Xiaohong harboured a feeling of nostalgia for Jimmy Chan, longing to sit in his Ferrari one more time, imagining her first orgasm with him, wishing they could do in the flesh all the things she had described to the police in a single impassioned encounter. Maybe it was her physiological cycle but her sex drive was at a high point recently. It was so strong that she even had a thirst for the sounds of Julia and West Gate Guard. But Julia had not seen much action recently and her guard appeared infrequently.

After a few days, Julia shifted her interest to target the East Gate Guard. He also had a friend who followed him everywhere. Julia asked Xiaohong if she had any interest in spending her free time entertaining him. She could guarantee he was clean, maybe even a virgin.

The nature of Julia's part-time work outside the hotel was something she never talked about. Only one mantra was ever on her lips: 'suffer for a few years and be happy for a lifetime'. Xiaohong didn't quite understand what she meant by this but it seemed as if it were no big deal. Julia maintained a cheerful outlook and nothing got her down. The more things that snagged on her, the higher she flew.

Lust is no dirty thing, though the actual transaction can be shameful.

It's like any other physical urge. When you're hungry, you eat. When you're tired, you sleep. It is all very ordinary. The different sorts of hunger are actually all quite similar. A diner partaking of fine delicacies at a banquet is like an emperor with three thousand concubines. But eating *mantou* or a bowl of noodles at a simple roadside stall, that's like the lowest forms of rutting. It's passable and, though *mantou* and noodles do have their own sort of excitement, it can't measure up to the upper-class lifestyle. Having sufficient food and wine is like the pleasure of having a steamy affair. But for the lower classes, when they fulfil their sexual desires, they do so only as to take care of a basic physical need. And so, the lower classes take what they can get – begging, borrowing and stealing – so that their basic needs are fulfilled.

At least, that was Xiaohong's philosophy. But as she thought it over, she couldn't decide which category she fitted into. Even as she stumbled into Liao's dimly lit room, she had not worked it out. She only knew she was hungry and that she wanted a hearty meal. Liao looked rather appetising, his two big hands stirring up some warmth in her as they offered her a drink.

He used disposable cups to brew some tea, rocking back and forth under the light. He smiled, his face always betraying a lack of confidence, as if it were Xiaohong's house and he were merely a guest who dropped in now and then. His police cap and uniform were on a hanger, looking like a person standing there. Liao sat down.

Xiaohong was not the least bit thirsty. She did not want a drink. She felt like a character on a movie set. She was the heroine of the tale who, not understanding a thing about sleeping with men, distracted herself with the act of drinking tea.

She began to feel the old hunger pangs in her belly. She casually glanced at Liao's bed. It was wide, so wide one could roll over three or four times without falling off. The bedspread was as clean as an unspoiled maiden.

An hour later, the pair of them had thrown the bed into a state of chaos.

SEVEN

I

She's back. Qian Xiaohong. She's been away for over a year, and now she's come home for the Dragon Boat Festival.

In this village, even without modern means of communication, news spreads like wildfire. Before a cup of tea had even flowed down her throat, people were coming to her door full of merriment. Some said she was thinner, some that she was prettier, touching her clothes and commenting on how different the style was. Once they had each taken a gift, they went away satisfied.

Her sister was the last to come and, at the end of the day, a big sister is still a big sister. She did not mention the past. When Xiaohong took out the clothes she had brought for her, she squinted at their dazzling brilliance and asked, 'Where would I go in those things?'

Xiaohong said, 'Wear them at home. Wear them when you go into town. Or just wear them when you go to work in the fields. I'll buy you more later.'

Her sister, turning a long-suffering smile on her, replied, 'Honghong, what have you actually been doing in Shenzhen?' She shook her head and continued, 'Don't lie to me. Everyone in the village says you... you... you do *that*.'

'I don't do *that*. I don't hook! I have an honest job! *Jie Jie*, others don't have to believe me but do you lack faith in me as well?'

Her sister continued to shake her head sadly. 'That's how it is. Girls go to Shenzhen and they always go down that path. Everyone knows it. Just look at you, so well dressed. Who wouldn't have some doubts?'

'You really don't know how horrible it is to hear you say that.'

Xiaohong was beginning to get angry. Those who had just left the house laughing happily, they were enjoying themselves at her expense, behind her back. But after all it was Xiaohong who had made her way to Shenzhen and seen the world a little. She had not spent much time keeping in touch with the village, nor had she been back. Let them make irresponsible remarks, then. But what disappointed her was that she had lost her childhood friends. They shrank from her like they were avoiding the plague. They dodged her questions, giving cold replies as if afraid she would corrupt the high moral standards and purity of all the women in town.

'Arseholes! Fucking arseholes! They're so blind!' she cursed quietly, looking down on those self-righteous pigs.

The first day she went round visiting as many of her neighbours as she could, despite the fact that her legs were a little unsteady after the overnight train journey.

Though Xiaohong's return may not have been a flash of lightning, it was at least a glowing fluorescent light. And she did bring a breath of fresh air. Over the next few days, more and more people dropped in at Xiaohong's house. Some came asking Xiaohong's sister to intercede with her on their behalf, begging her to help their sons or daughters find jobs.

On this front, the most prominent case was Aunt Chun. She came to both pull strings for others and to bring her own requests. She had a long pair of tear stains from an eye infection, forming a triangle across her face. When the wind blew, her eyes watered. The sad fact was that she eventually became so affected by the winds that she believed every piece of gossip that blew in on them. Regarding the rumour that Xiaohong was living in Shenzhen as a prostitute, she went further and actually fanned the flames, helping to spread the fire. She just wouldn't let it rest.

When she received a flowery clip as a gift from Xiaohong, she sat at home pondering for a long time, then took a look around her empty house and went back to Xiaohong's. In an unthinking manner, she heaped fierce praise, laced with a tinge of envy, on Xiaohong. When she had finished, she sighed and tragically added, '*Aiyah*. Everything costs money, even education. I can't afford to do anything. I've got a daughter at home and she has never lived up to expectations. Her results are poor, and the money we spend on her studies is wasted. All she does is sit at home every day. My Little Hong, take her to Shenzhen with you to work and earn a bit of money, OK?'

The woman was shameless. She had gone round telling everyone that Xiaohong was a prostitute in Shenzhen and here she was pushing her own daughter into the fire.

Aunt Chun wiped her eyes and pretended to be sad as she muddled through her request. Xiaohong tried to tear her away from the topic. Pretending to be surprised, she said, 'Aunt Chun, your eyes are still acting up every time the wind blows. I'll check when I get back to Shenzhen to see if I can find any effective medicine to bring back for you next time I come home.'

Aunt Chun replied, 'My Little Hong, you're so thoughtful! To tell you the truth, though, these old eyes are beyond fixing. Nothing can be done. But about my daughter... remember to help me.'

'Alright, Aunt Chun, if you're sure you can entrust her to my care.'

'If I can't trust my Little Hong, who can I trust?'

She stood there currying favour without even blushing.

'When I get back to Shenzhen and have checked things out, I'll write to you. You just wait for my news,' Xiaohong assured her.

Aunt Chun turned her rump towards Xiaohong and went home,

where she promptly packed up a dozen eggs and brought them over.

'My Little Hong, the hen at home lays eggs too quickly! Do me a favour and help me eat them up. Would you like some dog meat too? I can get someone to come over and slaughter the dog, if you want.'

'No! Please don't kill the dog. I'll be heading back as soon as the festival's over. I'll cook the eggs, but please don't do anything else. You've already gone to too much trouble.'

11

It was on the day of the Dragon Boat Festival at the dining table that Xiaohong saw her brother-in-law. Lunch was a typical holiday spread. Her father ate, feeling depressed, mostly because Xiaohong was leaving the next day, but also because everyone in the village thought his daughter was a prostitute in Shenzhen. He had lost face.

'This household is not penniless. Why would we resort to something like that?' He drank a little wine as he voiced what was on his mind.

'If others say that about me, it doesn't matter. If none of you trust me, then there's no hope! I'm not hungry anymore.' She threw her chopsticks down. '*Jie Jie*, Brother-in-law, don't you believe me either?'

Her sister sat there as silent as a vegetable while her brother-in-law chewed his food like a donkey, neither saying a word. He stole a glance at Xiaohong from the corner of his eye and found that she looked foreign, suddenly very far away from him. It was as if a bird he had held in the palm of his hand had taken flight and was now gone for good. He decided to go to Xiaohong before she left and he planned to do it that very night. He just had to be with her one more time.

Unable to eat another bite, Xiaohong sat weeping silently. Her heart had turned cold, along with the rice and vegetables on the table.

'On my mother's grave, I might as well go back to Shenzhen and 'sell', if that's what you all think,' Xiaohong suddenly blurted out and left the table. She hid in her room, intending to have a good cry. But after letting it simmer for a long time, not even one tear boiled over. She realised she wasn't even sad. In all honesty, she didn't care what others thought, including her family.

The villagers only cared about two things. One was money and the other was sex. Everything they talked about was somehow related to one of these two things. Of course, money and sex are two cornerstones of life, basic elements of comfortable living, so in one way, the villagers were not to be blamed. This sort of simple life might be worth continuing to live for them, but to hell with it if it had anything to do with Qian Xiaohong!

When she realized that she was not actually sad, she also discovered that she had already drifted away from this village and had no intention of returning to her roots.

III

There was a sudden booming of drums coming from the long, narrow boat slithering over the water like a snake emerging from its hole. Xiaohong remembered she had arranged to meet Sijiang at the river. With a sudden lurch, she left the bed that had bred so much sorrow and ran towards the sound of the drums on the Zijiang River. She did not know how long the river was, but the area where she lived was the liveliest section. Every year, the Dragon Boat Championship Race station was located here, the crowd of human bodies snowballing as it trailed along the banks behind the boats. From a high point near the river, one could see for miles. Seeing dozens of boats drifting like leaves on the emerald face of the water, the view gradually widened to take in the sounds of drums far and near as the boats seemed to emerge from the horizon, drifting slowly towards the crowd. Every patch of ground on nearby hills was covered with people as they grabbed a moment of respite from the heat and the exhaustion of dashing about.

Seasonal rains from the previous day had swelled the river to a self-assured, abundant flow. It set the perfect mood for the festival, a spirit of fun and joy best captured by the boats. Red flags inserted into buoys on the river fluttered, as if pushed by the distant vessels.

Everyone was brightly dressed and in high spirits, despite the rusty hue that tainted their skin. It was a fine day and they all wore caps or carried umbrellas to shelter them from the sun, readily parting with their money in exchange for ice lollies to suck on and gain a little relief as they sweated in the heat. It was a festival, a time to free their hands from their daily toil. Grandfathers carried grandchildren on their shoulders and boys carried girls on the backs of their bicycles. The young walked aimlessly about, filled with a youthful hope. Upstanding middle-aged citizens put aside their regrets for it was the Dragon Boat Festival. And thus the people came together at the Zijiang River, watching the same rickety vessels they had been watching all their lives. The sun was brutal and the ground bravely stood against its heat, baking people's trouser legs between sun and soil. Xiaohong, sunglasses donned, strode through the swelter, sweat creeping down her cleavage like a worm. As she stood amongst the crowd in the pavilion, she could not quite locate the feeling of Dragon Boat Festivals from years past. She looked at the crowd, she looked at the river and she found it all quite dull. At the jetty, after looking here and there, she saw Sijiang walking anxiously toward her, a little boy she held by the hand trailing along behind. 'This is my cousin,' she announced.

It was hard to tell if the right side of Sijiang's apple-shaped face was swollen or if the left side was shrunken, but Xiaohong felt that something was not quite right.

'Sijiang, it's been days now. How the hell you been?'

'I don't think there's any point to it all. When we were getting ready to come home for the holiday, I was so excited I could hardly sleep. Now that I'm back, there are some things that really piss me off!'

They sat on the stone steps in the shade beside the pavilion close to the river. The Zijiang seemed wide and open. Sijiang had to get her cousin an ice lolly before he'd settle down.

'Ah Hong, I gave my family three thousand *yuan* – nearly half a year's salary – and they turned on me really savagely. Once I'd put it into my dad's hands, he really laid into me. I'm just a piece of crap, completely worthless!' Sijiang picked up a stone and tossed it into the river. The drumbeats on the dragon boats intensified.

'Over my mother's dead body, you know better than that! You aren't worthless. If other people don't believe us, I really don't care. But when those in our own houses don't believe us, it hurts. Shit, I come home and I feel like a stranger here. I don't know when I'll come back for another holiday.'

Xiaohong's stomach began to rumble. The starting gun sounded and the dragon boats took off. Everything broke into a frenzy. The air was filled with voices screaming, 'Go! Go!' Sijiang's cousin, having devoured his ice lolly, could not sit still. He grabbed Sijiang's sleeve, pulling her towards the crowd.

'Ah Hong, I'll take him to watch the boats race. If it wasn't for him, I don't know if I could've got out of the house. My dad won't let me go,' Sijiang said helplessly.

'What? Sijiang, you mean you aren't planning to go back to Shenzhen?' This was a terrible shock.

'I'm worried. Of course I want to go back.' Sijiang once again looked confused.

As Sijiang led her cousin away, Xiaohong shouted after the retreating figure, 'Either way, I'll be there on time, waiting for you at the South Station!'

IV

Night came quickly and the Dragon Boat Festival faded into the darkness. All was silent, in contrast to the excitement of the daylight hours. It was like a dream, not quite real. Anonymous insects set up their ethereal orchestra and everything went on as if nothing out of the ordinary had happened.

The night was moonless, the sky grey. The shadows of trees covered the ground like ghosts. Any time, those branches might rub together and join the whispering chorus of the wind running through the leaves. There was not a peep to be heard from bustling traffic, no neon lights in the town centre, no one hurriedly coming or going. The trees and the insects alone hummed a lullaby, singing the village into a slumber as deep and silent as the grave.

Xiaohong stood on the balcony for several minutes. It suddenly hit her that she had already weighed her anchor and turned her course towards Shenzhen.

She finished packing, gulped down a cup of water, and decided she would depart early the next morning. She would wave her hand and slip out without disturbing anyone. She rummaged around to find some paper and a pen to write her father a note. A cool breeze blew the door open. Her brother-in-law stood in the doorway, eyes sparkling brightly.

Frightened, Xiaohong's chest began to pound. Pushing the paper and pen away, she said, 'What're you doing sneaking in here like a ghost? You trying to scare me to death? What the hell are you doing here?'

'You're leaving tomorrow morning. I came especially to see you, to keep you company.' He stood there in a white tank top, trousers and slippers. He casually closed the door, locking it with a swift thud.

'Hurry up! It's been a long time. If your sister comes in and finds us, it's going to be a big hassle!' he said, unfastening his trousers. He put his hand in his pocket and pulled out a handful of free condoms that he had picked up at the town's family planning office. He threw them on the table and continued frantically undressing.

'Put your clothes on! Are you crazy? What the hell do you think you're doing?' Shocked, Xiaohong spat the question at him.

'What the hell am I doing? The thing I haven't done with you for a long time, that's what! If I don't do it today, I don't know when I'll get to do it.' His hand moved a little more slowly. He stood holding onto his trousers at the fly, not quite sure what to make of Xiaohong.

'You still want to do *that* with me? You don't reckon you've already done me to death? On top of that,' she said, pointing at the condoms, 'you think I'm a hooker in Shenzhen. You're such a piece of shit!' Furious, she thought of how many times she had been done by her brother-in-law and a burst of nausea flooded over her. She could feel him in every pore of her body, a filthy dumb animal. She wished he would jump into the Zijiang River, cleansing himself once and for all.

'You think you've been mistreated here? I haven't given you the cold shoulder. What the hell are you going off at me for?'

His words enraged her so much she thought she would choke to death. She lunged at him and with a loud *pop* slapped him in one lightning-quick move. 'You fucking prick! You're nothing to me! Don't expect to even hear me call you 'brother-in-law' anymore!' She pulled herself up, her eyes wide as light bulbs.

He raised a hand, hesitated, then shoved her and said in a muffled voice, 'You hit me.' Knowing Xiaohong was not easily pushed around like her sister, he backed down.

'You listen to me. You better be good to my sister. If there's any more womanising, you better watch it or you'll find your balls cut off and thrown to the dogs.' Xiaohong accompanied the threat with a chopping gesture. Seeing the action, her brother-in-law gasped and involuntarily covered his crotch.

'My Little Hong, y-y-you... you've only been away for just over a year. How come you've become so wicked?'

'A year ago I was a stupid little twat. Now, I don't want any more of your bullshit. Get the hell out! I just want to sleep!' Her chest rose and fell dramatically. Her brother-in-law put the condoms in his pocket and, looking at her questioningly, turned and walked out, a shadow of his former self.

But how could Xiaohong sleep? She took out the paper, gritting her teeth against the stab of pain her brother-in-law had caused. Tears of humiliation dropped down her cheeks as she continued to write her letter to her father.

Dad,

I'm leaving. Today, I'll go to Changsha and get tickets for the night train. It will be a long, drowsy night at the train station after the two-hour or more bus trip. Everyone has badly misunderstood me, as if anyone who goes to Shenzhen can't possibly lead a proper life there. Others love wild speculation, and it's fine if they don't believe me. But my family thinks the same and that hurts. There are many things about Shenzhen that I don't have the time to tell you and I know you'll always be angry with me. I only have a few things I want to say, so I'm writing them here.

None of you have been to Shenzhen and you only go on hearsay. You hear bad reports but what you don't understand is how hard it is to make a living there. In the factories, it costs half a *kuai* to eat a simple meal of instant noodles or boxed rice. It's always endless overtime, working ten hours a day just so the monthly salary is sufficient. Even then, it's only three or four hundred *yuan*. Eight or nine people squeeze into one room and all year long you've only got cold water to wash up in. The beds are narrow and people often fall out of the top bunk at night. Some have been injured. Even

crippled! But the factory doesn't take responsibility. No manu-
facturer is ever sympathetic to the plight of their employees. All
they want is to see the workers live and labour like money-making
machines. At a metalwork plant, a boy had his hand cut off at the
wrist by a machine and the company only paid him a few thousand
yuan – and that's considered humane. Some manufacturers do
nothing, even if you're injured or killed and the labourers don't
even know where to go to report it. I'm doing alright, considered
pretty lucky, in fact. People have helped me along the way. When
I was in the factory, the hours were long but it was more relaxed
than a lot of places. I worked there for a few weeks then went to a
hotel as a front desk attendant. It's a lot better than factory work.

Dad, even if some people do *that* for a living, I really pity them.
It's not as if they like doing it, they have a really rough life. Maybe
it was just pushed on them. I know a few girls who have gone over
from our home province who are very pretty and very nice too.
One girl went and, in order to earn money to help her mother get
some medical treatment, she went down that route and became
one of those girls. Who are we to despise her?

And Dad, don't just focus on your projects. Take care of *Jie Jie*.
Take care of yourself too. Don't worry about me.

Goodbye, Dad.

Early in the morning, Xiaohong quietly left the village. She made her
way over some distance to the river and sat amongst the willow trees
on its bank. She sat until her backside was just about flattened and her
stomach was rumbling. Only then did she get up and run to the South
Station. She arrived before eight and went to the spot where she was

due to meet Sijiang. She was more than an hour early.

She ate a bowl of spicy noodles near the station, watching people come and go. Her mind wandered. It was nearly time. She got up and walked to the ticket counter inside the station and waited for Sijiang. Uneasily, Xiaohong wondered whether Sijiang would be smart enough to find a way to escape. If she was even a bit careless, it was certain she would be locked in the house for the whole day. Quarter of an hour passed, then half an hour, then an hour. Xiaohong exhaled heavily. She felt like she was standing in the middle of a battlefield and her comrade had fallen. She was suddenly very alone.

She turned to the bus, still dawdling. She finally boarded in despair. Just as she went through the door, she heard a familiar voice call, 'Ah Hong!' Sijiang was running towards her empty-handed, a look of shock on her apple-shaped face.

'Hurry up! Hurry up and get on! I'll explain on the way!' Sijiang pushed Xiaohong on, looking over her shoulder as if someone were in hot pursuit.

Eight

I

Any time a twenty per cent discount was given on a room, it required Mr Pan's signature, creating a measure of inconvenience for the girls and presumably for Mr Pan as well. When Xiaohong had accumulated a stack of such bills – enough to warrant a name change from the Qianshan Hotel to the Twenty Per Cent Off Hotel – she found that this was going to be detrimental to their little arrangement in the long run, so she discussed the matter with Wu Ying, Ah Xing and the rest.

'I have an idea. Say we forge Mr Pan's signature on some forms. If we do that, we only have to get him to sign some of those that we collect our share on. Then we mix in the forged forms with the real ones and we hand them all in together. What do you think?'

'Brilliant! Really brilliant!' Wu Ying and Ah Xing cried in agreement. 'But who's the best one to do it?'

They were all unequivocally agreed that it was a great idea but they each tried to push the other into the most dangerous role of actually executing the plan. In the end, they decided to put it to a vote and let the majority have its say. Wu Ying and Ah Xing both thought Xiaohong's penmanship best and that she would be most able to imitate Mr Pan's writing. Since she was most likely to pass the signature off as his, it was settled.

She bought some exercise books and practised throughout the night, writing Mr Pan's name until she thought she would drown in it. She wrote it at work and after work she'd go back to the dorm and write it some more, like a forlorn woman pining for her lover.

Julia's eyes noted this and her mind began to tick over. When she could stand it no more, she said, 'Xiaohong, wake up and look around! Mr Pan has a family and he's got a name in Qianshan Town. Just because you've got a crush on him, do you really want to go and make life difficult for yourself?'

Julia, wearing a skimpy rose-coloured tank top, wiggled her round hips. Her recently-dyed blonde hair made her fair skin glow all the more.

'Men just have to look at me once and they get a hard-on. If I coo at them and shake my arse a bit, they practically want to burst.' Julia boasted without the least hint of shame. Xiaohong found it a bit over the top.

Pretending that Julia had seen right through her, Xiaohong poked her friend as if in embarrassment. 'You're the one with a crush on him! Who knows perhaps he's already had a piece of you, the way you're always running in and out of his office. His desk is at least as wide as our beds.'

Julia laughed, the three pairs of studs in her ears sparkling. A fourth pair of earrings dangled, swinging in rhythm with her giggling.

'Even if he wanted to do me, he doesn't have the guts. Getting it on with your subordinates is one of the stupidest things you can do, don't you know? So you better not get any ideas in your head either. He's one of the top ten most upstanding citizens in Shenzhen, a real family man. Quite civilised. When that son-of-a-bitch does his womanising, it's strictly hands-off with his employees.'

'Please don't say anything. I have to have a way to get it out of my system, don't I?'

A week later, Xiaohong slapped her imitation of Mr Pan's signature on a form and took it along with a genuine signature to Wu Ying and Ah Xing for inspection. After looking them over carefully, they failed to distinguish the genuine from the counterfeit. They all agreed that, with this approach, they could pass the forms off as the real thing and that even Mr Pan himself would not notice.

11

Ever since the Qianshan Township's enterprises had been listed on the local stock exchange, delegations from all over the country had been coming to the town to study, research and pick up some tips. The Qianshan Hotel was almost always full of guests coming to seek their fortune. Being the town's high-end guesthouse, many civil servants turned their beady eyes on the hotel, where the staff did their best to accommodate the needs of these noble guests in style. As civil servants, they naturally did not care whether prices were low or high. In the morning, they slept in then had a late breakfast. Rejuvenated, they calmly set out for their daily tour, after which they happily returned to the hotel and descended on the restaurant on the second floor to devour their dinner, as they were passionate about the food in Guangdong. After they had eaten, drunk and relaxed to their heart's content, they carried the name of the Qianshan Hotel to the four corners of the nation.

The visitors had a long-lived fascination with Shenzhen's nightlife. At each event, the officials were led like a flock of sheep to green pastures. The schedule was always arranged with regimented precision. To put it another way, they all knew exactly what Shenzhen's nightlife had to offer, so there was no real danger of any of them unintentionally falling into a romantic entanglement that could derail his career. No sheep was left out of the fold and each was treated better than if he were some visiting head of state from a foreign nation.

Once, though, when Xiaohong and Wu Ying were doing the night shift, a guest, an official from Zhejiang, called the desk at eleven o'clock at night. 'Miss,' he said, 'can you send a few cans of San Miguel to room 807?'

Wu Ying had answered the call. She replied, 'I'll just need to go out and buy it for you.'

'Thanks,' he said, 'that's exactly what I had in mind.'

But what the official really had in mind was only made known when Xiaohong took the beer to his door. Room 807 was the deluxe suite and the fact that this official was staying there showed that he was a man of no mean status. When he turned on the TV, it was replaying a conference. Clad in a white vest and shorts, he moved in for a closer look. A bulge of white flesh appeared at his belly, round as a bucket of water. He was shaped like a capital letter 'S'.

Mr S was a big spender. He gave Xiaohong a sizable tip for running the errand, then said he would like to hear a little about her life working at the hotel. Xiaohong glanced at the money in her hand then, facing the large mirror on the wall, said, 'To earn fifty *kuai*, we have to work three shifts. Now, I've just walked no more than fifty metres and earned it from you. Working life is like that. Sometimes, money is only earned through sweat and blood. Other times, it comes easily.'

Mr S rubbed his hand over his bald scalp. Sweetly, he said, 'Which method of earning do you prefer?'

Xiaohong, having sensed his intentions early on, gave a knowing smile as she made her evasive actions. He was running out of patience, standing before this eighteen-year-old girl. Late-night passion was beginning to ferment in his swelling body.

'Let's talk. What number do you have in mind?' Meaningfully, Mr S moved in closer to Xiaohong. His full belly was the first thing to press itself up against her.

'Me? I don't know. I've never thought about it. What about you?

What number do you have in mind?' Facing Mr S with calm restraint, Xiaohong casually began toying with the fifty *yuan* note.

'For ten, I have to bring my own condom. For a hundred, I get any position I want. For a thousand, I get the whole night. For ten thousand, I get to do you to death. So Miss, which do you prefer?' Mr S smiled as if he had just delivered the cleverest little jingle ever spoken.

The thought of a romp on the pure white bed with its fluffy pillows and a night of ecstasy was certainly an interesting proposition. Sadly, though, the lead actor here was not award-winning material. Xiaohong bit her lip, putting on a pretence of childishness. She put a hand out and removed Mr S's tank top, then started to take off his shorts. Mr S immediately stripped and stood there looking like a frog. He reached out to undress Xiaohong, but she moved away and said demurely, 'Let me look at you first.'

The fifty-odd-year-old, S-shaped man stood naked – soft muscles, flabby arse, and round, fat belly all on display. At the spot where his smooth skin should have come to a gully, the thing that hung there looked like a seed dropped into a furrow in a ploughed field. It had begun to sprout, standing up just above the soil. In the heat, though, it was wilting, sagging hopelessly towards the ground. Xiaohong stood facing Mr S, and his round belly began to shake with laughter. She said in a deep voice, 'Uncle, I'm a virgin. I'm just curious about your body. I took off your clothes. If it's not too much trouble, would you mind putting them back on now? This fifty *yuan* is a tip for your trouble.' Xiaohong took the note she had been toying with for so long and tossed it toward him. Then she turned and ran out the door.

'You're too much, Ah Hong. You really humiliated him. At least he was good enough to tip you.' Wu Ying listened to the story anxiously, eyes wide with horror.

'No, Wu Ying, the tip was just bait. He wanted me hooked.' Xiaohong recited Mr S's jingle again and went on to say, 'He humiliated all women with that. He thought having a cock meant he could manipulate everyone else. But the money is the only life he's got in him, I tell you.'

The paternal Mr S seemed to suffer a setback in his spirits. From then on, when he went in or out of the Qianshan Hotel, he walked straight through the lobby without a glance right or left. He did not approach the desk for help again.

III

Though life seemed quiet and simple on the surface, it was full of complications and noise. In Wu Ying's case, her eyes were as black as a panda's and her ears had been ringing for three days. On top of that, she had backache. It was all because of her constant fighting with Yan. But Wu Ying still had a quiet demeanour, bearing these complex issues with a smile on her face as she went about her life and work. It was an ongoing process and no one really saw a clear linear development of the struggle. One afternoon while Ah Xing and Xiaohong were on duty, munching sour plums and chatting idly, Wu Ying came in excitedly.

'Hey, if you aren't busy, you got a moment for a chat?' she said, stopping in front of the counter.

'Of course we're not busy.'

Xiaohong said, 'Looks like Big Sister is about to make a great leap forward.'

Wu Ying came behind the counter and went straight to the issue of the twenty per cent discount. 'Sisters, there have been too many forms lately. Take it easy. There's no point fishing if the pond runs dry. Also, put more of Mr Pan's originals in when you take them up and less of Xiaohong's so that the fakes are hidden a little better.'

'Wu Ying, I don't believe you've come running in here all worked up like this just to talk about this.' Xiaohong winked at her.

'So I came in on my day off, you little monster. Is that such a big deal?' Wu Ying chided, smiling.

'Aha! Let the fireworks begin! You must have some news for us. Are you expecting again or something?' Ah Xing said with an air of mock graciousness.

'Not everyone is as happy-go-lucky as you, you little witch. Just look at the way you torture poor Li Xuewen! Lately I, Wu Ying, have been living the life of abstinence. I'm like a recently converted vegetarian, though I've known the taste of meat in times past. But I'll be liberated soon. He's finally agreed to the divorce,' Wu Ying said.

'That's great! Congratulations!'

'Yeah, Wu Ying, I think it's for the best too.'

Ah Xing and Xiaohong expressed their support.

'But he gets custody of Sparky. At the end of it all, he still wanted to stick a knife in my heart,' Wu Ying said, sadly. Immediately, though, she smiled and added, 'But never mind, I'm the one who gave birth to Sparky. Blood ties can't be cut. And now I have a free hand to go and learn something new.'

Sure enough, not long afterwards, Wu Ying was like a young girl all over again. She had her hair cut into a fresh new look and started carrying a stylish black handbag. Released from the pressures of home, parenting and relationships, her back straightened and her chest thrust forward as if it had never cradled a suckling infant. With gusto, she pursued an affair. No one really knew what was going on inside of Wu Ying, except that she wanted to sow her wild oats. Wu Ying herself said, 'I want to set out on a second spring!' She was like a young chick. Bursting from the fragile shell of her broken marriage, she found herself in this new world with all sorts of opportunities lying before her. She started a computer training course at evening classes. Whatever enterprise she might eventually put her hand to, the chick was starting a journey of growth.

IV

Unless he is a peeping tom, a man can never know the various shapes of the seductive Venuses who fill the female portion of a public bathhouse. Of course, he can picture them, but imagination is merely imagination. The open area outside of a public bathhouse, set aside for washing clothes, is as near to the bathhouse as it is to the imagination. There one may find many damp young women – legs bare below the knee and freshly clean arms exposed, clad in the fragrance of just-shampooed hair – their laughter and their jokes both dripping. Sometimes each of them was like a washer woman, humming as she pounds the clothes, breasts hanging freely in loose, open-collared pyjamas, inattentive, as she bends over her work, to the eye that might gaze through the neckline right down to her navel. If she does notice, she intentionally screams and pulls on the clothing of the one caught looking, casually fighting back with, 'What're you looking at? Don't you have a pair of your own?'

Doing their laundry after they bathed was, for the girls at the Qianshan Hotel, the moment of greatest leisure. So they slowly washed their clothes, scrubbing away their exhaustion and troubles.

Ever since the occasion at the bathhouse when Julia Wilde, her great white breasts jiggling, spoke disparagingly about Sijiang's two oranges, Sijiang stayed far away from the merriment of the showering area when it was crowded. She made a special point to avoid the place when Julia and Xiaohong and their big boobs met. If a mother has an ugly child, she might not mind commenting on it herself but it leaves a bad taste in the mouth if someone else says anything about it. Sijiang had never felt those two things had any significant impact on her, thinking of them no more than she did the pair of feet tucked away inside her shoes. She was not like Xiaohong and the rest, who might comfort themselves with an inspection of their breasts when they were bored, calling it a scientific investigation of the activity of tendons and blood. They touched them to feel the ecstasy, and as a way of showing off.

The bathhouse was an open bathing space. There was a long pipe, and water sprayed out from several lotus-shaped spouts high overhead, covering the women in a mist. Beneath each lotus, a devout group of followers always gathered to cleanse themselves. Sijiang looked the others over, noting which were alike and which were not. They were all familiar, and yet all strangers. She would always hide at the inner-most tap to bathe, casually washing herself as she carefully watched the others. This sort of bathhouse could not be found just anywhere and this sort of scene was not enjoyed by just anyone. She saw clearly all of the naked bodies of the girls at the Qianshan, grasping all the specifics of the breast size and shape of each. Summarising the status of both breasts and people, Sijiang came to a conclusion: one's fate lay in one's breasts. She thought about her two little oranges and became frustrated by the road ahead of her.

The fate of Julia, Xiaohong and the others was not the fate of oranges. Sijiang just wanted understanding. Burying herself in her self-study materials, she turned the pages of the book until they were frayed and dirty.

When October came, Sijiang's apple-shaped face had grown round. If someone who had not seen her in several months had bumped into her, they would certainly have been in for a surprise.

'Hey Sijiang,' Xiaohong said, 'what's got into you? Your eyes are looking really bright. If you could take a little flesh from your cheeks and move it to your boobs, it would be perfect. You can't imagine the killer image you'd have then!'

As always, Xiaohong was at her most charming when she praised Sijiang.

V

When Wu Ying took over the bunk that had been vacated by Ah Xing, things in the dorm really livened up. Julia joked that it would soon be as bad as student quarters, saying, 'Wu Ying, you're a newly hatched chick and need to focus on getting your wings under you. This slutty little Xiaohong has, surprisingly, also registered for self-study exams. Every day, you're both as serious as nuns, hitting the books as if you're preparing for the imperial exam. You two, when you're supposed to be studying, it's OK to work hard. But when it's time to go about flirting and enjoying a healthy sex life, you still work like dogs at your studies. There's something really wrong with that! The way I see it, you should take this opportunity to earn some money, then go back to your hometown and open up a little shop or something. You'll be all set,' Julia said, her breasts quivering at an unbelievable rate as she spoke.

'You little Jezebel, all you ever think about is your sex life. Sooner or later you'll be worn out. Pick up a diploma, learn something new first then worry about your sex life. Who knows how different things might be for you then. Look at Wu Ying. She got so worn out she finally left. Of course she knows what she should do with herself now.' No one but Xiaohong would have dealt with Julia this way. Wu Ying's mantra where Julia was concerned was simply, 'You're still young.' It was her way of laughing things off.

In late October, Xiaohong, Sijiang and Wu Ying went into the exam hall in high spirits. Coming back to the dorm, Xiaohong was like a rooster that had just lost a cock fight, moaning, 'That was so hard!'

Feeling depressed, she felt the sudden urge to find someone with whom she could have a frantic roll in the hay. When that was done, she could begin to regroup. She walked irritably to the Qianshan Hotel and went straight to Mr Pan's office. He was flipping through a book when she went in. He immediately picked up his pen, assuming she had forms for him to sign.

'Mr Pan, I'm here to see if I can borrow some books from you. I'm sure I didn't do well on my exams this time round. My reading has been too narrow. Or, maybe not narrow, but I haven't read anything with any real artistic or literary value.'

'You're doing the self-study exam? That's excellent. What books do you want to borrow? Have a look for yourself.'

'Why don't you recommend something, sir?'

Mr Pan's eyes lit up. 'You really want to read?'

Xiaohong nodded fiercely.

Mr Pan, leading her into a small inner room lined with books, said, 'Here are the literary works. You can choose anything you want from here.'

The windows of the study were stained the colour of tea, giving the light in the room a sort of dingy hue as if it had suddenly grown dark outside, creating in Xiaohong the sudden urge to go back to the dorm. She boldly turned her gaze to Mr Pan and was surprised to find a sort of perverted uncertainty there. She purposely moved closer to him, so close he could smell her breath. Then she pretentiously removed a book from the shelf, flipped through it and put it back. She did this four or five times, Mr Pan exhaling heavily through his nose as she did so. Xiaohong turned her head and saw Mr Pan standing with his eyes closed. It seemed he was struggling against his body's desires, but at the same time, he looked like he was savouring the passion that was so close at hand. At last, Xiaohong closed the gap between them and gently touched his arm, moving her hands to his chest when he wrapped her in a tight embrace. He hesitated, as if deciding whether or not he should take Xiaohong. She'd already started removing his shirt, as if dismantling his last line of defence. At first, they stood leaning against the bookcase, then crashed down onto the carpet. It would be fair to say that Xiaohong managed her manager quite well.

When Xiaohong left, she carried three books in hand. Having gone at it with Mr Pan, she was the very image of youth. When she passed the reception desk, Wu Ying stopped her with a dignified call then waved at her, hands flailing like a bear's claw, making Xiaohong uneasy.

'What's up?' Xiaohong asked, going behind the counter with a smile.

'The situation looks bad. I went to the finance office today to reconcile the accounts. The old man there was suspicious. He asked how come there were so many twenty per cent discounts. He said Mr Pan had too light a hand. He looked at each piece, one by one. I was so worried he would notice and that would really mean trouble.' Wu Ying's voice changed in her anxiety.

Xiaohong, feeling Mr Pan was attached to her, felt she was on solid ground. She knew no hint of fear. She thought, It was good timing to be with Mr Pan now. If he wants to make a scene, I can make it disappear just like that.

'Wu Ying, how much for each of us? Is it a large amount?' Xiaohong had never kept count.

'More than ten thousand,' Wu Ying answered quietly.

'Huh? For six of us, that makes sixty or seventy thousand! We're so evil!' Xiaohong was genuinely surprised. In a week of forging signatures, she had actually signed away tens of thousands.

'But Ah Hong, if we suddenly cut down, it will be obvious. We have to keep close to the current ratio and then cut back slowly.' Wu Ying had obviously given this a lot of thought.

'I think we've gone too far. If we stay at the Qianshan Hotel, we'll be

in constant fear. Why don't we make a quick killing, then all resign?'
Xiaohong's eyes sparkled.

Wu Ying nodded vaguely. 'But you know this job is not bad. It's a
waste to give it up.'

'We'll make a bit of money and we'll buy a bit of time. Wu Ying,
think about it – ten thousand! We'd have to work two years to make
that much! The Qianshan is just one station and we're all just passing
through. It might be sooner, it might be later, but eventually we'll all
be gone.'

It was Xiaohong who forged the signatures, so the bulk of the responsibility lay with her. She was clear about this. She began to prepare. The first thing she did was to remit eight thousand *yuan* to her
father and then she secretly began looking for a job. She couldn't tell
Sijiang about it yet, since Sijiang was, after all, also a member of the
staff at the Qianshan Hotel. What if she wavered? No matter how
close they were, this was a matter best not disclosed. It didn't matter
if she left. Especially since those who stayed behind might just be left
empty-handed.

VI

For two days, they did not see the quivering sensuality of Julia Wilde,
which left the dorm feeling a little empty. If Julia had got entwined with
some big-wig, it would not have been unusual. But while indulgence
was one thing, it was unlike Julia to be absent from work. She needed
this job more than anyone. She wore her work permit every day, silent
proof that she had legitimate employment. It made a good cover for
her part-time career. Xiaohong had a vague idea about what went on
in Julia's part-time working life. She suspected Julia desperately made
use of her flesh to earn some money. Occasionally, she probably even

played at love, such as the time she'd offered emotional comfort to that fellow who guarded the west gate.

'Wu Ying, this guy of Julia's wouldn't try anything funny, would he? There's something not right about her being gone all night. And she never misses work without reason. Something's wrong!' Looking at Julia's bunk, an inexplicable sense of foreboding overcame Xiaohong.

Wu Ying disagreed. 'Julia is a sharp girl. You don't need to worry about her. And she's always been loose. I'm sure she's just in bed with someone somewhere.'

'You don't know her like I do. Julia actually has very strict rules. There are some things she takes very seriously. She's a straightforward and good person.'

'I still say she's not as lovable as you. I don't like her melodrama or her promiscuity either.' Xiaohong had no response to this.

When Liao Zhenghu came into the dorm with a group of cops, Wu Ying and Xiaohong were so frightened their insides turned to jelly. The twenty per cent discount racket was always on their minds, a bomb ready to explode at any minute. They both stared open-mouthed at the cops entering the room, frozen speechless.

Liao smiled a greeting at Xiaohong.

'Which bed does Julia Wilde sleep in?' asked one of the cops.

Xiaohong pointed, not daring to speak.

'What sort of people does Julia mix with? Is there any way we can contact them?'

'Over at the Deer Hunt Bar, there's a fellow from Sichuan. He's her boyfriend. I've seen him, but I don't know his name.'

'Anyone else?'

'No.'

'Help us sort out her belongings. We'll bring them to the police station for her family to claim.' And with that, it seemed the police were done.

'What? Her belongings? All her clothes and stuff?' Xiaohong jumped to her feet. Wu Ying's face blanched with shock.

'Her belongings. Julia Wilde's belongings.' Liao's tone was unmistakeable.

'Julia's dead? She's dead? This... what happened?'

'Yes. It's a murder case and an open investigation. You two are not to discuss it with anyone.'

The police, taking possession of Julia's belongings, filed out of the room.

'Wait for my call. We'll need an interview.' Liao left a pager with Xiaohong.

Suddenly the room was filled with an icy chill.

'She can't be dead, Wu Ying. That little Jezebel was careful about who she went to bed with. That little slut! She said she'd take me to Mount Emei!' Xiaohong cursed softly, not even realising that tears were flowing down her face. She paced about the room, suddenly feeling that the empty bed had the vice-like grip of a coffin. Looking across at it, she could still see the shadowy form of Julia masturbating behind the mosquito net. Despite the hot day, Xiaohong shuddered and her hair stood on end.

'Ah Hong, the *fengshui* of that bed is no good. We shouldn't stay in this room. It's bad luck. We ought to get out of here or the sight of the cops might drive us mad.' No sooner had Wu Ying said this than the pager sounded, scaring them both out of their wits. Xiaohong clutched her chest with her left hand as her right hand held the pager. The screen displayed the message:

Hurry to The Storm Shelter teahouse. I'll meet you there.

'You want to know Julia's situation?' Liao asked carefully, his tiny eyes unusually quiet.

'Yes, I really do. She was my friend. Is she really dead? How did she die? Who did it?' Anxious and afraid, Xiaohong wanted to know the truth, even if it was worse than what she had imagined.

'Ah Hong, first I want to tell you that cases like Julia's happen all the time, mostly due to the influx of people from outside the city. That adds to the difficulty of investigating these cases. Like with Julia, we don't know who they mix with, what they do day in and day out. That leaves us with few clues and a lot of doubt.' Liao sipped his tea and sighed, both his voice and his eyes solemn. 'Julia's body was found five miles outside of town in the woods. She was naked and there was semen on the body. There were a lot of cuts and injuries to the lower body. The preliminary findings are that she was raped then killed. If we hadn't picked up her work permit in the field, she would have been treated as another Jane Doe.'

Thoughts of that night long ago when the tall fellow and Shorty had dragged her to that dark wilderness sprang to mind and Xiaohong shuddered.

'Do you want to see Julia? We took some pictures of the crime scene.' He took a stack of photos from his pocket and said, 'I'll pick out a couple to show you that aren't quite so upsetting.'

Xiaohong took one from him. It showed the upper half of Julia's body, her two large breasts bruised, one black and one red. There was a deep contusion around her neck. Apparently she had been strangled.

The other was a side shot of Julia's face, pressed against the ground. Her earring was missing, torn violently from the blood-covered ear. The mix of blood and pale skin on the corpse turned the contents of Xiaohong's stomach, making her want to vomit. She took a drink of water. Swallowing it, she finally said in a low voice, 'Oh God.'

What kind of place was this? What happened under the cover of darkness here? The dark of night took away real people. It placed a sort of fear and insecurity in those who woke up and went about life the next day.

It left the friends who survived with a sense of confusion and mystery.

'God, I can't stay there. I'll have nightmares that will scare me to death. Julia liked to sleep naked, like in the photos. I don't dare go back to that dorm!' Xiaohong's speech was incoherent, her mind spinning as if she were drunk.

How she came to spend the night at Liao's, she couldn't quite remember. There was an unknown wind pushing her as she drifted and he was an island. The island was breezy and sunny, with a sentimental charm. Xiaohong's nerves were on the verge of collapse and the relaxation of the flesh provided a slow release. He had meant to sleep on the floor but Xiaohong said, 'This bed is so big. Are you sleeping on the floor for appearance's sake? Julia's dead. Who knows when it might be me?'

When she'd said this, the atmosphere turned plaintive and sad. Infected by the mood, Liao suddenly said with feeling, 'I want to do right by you.'

He placed a special emphasis on 'do right', naturally overcoming his earlier inhibitions. He wanted to do it right and proper, like a man and a woman, like a lover and his mistress, like a husband and his wife. When Liao heard Xiaohong's moans of pleasure, he knew there was nothing fake about it. It wasn't difficult to hear the difference between the real thing and a fake. False moans of pleasure were for the benefit of another. True groans of pleasure came from deep inside, full of ecstasy. Xiaohong, trembling, called out an unfamiliar name. When they'd finished, he asked her about it.

Xiaohong answered, 'I called someone? Who did I call?'

'I didn't hear clearly, but it was definitely a name.'

'I called a name? I didn't call anyone at all!' Though Xiaohong firmly denied it, she was interested in whom she might have called when she was moaning. She thought carefully over every man she knew, but just shook her head at the possibility that she had called any of them. 'Forget it. No point arguing. Go to sleep. I've still got to look for a job tomorrow.' Xiaohong was a little irritated. She would really like to know whose name she had called.

'Why look for work? Aren't you doing well and getting plenty of time for your studies too?' Liao's big hands felt Xiaohong blindly.

'Julia's dead. I saw how she was when she was alive and I saw how she was when she was dead. I'm scared and I'm sad.' In a way, Julia's death was timely, giving Xiaohong a reason to leave the Qianshan Hotel on good terms. Liao lay thinking it over silently for several minutes, then felt that Xiaohong's idea was not unreasonable.

'Then do you have any interest in going over to the women and children's hospital as a receptionist?'

'Where is it?'

'In the suburbs. My uncle is chairman there.'

'Is it like a regular hospital?'

'Yeah, a hospital where you have to wear a big white lab coat. It's a much more serious occupation than working at a hotel. Of course, I'm not saying you're not serious. It's just that when you hear "I work at a hotel", it's not always actually the case.'

'Hmph! You're so biased.' Xiaohong rolled over and pressed against him.

'To tell you the truth, there are many university students waiting to get this job. If you don't believe me, go and have a look at the pool of talent available. They'll all be squeezed out of a job before they even apply.'

NINE

I

Sitting at a ninety-degree angle to the eight-storey women and children's hospital were the staff quarters. The main building was a mottle of colours, giving it the flavour of a site with some history. The structure that housed the staff quarters was like a new branch sprouting from an old tree, its white tiles always sparkling after a rain shower.

No one knew why the fifteen-year-old salon girl Ah Yue chose the women and children's hospital as her diving board. But there she sat, perched like a bird on the edge of the roof, crying, 'Don't come any closer! I'll jump!'

A crowd had gathered on the ground below and stood looking up at Ah Yue. Other than those patients who could not get out of bed, the hospital was empty. Doctors in white coats mingled with the crowd, mouths wide open in dismay. People seemed to be hoping for a quick resolution to the drama, preferably something shocking and exciting – the sort of thing that, even as they feared it, would satisfy those secret hopes they harboured for something out of the ordinary. Upstairs, along with the chairman of the hospital, Mr Liao, and those in charge of its offices, the emergency response police force had come, and more than ten people now stood facing the ledge where Ah Yue sat, all of them powerless to do anything. With Ah Yue sobbing as she despairingly talked about her conditions for surrender, no one could understand the rural dialect she spoke. Not understanding the dialect, the office manager reached out her right hand and kept saying, 'Come on, dear, give me your hand and we'll talk.'

Ah Yue, seeming to see this only as the right hand of deception, really let her tears fly then. Giving an untrusting shake of the head, she talked nonstop, apparently wanting them to promise to meet her demands. Another member of the hospital staff, upset, cursed, 'Shit! The city's top officials will be here soon to do a spot check. Why did she choose this place to jump? Why did we have to get mixed up in this nonsense?'

The more people gathered downstairs, the more nervous Mr Liao grew. For something like this to happen on hospital grounds, whether or not the person had anything to do with the hospital, would have a big impact. As word spread, things would be bad. And yet, he had no means of communicating with this girl.

'Mr Liao, I understand what she is saying.' Xiaohong stood on the floor below looking at the ledge where things were unfolding.

'Hurry, then, tell her not to jump!' Mr Liao wiped the sweat off his brow. It was a warm day, the sun at eight or nine in the morning already beating mercilessly down. The girl's dyed hair glistened in a golden fringe on her forehead. She was just a small thing – in years and in stature. Just a little child wearing a fashionable sleeveless t-shirt and cut-off denim shorts with long, frayed edges that barely covered the curve of her rump. Her face was black with dirt. She was not at all sexy. The clothes lay, practically empty, on her flat chest. She'd clearly experienced an earth-shattering disaster.

'Hey, little girl, don't move. Are you from Liqing?' Xiaohong asked, using her hometown dialect.

Ah Yue hesitated, then nodded.

'What's wrong? You can tell me and we'll all try to help you. Don't be afraid.' Xiaohong moved a couple of steps closer.

'Don't come over here. You can't help me!' Ah Yue shouted, taking a half step back.

The crowd downstairs roared.

'OK, you talk and we'll do what we can. You can trust me. I'm also from Liqing. Don't move. I really want to help you.' Xiaohong was also anxious. If Ah Yue jumped now, it would be a huge black mark against her, too.

'I... I was cheated into coming here. I work at a salon... I'm pregnant. The salon sacked me. I got no money... I... ah...' Ah Yue broke off, sobbing. Though she gave it her best effort, trying to burst into tears, the well had run dry. She maintained a posture of readiness, prepared to jump at any moment.

Xiaohong briefed the chairman on Ah Yue's situation. He finalised everything on the spot, saying, 'Tell her not to worry. The hospital will help her, without charging her a penny. We'll also help her solve her economic difficulties with a donation of a thousand *kuai*.'

Xiaohong relayed the chairman's message to Ah Yue, making his commitment known publicly. Ah Yue hesitated, still sceptical, but she had already let Xiaohong move closer to her and they stood together on the brink of death. Xiaohong pointed into the distance and said, 'Look over there. See that?'

Ah Yue looked around as Xiaohong pointed, then collapsed with a loud cry. Her wailing was like that of a motherless child.

When they had managed to pull Ah Yue back inside, the people downstairs poured into the hospital, clogging up the corridors so that it took some time for the blockage to clear. The doctors nervously examined Ah Yue, administering pregnancy tests and other health checks. They decided to do her procedure that very day then let her recuperate at the hospital for several more days. After that, they would give her a little money and send her on her way, hoping she would take the bad karma along with her.

Xiaohong was like an interpreter, following along in Ah Yue's wake.

'What kind of parents raised a child like this? She's infuriating!' Dr Chen Fangyuan said, shaking her head as she questioned Ah Yue.

'What's your name?'

'Lin Zhongyue.'

'How old are you?'

'Fifteen.'

'How long since your last period?'

'Two and a half months.'

'Huh? That's the problem. Not enough knowledge of family planning.' Dr Chen shook her head again.

After the results of the biopsy, the doctors, who had been impassive before, were suddenly stirred up and propelled into action. 'My God! Lin Zhongyue has a venereal disease. There's severe inflammation. It's not possible to do the procedure now.'

When Xiaohong told Ah Yue, the girl took the news stiffly, calm as a forest.

'You know what STDs are, don't you?' Xiaohong asked in surprise.

'I know. I've known for a long time.' Ah Yue smiled, showing a mouthful of yellow teeth.

'You aren't a bit scared? Not worried?'

'I'm scared and worried. I nearly jumped just now, you know. Your hospital said they'd treat me, so what's there to be scared of now? It's not like it's AIDS.' Ah Yue displayed a rare sophistication.

'How long have you worked in the salon?'

'Four and a half months.'

'You take in customers every day?'

'Pretty much. The money goes to the boss. I get about twenty *kuai* each time. When the boss found out I was pregnant and that I had an STD, he sacked me.'

'Go and report him!' Xiaohong encouraged her angrily.

'No point. There are still several girls there and if they get picked up, it'll be bad news for them. They all need to make some money.'

Xiaohong had no response, but a bitter feeling inside made her heart want to burst.

After this, Xiaohong, on a sudden impulse, wrote an article about the helping hand the women and children's hospital had extended to a working girl, Lin Zhongyue. She asked Mr Liao to edit it and then sent it to a local paper for publication. She had no real expectations when she did so, not thinking much of the attitude or the ethics of the corrupt doctors in this hospital. But where she had expected indifference, instead she got a red envelope with a little token of appreciation. The article became a hot topic and, as Mr Liao put it, it greatly improved the reputation of the women and children's hospital. The chairman convened a special meeting of the hospital's board and recommended that Xiaohong be transferred to the publicity and PR department. As a result of the situation with Ah Yue, within six months of working at the hospital, Xiaohong's prospects took a significant turn for the better.

Ah Yue was taking a daily dose of medication. Never had anyone seemed to find medicine so appetising. Of course, the other way of looking at it was that she was eager to take care of her disease as soon as possible. The hospital's cafeteria food also seemed to suit her tastes just fine, and she ate at least as much as the young male doctors.

At first, the hospital arranged a bed for her, with the intent of handling her family planning needs within a few days. The problem was, many women flocked to the hospital and even the corridors were filled with beds for the patients. When the situation got that bad, Xiaohong offered to let Ah Yue stay with her, hoping to alleviate some of the stress on the hospital. For this, she also received the chairman's commendation, making her a rising star in the hospital, second only to Ah Yue in fame.

Oral, topical and injected medications were all used to treat Ah Yue's venereal disease, taking a multi-pronged approach. After two weeks, the doctors performed an abortion on the three-month-old foetus in her belly. Just to be sure there were no mistakes, they had assigned the famous Dr Lei Yigang, an obstetrics and gynaecology surgeon who had been wielding the scalpel for more than a decade, as the lead doctor on the case.

The hospital gave Xiaohong three days off especially to take care of Ah Yue and the doctors also took extra care to visit the patient, doing everything humanly possible to express their sympathy. When Mr Liao came and put a thousand *yuan* into Ah Yue's hand, the girl was so touched she started crying all over again, even as she laughed. She seemed to have a renewed confidence in life.

'Ah Yue, when you've fully recovered and you leave this place, don't go back to the salon! Go and study. Plant some seeds and let them grow.' Xiaohong saw that Ah Yue's body was recovering quickly and her spirits were lifted and she wanted to encourage her.

'When I got out, I got out. What the hell would I go back there for? And study? I don't have the money. My mum always said studying isn't any use. Better to keep the money you got in your hand than spend it on studying.' Ah Yue faced the mirror, flipping her hair up and down against her forehead, as if she didn't quite know what to do with that lock of blond hair.

'Then what do you plan to do? The hospital spent a lot of money, gave you a lot of treatment. It's only fair you do your part now!' She hadn't been there all that long, but Ah Yue was already taking so much of the room and board that there was hardly anything left for Xiaohong.

'I won't forget all of you. Tomorrow, I'll go. I'll go back to my hometown and do whatever the hell kind of work I can find.' Ah Yue seemed to be full of confidence about the future.

The next day when Xiaohong got home from work, she found that Ah Yue had left without a word of goodbye. Her room had been cleaned out by the girl. All her nicest clothes and shoes, her digital camera and the hundred or so Hong Kong dollars she'd stashed in a drawer had all gone missing with Ah Yue. She had helped a fellow villager, only to be stabbed in the back. She wanted to fiercely curse the little bitch, but she couldn't bear to let out the stream of abuse that was welling up in her. This fifteen-year-old little girl speaking her dialect – she really didn't have that sort of rage to direct at a child. She just felt heavy. She exhaled deeply, looked out the window towards the centre of town and thought of her own barren hometown. And she was sad.

I I

Every time she went in or out of the hotel, Sijiang would turn and look at the giant golden letters on the sign reading Qianshan Hotel. It had become as habitual as making her bed each morning. Sometimes feeling settled and sometimes feeling a void inside her similar to sexual desire, her mood swung back and forth and was nearly impossible to handle day after day. She had lost some weight, suddenly showing people that she had a good figure as she walked along the road. Her tiny ever-virginal eyes gradually took on the look of someone with a naive, weak temperament.

On Tuesdays, Thursdays and Saturdays she went for her classes at the youth centre, and she'd begun to attract the eye of a young man. She was not like Xiaohong. Anyone who wanted to gain Sijiang's affection had to go about it with a patient sincerity. So the bespectacled boy, Wu Chengjun, spent about half a year working on her before he finally heard outright laughter from Sijiang. Specs, as Sijiang liked to call him, was from Jiangxi, and had graduated from a teacher training school, after which he had taught in a primary school for two years. Now he was working for an insurance company and studying for a diploma in his spare time. It was at his training classes that he had come across Sijiang. She observed Specs for a long time. Ever since the incident with Bud Kun, she had been wary, practically resorting to an old style self-criticism full of revolutionary zeal.

But this was love. Wu Chengjun and his specs had a certain power. Sijiang was often uncertain whether it was a reflection from his lenses or an actual sparkle in his eyes, but it left her constantly dazzled. Love had unwittingly hit her without warning like a bout of the flu. She didn't even know when it had happened or from whence the infection had crept up on her. After Xiaohong had left the Qianshan Hotel, Sijiang got a new partner and that was the only real change in her. Specs had never met Xiaohong and only knew of her existence from the constant mentioning of her name by Sijiang. It left Specs with some high expectations.

The Qianshan Park was serene at night, its path lit by lamps about a foot tall, illuminating the gravel beneath their feet. The moon was a round, lonely figure but the park was not quiet. Sijiang, holding on to Specs's right arm, walked over half of the grounds, and still they had not found a suitable spot, the ideal place to sit kissing and cuddling. Other couples must have come earlier, marking off their plots, each three paces from the other so as not to interfere in one another's business.

Despite the cover of darkness and the skill of the kissing couples in controlling the sound of their activity, the ears of the lovers were extremely sensitive. Specs and Sijiang had heard enough to set their blood bubbling, even picking up the groans from an especially thick patch of bushes. Specs was reaching a state of urgency and the sounds of the night were doing nothing to ease the situation. Practically gasping, he said, 'Would that empty spot by the pond do?'

'Alright. It's like the later it gets, the more people there are.' Sijiang's voice was as low as the buzz of a mosquito and soft as a blanket. The ground wasn't very even, so he shifted a little, and finally she sat down in the space between his legs, settling herself against his most vital parts. Having wandered amidst the sound of embracing, kissing and love-making, Specs and Sijiang had no problem entering the flow of the action in the park. But no sooner had they engaged in their first kiss than they were accosted by a low voice.

'Don't make a sound. Take out your wallet. Hurry up!'

When they fell apart, shocked, the first thing they saw was the flash of a dagger in a short man's hand. He moved in closer, ready to stab them at the slightest provocation. Specs quickly determined that the man did not have an accomplice. He could not say whether it was because he wanted to look like a hero in front of Sijiang, or if it was for the sake of the month's salary he had in his wallet, but he thrust Sijiang behind him and poised himself to fight with the short man. His assailant, saying nothing, made a random stab, knocking his glasses to the ground. Immediately, everything in front of him became a blur. The short fellow took the opportunity to make a couple of more swipes at him, deftly reached in to take the bulging wallet from his back pocket and quickly disappeared.

Sijiang was scared speechless. By the time she thought of calling for help, the short guy had long since vanished into the darkness and was sitting somewhere counting his swag. But she cried out, mostly to release the fear, then at once collected herself enough to take the bloodied Specs to the hospital. He objected to her using two hundred *yuan* from her own pocket but his injuries, though not terribly serious, were not negligible. He was in the hospital for two days, and needed an additional two weeks to recover. As soon as she knocked off work, Sijiang would cook up nourishing meals to take over to him. Putting aside any pretence of shyness, she openly stayed by his side.

'Why didn't you just give him the wallet and forget it?' Sijiang was a little confused.

'I'm taller than him and I thought I could take him. Who knew he'd come after me so quickly? Then my glasses fell off and everything was blurry. If not, I'd have really shown him!'

'Didn't you see that he had a weapon? Next time, just do what he says. Give him the wallet. Why try to be a hero?'

'Next time? Next time, stuff the money into your bra.' The two of them turned the excitement of the incident into flirting. Having experienced this catastrophe, they had more of a feel for each other as they passed the time together.

After Specs had recovered, he suggested they move in together but Sijiang wasn't sure it was a good idea. 'Good or bad, how will you know if you don't try?' Specs said, who was all in favour of giving it a go.

'We don't need to rent. We've both got places to stay.' Sijiang hated the idea of paying rent. Money wasn't all that easy to earn.

'Yeah, we've both got places to stay. But I want to share a place. So we can eat and sleep together. I mean, we both have needs. Don't you want to start our life together?' Specs knew that Sijiang wasn't really refusing him, she just needed reassurance. Or, you might say, it was all for the sake of a girl's self-esteem. Sijiang chewed on her lower lip, her tiny eyes squinting in thought as she glanced at Specs. After a moment, she pouted and said, 'Is it marriage?'

Specs, elated, said with an innocent smile, 'We're going to be married.'

Sijiang's face, though no longer quite as fresh and round as an apple, perked up. He might as well have put a ring on her finger.

'Sijiang, let's wait till we get our diplomas, then we'll get better jobs, improve our finances, rent a nicer house – maybe even buy a house! – then we'll really have a better life. We'll work hard, OK?'

Sijiang nodded fiercely, saying, 'I've already planned to open a salon, to earn a bit of money to send home and buy myself some prettier clothes.'

Sijiang's heart was warmed, and she softly burrowed herself against his chest. Suddenly she thought, I wonder if Xiaohong has a lover.

III

'I'm in the publicity department.' When Xiaohong phoned the Qianshan Hotel to tell Wu Ying and Ah Xing, she felt like she was saying, 'I'm a crusader'.

Ah Xing, pleasantly surprised, said, 'You're an advocate for public good. Congratulations!'

Wu Ying grabbed the phone and said, 'Public education is important.'

'Public education is for the birds,' Xiaohong said laughing, 'or at least, we get to talk about people's cocks all day. Anyway, whenever either of you is ready to have kids, or if you want to get your tubes tied, or if you have any problems in your sex life, you can come to me for help!'

Wu Ying teased, 'You take care of your own sex life first.'

'My own sex life is basically non-existent. I rely solely on the hand.'

Ah Xing said, 'It's like you've been unleashed in that job!'

Xiaohong asked how things were at the hotel. Ah Xing said everything was fine, and that nothing had changed much, the coast seemed clear for the twenty per cent discount scheme.

'Then I don't have to worry anymore about the security of my comrades. A guilty conscience is a real burden.'

Xiaohong was moved to the publicity room, chased out of the mindless routine of her clockwork life, like a duckling herded into the water for the first time. Her thinking and habits had been shaped by a different sort of experience. She was tense, but as she began to settle in, she found that if she took the time to get familiar with her surroundings, she could get used to this aquatic lifestyle, learning to swim with ease.

Before long, she had a good grasp of all the hospital's so-called publicity materials. Really, it was just a patchwork of writings on family issues or a hodgepodge of stuff about one's private life for people to read. For instance, every week they recycled the publicity and public education material from old newspapers and presented it as new material. Of course, it all had to do with medicine, women's issues and reproductive health concerns. Then there were the notes scribbled onto the bulletin boards. The headers rarely changed, the content in the reports was always small and inconspicuous, and the fonts and art work were all pretty mundane.

She had numerous errands to run, such as customising banners for important campaigns. She also managed the medical health section for a local newsletter, teaching readers the best positions, how to have a smart baby and how to manage reproductive health. It was as if this small newsletter had some key part to play in changing the world, like it really made a difference.

With the addition of Xiaohong, the original publicity manager, Xia Jifeng, who had always worked single-handedly, was no longer alone. He had explained the basics of public education work in ten minutes and then he had begun an endless stream of phone conversations. So the only perspective Xiaohong really got on the ongoing work of family planning propaganda from Xia came from his chatter on the phone.

He was about 1.7 metres tall, no more than thirty-years-old and a little on the stout side with a prominent nose. At a glance, he looked a little like a Hong Kong pop star but Xiaohong couldn't quite work out which one.

'Xiaohong, since you came, things are much easier for me. Before, I was like both father and mother. I'm not cut out for that!' Xia's eyes were set far apart, giving him a slightly awkward appearance. It made his expression one of perpetual sentimentality, softening his features even as he complained.

'Is that so?' Xiaohong asked, smiling at him with a somewhat threatening expression, as if possessing some secret she could use against him.

'What's wrong?' Xia, looking innocent, wiped the sweat from his face.

'Nothing's wrong.'

Xiaohong continued to smile. She wasn't yet ready to say she liked Xia and his muscular form rippling under his black t-shirt. Having just two people in such a cosy office, she felt that they would end up in bed together sooner or later.

IV

Xiaohong had much more freedom working in the publicity department. Unlike being on reception where she was chained to the desk, now she could saunter to the lab to chat or make her way next door to the outpatient obstetrics and gynaecology clinic. She became like those doctors who are in the hospital so frequently that they acquire a liking for its peculiar smell.

The hospital was relatively quiet. Including the doctors, ninety per cent of whom were female, there were dozens of women – too many women to count, a sea of women, of all shapes and colours, as if a floodgate had been opened without warning.

In the lab, Xiaoqiao and Youqing were the youngest girls. They wore the shortest skirts which, like their white lab coats, barely touched their knees. Along with He Jianguo, the only male technician in the lab, who had a prosthetic leg, they often talked about maternity-related issues. Every time Xiaohong went to the lab, looking through the window past the white plastic sample cups, she would always see faces lit up with laughter amidst the small talk that, like the urine and stool samples contained within those white cups, was so muddled you couldn't distinguish one from another.

'Ah Hong, come here. That girl with the STDs, what's she doing now?' the short-haired Youqing asked brightly as she lifted her face, round as a melon, from her newspaper. She always made a great effort to put on a pleasant expression, though one could never tell whether it came from confidence or artifice.

'Oh, don't talk about her. I don't know anything about what's happened to her since she left!' Xiaohong pulled over a stool and sat down at a little bit of a distance from the specimen cups.

'You should get checked out and see if she passed her STD to you.' Though joking, Youqing spoke in earnest tones, sounding a bit harsh. Her attitude toward Xiaohong was different from others. She was arrogant, perhaps because her father worked in the Environmental Protection Bureau.

'Give us a urine sample and we'll take it to the lab for tests.' Xiaoqiao's interest was piqued.

'Wow, you guys! I bet every time I leave here you sterilise the stool I sat on, right?' Xiaohong went and touched Xiaoqiao's face when she had said this, shouting, 'Let me give it to you, then!'

Jianguo laughed the whole time. Having nothing better to do, he plucked at the few scraggly whiskers forming a sparse goatee on his chin. His eyes distractedly fell on Xiaohong's face, as if he were pondering some philosophical proposition.

Xiaohong, of course, did not give them any samples. She had already disposed of everything Ah Yue had used, even the wash basin. Xiaohong said nothing about the clothes and money Ah Yue had taken. She didn't need anyone's sympathy, and she certainly didn't want to hear people say things like, 'You Hunan people.'

The consultation room in the obstetrics and gynaecology clinic was perfect for an afternoon nap. The examination table was soft, the air conditioning was cool and when the curtains were pulled, it was as good as sleeping at night. Lying in the dark, questions surrounding Jianguo's prosthetic leg would often blow into Xiaohong's mind.

The coolness of the room especially suited the fleshy form of Chen Fangyuan, who made quite a racket with her snoring. She had a daughter in one of the top secondary schools in the city and her husband was a chief of something-or-other at the Public Security Bureau. She seemed to have no regrets in life and always had energy to spare when it came to helping others. She practically flew through the corridors as she walked, as if she were forever about some business of earth-shattering importance. Dr Chen was always very friendly to Xiaohong, perhaps because of her connection to the hospital chairman, perhaps because she was temporary and posed no threat to her colleagues. Or maybe it was simply because of Xiaohong's small stature and straightforward temperament. For whatever reason, Dr Chen was particularly fond of Xiaohong.

'Xiaohong, my girl, He Jianguo hasn't always been a technician. He used to be a driver. After he broke his leg, he became a lab tech,' Dr Chen said, lying flat on the bed. Her body filled the exam table. She turned her head to face Xiaohong, an ultrasound scanner between them. She stretched her muscles as she spoke. Seeing Xiaohong's interest, she went on about the Jianguo affair, how he had fallen from the fourth floor and broken his leg, leaving him unable to drive. 'And that's how come he's stuck in the lab. Basically, you've got to take care of yourself.'

As she talked on, Xiaohong grew drowsier, only grunting in reply. She gradually realised that Dr Chen's greatest hobby was gossip. Every afternoon, the doctor just had to tell her stories, as if it were another meal to be digested, slowly torturing everyone's ears. Sometimes it was all nonsense, but sometimes she really had a scoop. For instance, she told them how Youqing had stopped menstruating for two years and had gone to all sorts of doctors for medication. When this news came out, everyone was dumbfounded. Youqing's boyfriend was a decent sort of guy but, significantly, he was not exactly stable. Since he was doing contract work, he could not quite settle down and that created a fair bit of uncertainty from one day to the next.

'None of you have met him. Because of Youqing's physiological problems, the guy seems to have backed off several times. No one knows why they haven't separated yet. But I guess he's a smart fellow. He saw her father's position and saw a way to transfer to the city.' Dr Chen proposed this theory, making things really lively.

Xiaohong listened and observed, and tried to imagine what Dr Chen would look like making love to a man. She was at that *thirsty* age. The way she looked, certainly no other man would have any interest in her. Only her husband would be dutiful enough to be with her until the end. So did that mean she had no interest in being with other women's men? That was a question Xiaohong did not care to ask. With that question, she dozed off.

V

What a let-down! For some time, Liao Zhenghu had been storing up his energies until he could see Xiaohong. But when the time came, all of the passion he had hoped to offer to her in a prolonged outpouring came out in a single shot. The poor fellow just couldn't contain himself, which was beyond even his own imaginings. The frustration was indescribable. The worst of it was that he was not even sure that his quick ejaculation hadn't found its way into Xiaohong.

'Think! Think carefully!' Xiaohong was frantic.

'Well, what about you? Do you feel like it's OK?' Liao retorted.

'Feel? I didn't have time to feel anything! If it's going to always be like that, what's the point? Might as well just masturbate.' Xiaohong was unusually agitated. Liao wanted to offer her some comfort but she left him grasping at an empty space on the bed as she got up and went into the washroom to take remedial action.

Liao rolled over to her half of the bed, feeling depressed. He thought back over everything carefully, trying to figure out why he had made such a quick, clean end of the matter.

When Xiaohong had spent five minutes squatting over the toilet, she came back to lie on the bed. Liao suddenly found an answer. He passionately reached for Xiaohong and said with feeling, 'I love you!'

Xiaohong shuddered. What a fresh phrase! It was the first time she had ever heard it.

'What did you say, Ah Sir?' she asked, giggling.

'I said I love you, Qian Xiaohong.' Liao looked at the ceiling as he spoke. It was very white and there was a stain where it had apparently flooded before. It looked like a map.

Liao sat up. He glanced around Xiaohong's one-room, one-bath quarters, the powdery white walls bare of decoration. It was empty and pale. The bed squeaked. The desk wobbled. It was a second-hand piece discarded from the hospital after who knew how many years of use. The simple wardrobe bulged, tilting to one side under its overwhelming load. The fat magnolia leaves outside the window were turning black. Lazy and heavy, they swayed in the breeze.

'What are you sitting there for?' Xiaohong swatted him on the thigh. It wasn't that she hadn't understood what he had said, it was just that she wasn't sure whether what he had spoken of actually existed or whether he had just said it on impulse. There was no reason for him to really love a girl who had worked in a salon and a hotel, nor was there a reason for any man to. Liao had spoken out of a moment of compassion, wanting to make himself look good.

'Are you going to hate me if I don't marry you?' Liao seemed poised for a long conversation.

'Why would I hate you? The thought hadn't crossed my mind.'

'Then don't you feel like you're losing out?'

'Losing out? I never thought of it like that. It's not like you forced me.'

'You're a girl. It's always to your disadvantage if someone *does* you.'

'If I remember correctly, I've always been the one on top.'

'But it's still *me* doing *you*. I just did it more pleasantly.'

'It pleased me too. I didn't do it as a service to you.'

'You did it to serve desire.'

'You could say that. We were satisfying our bodies.'

'Of course, I'll cherish the person who fulfils my desires. That's the essence of all affection.'

'Prostitutes and rape victims lose out in the sex act. I'm not a prostitute. You're not my customer and you didn't rape me. I don't see how you can say I lost out, especially not if I enjoyed it as much as you did.'

'If all women thought like this, wouldn't the world be a mess? All hell would break loose.'

Logically, Xiaohong was the ideal partner for anyone to get along with, since she had no ideological baggage. But Liao felt awkward and this affected his thinking.

'It would be more balanced. Otherwise, it's only women's worlds that are a mess. Like my sister with her loyalty to her husband. Though I guess her world has some sort of blind order.' Xiaohong's voice grew husky.

'What have you been reading? Where'd you pick up this way of thinking? Why do I find that I can't keep up with you?'

'I'm still talking about the question of whether or not I'm losing out.'

'Alright, alright. Let's not talk about losing out. Anyway...'

'Anyway, you're a good guy. I know.'

Liao was afraid Xiaohong hadn't got it. Despite her ideological work, he'd never imagined she'd start lecturing him. In all honesty, he thought that being involved with a girl like Xiaohong would save some trouble. He never actually thought about marrying a working-class girl. For her, it was a constant struggle for employment, for permits, for diplomas. Now he finds out she didn't think she was losing out. It must be because she thought he at least had real feelings for her. As soon as she realised he was just having his fun with her, the feeling of loss would come.

But what about him? Why was he so obsessed with her? That was the real question and Liao was constantly seeking an answer to it.

VI

People perpetually surrounded by sickness and suffering appreciate life and health more. And so hospital employees, forever hearing the moans and groans of worry and anxiety, often become philosophical seeing so much fear and despair. Though the younger employees are already like that, it is particularly obvious in the older doctors, showing up in their speech and behaviour and their general take on life. It's as if the hospital becomes their whole world.

As for that young, energetic guy Xia Jifeng, though he was not a doctor, Xiaohong felt he should go out and see the wide world and not just sit around in the hospital flirting with the nurses, as satisfied as if he had personally done every one of them.

Xiaohong's and Xia's desks were next to each other. When they were both in the office, it was like they were in a café having a drink. The air conditioner constantly buzzed, steady as the heartbeat of someone at rest.

'There's going to be a big campaign in a few days. We need to come up with a float and a dozen or so brochures. We'll need to work overtime to get the content for the brochures ready. You need to find some information quickly and pull together our best stuff. And make sure to cover all aspects.'

Xia stood in front of the desk as he said the first part and by the time he had finished talking, he had walked into the corridor. Over the previous few days, he had seemed to be avoiding sitting down facing Xiaohong. This clever disguise actually unintentionally revealed his carefully hidden secret. Xiaohong sometimes pressed her chest against the edge of the desk, and in that posture chatted casually with him. Xia felt he, like the desk, had to endure certain pressures to which Xiaohong subjected him.

Xiaohong drank some water, her mind a little unsettled. This sort of campaign was nothing, really. It was ridiculous the way they drove along the bustling streets, stopping in the corner of some square, piling their belongings up like wandering hawkers setting up shop. All those public education brochures, who would stop and read them? Anyone who spent ten minutes doing so had to have thick skin. Who would want to have others suspect they had some illness, especially an incurable disease? Everyone likes to put on a front of health and happiness, mocking things like impotence, premature ejaculation, prostatitis, vaginal discomfort or gonorrhoea. Only stealthily, under the cover of darkness, would they enter a hospital for a check-up.

The women and children's hospital had a private clinic for men. Every night after ten, male patients, pale as ghosts, came in and out. Even for a normal procedure like circumcision, they would only have it carried out at night. They were the sort of people she saw on the streets, each one cockier than the next and each one more *normal* than the next. Xiaohong would see those high and mighty fellows and she would have to wonder about their physical condition. Sometimes it made her laugh, as if she had access to all the secrets of another person. But beyond all doubt, if the upper body was not stable, then everything below the waist would be a secondary concern. Those problems were less obvious.

In the evening, the sunlight gave way to the fluorescent bulbs. Xiaohong flipped through a medical book, selecting the useful information. She skipped here and there, her mind suddenly full of reproduction, diseases and sexuality. The edginess inside her intensified. When she couldn't stand it any longer, she went to the dining hall for dinner, then paced around the hospital lawn a few times. At the corner of the yard, she saw Youqing and Xia in conversation in a small pavilion about four or five feet away. When Xiaohong approached, Youqing turned her lab coat clad rump toward them and walked away. Xiaohong noticed that she was very short, maybe even shorter than herself.

'You had dinner yet? The pork rib stew is pretty good today,' Xia said, making conversation.

'Why are you eating in the canteen?' As soon as she said it, she regretted asking. She just remembered Xia was divorced.

'How's the preparation of the materials going? Try to keep ahead of schedule, so you can have a bit of leeway in case you need it,' he said as they walked back to the office. Xiaohong walked behind him, giving her about ten seconds to quietly look him over. Stung by his indifferent, businesslike attitude, she thought back over his expression when he had first started speaking, trying to find any chink in the face's armour, but his expression was forever ambiguous.

'I'm a bit scared working overtime in the hospital. The day before yesterday, someone in the maternity ward died and it was like there was constant crying. Then, last night, it was weird. One of the duty nurses was stuck in the elevator. She was trapped there in the dark for over an hour.' Whether the fear was real or feigned, Xiaohong herself could not actually tell. Whichever way, she faced Xia and spoke to him in this pitiful way.

'The lift is old. It's got nothing to do with the death. Don't be so superstitious.' In the empty campaign work room on the sixth floor, Xia's shadow seemed to dangle on the wall. As he spoke, he selected a few suitable signboards. He rapped on the boards with his knuckles.

Xiaohong flipped casually through the propaganda posters, attaching each one to a board with thumb tacks.

'This is the good life—, ouch!' Xiaohong had pricked her fingertip. She shook her hand, a little angry.

'You've got two options. You can use the hammer or you can wait for me to come and push it in. You do something else.' He was attaching another poster to the board.

Finally unable to stand it anymore, she plopped down on the campaign room table, one leg resting on the floor while the other dangled in the air. 'You seem to have some objection to me. Did I do something to offend you, Xia? It seems like you can't even bear to look at me!'

Xia, bending over his work, turned and caught sight of the open gap at the front of her skirt between her thighs. A wave of heat coloured his forehead and he buried himself deeper in his work.

'Go on, say it. I'm careless. You tell me what you think and I'll examine myself, alright?' Xiaohong said sincerely. She had worn a very short and very tight skirt today. She wasn't a doctor so dressed a little more freely. She hoped he would look up and then he would certainly be done for.

He continued to keep his head bent over his work. It was as if he would spend a lifetime like that, never looking up.

Whack! The lights went out. The streetlights outside the window were bright, the words Royal Hotel flashed through them, flickering on and off. The night's lights cast a glow of indeterminate hue over the work room.

'Eh? What's this? There's power upstairs and downstairs.' Xia searched for the light switch and found Xiaohong standing devilishly beside it.

'The fuse has gone.'

'I'll have a look.'

'Even if you have a look, it's still gone.'

'Even if it's gone, I'll still have a look.'

'Then have a look.'

'I don't want to have a look.'

Xia had fallen into the trap.

Finally displaying the strength reflected in those muscles, he force-fully squeezed Xiaohong's big breasts. He plonked her onto the table and there atop the family planning, reproductive health and STD propaganda posters, he could resist no longer. He resolutely ravaged this demon that had provoked him. Using his own bodily fluids as glue, he stuck the posters to the board, nailing them down so hard no wind would blow them away. Soon, they would make a brilliant display in the streets.

VII

A new fellow named Xiao Yuan came to work in the administration of-fice at the hospital, acting like a big shot. It turned out he was Youqing's boyfriend. He had been employed before HR had assigned him a post, since they had not yet shuffled things round to accommodate him. It was all a game of musical chairs, really. Clearly, since Youqing's father, the bureaucrat, had taken in Mr Liao's son, Mr Liao had had to take on Youqing's boyfriend, so as not to owe any favours or be indebted in any way. It evened the score and everyone was happy. It was an excellent idea, but no one could say for sure who had thought of it.

Of course, the suggestion almost certainly had come from Youqing. Only she was smooth enough to think of a solution that was so mutu-ally beneficial to both parties. And in discussing the business with Mr Liao, only if she personally came up with the solution would there be any results. Most people, no matter how hard they worked, could not get things done, but some people needed only play their little games and everything was settled. In the course of a single meal, she could secure jobs for two people and get another promoted.

On her way to the washroom, Xiaohong ran into Xiao Yuan. They parted ways at the toilet door, one going to the left, one to the right. Xiao Yuan turned back to Xiaohong and smiled, his features rough, facial muscles taut, smile uneven. His actions were so like those of a bashful virgin that Xiaohong thought for a moment that he might go into the ladies' washroom.

Youqing had shown up at work that day, exceptionally beautiful in both appearance and mood. She hummed and tapped her feet, instead of walking at her normal haphazard pace. She greeted Xiaohong warmly with a friendly smile, as if they'd always been close friends without any rift between them. What prompted her to be so forgiving and accepting, forgetting all past unpleasantness, and loving the world with such limitless passion?

'It's come! I've got my period!' She announced with the same enthusiasm a woman who had been married for a long time would announce her pregnancy, causing a sort of emotional shock throughout the hospital.

'Congratulations! Now you can get married and have a baby!' the male doctors said.

She was like a treasure, with everyone asking all sorts of questions about her. 'How is it? Is it heavy? Is it a bright red? Does your back hurt?'

The female doctors crowded around her, holding her little right hand, greatly concerned. Because of the situation surrounding her period, Youqing was something of a celebrity. Though beside herself, she calmly answered all of the questions the female doctors fired at her, going through every detail of the onset of the symptoms of her period through the feeling of its actual arrival. She spoke on and on about it at a snail's pace, slow and meticulous. You have to understand, the arrival of Youqing's period was like a child born to a couple advanced in years, worthy of celebration. She and her boyfriend had already made preparations for their future and were only waiting for the arrival of her period so that they could proceed.

Xiaohong's nausea started at the same time that Youqing's announcement was being made. She suddenly felt these people were like a hunk of fatty meat, producing both nausea and irritability as the stomach turned. Her belly longed for the leeks that grew from the soil in her hometown, so green and fresh, like a breeze blowing through the window into the house, bringing a cheerfulness with it. But when a real gust of wind blew, a real desire to vomit came with it, sticking in her throat. She held her breath, walked to the washroom and spewed into the sink. When she was finished, she calculated and found that her period was a week late. From her own experience with her body, she was sure a little worm had settled down and made its home inside her.

'What's this? Why are you having such a big reaction to my period?' Youqing's voice came to her suddenly. She leaned over the basin and pretended to wash her hands, drawing nearer to stare at Xiaohong. Then she calmly turned and left.

Xiaohong was surprised and a little embarrassed. She figured Youqing had heard her vomiting, but could not be sure the other girl had guessed why. The look on her face and tone of her voice when she spoke made it seem she had come pretty close to the mark. But, even if she knew Xiaohong was pregnant, she couldn't say for sure who was responsible for it.

Who *was* responsible for it? At that thought, Xiaohong was a little confused herself. It might have been Liaos fluid that had got into her. Even just a drop could have this outcome. On the other hand, it could have been that Xia's withdrawal had not been complete. A drop then could also have led to this result. So, which drop was more likely? Which drop? Which travelled faster? Which was more robust? Only that drop knew, only that secret path knew, only the womb knew.

'Men are such shits!' she scolded furiously. 'Fuck! So careless. This is no small mistake. It's huge! And to be mixed up with two men is nothing, until this sort of thing happens!'

✳

Not long after Youqing had shouted, 'I've got my period!' she was caught up in a new type of distress. The flow went on for two weeks straight, creating big problems for her potential sex life. The menstrual cycle, if it didn't come, was trouble. When it did come, it was even more trouble. Youqing's period failed to come and it made her not quite a woman. But then, when it did come, it made it impossible to achieve another form of happiness as a woman.

Similarly, when Xiaohong's period failed to come, new anxieties and worries welled up inside her. She could get married. But, to Xia Jifeng or Liao Zhenghu? If she chose the wrong one, sooner or later it would mean trouble. Nor could she be sure either would marry her. Actually, even when she was in the washroom vomiting, she already knew it was her fate to undergo an abortion.

When she knocked off work, her stomach churning, Xiaohong suddenly remembered how Xia had said, 'The pork rib stew is pretty good.' Unable to contain the violent wave of nausea that overcame her, she ran to the washroom and quietly cleared her belly of its contents. She wanted to go onto the rooftop and get some fresh air, to enjoy the breeze in solitude. Or, rather, to enjoy the breeze with the little fellow in her belly that was making her so exceptionally uncomfortable.

She made her way up the stairs.

✳

'Xiaohong is a flirt. She is such a bloody flirt.'

'Don't make wild guesses and don't just go around talking about people for no good reason, OK?'

'When did I ever talk about anyone for nothing? You're with her in the office all day long. I can't believe she hasn't seduced you yet. I'm telling you, when I saw her puking that day in the washroom, I immediately thought of you. Did she do it with you?'

'I... Youqing, you are still talking nonsense. You see someone puking, you can't assume they are pregnant. You're a girl too. Please don't just go around saying such things.'

'I think you smell of her. You still say you don't like her?'

'How could I like her? Will you stop going on about it? Now that you've got Xiao Yuan into the hospital, what do the two of you plan to do?'

*

The wind carried the voices from the roof into the stairwell. Xiaohong, nauseous, walked away. Spitting, she began to consider her options. One, tell Xia she was pregnant with his baby. Second, tell Liao she was pregnant with his baby. Third, just quietly pretend nothing had happened and go to the People's Hospital for an abortion. Plans one and two might be explosive and the outcome less than ideal. The third was the quietest, like swallowing your front teeth when they have been knocked out. After all, she had to live and being single and pregnant was never going to yield a happy outcome. Forget it then! Next week, she would take time off, go to the People's Hospital and get this matter cleared up.

The next few days, Xiaohong's mouth was preoccupied, silently chomping on sour plums. She had takeaway meals and ate in her room, holding her nose as she took a few mouthfuls, then running again to the toilet to wash it all away. She wracked her brain, asking herself what she could possibly eat. Then, suddenly, she would have a terrible craving and for as long as she had this voracious appetite, she was extremely comfortable. Once she got what she wanted and finished it, she could survive the day.

VIII

During her recovery period, Xiaohong was conflicted. Restless, her mind began to wander.

On the one hand, she wished for a little comfort from Liao, but she feared he would want to sleep with her. After she had taken it upon herself to settle the matter of the little worm, she suddenly began to regret it. She felt she should have talked to him, since he played the leading role in her sex life. Even though she had been with Xia that one time, it was Liao who should take primary responsibility for this. But the matter had passed just like that, leaving her more or less in good health. No one knew the secret thing Xiaohong's body had experienced. That time Youqing had seen her in the washroom vomiting had become nothing more than an illusion.

Her mind drifted to Youqing. Why would she want to bring a time bomb into the hospital, putting Xiao Yuan where he would cross paths with her and Xia? Perhaps she had some sick obsession with seeing men fight over her. Xiao Yuan was from the northeast and was something of a pet project for the little southern girl. And his friendliness toward Xiaohong seemed to raise a heartfelt jealousy in Youqing.

It was November now. The weather was finally cool enough for a light sweater this late in the year. At this time, Xiaohong's body was particularly vulnerable to fatigue and sometimes she experienced a sensation of vertigo. For a girl so young, this was a little strange, she thought. Xiaohong started wondering if it was anaemia, but then found no problem when she had it checked. She could not think of when the seed of this problem had been planted. Was it cancer or was she suffering from AIDS? Was she dying? These random thoughts troubled her and she suddenly became quite pessimistic. It finally produced in her a wave of self pity that was quite unprecedented.

Autumn had passed and winter seemed to be hiding inside her body, though it had not yet begun its full assault.

On her day off, Xiaohong's forehead began to sweat and her breathing became uneven but it only lasted a moment before it all went back to normal. She went to a little fruit market and bought a bag of apples. Not bothering to peel it, she washed one of them and bit into it. When she had taken the bite, her eyes drifted to the stain on the ceiling. She recalled the day Liao had said, 'I love you'.

The teeth marks on her apple had a slight bloodstain.

Her appetite left her. She threw the rest of the apple away.

It dawned on her that she had not seen Sijiang in a long time. The last time was when Specs had come with her to the hospital. Since then, they had only talked on the phone once. Specs seemed an honest, loyal sort. A shy, quiet echo of Sijiang. There should be no trouble between those two.

She didn't know what that pair of dear old sows Wu Ying and Ah Xing were up to either. Wu Ying had found another job and Li Xuewen had opened a small bookstore for Ah Xing. They had all left the reception desk where they used to sell their smiles, and were in contact less frequently, naturally falling out of touch with one another.

She thought of going to Qianshan Town, since it wasn't far. She could get there in half an hour on the bus. But she couldn't get up. Lying there groggily, she dozed off. She slept, feeling she had found her way to the big comfortable bed back at home, smelling the fragrance of the rape fields, listening to the buzz of the bees' song.

When she awoke, she found herself lying on a narrow bed in a foreign place, greeted only by empty walls and a simple wardrobe that sagged to one side.

Ten

I

Spring came like the evening tide, quietly and quickly, a patch-up job to repair the decay of winter. For those who were not particularly sensitive, the change of the seasons in this city was vague and they were completely oblivious to the arrival of spring. Most people lived in this distracted way, the change of seasons having nothing to do with them. There were only two sorts of people who felt strongly about the changing seasons. One was the lonely woman who was excessively tied to a luxurious lifestyle and the seasonal changes in fashion. The other was the rootless vagrant whose only concern was the business of survival. These two types of people had very different feelings. The sensitivity of the former was only skin deep, while the latter's was from the soul. In the former, the change of seasons led to sentimentality but in the latter, it shaped the basic tenor of life.

Spring, a time of growth, the crazy mating season, was also the time for the annual peak of public education activity at the hospital. Those who exceeded the bounds of family planning policies and found themselves pregnant again had to have abortions. After the second child, it was time to talk permanent solutions. Each couple needed to make arrangements for husband or wife to have a procedure. Either would do. Normally, the woman would have a tubal ligation, hysterectomy or some other method of sterilisation. If the woman was really not able to do so, the man would have to pay the price and go under the knife. Although the campaign had been an aggressive one, there were still many people hiding out, waiting to have a third – or even a fourth – child. Often they persevered until they had a son, after which they would be happy enough to go and see the doctor and his scalpel.

The little cock. It was forever the ideal, the pride of life, a sustained revolution. When it was grown, it would bring both ecstasy and catastrophe to women. It would bear and bring forth all sorts of worries, excitement and joy.

This spring, Zhu Dachang accompanied his wife, the dark-skinned teacher, to the hospital. He was lucky – his wife had given birth to three sons all at once. She was unlucky – she had given birth to three sons all at once, so had to submit herself for the operation.

As it turned out, her luck was not all bad. The doctors reported that she had a rare condition that made her unable to go under the knife. She felt as if a glimmer in the dark of night had burst forth into the bright light of morning.

Dachang said at once, 'Don't you think I'm done here? I've got three boys. Even if you paid me to do it, I wouldn't want to father anymore!'

'No one can say for sure. But if you're slated for an operation, you've got to have the operation. It's official policy.'

While his wife was resting and the three babies were asleep, Dachang left the milky-smelling ward behind and went out for a walk. The smell of milk lingered even on his own body. He wandered out onto the lawn. Red and gold banana trees blazed, as brightly coloured as a bride in her heavy makeup.

Dachang suddenly remembered that some time back, Xiaohong had called and told him she was going to work in a hospital. He had been very pleased for her. He could not remember which hospital she was at, nor did he know how things were going with her. As he thought about it, he felt some regret. He should have taken care of this girl who was so far away from home. Even if his wife was jealous and even if he had promised not to speak to Xiaohong, all the same, he should have taken more care of her. Thinking back to the first time he had met the pathetic girl in the detention centre, Dachang felt that, in the face of the hard realities of the world, she really was too small and too weak. In Shenzhen, there were many small, insignificant people like Xiaohong. It was hard to see how these blind little girls overcame the difficulties they faced in life.

Walking round the lawn, Dachang looked up and saw a head sticking out of one of the windows in the hospital, looking at him. Then a hand came out next to it, desperately waving. He looked round to see who the person in the window was beckoning to and realised he was the one being hailed. Only then did he notice that the person looked like Xiaohong. Just like her.

'*Zhu Ge*, I was looking for you. You have triplets! It's all over the hospital. Everyone is envious.' Xiaohong was like a wind blowing over him.

'I'm happy for both of you, too,' she slowly added.

'It's going to be a real hassle,' Dachang said, conflicting emotions playing on his face and in his voice. As for what kind of trouble, he was too embarrassed to say. For a man to undergo this sort of operation, it was as humiliating as suddenly being castrated. Although the physicians had constantly reaffirmed that the procedure would not affect the normal functions of life, who believed that?

Xiaohong also didn't ask what sort of hassle he meant. She only wanted to show herself to be quiet and thoughtful with Dachang. She was a bit stiff. It was a strange thing. She couldn't explain it. A few years had passed and then they met like this, stood face to face like this, chatted like this. There were traces of sadness about each of them and they were left not knowing how many years would pass before they met again. Perhaps a lifetime. It was a sadness that hinted at autumn and the end of comedy.

'You're... alright? Looks like a good place to work. You need anything, I'll do my best to help,' Dachang stammered.

'It is good. Really good. I always remember the help you gave me.'

'There'll be a typhoon in a couple of days. Remember to secure the windows. It's best to stay indoors. Don't go out.'

'Alright.'

'You need to apply for your temporary resident's permit?'

'No. The hospital took care of that for me.'

'If you need anything, call me.'

'OK. Oh, do you know anything about the case of the girl who worked at the Qianshan Hotel, Julia Wilde? I don't know if there's been any resolution to that.'

'From what I heard, there haven't been any leads.'

'I guess there's no hope. Oh well.'

'You take care of yourself. Don't worry too much.'

'You too.'

II

Several months flew past and, before he knew it, autumn had arrived and Dachang found himself at the hospital again. The shadows of two figures were visible on the other side of the screen. Zhu Dachang sat facing Dr Chen Fangyuan, answering her queries, under diagnosis.

'Stand up. Take off your trousers,' Dr Chen said in sanctimonious, majestic tones.

Dachang had gone under the knife in the spring, but his wife had recently become pregnant again. Suspecting the worst, Dachang decided to first go for a check up himself. He thought that if there were a few guerrilla forces lurking in his own body, he could do nothing but laugh it off. But if it were confirmed that his troops had indeed been defeated, then it was a big problem and his happy marriage and peaceful family life would face a severe test.

Dachang listened tensely to Dr Chen's instructions, holding his breath as her hands prodded and pinched at him.

'Has it had any effect on your relations with your wife?' Dr Chen's expression was like that of a blind fortune teller.

Dachang wanted to say it hadn't but he sort of felt it had, so he answered noncommittally. The screen was suddenly pulled a bit and another female doctor came in, obviously on urgent business.

'How can you just come in like that?' Dachang, startled, quickly covered his most sensitive parts.

The doctor looked at him with a pair of panda eyes and said, 'I'm a doctor! Is there any real reason to cover that thing up?'

The doctor muttered something at Dachang. Then turning a backside as round as a panda's in his direction, she left.

'Female doctors are still women, aren't they?' he said, as if in a trance.

Dachang reluctantly uncovered his nether regions once again, returning to face the reality of a check up by Dr Chen. Using the fingers to pinch and confirm that the vas deferens had in fact been cut was a particular strength of Dr Chen's, but she seemed to be encountering some problems this time. After spending about ten minutes prodding about, she gave a depressed sigh. 'Strange, it's not standing up. I can't reach the vessels at all.'

Dachang had not thought that she might want it to stand. Why wasn't it erect? He didn't understand it either. But he did know it would be difficult to manage much of an erection when faced with Dr Chen.

In the end, she said, 'We'll test the semen.'

Dachang felt insulted. He thought she could have avoided the embarrassment of making him remove his trousers and just taken some samples of his bodily fluids.

'It's not the same thing,' Dr Chen said. 'We need a multifaceted check up.'

She arranged for a small room for Dachang. Inside was a small colour TV and VCR. It was a very professional setup.

She turned on the video but didn't leave right away. Two naked people started kissing on the screen. Turning a blind eye, she handed him a plastic cup and said, 'You just enjoy the show.'

Dachang stared blankly at the cup. It suddenly hit him what it was for and he began watching earnestly. But the more he watched the blue movie, the limper he became. This upset him so much that he turned positively soft. After fifteen minutes, Dr Chen knocked and came in to have a look. The video was rewinding, the cup was empty, and Dachang's face was unhappy.

'Oh, you got so involved in watching that you forgot about the real thing, huh? Then how will we do the tests? If the video's no use, would you like us to call a prostitute for you?' Obviously, Dachang was wasting too much of her time. She added, 'I'm serious about the prostitute. Once we had a guy who came in for a check up and he couldn't squeeze out a thing, not to save his life. His wife wasn't here to help extract anything either. In the end, we had to call a prostitute before he could manage it.'

'Doctor, I am very sorry. If you'll just give me twenty minutes, I'll give it my best effort.' He was very embarrassed. Dr Chen stared at him a moment, eyes protruding, then turned her fat rump and went out. Dachang simply turned off the video. He sat stewing, and after several minutes, Xiaohong's face popped into his mind. He immediately picked up his mobile phone and called. When she answered, it was obvious she had been napping in the office, but she quickly perked up when she heard Dachang's voice.

'I'm at your hospital.'

'No. Don't tell me you're expecting again.'

Dachang fell silent for a while. Finally overcoming the difficulty, he poured out the story in a rushed whisper, telling her everything.

'I... what can I do to help?'

'Xiaohong, your voice is so nice. Use your voice...'

'Really?'

'Really.'

'...'

'You like me, don't you?'

'Yes.'

'That time... that time... I almost...'

'You almost took me...'

'I couldn't...'

'I know. You're the best man I've ever known.'

'Xiaohong, talk to me. Talk dirty to me.'

'I... you... it...'

'Yeah...'

After a few minutes, like a tide coming in from the sea, it poured out like the pounding of hooves from a herd of wild horses, silently galloping across the great expanse of the universe, free and unbridled. All the clouds in the sky rolled up into a heap, white and billowing. His breath was like a torrent, coming in waves, then suddenly her ear was filled with the sound of wind. Xiaohong, unable to contain herself, groaned. Then, laying her head on the table, she wept uncontrollably.

When Dr Chen returned, she only saw the retreating figure of Zhu Dachang leaving the video room nonchalantly. Suspicious, she went in and looked around, then followed Dachang out and went to the lab. She stood looking at the contents of the plastic cup, trying to judge whether or not it was the real thing. Her eyes protruded even more than usual.

The test results were normal, showing no traces of sperm in his specimen. Stunned, he found himself in a wash of mixed emotions. He did not know whether to burst into laughter or drown himself in tears.

He had no idea how he would manage things at home.

ELEVEN

I

Who'd have thought that Mr Liao would be leaving? The 35-year-old top surgeon Dr Lei Yigang was promoted to take his place as chairman. He was from Guangdong, practically a native of Shenzhen. People from Guangdong usually gave one the impression of leanness that bordered on flimsiness, but Dr Lei was not like that at all. On the contrary, both his stature and his family background were quite solid. He was not too short and his weight was well proportioned to his height, with just a small surplus. His chubby face was always a picture of the good life, someone who enjoyed a lifestyle of ease. He had not the slightest sign of a beard on his face. This was not because he shaved himself closely but because his beard would not grow anymore. It was often said that this was closely connected with a breakthrough in his research. Contributing to the advancement of gynaecological medicine, he had successfully developed a new type of blade that could lessen the suffering of a woman undergoing a sterilisation procedure by forty per cent, shortening the time required for the operation to fifteen minutes and speeding the recovery time to a mere five days. As for medical expenses, of course, it would save a fortune. This matter would have a great social impact, especially for women, much like the release from the tradition of foot-binding. So, Dr Lei always wore a smile on a face shaved beardless by that blade. Some said it was a humble face, some said it was the gaping grin of a tiger, and some said it was a cunning look. Only Lei Yigang could know for certain what it hid.

With the hospital's personnel changes, all the departments were shuffled and this meant promotions in the publicity room. Staffed with just two employees, Xia Jifeng was the obvious one to promote to Publicity Director, which opened up a vacancy for a very lucrative post. To use a negative example, this lucrative post was like an enemy bunker, with countless elite forces all eyeing it, preparing themselves for the noise of battle. Many lurked in the dark, waiting to see who would finally capture it.

Xiaohong's propaganda work had been impeccable. Of course, this was credited to Xia, according to an unwritten rule. When one person stands a step higher than another, it's only natural that he will be the taller of the two.

When Dr Lei took over his new post, he wasted no time in placing great emphasis on publicity. There was always room for more publicity in his office and thus he needed to have more contact with his PR people. That is to say, he had plenty of reason to be frequently in touch with Qian Xiaohong.

'Hi, Xiaohong. Why don't you come over to my office and sit down and talk for while.' Dr Lei said to Xiaohong on the phone. When she arrived, he opened a small window and a leafy branch began tapping gently against the blinds. His beard had still not grown, which always made Xiaohong feel a twinge of regret.

'I'm here, Dr Lei, sir.' Seeing his posture, she knew this was not just another casual chat. It made her a little anxious.

'You've been doing publicity work for quite a while now.'

'Over a year, sir.'

'Then you should understand the hospital's situation quite well.'

'Um, I guess so.'

'Recently the hospital has decided to introduce some reproductive health services and the publicity needs to be handled well. I've assigned some specific work to Mr Xia and I want you to cooperate closely with him on this.'

Xiaohong nodded, feeling Dr Lei was being rather vague. Ever since that one night, she and Xia had seldom been in the office together. It was like they were following each other through a revolving door. When Xiaohong came in, Xia went out. When Xiaohong went out, Xia came in. A bit like their love-making, in fact.

Dr Lei smiled, looking like he was hiding some scheme.

'Also, I need to give a report at the board meeting next Friday. I want you to help me do the summary. Just get the materials together for me. If you have any questions, you can call my mobile phone any time.' The same innocent smile emerged on his baby face.

Xiaohong answered nervously, heart pounding as she pondered. This sort of thing had always been written by Xia. How had it suddenly fallen on her head? Was Dr Lei just trying to make things difficult, or was he trying to get something out of her?

Dr Lei's beardless smile had no regularity to it. It was so smooth that he looked pitiful, and it made his smile so sinister that it sent chills down her spine. Xiaohong saw the folds and wrinkles of his face as ditches and gullies. His lips were not red, but glistened as if they had been dipped in oil.

This matter weighed heavily on Xiaohong's mind. She thought, Fuck! Obviously Dr Lei is screwing me over. If I screw up this article, it's going to come to a bad end. How the hell am I going to get a report of more than five thousand words done?

'*Xia Ge*, can you lend me the original materials to refer to for my report? I'll use that material in my write up.'

Xia was a little stunned when Xiaohong asked him this. He thought, How is it that the report is to be done by her? If she does it, what's left for me to do? What is Dr Lei up to with that girl?

'What are you doing?'

'The summary report for Dr Lei's meeting next week.'

'What did he say about it?'

'That's all he said.'

Things were definitely not that simple. Xia felt Xiaohong must be hiding something big. She was obviously wary of him. She must be playing her own political games, secretly scheming to obstruct him. Xia's good will towards Xiaohong and the passion he had felt that night made him ashamed. He reluctantly dug out some materials, like a farmer grudgingly parting with some of his seed crop to share a few sprouts with someone else.

'Basically, it's like this. You see if there's any value to the information here.' He handed her a few photocopied documents in a file, as devoutly as a girl giving away her virginity. Xiaohong took it, full of gratitude, and began to read, not overlooking even the tiniest of punctuation marks. When she had finished reading, she did not understand a thing. She could only remember that there were a great number of sterilisation cases and that the volume of human traffic was even more alarming. Then it suddenly hit her. People mated every day. Gorgeously apparelled, they flirted all day and went about their night-time business without a stitch of clothing on. This sort of healthy reproductive life led to a whole lot of problems.

She bit the bullet and worked that evening until five or six. When she knocked off, she only had about a hundred words of an introduction, nearly eighty of which were dug out word for word from the summary.

'If it's a rooster, then it's a rooster. No matter how long you wait, it won't lay an egg.' Xiaohong finally understood what lay behind that old expression from her hometown. She was now just a rooster, incapable of laying an egg. She'd been put to roost by Dr Lei.

'Lei Yigang is such a prick!' Xiaohong mercilessly pounded the desk a couple of times then, quivering, paraded around the office, chest thrust out. She decided not to waste any more time on the report. She would show him. She was a rooster. She couldn't do a hen's work.

On the phone with the chairman, all was quiet in the background, as if he were in the car or at home. This gynaecologist's voice was always soft, like he was treating one of those sensitive illnesses. It was the same touch he used when caring for all the female genitalia he handled.

'Let's talk more specifically,' Dr Lei said, as if just talking would settle Xiaohong's problem.

'It's hard to say it clearly over the phone, sir. This report is very important to you, and I'm afraid I'll hold everything up.'

'We've still got time. Come on round and we'll talk about the specifics.'

'Where are you? And do you want me to bring the materials?'

'Yes, bring it all. I'm in my office.'

II

Dr Lei was in his office. Xiaohong had not expected this. Nor had she expected to find him sleeping. What was he doing sleeping now, she wondered. His freshly awakened beardless face was especially flushed and boyish. A face like that on a man was unbelievable. His lips were even redder and wetter than usual, always looking as if he had just had a drink.

Breezily, the door swung open. Dr Lei carelessly knocked against Xiaohong as he casually plopped down on the sofa, blithely waving for her to randomly select a spot to sit there as well. The sofa was like plastic, making her backside warm. As her posterior heated up, she inevitably moved, and in moving, the two rear ends were suddenly in quite close proximity to one another. Before they had even started talking business, the pair of arses had already begun a vague dispute of their own.

'How should I put it? This material is both easy and difficult to write. If you've never done it before, it's quite hard. But once you've got started, it gets easier,' he said, not offering any insight that was of much use. Xiaohong was not awkward this time. She actually looked at Dr Lei and smiled, as if his advice was full of wisdom. She looked very appreciative as she listened. Dr Lei mentioned very specifically his own outstanding contributions to medicine, saying that this could be one of the more important accomplishments of the hospital to focus pen and ink on. It was necessary to look at what had happened before, he said, in order to focus on future advancements, highlight programmes and show the municipal leaders the sort of development the hospital was aiming for.

'Got it?' Dr Lei once again seemed to be full of hot air. 'Xiaohong, you write it up. When you're done, I'll have a look and do some tweaking.' Dr Lei casually reached over and took the material from Xiaohong's hand. Xiaohong noticed that his hand was as white as if it had been sterilised. On the back of his hand, miraculously, there were a few black hairs. Thinking of how that hand had taken the scalpel to countless women and of the relations it had had with a multitude of women's private places, Xiaohong felt nauseous and seemed to detect the smell of blood.

'Dr Lei, your help has given me some inspiration. I'll go and write it up.' Xiaohong peeled her backside from the sofa. His hand struck a moment too late. Failing to get hold of Xiaohong, his nails merely grazed her skin. She smiled airily and, gently opening the door, casually went on her way.

Dr Lei drifted up from the sofa.

III

The atmosphere was a little tense, those days. Even the slightest thing would cause idle tongues to pounce like flies, buzzing about finding fault and making irresponsible remarks.

Youqing was secretly entangled with two men and her face grew longer and sharper. Her menstrual cycle was suddenly enshrouded in mystery. She no longer gave regular reports. It was as if, once she was on the right track, the matter was gradually forgotten. Youqing seemed to have some difficulty managing her own private life, such as her relationship with Xia. Unfortunately, Xiaohong had discovered it and, although she was too lazy to expose them, Youqing found it harder to carry on the charade.

That day on the rooftop, when Youqing had cursed Xiaohong for closing in on Xia, Xiaohong had heard everything clearly. Xia had said he could never like her. She understood. Whatever the pair had said after that did not matter. He was dodging her, which just proved how powerless he was. A man who was afraid to face a woman was at the very least weak-willed. Xia was also very hypocritical, his love life mixed up with a wide range of factors. He wanted to go to bed with Xiaohong, but he hid it, always looking over his shoulder as he slunk around. Xiaohong remembered that night very clearly, all of his trembling excitement. If he had not had the desire for some time, if he had not felt some real emotion, then he would not have been so frantic. The way he suppressed his desires, Xia's life must be devoid of passion. What a flaccid existence!

As Xiaohong brooded over the report, Xia and Youqing were wondering how Dr Lei had come to give the assignment to Xiaohong. When Xia and his ex had divided up their assets after the divorce, he ended up with the apartment. Three bedrooms and a family room in a housing estate that was not too shabby. The lawn was green and full of red flowers throughout the year. Living here gave one a sense of satisfaction, naturally increasing one's sex drive. So as soon as the pair had decided that Xia should go to Dr Lei at the hospital the next day to discuss the matter of the report, they embraced and made their way to the bedroom. Once they had taken care of things thoroughly there, they continued discussing the feasibility of the plan.

'Youqing, tell me specifically how you think I should go about it so as not to let Dr Lei misunderstand my intentions. I know he's an extremely perceptive man, not the usual sort of guy at all. Once you offend him, that sweet, warm smile won't be turned on you again,' he said, trying his best to see into the future.

Youqing looked up at him, feeling he was a good man, mature and attractive. Xiao Yuan, in contrast, was still green, sometimes even a little rash. How was it that Xia was a divorcee, she wondered, letting out a faint sorrowful sigh.

Seeing Youqing silent, he shrugged his right shoulder, where her head lay.

Youqing, jostled by his shrug, bit her tongue. She yelped, pushing him away, and sat up, putting her hand to her mouth as her eyes teared in pain.

Xia, tired and not inclined to comfort her, lay thinking about his own troubles. Youqing's eyes had first started tearing because of the pain but gradually she began to really cry. And as she cried, she grew melancholy. Uncertain what had happened to her, Xia was puzzled by her behaviour.

She finally said, 'If you don't care about me, why should I bother so much about you? Xiao Yuan wouldn't be so callous.'

At this, Xia grew jealous. 'Then go to Xiao Yuan if he's so good. We've been involved in politics from the start, and now you want to get all emotional about it. Before you know it, I'll have no room left to ma-noeuvre.' He wanted to get up but was afraid Youqing would be angry.

'Tomorrow when you talk to Dr Lei, don't give anything away. Just shoot the breeze, test the waters, OK?' Youqing reined in her temper and thought to herself, Who asked me to fall in love with you?

'Shoot the breeze? How? I don't normally just chat with gynaecologists. I'll have to watch myself. He's got backers who are quite influential too.'

The next day at work, Xia monitored the movements of Dr Lei's office carefully. He did not find a suitable opportunity the whole morning, with Dr Lei talking on and off with various people.

Xia was preoccupied, as if he were suppressing something. Every time there was the sound of footsteps in the corridor, it would attract his attention. He would look up then turn back. Xiaohong, involuntarily affected by his actions, followed his lookings up and turnings back. Before long, feeling a little dizzy, she began to see stars.

'You're looking for Dr Lei?' she asked, biting at the tip of her pen, making Xia pause for half a beat.

'He seems especially busy today. How's the report going?'

'Eh. Not so well. You want to look it over for me?' Xia held out a hand, and Xiaohong passed it to him. He scanned it for a couple of minutes, then handed it right back to her.

'That's about right. It's got plenty of information.'

'You mean it's OK as it is? You don't have any advice? Points one, two and three that need changing?'

'You've done fine. Better than I'd imagined.'

She looked at him and asked, 'Are there any awkward sentences? Any mistakes? Help me brush it up.'

'It's pretty smooth. Stronger than when I started writing.'

'Encouragement isn't any use, Xia. See it through Dr Lei's eyes. Where do I need to change it?'

'I'm not Dr Lei. Of course I don't know what he's thinking.'

A figure went past the door. The last person in the chairman's office was leaving. Xia pushed the chair away with his hip, stood up and disappeared in a flash. In another flash, he returned. Silently and sulkily, he settled back into his chair.

Xiaohong took the report and stood up. She likewise disappeared in a flash. About ten minutes later, empty-handed, she quietly went back to her own chair. 'Your turn. Dr Lei wants to see you.'

Xia said a quick 'Thanks' and went out in yet another flash to Dr Lei's office.

'What do you think of Qian Xiaohong's report? Have a look.' Xia stood and courteously took the report with both hands from the chairman. All the lights in the office were always on. The bright mosaic of dozens of pale fluorescent bulbs on the ceiling made Xia rather uncomfortable, as if every sweat gland and every pore was exposed. Feeling a little awkward, he was not really looking carefully at the report. Rather, he was thinking of what terms could more perfectly express his own views. He did not want to be seen as substandard, nor as purposely critical. And he wanted to get a clearer idea of Dr Lei's thinking. After ten minutes, Xia raised his head and smiled sheepishly, as if to say that if the report were not up to standard, he was partly at fault.

'The material is a little convoluted, not a lot of weight to it. Some phrases don't quite flow. And the content's confusing. That's my general feeling.'

'Ah,' Dr Lei said in a nasal tone. He got up and poured a cup of water, the bubbles in the dispenser rising at full speed.

'It's worse than I imagined. I thought it could be used, with slight modification. But now that I read it properly, there are too many places that need corrections. So, I want you to rewrite it.' Dr Lei put the cup of water in front of Xia, who scrambled to politely accept the cup with both hands.

'Of course. It's my duty.'

'To engage in PR, you need a certain level of culture. At least a university degree.'

'You are right, sir. PR has always been about culture, cultural publicity. Sometimes I also feel she's not quite strong enough.'

'Hmm. Or maybe what's needed is simply some specialisation, and then she'll be steady enough.'

'That's true, sir. For PR, in this line, it's best to be multi-talented.'

'You think it over. We need to plan out the personnel requirements for the PR department. You're the head. You can make a proposal to the department.'

Dr Lei dropped the hint, and Xia implicitly understood. He also had a gut feeling that Dr Lei had his own plans.

IV

The rain fell in thin sheets, setting up a pinging rhythm on the bonnet of a car. The wind whistled past, then whistled back again. It was a heavy downpour. It had been a long time since it had rained like this. The drops splattered onto the window, splashing onto the tip of her nose. Xiaohong stopped and stared, watching the beads of rain hit against the flat part of the leaves, against the umbrellas under which people sheltered, against the slanted billboards, and against any exposed patch of earth. As she watched the rain like this, everything that it beat down upon, instead of becoming soggy and saturated, perked up with a vibrant energy. Time passed and still she felt antsy. Though the rain had come and gone, it left everything just as it had been before. Xiaohong felt she should do something with herself, but when she pulled out the necessary books to study for exams, looking seriously at a few lines, she grew more restless than ever. Once boredom had her in its grip, all she could hope to do was find something even more meaningless to occupy her mind.

Looking out of the window, the late afternoon sun had come unself-consciously out, and life continued on in its light. Xiaohong made her way out of the house, airing herself out in the sun. Motorcycles and cars obnoxiously emitted clouds of exhaust, humble bicycles making their way amongst them, while pedestrians stuck to their own paved walkways. The street was wet and steaming, and music blared from the CD shop. Pagers were advertised at huge discounts and wind chimes swayed in front of an everything-for-eight-*yuan* shop.

A few fluffy-haired girls from the nearby factories walked by, holding hands. Their rubber-soled shoes sticking to the spot as they stopped, apparently listening to the wind chimes. Xiaohong passed them and a pungent odour of armpits mingled with the chimes attacked her senses. Both ear and nose suffered the effects and then it passed back through her system for a second round. Practically suffocating, Xiaohong thought that at least the smell was not coming from her. She took some comfort in the fact that her own body odour was not quite so strong and that she was cleaner than those factory workers.

She felt good. No wonder people said that a nice walk was a cure for boredom. The effects were obvious enough to see, at least initially. Xiaohong walked with a light step, chest out and head thrown back to see the azure sky. She was surprised to find that one of a few stray clouds had wrapped itself round the spire of a building.

What shall I do? It would be a shame to do nothing and waste weather like this. With this aimless thought, her right arm, swinging by her side, nearly hit several cartons of cigarettes on a stall on the pavement. There must have been about a hundred different brands of cigarette, all wrapped in packaging that dazzled. Xiaohong stopped, tilted her head and beginning with the first row, carefully counted all the brands – foreign and domestic, cheap and dear. There were exactly a hundred and eight varieties.

'Want some smokes? There are some especially suitable for girls to puff on, like this one here,' a woman said, dark and thin and with a little boy tucked under her arm like a bundle of straw. She spoke with such confidence and sophistication that Xiaohong guessed she must have been smoking for decades.

'You've tried it?' Xiaohong took the small, delicate packet.

'All the girls smoke this one.' The woman reined in her confident air and it was replaced with a trace of regret on her face. The child in her arms wiggled like a crab, looking around with wide eyes. As she spoke, a little girl ran out from the shop and said in broken Mandarin, 'Ten *kuai*, ten *kuai*. Ten *kuai* a packet.' She stared at Xiaohong, waiting for payment.

When she had bought the cigarettes, Xiaohong walked off, glancing back at the stall. She could not see anything clearly through the clutter there. As she was about to walk away, a girl grazed against Xiaohong's waist as she ran past, shouting, 'Mum! I'm home!' She tossed her red rucksack to the woman.

How many kids do you have? Xiaohong wanted to ask. But by the time she thought of it, she had already left the cigarette stall. Day had eased into evening without pausing for twilight. In a half-dream state, Xiaohong walked along, packet of cigarettes in hand. When she crossed the pedestrian bridge, she noticed that a man seemed to be following her and had been for a while. He had very large feet. Xiaohong stopped and leaned against the railing, waiting to see what he would do next. Bigfoot stopped on the opposite side of the bridge and, leaning against the handrail there, looked idly around.

The neon lights flickered to life and the cars passing underneath the bridge likewise began to switch on their headlights, the glare shooting before them like flames. Xiaohong shifted her weight, finding that her hands and feet were growing numb from being in the same position too long. Her feet were like cotton wool and she felt like she was floating.

As it was getting dark, Bigfoot came closer. 'Can I scrounge a smoke?' His voice was not evil. He sounded like someone with a legitimate profession. Xiaohong looked him over sternly. She found him good-looking in spite of herself. He looked nothing like a predator slinking along the streets.

'Got a light?' Xiaohong said, trying to open the packet but failing to find the seal and fumbling with it.

'You don't smoke, but you bought cigarettes.' Bigfoot took the pack from her, their fingers touching. He tore open the clear plastic film, which flashed as he dropped it onto the bridge. He handed Xiaohong a cigarette, as if he were a master smoker.

'Why are you following me?' Bigfoot pulled a lighter out of his back pocket and lit the cigarette for Xiaohong. Elbows glued to the railing, she began to puff on it chaotically.

'What makes you think I'm following you? It's just a coincidence. I've just broken up with my girlfriend, so went out for a walk. Then I saw you and that's all there is to it. You can't expect to be the only person to occupy the streets as if you're the only one who's got things on their mind,' he said seriously. He kicked the railing with his oversized foot, as if he wanted to make it share in his pain.

'What do you do? How long you been in Shenzhen?' A white car shot out below Xiaohong, driving straight ahead and joining the flow of traffic.

'I work in a securities company, a stock broker. I've been in Shenzhen eight months.'

'Oh. You've only been here eight months and you've already had a girlfriend and broken up with her. I've been here two or three years and I haven't even had a boyfriend, not to mention a break-up. You're much better off than me.'

He looked at her then withdrew his gaze. After a second, he suddenly turned back and looked again. Xiaohong opened her eyes wide, intrigued.

'She was a whore, you know. At least, she sold herself. After she made some money *that* way, she went into shares. Now she's climbing the ladder with shares worth over half a million. But I wish she'd never made that half-million!' He poked his big foot under the railing. It looked as if it wanted to take a suicidal plunge.

'You fall for her because she had half a million. Then after you fall for her, you despise her half-million. Or, you mean, if she'd made that money innocently, then everything would be perfect? I doubt that.'

Bigfoot pondered for a moment, then withdrew his foot and said, 'How do you work that out? That's not true.'

'I bet it is. You just don't want to admit it.'

'It's getting late. Let's go to The Bean King and I'll buy you some soya milk and bread sticks. They've got good dumplings too.'

When they had finished their late night snack, Bigfoot inveigled Xiaohong into watching a video. The video hall had several private rooms with comfy seats. A person could get stuck there all day without moving. The room had been put together with a very scientific approach. No one was to be seen in front of the viewers, nor was there a shadow of other people to the right or left, and the only thing visible upon looking over your shoulder was the back of the seat. It seemed to be a Hong Kong film and it was full of nude scenes. As they watched, it was difficult to say whether it was because of the comfy seats or the steamy scenes, but desire was born. Perhaps the whole point of this sort of lovers' nest was to foster something between them. It started with an innocent touching of hands, a grasping of hands and then a squeezing of hands. Then Bigfoot's arm snaked its way around her, pulling Xiaohong into an embrace.

Their lust was ignorant and it was normal. And it made the video no longer something to be relished but something to be dispensed with. All the people in the various rooms followed the film's touching and kissing. And while their moves might not have been as artful as those onscreen, they were more spontaneous. From time to time, a careless sound escaped from one of the rooms, serving as a catalyst to stir up even more shenanigans in all the other rooms.

When the film was over, the wind blew along the night streets, sweeping amongst the fluttering shadows, all of which were rushing to one place or another to mate. Xiaohong's hand was continually in the grip of Bigfoot's, making it a little damp. They went into the night streets, not saying a word, only looking for a taxi. It was as if Xiaohong were just an article of his clothing, never even asking where they were going. Not even a simple, 'Your place or mine?'

When they got to his flat, Bigfoot took Xiaohong and, like an article of clothing, flung her onto the bed.

Midnight is always a time of confusion.

V

Monday, 18 September. Gregorian calendar. And what's so special about that date? Why, it's Qian Xiaohong's twentieth birthday.

Seeing Bigfoot in the doorway of the office, a smile came over her face. She knew he wanted to be with her a second time. But for now, he was dressed smartly in a grey t-shirt and brown slacks, and his behaviour spoke of culture and cultivation. Even Xia was a little jealous, which made Xiaohong's face glow more than ever. She greeted Bigfoot with the warmth of an old friend and poured him a cup of tea. Xia took the hint and beat a hasty retreat.

'The environment here's not bad,' Bigfoot said casually, glancing about the office. His mouth was not small, but very sensual. His teeth were white and clean. From the night they had spent together a couple of weeks earlier, Xiaohong could not quite remember the taste of that mouth. She thought back for a moment, but still could not recall it.

'What are you doing here?'

'Shouldn't I have come?'

'It's a bit of a surprise.'

'You knew I'd come.'

'You might as well say I knew you'd want to sleep with me again.'

'I won't pretend to be noble. I wanted to come, so I came.'

She giggled.

'Let's start again,' he said.

'Not continue? Why turn it into starting again?'

'There was so much going on that night.'

'You mean you want a relationship?'

'Why not?' He paused for several seconds, his big hand scratching his ear and his big feet shuffling over the floor.

'I suppose it's likely enough.' Xiaohong stared at his shoes. They were very clean.

'I'm just on my way to work. I'll meet you tonight. We can go for karaoke.'

At six, Xiaohong went to the McDonald's where they had agreed to meet. It was nearly dark and the rush hour traffic clogged the whole area. There was a hubbub of noise from the crowd, as if everyone were out in force to attend some grand event. The whole world was turned upside down, so why not eat, drink and be merry?

In the restaurant, there were no empty seats. It was packed with people milling about as freely as the aroma of spicy wings and burgers. Xiaohong felt as vulnerable as if she were in a crowded train station, overwhelmed by a sense of annihilation, loss and loneliness. After a moment, she suddenly spotted the flash of his white teeth amidst the sea of black hair, his mouth like a ship floating on its surface.

'You go and have a seat. It's across from the washroom. I've saved a place for us there,' Bigfoot told her, then frantically made his way straight to the counter.

Sure enough, they were facing the men's WC. The door was quite beautiful. The smell of spicy chicken wings and hamburgers floated in the air, and everywhere she looked, people were clasping their cups of cola. Xiaohong sat watching with interest, feeling herself lucky, as Bigfoot used his two great feet to force his way through the crowd, carrying a tray.

'Fries, chicken wings, burgers, cola, ice cream and ketchup.'

Xiaohong, perhaps affected by the thought of all the exposed rears in the WC, noticed that Bigfoot's face was even smoother than a baby's bottom. A clean-shaven man was one who was ready for business, showing himself to be serious and conscientious. It was a sort of silent oath. Xiaohong was a little touched, though she was not really sure if it was because of that face shaved smoother than a baby's behind or because of the meal. She only knew she was touched, and that what lay behind the feeling was this big-footed man with the charming smile. With his sparkling white teeth, he took a bite of the hamburger. As if in response to the smile on Xiaohong's face, he said vaguely, 'I'm hungry! Come on, you eat too.'

Xiaohong liked eating with him like this. What she most disliked were those men who were prim and proper as eunuchs, eating a dainty little bite, then wiping their mouth carefully with a napkin. God, they wiped their mouth as vigorously as wiping their arse! It was better to eat like Bigfoot, nice and easy-going.

Xiaohong poured out some chilli sauce, then dipped one of the tasty, tender wings into it. When she had finished, she stuck her fingers into her mouth, acknowledging both her love of the chicken wings and her appreciation to Bigfoot. She took a swig of her drink then repeated the process, eating the fries in a more flirtatious manner. The fries were long and thin, not easily eaten in a single bite. After she had eaten half of one, she would dip the remaining piece into the sauce, making it all a very complicated process.

'This was a perfect birthday dinner! Thanks a lot.' Xiaohong smiled happily.

'It's your birthday? Oh! Happy birthday! What do you want to do now?' Bigfoot asked enthusiastically.

'I'm full. About to burst. Let's go for a walk.'

'It's not even seven o'clock yet. Let's go to the park and walk off our dinner. Karaoke doesn't start till eight.' Bigfoot turned the romance of a stroll in the park into a mundane thing, a walk to aid the digestion. There was no ambiguity. It was as simple as the chicken wings they had just eaten.

'Mister, buy some flowers. Flowers for the lady.'

As soon as they reached the park entrance, Xiaohong and Bigfoot were stopped by two five- or six-year-old girls. Each had a large bouquet of roses in her hand, with each rose wrapped in plastic. They were all wilting, as if they had been salvaged from the rubbish bin.

Bigfoot said, 'I'll buy you one. Today's a special occasion.'

Xiaohong firmly blocked his way, saying, 'You might as well just give her the money. Look at them. How can you even call those broken things flowers? Let's go. Don't bother!'

As he took a step, Bigfoot found his leg embraced by one of the girls. Her whole body clinging to him, she cried, 'Buy one! Buy one! I'm begging you!'

Bigfoot did not move and a crowd began to gather. Left with no choice, he took his wallet from his back pocket and by the light of the streetlamp took out five *yuan*. Only when he had pulled a drooping rose from the bunch did the little girl let go of his leg. He walked away, carrying the pitiful flower. He didn't dare give it to Xiaohong. When they had entered the park, following several turns of the path past a sculpture of a giraffe and over a little bridge, he finally shoved the rose into the rubbish bin. He pointed to a bench by the pond and said in a relieved tone, 'Let's sit there.'

Bigfoot walked across the lawn to the bench, passing countless shadows of people huddling in the dark. He plopped down onto the white stone seat, facing the dim light of the pond with a faintly stunned expression.

'You still want to sing? I'm not in the mood.'

'I'm not really up for it either.'

'Something bothering you?' Xiaohong asked, noticing his silence.

'She wants to marry me. I can't decide.'

'You can't decide to marry her but you can't decide *not* to marry her either.'

Shaking his big feet, he did not reply.

'You love her. And you are bothered by her previous life. It's obvious you're a hypocrite. You want to have a good reputation and you want wealth too.'

The willow branches swung freely, tips dragging along the water.

'I don't want her money. I've already decided on that.'

'She and the half-million are linked.'

'So, I don't want a single *kuai* from her.'

'That's up to you. I can't console you.'

'I want to be with you.'

'Then you'll really lose out. I'm no virgin myself. I've been with lots and lots of guys, and I don't have half a million to show for it.'

TWELVE

I

After watching a film at the Qianshan Theatre, Specs was a little excited. All he could think of was getting back to the flat he had rented with Sijiang. Her small eyes glared at him, not showing the least sign that she shared his desire and she pulled him along to Ah Xing's bookshop.

Ah Xing was noticeably pregnant, her tummy protruding like that of a potbellied teddy bear. In slippers, she lazily moved about, clumsy as a penguin. It was no more than ten paces from one end of the bookshop to the other but Ah Xing needed twenty to waddle across it, her hand constantly rubbing her rounded belly, comforting the unborn child there.

'Looks like they're about to close.'

'Hey Ah Xing! How long till you're a mum?' Sijiang tittered, feeling Ah Xing's belly.

'According to the doctor, about another thirteen days. Have you two started making plans yet?' Ah Xing's face was plump and ruddy, with a hint of freckles scattered over it. Sijiang looked at Specs, not sure how to respond.

'You take your time and have a look round. You're our last customers today.' Ah Xing supported her belly as she sat down, picking at her teeth with her nail, as if without a care in the world.

Specs browsed through the section with martial arts novels. He looked through *The Swordsman* then reluctantly put it back.

'Hey come here. Look at this.' Sijiang held up a book called *The Pregnancy Encyclopaedia*. It was at least as thick as two copies of his coveted volume of *The Swordsman*. On the cover was a beautiful woman with a sunny smile.

'I'm going to buy this,' Sijiang said happily.

Specs turned it over to look at the price tag. 'Thirty *kuai*. That's expensive! It's still early. Do we really need to buy it now? Can't we just learn from Ah Xing, Wu Ying and the others?' He looked distractedly back at *The Swordsman* series.

'Eh? That's no good. There's so much to learn and it's annoying to others if you keep pestering them.' It was the first time Sijiang had been so firm.

From where she sat, Ah Xing laughed. 'Just buy it. I'll give you a twenty per cent discount. I don't earn anything from the sale but, you know, just to show my support.'

Specs had no response to that. Sijiang said, 'We'll buy it and *The Swordsman*.'

Specs hesitated, then joked, 'That's a lot of money. We'll have to eat nothing but vegetables and tofu for a while! Sijiang, I don't want the novel. I'd rather eat meat!'

Ah Xing clacked away on a calculator and said, 'Eighty per cent. Just make it fifty *kuai* then.'

Sijiang took a wad of folded notes from an inner pocket, smoothed one out and handed it to Ah Xing.

Specs was still saying, 'Sijiang, don't buy the sword-fighting novel. I was just flipping through it.'

'Come on, don't take the fun out of it. I've known for a long time how much you like to eat meat. Actually I wanted to buy *The Swordsman* for you before but I used the money for meat instead. If I just cut down on the household expenses, it should be OK.'

As Sijiang glared at him, he noticed that her tiny eyes made her a classic beauty, like the famous women of ancient times. He couldn't help but love her all the more for it.

At night when they were back in the dim light at the rented flat, he sat down to study the pregnancy book with her. Specs became unusually serious and excited, as if Sijiang were going to deliver a baby the next day. They were bathed in a special kind of happiness. They turned the pages slowly, lingering over each one, spending half the night poring over the book. When they had just crawled into bed and cuddled up to one another, there was a sudden ruckus. Someone was banging on their door.

'What the hell?' Specs shouted boldly.

'ID check! Let's see your papers!'

'Sijiang, quickly get dressed.' Specs, half-clothed, opened the door. Several men in camouflage uniforms burst rowdily into the room. All had work badges on, but the couple could not see clearly what department they were from. Or, rather, neither Sijiang nor Specs had the guts to look carefully enough. One fellow who seemed to be the lead officer stood in the centre of the room with his feet spread wide apart. Behind him, the others stood ready to be deployed.

'Papers.'

Specs found both of their IDs and temporary residence cards.

'Take out your Family Planning Certificate and let me see that too,' the officer said, looking their documents over slowly.

'Family Planning Certificate?' Specs stammered. He shook his head.

'What's that?' Sijiang was at a loss.

'It's a card for those who aren't married,' said one of the camouflaged men. Like dogs, they had immediately sniffed trouble and were closing in. Sijiang felt their breath crashing in around her like the wind of industrial-sized exhaust fans.

'You don't have it?' the officer repeated again, with difficulty.

'No. We didn't know we needed it. We'll go and take care of it first thing tomorrow.' Specs didn't know much about these guys.

'Take her in!' The officer waved his hand and four of the camouflaged men moved in, breathing heavily. They took Sijiang's arm, pulled her up and bustled her out the door. Outside, there was a car, sleek and black. No sound was to be heard, aside from the running of engines. There were red lights flashing on the car, like a police van.

'Why are you taking her away? Where are you going with her? What are you doing?' Specs grabbed the officer.

'The women and children's hospital. Remember to bring some money. She'll need to stay for three days.'

'Days? What are you doing to her? What does she need to go to the hospital for? She's not sick!'

Specs cried out in his panic, but in a brief moment, the officer and his car were swallowed up in the darkness.

II

When Specs had rushed to the hospital, everything was brightly lit and overrun with people. It was blazing hot. Every window was lit up, and everyone seemed to be shouldering a heavy burden. Specs was at a loss, not sure where Sijiang had been taken or who to ask. He ran up several staircases, through various departments and finally found himself in a crowd milling around in front of an operating room. Every single seat was occupied and no one seemed the least bit sleepy. People hustled and bustled around him, walking hurriedly, as if it were a clinic on the front line of a war zone. Everything was tense and everyone was anxious.

Specs turned to ask an old woman sitting on a nearby stool. 'Auntie, it's late. What's everyone waiting for? What surgery are they doing here?'

The old woman looked at him a moment, slow to answer. 'I'm waiting for my daughter-in-law. The surgery is sterilisation.'

'Sterilisation?' Specs, feeling he had suffered a staggering blow, almost fell to the ground. Just then, he saw a familiar pair of slippers hanging from a hook on the wall. He picked them up and looked more closely. They were Sijiang's. Blood rushed hotly to his head. He turned and ran to the door of the operating room. Unfortunately, it was locked. He dashed his fist against the words No Admittance printed in red along the glass door. Immediately, he was caught by two men in camouflage.

'What are you doing? Try that again and we'll haul you in,' the men pushed Specs aside with a stern warning.

'I'm looking for my girlfriend. Where is she?' His legs felt weak. He dropped to his knees, as if kneeling before them.

'We don't know. Don't go around making trouble in the surgical ward.'

'You've got the wrong person! She's just a girl! You can't sterilise her! I'm begging you! Doctors! Doctors, I'm begging you! Please let her go!' Specs quaked, crying as he desperately tried to break away. He wanted to go into the surgical ward and to the doctors' offices. He wanted to pull Sijiang off the operating table, but his hands were wrenched firmly behind him by the guys in camouflage, like some criminal they had subdued and contained.

Just then the old woman sitting on the stool, whose face had been so cold moments earlier, stood up and said to Specs, 'Is she a round-faced girl? She was barefoot. She really put up a fight. At the door to the operating room, she yelled for all she was worth. It took four men to come and drag her in, carrying her by the arms and legs. They should be done by now. You're not married? What a shame!' The old woman sighed and, looking ancient, walked back to where she had been sitting.

Specs fell silent. The men in camouflage released their hold on him. He went limp, tumbling to the ground like a mound of wet sand. His glasses slipped. Those plain, cheap glasses that he had bought purposely to make himself look more professional when he went for interviews, were now being trampled underfoot into a crooked heap.

Many pairs of eyes looked on, blank and puzzled, in a sort of numb confusion. They all sat there together in mutual sympathy.

Before the peak season of sterilisations had come round again, Xiaohong had been deployed to another department in the hospital. To be more precise, she was sent to the kitchen. She would wield a knife there, or at least accompany the person wielding the knife to prepare the meals, while the hospital used the opportunity created by the additional traffic to earn a little extra income. It was important to look after the welfare of everyone in the hospital and improve the lives of the working class in this way. Before the hospital chairman Dr Lei had gone into battle, knife in hand, he had sought out Xiaohong for a talk. He made it clear that if she did a good job on kitchen duty then, when the peak season for surgery was over, it would be for the good of the cause. They would all, whether they took up the knife in the kitchen or the operating room, be comrades in the heat of strife, and both jobs were equally glorious.

When Dr Lei broke the news to Xiaohong he said, 'send you down'. It was a loaded phrase. If going to work in the kitchen was really nothing to feel ashamed of, then this silly charade was full of a unique sort of significance all its own.

'I'll do whatever's assigned to me,' Xiaohong said. She felt strange and unhappy, but when the higher-ups so solemnly 'send you down', it doesn't matter whether you feel good or bad, panicked or relaxed, you've just got to knuckle down and get it done.

Next, it was Xia – or the new Publicity Director Mr Xia – who sought out Xiaohong for conversation. Though he had not yet officially been notified of the appointment, he was already starting to break in the new job title. Xia's message was the same as Dr Lei's, almost quoting him word for word, in fact. His performance skills, however, were not quite up to scratch and he gave rather a bad imitation of the doctor's precise accents and emphases. When facing Xiaohong, he was not quite up to acting the part of the hospital chairman.

Xiaohong went straight to the kitchen. She washed vegetables, washed bowls, served vegetables and served rice. Wherever they were short-handed, there she went, flitting here and there like a nightingale. On the third day when they opened for lunch, Xiaohong rolled up her sleeves and in deft movements ladled out the soup and scooped the rice. She collected meal tickets without even looking at the faces of those she took them from. She was too busy to care. It was not at all easy work to serve food during the peak hours. When she finally relaxed, wiping the sweat from her brow, she suddenly noticed Specs lingering outside the window. He had a meal ticket in his hand, but it seemed he didn't know what he was supposed to do. He was not wearing his glasses and he looked like he hadn't slept all night. From his lifeless eyes, she knew for sure something was wrong. She called him but there was no response. When she had called him for the third time, he finally walked over to the window.

'What are you doing? You want something to eat? Who's ill?' Xiaohong fired a volley of questions through the gap in the window.

'Xiaohong. You're here. Sijiang's ill. She's ill.'

'What? Not pregnant!'

'No. *Not* pregnant. She's...'

'Well, go on. What're you stammering for?'

'Ah Hong. Last night, she... she was sterilised!'

'Oh God! Fuck!' Xiaohong slipped back into her hometown dialect as she cursed. She threw her spoon, splattering the carrot and pork rib soup everywhere. She wove her way through the kitchen on her two slender legs and followed Specs hastily to the Inpatient Ward.

III

The Inpatient Ward was calm and peaceful, like the rhythmic toss of a boat enduring a storm. Patients and their relatives laughed softly, chatting about the past, reviving family memories and renewing the ties of kinship. Occasionally, a woman would groan. Mostly it was just whining, since the physical pain was only minimal, as if to remind her loved ones she had gone under the knife and of the sacrifice that she had made. Ninety per cent of the women here had undergone the sterilisation procedure. The ones who had endured the knife lay on the beds like cut grass scattered across a field. Xiaohong and Specs were like farmers planting rice. When they traversed the field, it was not a smooth path. They squeezed between the wall and the row of beds, knocking their shins countless times as they crossed the room, advancing toward Sijiang's bed.

The air was full of a smell, an odour of complex nuances. Not just the clothes stained black as mud, and not merely the smell of unbathed human flesh caked with filth. No single odour could be identified. It was more like the odour of pus in a wound, a fatty, sour, fermented smell. Xiaohong controlled herself, suppressing the impulse to puke. After a moment of gaining her composure, a fresh wave of overwhelming sadness hit her, renewing the desire to vomit.

Living people, but dirtier than animals. In the pig sty at home, with a sow and her dozen or so piglets, eating and drinking from a common space, the smell was not even a tenth as disgusting as this place.

People valued less than animals. Even a pig set aside to be spayed was allowed to wait until its proper time. Sijiang was just nineteen, and here she was neutered like an old sow.

Sijiang would have cherished the feeling of being a new mother more than most. Someone who would especially relish the whole birth experience, if sterilised, would definitely feel the pain of the blow more acutely than most. Oh, Li Sijiang! Xiaohong didn't dare to think about how her friend might actually be feeling right now.

A few years ago, something similar had happened back in Xiaohong's village. The Family Planning Office made a surprise attack in the middle of the night to round people up. It seemed that a woman who had three daughters escaped, so the staff took the youngest girl and sterilised her. Whether it was a case of mistaken identity or a matter of spite, the outcome was that she was barren, plain and simple. She would never be able to bring another labourer into the nation's workforce. Who would want to marry her? The girl finally ran to the river and killed herself, making the outcome plainer and simpler still.

Xiaohong, worrying as she walked, suddenly saw the homely form of Sijiang, lying on a white bed. She didn't know why, out of so many white beds, her eye found Sijiang at a single glance. The girl lay there blankly, limbs flopped carelessly on the sheet, blandly staring up at the ceiling until Xiaohong reached her. Two tears plainly flowed down her cheeks.

'Hey Sijiang, don't lie there like this,' Xiaohong advised, suppressing her own tears as she persuaded her friend. She just wanted to cheer Sijiang up, but even she felt it was all a load of crap. If she were the one who had been sterilised, she would be even more deeply in despair than Sijiang was. She would snap at anyone who came near.

Xiaohong tried to quell the anger in her belly. She kept herself from cursing aloud. She knew this was not the time for cursing. This was the time for easing Sijiang's suffering. Sijiang couldn't move – didn't want to move – and so just lay there, face becoming more drawn. She was no longer that young girl from the days at the salon, face fresh and round as an apple.

Specs sat quietly on the bed watching her, looking even more un-comfortable than if he had been castrated himself. In fact, as a man who had failed to protect his woman, he *had* been emasculated. He felt guilty. And, with his woman's sterilisation, he was as good as castrated anyway. He patted Sijiang's hand a moment then put a hand on her forehead, as if hoping to bring back the old Sijiang with his touch. Her listless eyes looked straight ahead, hoping for a miracle. After lying still as a block of wood for a long while, Sijiang suddenly showed a ruth-less urge to cry, but that pulled at the wound and the physical pain it caused made her restrain herself. She slowly resumed that wooden gaze.

There were six beds in Sijiang's ward. The room was bright and clean. Even the flies were too ashamed to stay, wandering in only to make a single circuit before flying back out of the window. Having seen the place they had passed through, the mixed ward with dozens of patients, Xiaohong and Specs could tell this place was a level higher. Sijiang was enjoying superior treatment. No doubt about it, this was a clear sign that someone was trying to cover up a guilty conscience.

The faces of the nearby women who had also gone under the knife were all full of sympathy. They were able to take a little comfort from Sijiang's situation, feeling that at least their own surgeries were 'justi-fied'. And, furthermore, the prospects for their own sex lives after this ordeal still looked bright. As they ate apples, they politely offered some to Sijiang. Xiaohong, feeling that this friendliness vaguely implied complicity, politely refused.

Lying in the second bed was a woman of about thirty, seemingly the wife of a wealthy local farmer. She lay casually, and when her child needed to be breast-fed, unable to sit up, she simply laid it across her body in a chaotic arc. Several people attended her, coming in and out in a constant stream.

'First let your wounds heal. Don't develop any other complications. As soon as you recuperate, you should sue them for compensation, at least a hundred thousand *yuan* or so,' the breast-feeding woman said.

'Yeah, you definitely gotta get some money. You can't have kids. Who's gonna marry you? Who's gonna take care of you when you're old?' The breast-feeding woman's mother-in-law looked on with a worried expression, hitting right at the heart of the matter with those few words. When she had finished, she clucked her tongue and shook her head, then she took up the nursing child in her arms, turned it towards her and kissed it twice before continuing to play with it.

What the old lady had said hit a tender spot with Sijiang, renewing her grief. Tears gushed violently from her.

'I'll marry you, Sijiang. Don't cry. Crying is going to make the wound worse. I want to marry you!' Specs clumsily wiped Sijiang's tears, his movements heavy, as if scrubbing at a particularly stubborn stain.

His calm tone shocked Xiaohong. She suddenly felt this humble-looking guy was such a beautiful, shining light. Xiaohong became more emotional and the second round of tears fell more heavily than the first. Wiping her eyes, she turned to Specs and said, 'Let's go. I'll take you to the head of the hospital.'

IV

Dr Lei was not easy to find at all. He was right in the middle of the peak season's increased activity. The fourth time they knocked on his office door, he finally heard and that mouth that couldn't grow whiskers of any length called out a deep, 'Come in!' On his head was a white cap, and a surgical mask dangled from his ear. He drank water from the cup of his stainless steel thermos. When he saw Xiaohong and Specs, he was a little caught off guard. His face was too pale, and that surprised expression was all too clearly seen, like a shadow passing across it.

'You two... have a seat. What can I do for you?'

Xiaohong glanced at Specs, indicating that he should speak up.

'You all... sterilised her... we aren't even married yet... you all... have gone too far!' Specs had too much to say and not enough breath to say it.

The chairman looked very confused.

'Dr Lei, you got the wrong person. His girlfriend, her name's Li Sijiang. She's not married yet, and the hospital sterilised her!'

'I heard about that, but it's nothing to do with the hospital.' Dr Lei was quick to shift the blame.

'But sir, this happened at our hospital. It's our hospital that did the surgery!' Seeing Dr Lei's flippant manner, a fury began to well up in Xiaohong, smouldering inside.

'I can tell you this. Li Sijiang's name was swapped for a local farmer's wife who has four daughters. She was trying to hide, wanting to escape the family planning regulations. No one thought they would stoop to such trickery. It's very wicked. But don't worry, they'll find out exactly who is responsible. The authorities will investigate carefully. The hospital merely performs the procedure. If the surgery goes wrong or there are complications, that's the hospital's responsibility.'

'I want to know, who performed Li Sijiang's operation?'

'Yeah, who did it?' Specs echoed, as if just striking upon the crux of the matter.

'Whoever did it, it's all the same. There's no personal liability. When something like this happens – and this is the first time – we give it careful attention.' Dr Lei didn't think this pair of common wage earners was worth a second thought.

'Why won't you admit that it was you who did it? I went and checked with Xiao Yuan. You were on duty. You did the surgery. That day you performed eighty-eight operations in all. You broke the previous record for the most operations in a day, didn't you?' Xiaohong laid her cards on the table. In one day, eighty-eight women underwent the sterilisation procedure and yet only one person walked carefree out of that operating room, and that was Chairman Lei Yigang.

Dr Lei was surprised Xiaohong could remember the figures from the report.

'Is it possible you didn't hear her screaming? She's just a girl! Why didn't you hear? Are you all deaf? You didn't see her struggling? And just like that, you ruined her, without even the least bit of pity! Even veterinarians wouldn't behave like that!' Specs stood up furiously. He thought of the four butchers heaving Sijiang to the operating table and this animal surgeon taking his knife so nonchalantly to her. He began to tremble in his anger. But he just stood there with his arms spread wide, uncertain what to do with his two huge hands.

'When they come in on the gurney, they cry and they shout. They all do. After you give them the anaesthetic, they quieten down.' Dr Lei had obviously received a shock. He leaned his head back several centimetres. He looked at Specs and seeing no further action from that quarter, the colour returned to his face. He went on to say, 'Let me add, I really do sympathise with your situation. The hospital won't charge you any fees for the surgery, medication or hospitalisation. Just relax and recuperate.'

V

During the peak season at the hospital, those who were busy were extremely busy and those who were not were bored to tears. The busy ones went madly about their work updating statistics, recording the number of those being sterilised. How many were sterilised in the morning, in the afternoon, at night. Whether there were complications. Whether there were side-effects. All over the hospital, the talk was about nothing else but sterilisation, reproductive organs and women's issues, and there was unprecedented attention to the way of going about it all.

Xia was suddenly occupied with important matters, which came as something of a surprise to Youqing. It was the administrative offices and labs that were the most leisurely. For the time being, no one bothered about Youqing's menstrual problem or her fiancé's work assignments. She was idle and lonely. At first, she wavered between Xia and Xiao Yuan, considering the advantages she liked so much in each of the two men and mulling over their shortcomings. She hated that she could not bundle the two up into one, making the perfect man, just for her.

In the morning, Xiaohong was in the kitchen washing vegetables when she felt something wrong. Her period had come. She wiped her hands and hastily went to her dorm to sort herself out. She had just climbed halfway up the second flight of stairs, when she saw Youqing's door on the third floor open, and a man's heel came into view, followed by another, then by the legs, back and finally the head. Obviously the couple was still completing their goodbyes.

'Alright. Hurry up. It's about time for work. If people find out, it will be bad.' Youqing finished her whining speech, then kissed him a couple of times, pushing him out and closing the door. Xiaohong rushed back a couple of steps to the floor below then pretended to be just coming into the stairwell. At the point where the staircase turned between the second and third floors, she 'bumped' into Xiao Yuan.

'Hey! Good morning.' Xiaohong smiled in a tacit understanding then noticed that Xiao Yuan's zip was only half closed, as if it had been hastily done up. In snatching some pleasure during working hours, Youqing had rushed him a little too much. Or perhaps he was the one who was a little too hasty, making love as quickly as clearing his bowels rather than taking the time to enjoy himself. Xiaohong gave another knowing smile and pointed at his crotch.

Xiao Yuan looked down and, as he zipped up his fly, said jocularly, 'Hey, you shouldn't be looking.'

'I thought you were showing it off on purpose.' Xiaohong found dealing with men to be a simple thing, joking easily like this with them. With women, especially the doctors and staff at the hospital, it was different. Just take her relationship with Youqing. It was as hard as uncooked rice, no matter what she did.

'What're you doing here anyway? I'm off to work.' Xiao Yuan said as he walked down the stairs. When he tried to pass Xiaohong, the staircase was too narrow. She did her best to pull her breasts in close but still brushed them up against his arm. Or rather, let his arm brush up against her chest.

'My period came,' Xiaohong said provocatively. Xiao Yuan smiled shyly at her and walked off quickly. Xiaohong watched him go down the staircase and open the door. She noticed that his arse was like a woman's, full and sensuous.

VI

When Liao dropped in, Xiaohong's holiday was over. She pretended that her back was hurting so that Liao would not dare act rashly. He was becoming more urgent, always reaching an end just as Xiaohong was beginning to get excited. The duration was shorter each time. It was like an incurable disease. He just could not help himself. The more he worried about his endurance, the more quickly things came to an end. The more Xiaohong concentrated on reaching a climax, worrying that he would come to an early finish, the more unlikely she was to climax at all. Over time, it became a vicious circle. Xiaohong put up with it for a while then grew irritable. She had lost the morsel of interest she had once taken in Liao's body. All the same, even if they didn't engage in physical relations, Xiaohong was willing to carry on with him. He had plenty of fresh ideas, was always full of good advice and knew a lot about life. What he didn't understand was why his cock had become so powerless.

He chatted about some of the recent cases he had encountered. It all sounded a lot like the hospital. Other than the doctors, there were no healthy people. Hearing about the cases just created a feeling that the world was in turmoil. There was murder, arson, adultery, prostitution and gambling everywhere. He mentioned Julia Wilde now and then, and how time just ticked on without regard for human suffering. As he chatted casually, he took some pleasure in Xiaohong's upper body.

Xiaohong's breasts were not as sensitive as before. She was virtually numb as Liao caressed her. Later, he rubbed his naked thigh back and forth over hers, slowly finding some satisfaction. Suddenly, he seemed preoccupied. He sighed, then stopped stroking her and said, 'Xiaohong, I'm getting married.'

Xiaohong remained silent.

'I'm getting married!' he repeated loudly. Then he buried his face into her large bosom. The room was dark and he could only see the curves of her body. She seemed to be asleep. Liao shifted so that there was a space between them, then moved to the other side of the bed and lay there.

'You should get married. Don't waste your youth and your lively sperm. When you're married, you will have a perfect place to store them.'

Xiaohong was wide awake.

VII

Prior to being discharged from the hospital, Sijiang suddenly came down with a high fever. She came very close to registering her name for the afterlife. It left just as suddenly as it had come on. It scared the hospital staff half to death. If Sijiang got ill and died like that, this surgical procedure would become an even more complicated issue. Sijiang became an object to be carefully protected. The doctors and nurses came in turn, touching her forehead and checking her temperature. They did everything they could, acting as if Sijiang were their own daughter.

Dr Lei, representing the hospital, came especially to see Sijiang. The visiting envoy had a huge team with him. Lined up in order of priority behind Dr Lei were the hospital's vice president, chief executive officer and several departmental heads who had come spontaneously to support the rest. They surrounded Sijiang, looking down at her in turn, as if paying respect to her mortal remains. She felt like a martyr returning home from some heroic battle. They stayed for a few short minutes, expressed brief words of earnest expectation then filed out. Their white forms receded from the room like a solemn row of priests, slowly disappearing into the ward.

Sijiang's hair was dishevelled. Her face, once the fever was gone, wore a faint smile. It was the first time she had done so since the operation. Her smile brought a happy tremble to Specs's lips, and he cried, 'Sijiang! It's good to see you smile!'

Specs held her clammy hand, looking like he would never leave her side. Her body had begun to give off a thick odour of sweat, like a length of nearly rotten meat. But this cut of meat could move now and its fingers were flexible once again. When Specs told her that the hospital fees and medication were all to be absorbed by the hospital, she curled those fingers round the medicine and popped it into her mouth, looking much more relaxed. Perhaps the drugs had numbed her. No matter how tough the pill was to swallow, it also had a wonderful aftertaste to it. Once she was given injections in her hip, or some liquid medicine, she no longer looked like she was going to join the heroic ranks of martyrdom.

'Sijiang, we'll work out what to do when you're out of hospital. We can sue them, get compensation and an explanation,' Specs said quietly but firmly, almost as if he were shaking a fist.

Sijiang nodded, fully empowering Specs to act in the matter, just as if he were already head of the family.

Thirteen

I

Youqing, the little bitch, was kind of pushy. Making use of the hospital's karaoke room for a party, she called all the doctors and her friends together to celebrate her twenty-fifth birthday and went on about it constantly. The karaoke room was big and equipped with a fair-sized dance floor. The older doctors took a few turns then went home to their wives, leaving the younger singletons to carry on partying. Youqing had taken extra care in making herself up. Hair washed, blow-dried and swept across her forehead in the most fashionable style, she was quite charming.

Xiaohong had not intended to join the party. She hesitated for a long time but seeing as Youqing had invited her, she felt she should at least go and offer her congratulations. When Xiaohong came sauntering in, she saw Youqing dressed in a perky white dress, looking like a butterfly spinning proudly across the dance floor. Xiaohong sat down, peeled a banana and drank some tea. She took out a present wrapped in bright paper, waiting to give it to Youqing when the dance was over. Youqing swayed in Xiao Yuan's arms, dancing slowly. She turned, gliding to one side then twisted the other way before returning to his embrace, like a yo-yo reaching the end of its line before coming back to the palm. Xiao Yuan handled Youqing's body with a delicate touch, as if he held a little chick in his hand.

When she had finished her turn about the dance floor, Youqing saw Xiaohong. She tossed Xiao Yuan aside and went over to the table.

'Ah Hong!' she said, 'you just arrived?'

'Happy birthday, Youqing. I had something I needed to do, so I'm a bit late. Here's a lipstick case, just a little something for you,' Xiaohong said, handing the pretty little package to her.

'You didn't have to do that. Here, have an apple.' Youqing took the gift from her as she welcomed Xiaohong like a courteous host.

'Why don't you dance?' Youqing said to Xiaohong, waving to the men.

When the light from the dance floor flashed across Youqing's face, Xiaohong suddenly saw on her earlobes a pair of green studs. Other than the colour, which she could not see very clearly, the earrings were just like those Julia Wilde had always worn, exactly the same size and style. The image of Julia in those studs leapt into Xiaohong's mind.

'Hey, Youqing, those earrings are really pretty! I like them.' Xiaohong laid hold of Youqing. Moving in closer to look at the earrings, her fingers squeezed tightly on the other girl's arm. When the lights flashed on them again, illuminating Youqing's face, Xiaohong was almost certain that this was the same pair of green earrings.

'I like them too,' Youqing said, smiling happily.

'Where'd you buy them? I'd like to get a pair,' Xiaohong said casually.

Youqing, smiling sweetly, was invited to dance with one of the men. Xiaohong sat down slowly, her heart pounding. She was excited by the mystery, so excited she was filled with a sort of terror. It was as if she had just seen Julia Wilde herself walk into the party, making her hair stand on end and her skin crawl. She felt like she had seen a ghost. She suddenly began to tremble violently.

She looked through the crowd at Xia, who was weaving his way through the tables and chairs on his way out of the karaoke room.

11

Xiaohong tossed and turned on her bed for half an hour, trying to sleep. She suddenly felt something caressing her chest, then a wet tongue was dragged across her breast, licking and sucking on it. She had just begun to feel very comfortable when the licking and sucking turned into a pair of manly hands, poking, prodding and pinching with fingers hard as dead twigs. She felt the pain, and cursed angrily. Jolted into wakefulness, she heard the last of the cursing escape her mouth, 'Fuck!'

She got up. Without bothering to turn on the light, by the dim glow from the window she flip-flopped in her bedroom slippers to the bathroom to relieve herself, listening to the splashing sound through her sleepy daze. She straightened up, rubbed her eyes, went back to the room and plopped down onto the bed again. Feeling her pyjamas were a bit tight, she tugged at the front, then the back, yanking at the fabric. As she pulled, she discovered that her breasts were swollen, as if her body were inflated. She probed her breasts and found that they were tender to the touch. She might as well bare her breasts, the way they were swelling, as if demanding to be released. They bounced a couple of times, like balls falling to the ground. She pressed them with both hands and felt they had grown. Inspecting them again, she did not find any lumps. They were as soft as they had always been. She took comfort in touching them for a moment and it occurred to her that the swelling might have been caused by ovulation. Putting the matter out of her mind, she went back to sleep.

The next morning when she was putting on her bra, she realised that she had not imagined the extent of the swelling. Practically speaking, her bra could not cover her breasts. The flesh spilled over the bounds of the garment. Like flowing oil, they refused to be bound. Xiaohong undressed and stared at the things she had been carrying for years. She could not understand why this cycle of ovulation was causing such a major change. She sat down again and examined them carefully. The flesh was white with the small blue lines of blood vessels showing through like earthworms crawling under the surface. She noticed that the nipples were redder than normal and that they stood up as if excited. The look was that of a balloon not fully blown up, with plenty of room left for expansion.

Xiaohong tossed the bra aside, picking up some loose-fitting clothes to put on. It did not cross her mind that, from now on, her breasts might only live without the confines of a bra. She walked slower than usual, so that the unfettered swing of those two fellows inside her clothes wouldn't be too extreme. She felt like a woman suffering from engorged breasts, but without a child to nurse.

'Wow, you're not wearing a bra anymore. Fashionable.' Youqing was not the first person to discover that Xiaohong had not worn a bra, but she was the first to announce it in shrill tones. Xiaohong had just plopped two scoops of rice into a bowl and handed it to Youqing. With the movements of her body, her breasts glided here and slid there, like bowling balls on a well-waxed alley. Laughing, Xiaohong scooped her own rice and went to sit with Youqing.

'Where'd you buy those earrings? I really like them.' Now out of the dance floor lighting, Xiaohong could clearly see the earrings Youqing was wearing. They were light green. She knew without a doubt that they were Julia's.

'My lover gave them to me. I'm sure you can't buy them.' Youqing's arrogance reared its head again.

'Which lover? Can I guess?' Xiaohong sipped at her soup, only half-joking.

'You'd never guess.' Youqing smirked. Her hair was still the same as it had been at her party. Obviously she had not washed it since then.

'Give me three guesses.'

'What makes you think I've got three lovers?'

'I only know of Xiao Yuan. So, can I guess?'

'Sure. But if you don't get it right, you have to eat four more scoops of rice.'

'Xia Jifeng.'

'What the hell?' Surprised, Youqing denied it sharply.

'Then it's Xiao Yuan?' Xiaohong said with a weak smile.

'*Non.* Last chance.'

'Or.... Xia Jifeng.'

'Uh—!' Youqing coughed as if she had swallowed a jar of pepper. She sputtered, her face turning red and her eyes beginning to water.

III

The peak season had passed and the powers that be had not notified Xiaohong to go back to the publicity department. The hospital seemed to have forgotten the matter. Xiaohong waited several days and, while she was waiting, received a telegram from her sister saying her father had died. Xiaohong, feeling that the world had turned black, took a week off work to go home for the funeral.

She called Liao from the train station and told him about Youqing's earrings. She said that they were just like those Julia had often worn and that, since they had been a family heirloom, it was not possible to buy them in a market today. Perhaps this was a clue, she said. Liao replied enthusiastically, 'We'll investigate. If they really are Julia's earrings, it's certainly a very important clue that could be the key to the case.'

'I'm at Guangzhou train station. My dad died. I've got to make a quick trip home.' Xiaohong hung up, biting her lip. She fought to hold back the tears, her throat tight, and walked calmly through the crowd.

When she got home, her sister told her that their father had had an accident at the construction site. A heavy object had fallen on him and he had drawn his final breath on the way to the hospital.

As her sister spoke, she looked at Xiaohong's chest with eyes that were red from crying. 'Why're they... like that?' She noticed the unusually large breasts.

'I don't know. It's like they get bigger by the day. They don't hurt. I don't feel anything at all.'

The shape of her sister's worn-out bra was visible through her silky-thin blouse. She sighed, not knowing what to say.

The older sister pondered for a long time and finally added in a hesitating tone, 'You're already twenty. You shouldn't still be developing.'

'Alright, alright. Let them grow. Let's see how big they want to get,' Xiaohong answered irritably.

Thinking she had angered Xiaohong, her sister closed her mouth and silently stared at their father's coffin on the other side of the room where the wake was being held. There were three photos of the household's deceased. They were arranged in order, Grandfather's first, then Grandmother's then Father's. Only Mother's was missing. They wondered why her photo was not hung with the rest. They had never thought to ask their father while he was alive. He was the only one who knew the reason and now he would never be able to sit down and explain it all to them.

'Have you started making plans with your boyfriend yet?' To her sister, Xiaohong was no longer young. After all, when she was Xiaohong's age, she was already a wife and mother.

Xiaohong searched her mind for a moment, thinking through her relationships with the men who were close to her but she could not reach a satisfactory conclusion. She could not even think of one worth calling a boyfriend, so how could she make any plans? She wasn't even sure what sort of plans she should be making. Maybe her sister had asked the wrong question. She should have just said, Have you slept with other men? That was a question with a clear answer.

Finally, she settled on an answer. *'Jie Jie*, when I decide to make plans, I'll bring him here to meet you.'

Xiaohong was a little depressed. She suddenly felt her sister's life was a happy one. Even though her brother-in-law liked to have his fun, the couple always slept side by side, quarrelled with one another, made love and worked together in the fields.

A clucking sound bubbled over. A hen that had just laid an egg hopped out from the coop, proudly singing. It strutted about the empty ground with its head held high. It greeted the sun and the sun dropped the colours of youth upon it. Recalling for Xiaohong the warmth of her grandmother's lap, it shone onto the canopy that sheltered her father's wake. Tears began to fall, streaming down her cheeks.

'Don't cry. Save your tears for the funeral procession.'

The voice was that of the bearded Jin Haishu. He pulled a hemp rope over the coffin, preparing to carry it out of the hall where the wake had been held. The veins on his arms protruded with the heroic level of effort it required. About thirty-five, Jin had been a soldier for ten years. After his demobilisation, he had returned to the village and entered the ranks of the cadres. He was a powerful man, in a position of authority. Practically every woman in the village idolised him.

Jin's words did not seem to be coloured with emotion but Xiaohong heard in them the concern of the village leaders. Her tears seemed to shut off like a tap. She looked at Jin and he averted his gaze from her bust. He caught her eye and smiled vaguely, his longing turning to affection. A dizzy feeling flowed from Xiaohong's mind to her chest, making several rounds of her body's private places and giving rise to warm fluids.

'When you were little, I used to carry you,' Jin said.

Xiaohong did not answer, picturing in her mind the image of Jin holding her.

'I'd often pick you up with one hand, or throw you into the air. You'd laugh so sweetly. Ah, and here you are now, all grown up in the blink of an eye.' When he said 'grown up' his eyes fell to Xiaohong's chest, as if to indicate the growth of her breasts.

Xiaohong looked at his big hands but didn't say anything.

'What day is my dad's funeral procession?' she asked, suddenly thinking of it.

'Tomorrow. If there are still other relatives we need to wait for, we can hold off until the day after tomorrow. Tonight, we'll keep vigil.'

'I'll stay up.'

'You should.'

IV

As Specs was leaving the newspaper office, he felt he was like a ball, bouncing rhythmically and reaching a great height.

A newspaper reporter had prepared an interview concerning Sijiang's situation. He hoped that, when the report appeared, it would stir up public interest and build some momentum, finally resulting in a wave of public opinion that would help Sijiang reach a favourable outcome to her case.

When the reporter came to their flat, Sijiang did not want to speak to him, feeling that sacrificing that much of her privacy would be unbearably embarrassing. She was even more reluctant to reveal her real name. She evaded him for some time, while the reporter emphasised over and over that by making her name known publicly, she would get better compensation. Sijiang began, reluctantly, to answer the reporter's questions. When he asked her about how she felt after the surgery, she wept as desolately as if facing her own father with this news. She cried until her throat was raw. Gasping, she answered, 'I wanted to die.

I desperately wanted to die. If it hadn't been for him standing beside me every minute, every second...' She could say no more. She stopped, burying her face in her hands.

'Go on, let it out.' As she cried, Specs reached over and patted her back, as if doing so would speed up the grieving process. The reporter, turning his attention to Specs, asked how they'd met and fallen in love. He sighed a lot, recognising the sincere feelings of stress expressed by Specs.

'Simple working class folk with such a deeply moving love story. It's the paper's obligation to report this. It's our duty to spread light and love. People everywhere need to know the truth.'

Even the reporter seemed to be moved nearly to tears. He looked back over his notes, thinking carefully, afraid of missing anything and considering whether there was any additional little nugget he could dig out.

Specs smiled humbly, as if to say that it was a small thing. If you love someone, isn't this how it should be?

As the conversation between Specs and the reporter went on, Sijiang gradually stopped crying. It was like she was stepping into a role. Perhaps it was as the reporter had said and she was indeed the heroine in this love story. She no longer felt it was a stigma. Her eyes brightened and she found the courage to face the reporter.

'You can't have children. What do you plan to do?' the reporter asked, turning first to Sijiang, then to Specs.

'We'll adopt,' Specs said.

'It'll be just like having our own,' Sijiang added. The reporter looked from one face to the other, feeling they looked pretty unconcerned, considering all that had happened. He nodded as he took a glance around at the environment, looking just a little envious of their love nest.

As the reporter was leaving, Specs seized the opportunity to ask him a question. 'How much do you think is appropriate for us to claim?'

The reporter turned back and thought a moment before replying. 'I've never seen a situation like this before, but I'd say sixty or eighty thousand should be possible. Of course, there are some things that cannot be compensated.'

'Well, we'll settle for eighty thousand, then, and we won't stop till we get it,' Sijiang said to Specs after the reporter had gone.

She suddenly found that Specs had a cigarette in his mouth, and he was acting like he knew just what he was doing with it. She didn't know where it had come from. She cried sharply, 'You smoke? How come I didn't know?'

'It's not mine. That reporter gave it to me just now. Seems a pity to waste it. Can you find a match for me? I'm going to smoke it,' he said.

'Don't. It's addictive.'

'How will I get addicted? I'm going to smoke this one. You afraid I'm going to smoke us into the poorhouse? Silly girl. Wait till we get our eighty thousand. We won't be poor then. By the way, what do you want to do once we've got it?' Specs seemed to have all sorts of plans, as if he already had the cash in his hand. He dragged on the cigarette like an old pro.

'I'll go to beauty school. I want to open a salon. There should be plenty for a salon. Then we'll rent a nicer flat too, save some money, and buy a place later.' Sijiang's calculations were always very down to earth.

Specs released a smoky breath, not quite agreeing with Sijiang's plan. He inhaled so deeply that his eyebrows wrinkled up and his eyes narrowed to a thin line. His Adam's apple moved up and down, as if swallowing a word. Catching a glimmer of hope in his face, she began to initiate some affectionate intimacy with him but he was not particularly interested. He held the cigarette butt, dragging on it desperately. Even when it had burned nearly all the way down, he still put it fearlessly to his lips. Sijiang took it and tossed it to the floor, placing her own mouth to his. Specs sat passively, like a woman waiting to be stirred to the point of excitement, numbly waiting for the feeling to find him.

V

Dr Lei had been looking haggard recently. With the peak season of surgeries over, he seemed on the verge of mental collapse. In fact, it was quite odd to see him like this. The other doctors had been through the same peak season and none of them were showing signs of collapse. As head honcho, he could have easily taken some time off. All the doctors who met him would say, 'Dr Lei, you're overworked! Take a few days off.'

It was as if all the work had been done by him, all those tubes cut by his own hand. Dr Lei would just put a smile on his hairless face and say, 'Everyone's in the same boat. We're all overworked.'

Three days after Xiaohong had left, a new girl of twenty-two or -three was promoted to the publicity department. Xia helped her clear out Xiaohong's desk, putting everything from the drawers into a pile and laying it aside. The girl sat on Xiaohong's chair. Rolling it back and forth over the floor a couple of times, she said to Xia, 'I don't like these moving chairs.'

'Then we'll buy one that doesn't roll,' he said.

'I don't like the desk facing the door,' she said, still not satisfied.

'Then we'll move it,' Xia said and immediately got to work moving it.

*

When Liao and his partner entered the door of the publicity department, they heard the sound of desks being dragged across the floor. Liao knocked on Dr Lei's door. The chairman was sitting in his large boardroom-style chair with his eyes closed. When the two armed police officers came in, Dr Lei stood up hurriedly, nearly sweeping his mug off the table as he did so.

'What do you need... can I help you?' He started to pour tea for them.

Liao held out a hand to stop him. 'Sorry to trouble you. We need you to find Yu Youqing for us. We need her help in our investigation of a case,' he said.

'Yu Youqing? The lab technician? Oh, well, wait a moment.'

He picked up the phone and called the lab. 'Ask Yu Youqing to come to my office, please.'

As they waited for Youqing, Liao asked the chairman a few simple questions about the girl's situation. When he asked about her love life, Dr Lei said, 'I don't get involved in the private lives of my employees. I don't know anything about that. You'll have to ask her yourself.'

Liao nodded, appreciating Dr Lei's respect for his employees' privacy.

There was a knock on the door. Dr Lei's 'Come in' seemed to get stuck in his throat. At first glance, Liao noticed that she was wearing the light green earrings.

'You're Yu Youqing?' Liao began. She nodded, looking at each person with an exaggeratedly bold expression.

'Please take off your earrings and let me have a look,' Liao said, pointing at Youqing's ears.

She removed the earrings and put them on Dr Lei's desk. Liao picked them up to have a closer look, put them back down, then stood up to top up his tea with water.

'Where did you buy these?'

'I didn't buy them,' Youqing said.

'Please explain in more detail.'

'Why should I? It's my own private business.'

'We'd appreciate your cooperation. It is crucial that you tell us.'

'A friend gave them to me for my birthday.'

'Who's your friend?'

'A man.'

'Be more specific. Give me his name. Occupation. Employer.'

Youqing did not say anything. She wore a pained expression.

Liao glanced at her. She was staring at Dr Lei.

'I think this is a matter of Ms Yu's privacy. We should respect that. We cannot let this matter violate the privacy of innocent people,' Dr Lei said, thinking the police had pressed too far.

'Dr Lei, the case we are investigating has cost another woman her life. Life or privacy? Which is more important? Ms Yu, please continue. We need you to cooperate.'

'Her life?' Youqing's shocked expression made her face taper to a point at the chin.

'Yes, her life. It's a serious matter.'

The water in the dispenser started to gurgle, bubbles rolling to the surface. A car horn sounded as it passed beneath the open window. A breeze came through the window, ruffling the official documents on the desk. It was warm. Dr Lei's pale face began to sweat, perspiration trailing down along his ears, drawing two thin streaks down the sides of his face. He shifted his weight in the chair, remaining seated behind his desk.

Youqing twisted her fingers together uneasily and faced the window. The clock on the wall ticked crisply as it marked time.

'It was... Dr Lei who gave them to me,' she finally said.

Dr Lei's chair creaked underneath his weight.

VI

Aunt Chun and her long triangular tear streaks changed her tune very quickly. Because of her daughter's situation, she was especially critical of Xiaohong, who hadn't found a job for her daughter. It eventually developed into contempt for the whole city of Shenzhen and a complete rejection of Xiaohong. She looked down on anyone who left their home soil and went far away to hang out with God-knows-what-kind of people. She said Xiaohong's nose had turned up, just like a monkey's. And so, Aunt Chun didn't bother to visit Xiaohong anymore. She scorned the girl, as if in an attempt to recapture her own lost dignity. When Xiaohong's father died, Aunt Chun still said, 'My daughter won't set foot in that little goblin's place. Who knows what sort of misfortune might come her way there? If she does, her father will beat her half to death!'

Whenever Aunt Chun got excited over such things, she had a habit of spreading the word around, as if she would choke on it if she didn't. At the funeral, when she saw Xiaohong, she thought the girl's mourning was not sufficiently distraught and began once again to spread news of the girl's misdeeds. The story she cooked up this time was that Xiaohong must have borne a bastard child in Shenzhen and that was why her breasts were so swollen now. Even outside of the village, news hopped from here to there, like corn popping in a pan. Even when the scrap metal collectors came round, Aunt Chun told them all about it, letting the topic slowly wander to Xiaohong's body. She relished this rendition of the tale and when she had concluded, both speaker and listener were satisfied, each enjoying their own role in the game.

'Things in Shenzhen are not normal for Qian Xiaohong.'

'Qian Xiaohong's breasts have grown so much because of it.'

Xiaohong herself knew nothing of all of this.

From early on, Xiaohong had no intention of returning to the village to live. She couldn't get along with the old fossils here. That was her reasoning and she was proud of it.

The morning of her father's funeral procession, Xiaohong could clearly feel the increased weight of her enlarged breasts. They were falling forward, pulling her down with them. They pulled until she felt she would fall to her knees, crouching forward on the ground. It was as if she had no choice but to acknowledge her imagined guilt before the whole village. Xiaohong began to feel it was as cumbersome as carrying around a pair of boulders. She tried to put on a snug-fitting camisole, tightly binding her breasts in place. It turned them into shapeless fatty lumps, no longer looking like breasts at all. She felt oppressed and sad, all her self-confidence collapsing into frustration. Finally, she decided to just release them, preferring to let them swing.

Along the route of her father's procession, according to village customs, she continually stopped to kneel, get up, and walk a little further, before repeating the whole procedure. She was breathless with exhaustion. Perspiring, she felt even her tears had turned to sweat. The two mingled together, falling from her face to the road. Along the way, accompanied by the hammering, humming chant from the temple, she kept pace with the slow, steady rhythm of the pallbearers. When they were supposed to cry, they cried. When they were supposed to speak, they spoke. When they were supposed to be silent, they gritted their teeth and kept quiet. Because of the weight of the coffin, they could not speak anyway.

Jin Haishu was the lead pallbearer. He walked on the front left corner of the coffin, with a towel on his right shoulder to prevent the wood from chafing his skin. He had another long towel across his shoulders, with which he constantly wiped his sweat away. Like everyone else, he wore no shoes. His bare feet moved forward, one step at a time. But unlike the rest, his eyes were always on Xiaohong and the pair of breasts that were weighing her down.

Xiaohong's sister wept in a most professional manner, tears streaming down her nose. Every performing artist in the world would be put to shame by the stellar performance this uneducated woman put on in portraying her grief. She was simultaneously in high spirits and in despair, both of which were important to her sense of rhythm. It was a tedious process. Xiaohong had never noticed before but her sister was an artist. She was a folk singer and a dancer. Her mourning voice made the flesh on Xiaohong's back creep.

Her sister's confused cries were like the chattering of a life. It made Xiaohong want to laugh. She stood beside her sister offering what comfort she could, but felt like an outsider who had nothing to do with the funeral party at all. Infected by her sister's mood, Xiaohong gazed about her. Each time she saw Jin Haishu's gritted teeth and sweaty form, she somehow felt he was a part of her own family tree. Which branch of the family, she did not know. She only knew she felt a warmth for him. This warmth was too vague to identify but, to put it bluntly, Xiaohong wished that those gritted teeth and that perspiring body would do her. Do her with this silent momentum. And that he would do her to death. She was aware of her physical desire growing stronger recently, as if her body had suddenly discovered some new hormone.

The men in the village were not slow to pick up on emotions. On the contrary, they had a rather keen sense for it. How could Jin not sense what she was thinking now? Even if he couldn't see into her thoughts, he could certainly see what those big breasts had in mind, loafing like vagrants inside Xiaohong's clothes. Were they not just waiting for a chance to be engaged in a good day's work? Jin picked up that message easily enough and he quietly gave his reply.

'Qian Xiaohong, when you come back, I'm going to marry you and settle down,' he said.

Fourteen

I

Xiaohong had not answered Jin Haishu. After a few days, she hit the road, carrying her huge breasts. 'Carrying' being the operative word. They had grown again, quite severely, and were also drooping quite badly. Before long, she would not be able to see her belly or her knees when she walked. From her point of view, it looked like she was floating over the ground, except that her body was heavy. She wished they would just turn into Sijiang-style oranges. Honestly, oranges would be absolutely fine.

Thinking of Sijiang, she temporarily forgot about the weight of her breasts. She wondered if Sijiang had recovered and been discharged from the hospital, and whether Specs had made the complaint yet. Logically, Sijiang should receive some compensation.

And then there was the matter of Youqing's earrings. Were they Julia's? Had the murderer been found? That pervert! They ought to let him be raped by a bull, then chop off his cock and feed it to the dogs, she thought.

As Xiaohong pondered, she grew angrier. Despite her anger, she took in the rural scenery as she went. She suddenly felt that the landscape had undergone a great change. There were no more wide vistas. The land that had been empty before now housed newly built residential buildings. The windows were plastered with the sort of banners normally seen at weddings, with colourful words slapped on them. The young never like having the elderly hanging around them, preferring, instead, to be surrounded with their own kind. Nowadays, the younger generation think of all sorts of ways to live in separate quarters from the older generation of their relatives. Thus, their sex lives can be free from restraint and they can enjoy their freedom under their own roof. Once they married, they were all anxious to have children, at least two, and so the sound of a baby's cry was as common here as a dog's bark. Either could creep into the ear at any time.

When she had boarded the bus to the train station, Xiaohong leaned against the window on the right side, staring out of it. Suddenly, the scenery on the road seemed very familiar. Two minutes later, the bus turned into the road where Mr Tan, the scrap metal dealer, had his shop. Xiaohong saw two men and a woman at the door. The woman was well on her way to having a little one. The men, chewing on betel nuts, shook hands with her, and they all parted. Xiaohong saw the bald head and proud demeanour of Mr Tan and could almost hear his raucous laughter. Seeing this brief scene, like a shadow from her past, Xiaohong decided, When I get back to the hospital, the first thing I'm going to do is go for a check up and find out what the problem is.

Dr Chen was the one who did the examination. She seemed like the type who could do it all. With her index, middle and ring fingers, she pressed the area around Xiaohong's breast. Her mind elsewhere, she pressed the breast down, letting it spring back up, then pressed again. After she had done this a dozen times or so, she said mysteriously, 'Youqing was cheating with Dr Lei, did you know?'

Xiaohong was used to the way doctors would talk about matters completely unrelated to the check-up they were carrying out. Hearing Dr Chen's news, she said, 'Dr Lei was cheating with all the female doctors. It wouldn't surprise me if he'd had an affair with you too!'

'Dr Lei, that satyr, I can't seem to get away from him! He was hauled in by the cops. You didn't know?' Dr Chen leaked out all the information she knew.

Xiaohong was shocked. She grabbed Dr Chen's hand and held it. Amazed, she asked, 'What had he done?'

'Raped a prostitute. Then murdered her so there wouldn't be a witness.'

'No! What do you need to rape a prostitute for? Just give her money and you can have your way.'

'It's not that simple. Could be he did it and didn't want to pay so the hooker objected. Anyway, he got caught. What the circumstances surrounding it were, I don't really know. I just heard that Youqing had some earrings that belonged to the dead hooker.'

'Oh!' It suddenly hit Xiaohong and she grabbed the three fingers Dr Chen was pressing against her breast, saying, 'You mean Julia Wilde's murderer has been caught?'

'Ah Hong, what're you so excited for? You mean to say that prostitute was a friend of yours?' She extracted her three fingers from Xiaohong's grip and pulled out the mammogram reader. She looked at it for about ten seconds then turned it off.

'Anything wrong?' Xiaohong did not understand the grey lumps she had seen on the screen.

'Nah. You're alright. A bit of breast hyperplasia. I'll give you a prescription for some medicine you can take. Make it a habit to do some massaging before you go to bed and then again when you get up. That'll increase the blood circulation. When you bathe, make sure you scrub yourself thoroughly.' From Dr Chen's reply, it seemed as if she had seen a lot of such cases.

'Dr Chen, do you think they're a lot bigger than before? Will they just go on growing and growing like this? That's too scary to think of!' Xiaohong didn't quite trust the machine and she was also a little sceptical about Dr Chen.

'Ah Hong, you've got quite an imagination. That's just an old wives' tale. You think they'll grow so much they'll be like sacks of rice? If that ever happens, you'll certainly make the news! Silly girl.'

Dr Chen said the final two words in a drawling Cantonese. Amused, Xiaohong punched her playfully, saying, 'Give me a cheaper, more effective cure. If you can save me a little money that would be best.'

II

The fellow with big feet was mysterious. His senses were better than a dog's. The previous time he had come to the hospital, he had caught Xiaohong on her birthday. Now, having just returned from the funeral, here he was again. She had spent half a day on the bus, then taken the overnight train. Her legs were sore and her bones ached. All she wanted to do was sleep as soon as her shift at the hospital finished. And yet, here stood Bigfoot, having gone to the publicity department looking for her again.

He ate half an apple, fidgeting constantly. He'd just begun his ma-noeuvres when Xiaohong said in an indifferent tone, 'Please don't come here looking for me anymore.'

'Why?' he asked incredulously. 'You've changed!' Frustration shaded his face.

'No reason. And I haven't changed. It's no different from the way I slept with you without any reason. Whatever happens just happens. I don't force myself to do anything.'

Xiaohong could not even really explain it to herself. Why had she gone to bed with Bigfoot so easily, without a second thought? It was as if she were as easy as a prostitute. But, in another sense, she wasn't like a prostitute at all, in that she didn't need anyone to give her money to do it.

Xiaohong really wanted to shed some light on the matter, but felt it was no use. Bigfoot would just give her a good scolding anyway. But then, hadn't Xiaohong herself just said she was like a prostitute? What suitable words could he find to curse her after that? All the same, he did want to curse her.

'Fuck! I've been duped!' Humiliated, he tested the room's floorboards, stomping up and down. 'You women! Such bitches! You're heartless!' His gait was like Charlie Chaplin's, though not quite as exaggerated.

Strangely, only now did Xiaohong take in Bigfoot's appearance clearly for the first time. She looked at him carefully. This was the third time she had seen him since they had met. After they had parted on the previous two occasions, she had not been able to recall what he looked like, no matter how hard she tried. Even the feeling of him against her body was only a vague impression. She had never given him a serious thought. He had come to look for her again, which she found quite incredible. She really didn't want him to come back. She didn't want to carry on with him, so there was no reason for them to meet again.

'Am I toying with you? Did that woman you lived with toy with you? Isn't it you who didn't want her? I haven't played with your feelings at all. Did I ever say I loved you? Did I even say I *wanted* to fall in love with you, or to marry you?' Xiaohong got more upset as she spoke. She felt the swelling of her breasts. They were tight and numb. She felt an urge to massage them.

Bigfoot still stood there staring at her, not moving. It seemed he could not make himself believe that this was actually happening.

'Bitch! *Bitch*! You're all bitches!' Bigfoot stomped as he cursed.

'If you're not leaving, I'll go. When you do go out, please make sure you close the door behind you.'

Xiaohong turned to go, but as soon as she had spoken, Bigfoot manoeuvred his way in front of her and squeezed past. She heard the pounding of his feet as he ran down the stairs.

III

Xiaohong dragged her feet as she exited the publicity room. She leaned against the wall. It was cold. Her muscles seemed to latch onto it and she immediately felt more comfortable. She overheard the new girl in the publicity department saying, 'Her waves are huge. When you men see such big waves, what do you think?'

Xia retorted, 'When you see a strong, muscular guy, what do you think?'

The girl immediately responded, 'I want to do him! I want to do it with him!'

Turning the corner, Xiaohong could not hear Xia's response. As she started down the stairs, she noticed she had left a handprint in the dust on the handrail and that there was a thick layer of dust on her hand. So she kept hold of the handrail and walked down the stairs, revealing a freshly cleaned coat of red paint as she went.

Before Bigfoot had shown up, Xia had told her, 'Personnel decisions were made by Dr Lei and the hospital – though Dr Lei isn't here at the moment. If you want to change jobs, you'll have to wait for him to come back or until a new chairman takes office.'

Xia, that cocky bastard, looked at her helplessly. She was on the verge of blowing the whistle on him and Youqing but her swelling bust always seemed to hurt more when she got angry, so she dropped it. She tried to keep herself calm.

Xiaohong realised that Dr Lei and Xia had ganged up on her and she had been taken in. They had sent her down to the kitchen then conveniently arranged a replacement to come in and take her place, squeezing her out. And it was all because she had been appointed by Mr Liao, Dr Lei's predecessor. With the change of regime, the fate of all the common workers and petty officials hung in the balance. When Mr Liao had been around, Xiaohong could jump from the reception desk to the publicity department, where she was in close contact with the powers that be, as well as staying in touch with the masses. When Dr Lei took office, Xiaohong had been relegated to a life of washing vegetables in the kitchen.

Finally, Xiaohong couldn't stand it anymore. She thumped the desk but the sound was not very loud. She had not said a word, though in her heart she had roared furiously, If I'm gonna wash vegetables and dishes, why the hell don't I just go back to washing scalps? And you lot who are just wolves in sheep's clothing, what'll come of you? Xia, you've backed the wrong horse. If you think Dr Lei's coming back here to be hospital chairman again, you really are an idiot! As for that pervert, if he doesn't get executed, it'll be a waste of the justice system. Xiaohong's breasts quaked, undulating under her blouse like stones falling in a landslide.

As she reached the first floor, the lift opened to deposit the next batch of sickly people at their destination. A familiar face with high cheekbones and tiny eyes was among them. The face was covered in a layer of skin deadened by acne. The hair was now cut short and the stomach protruded, though not necessarily in a way that indicated that she was pregnant. Yet, somehow, one could tell she was expecting at a mere glance.

'Zhang Weimei!' Xiaohong called.

The pregnant woman turned and saw Xiaohong and was so surprised she nearly dropped the box of medicine she was carrying. She looked like she wanted to hide. Xiaohong caught her and said, 'You're married!'

Weimei smiled reluctantly. A man of thirty or forty stood behind her, a vacant look on his face.

'Your husband?' Xiaohong whispered.

She shook her head.

'Let's go and get something to drink and have a chat.'

Meeting Weimei now, Xiaohong felt very warm towards her. She would never have expected this herself, nor would she have imagined Weimei would be so annoyed to see her. She would have hoped at least to provoke a trace of happiness. Xiaohong could not quite tell what she was thinking, so she grabbed the other girl's hand and took her to the canteen.

'They're... big!' Weimei hesitated a moment, but still went ahead and said it.

'They've grown a lot. A real burden. I had them examined. It's breast hyperplasia. I have to take medicine for it.'

'I see. How're Wu Ying and everyone? Still working at the Qianshan Hotel?'

'Nah. Wu Ying got divorced then went to work in a factory. I haven't heard from her in quite a while. Ah Xing's a mother now. And married to Li Xuewen, of course.'

'Mm-hm.'

'You got your residency card settled?'

'Nope. Can't afford it.'

'Even with that twenty thousand Hong Kong dollars?'

'What twenty thousand? Where do you think I picked up twenty thousand from?'

'That day when the cops investigated, they said it was twenty thousand.'

'They're full of crap. There was less than eight thousand.'

'So little? That's not even worth the trouble. Especially since you've had to stay in hiding for so long.'

'There was over twenty thousand to begin with. But they took most of it and lost it gambling before I ever saw it. Anyway, I guess I should go. He's waiting.' Outside the window, the man of thirty or forty stood shifting his weight from one foot to the other, frequently looking at his watch. Weimei looked a little helpless.

'Who is he, not your husband?'

'No. I'm not married.'

'The child's his?'

'I'll give it to him when it's born. He'll pay me for it.'

'You're a surrogate for him?'

'According to the ultrasound, it's a boy. I'll get twelve thousand *kuai* for it. The previous one was a girl. Only eight thousand.'

'Weimei!'

'Oh, it's alright with me,' she said quietly, putting a hand on the table to push herself up. She fiddled with her blouse, then stopped and said, 'Ah Hong, would you be up for it? I can talk to him. You're pretty. You'd fetch a higher price.'

Xiaohong immediately shook her head.

Weimei scrunched up her face, turning away awkwardly. Xiaohong watched her waddle out.

The girl disappeared from view.

IV

The sun seemed swollen as it dropped towards the horizon, like a head burying itself under a blanket. It had a choking effect, making even the trees and plants look heavy. People walking along the road squinted. Only, having left the hospital for good, Xiaohong felt like she was floating. Her breasts were like wings, bearing her up over the city to fly in the air above. A bird's eye view spread out beneath her. The air was cold and the wind grazed her ear. She was like a mermaid, trailing her tail behind her as she floated.

Xiaohong grinned. Something salty trickled into the corner of her mouth. She wiped it away and found that she was covered in sweat. Her feet were still plodding forward at a steady pace, like an old beggar woman. She stopped on the pavement in the shade of a tree, using her hands to fan herself. She saw a bus stop about five hundred metres away. Five hundred metres! But honestly, even if it was just five metres, she wasn't sure she'd be able to make it. She couldn't carry on, couldn't manage to move those two sacks of rice any further. She no longer thought of them as breasts, but as two beggar's sacks, waiting to be filled up with life and achievement. They were not a source of happiness or pleasure. They just kept weighing her down, pulling her down towards the ground. She doggedly supported herself, not believing she could be crushed by parts of her own body. She had stopped caring long ago that no one touched them anymore. She didn't bother about them any more than she did her feet, coldly ignoring them. And she didn't even mind about those men who had climbed upon them. She only minded that they were still growing.

Why did they just keep growing?

It was only half-an-hour's bus journey to Li Sijiang's, but it was more trying than travelling from Hunan to Shenzhen. She stopped her flight, descending to earth once again so she could board the minibus.

As she boarded, her right leg got caught in the door as it closed behind her. She thought that, with a bit of effort, she could force it free, making it keep up with the left leg as normal, and go and find a seat. But, after several tugs on it, she realised that each pull was weaker than the last. The people at the bus stop behind her just stared up at her arse, pressed up against the glass door of the bus and twisting this way and that, her left leg jerking inside her oversized trousers as she turned her hips. She just could not free it from the door.

Finally, a kind man behind her gave her a push and she managed to get on to the bus. As she moved along the bus, she saw there was no seat. Breathing heavily, she leaned against the back of a seat and wiped the sweat away. When the bus moved, she began to shake badly. To be more accurate, it was her breasts that quivered badly, as if they'd come to life. Xiaohong was shoved further down the bus. She planted her feet firmly on the floor, one hand grasping the pole. But in the end, she could no longer hold on. When the bus accelerated again, she fell, breasts first, against the man who was sitting in front of her. He stood up, primly offering her his seat. She had never felt such sweltering heat. She sat, putting her breasts on her lap and wiping her sweat. Her clothes were soaked.

The gate at Li Sijiang's apartment was not locked. Xiaohong leaned against the wall and weakly knocked on the door. She thought Sijiang would open it immediately and offer her a cup of water to gulp down. After her bus ride in the heat, she felt she would die of thirst.

But no one answered.

She knocked again. Still no one answered. Xiaohong felt something was wrong. She pressed her face up against the window. Through the glass, she saw Sijiang lying on the bed. Her hands and feet were spread out, rigid. She looked dead.

'Li Sijiang! Open up!' Xiaohong beat on the door with all her might. She banged on the window, but Sijiang was motionless. Xiaohong's head was swimming as she tried to force the window open. She shouted for help. A few blue collar workers rushed over from the neighbouring flat. They smashed the window and climbed in.

For a moment, Xiaohong was not even sure this girl was Sijiang. Her face was similar to Sijiang's, but it was long, not round. The lips were pale, the face blanched. Blood ran constantly from her left wrist. Her tiny eyes were like a thread. She opened them a moment.

'Sijiang! What have you done? Fuck!' Xiaohong saw that familiar pair of eyes and she could not keep from swearing and crying. Someone wrapped Sijiang's wound and several people rushed her to the hospital. Xiaohong's tears flowed down her face. Her heart broke, shattered, splattering like a pile of pig manure dropped on the road.

'Sijiang, Sijiang! What happened? What happened?' Xiaohong moved as quickly as she could, following them to the hospital. It was like she was trying to keep up with the answer to that question. The blood from Sijiang's body made her despair. Her clothes clung to her, clammy. They were wet, then dry, then wet again. She was cold. She wanted to burst out into mourning right there in the street. This gave her a strange expression. She was like a grief-stricken penguin. Her head and feet were small and her midsection inflated. She struggled to move her feet, paddling along with her legs. Where was she going? It wasn't like she was trying to catch up with the half-dead figure of Li Sijiang at all. Rather, it was as if she were making her way to the vast sea to swim away.

Sijiang woke up again just as the poignant light of dusk was entering the ward. Her face was tinged with sorrow. The sheets, not quite white, were stamped with a red cross. Sijiang's left wrist was bandaged and her fingers, pale and weak, rested on the red cross. On the wall, the shadows of tree branches swayed. Sijiang wanted to speak but her lips were stuck together.

'Don't talk. I'll get you some water.'

Xiaohong tried to stand up. But it was as if her clothes were nailed to the chair. When she had raised herself just a few centimetres from the seat, she felt a weight pressing her back down. She turned awkwardly and slowly poured some water. Supporting Sijiang, Xiaohong wet her lips and let her have a sip. Her eyes opened wide and she looked in astonishment at the behemoths on Xiaohong's chest.

'Sijiang, why didn't you call the police?'

'I called 110. They said, "Your domestic problems are not our business."'

'But you can't let Specs get away with this.'

'Honghong, without him, I wouldn't have got the sixty thousand in compensation anyway. It's not losing the money that I mind. I just don't like being played for a fool.'

'*Aiyah*. People in this world, they've either got designs on others or they're the victims of other people's designs. Either they scheme or they're the victims of others' schemes. You've always been too trusting.'

'I wanted to kill him.'

'You wanted to kill him, then why did you end up cutting your own veins? Idiot... Sijiang, I'm really sorry. I should never have asked you to come to Shenzhen.'

'Honghong, what're you talking about? Look at yourself. They're... what is it they've grown into?'

'I don't know. Before long, I won't be able to stand up. Bloody hell! Hey Sijiang, look... if you want to go back home, you should go. Although there's nothing much there to go back for.'

V

Throughout the journey, tears streamed down Sijiang's thin face. When they had walked to the pedestrian bridge, Sijiang put down the bag she had carried with her when she first came to Shenzhen and wiped her face a couple of times with the back of her hand. On her wrist, a white scar wormed its way across the flesh. The spots on her long face were less obvious.

'I'll write to you when I have time. Don't cry!' Xiaohong kept repeating this refrain. But Sijiang was taking all her first-time experiences and leaving them in Shenzhen. If she didn't cry, what was there to say?

How had her fresh, apple-shaped face turned into this old pumpkin seed shape? No one could say for sure any more than they could say why Xiaohong's breasts had suddenly become so huge.

A plane flew overhead, drawing a line of smoke across the blue sky. Their loneliness was like the plane, no bigger than a solitary bird, drifting across that vast empty space.

'Don't cry. Stop crying or I won't be able to stop myself either.'

Xiaohong suppressed her grief, desperately biting her lip as her eyes started to redden.

'Honghong, work out what you're going to do. Take care of yourself. I'll go on my own from here.' Sijiang nearly collapsed under the weight of her luggage. Resolute, she collected herself and strode ahead as quickly as she could.

A minibus stopped. Opening its mouth, it swallowed Sijiang up and turned towards the train station.

Xiaohong rested her breasts on the railing, watching the rear end of the vehicle carrying Sijiang until it was out of sight. She laboured, using her hands to lift first her left, then her right breast. Suddenly, she lost her balance, tilting under the weight of her right breast. She fell to the ground under the weight of her own bust. She clasped the railing, trying to stand up, like a boxer pulling himself up on the ropes. One... two...

It was like her breasts were nailed to the ground. She could not move them. She was weighed down by them, kneeling with her face just inches from the ground.

She heard the sound of footsteps and the wheels of cars. They banged past, shocking the eardrums. A deafening sound came from the gutter like the lecherous laughter of waves crashing against the shore.

She sagged yet closer to the pavement. She found herself surrounded by a crowd of feet, some in shoes, some in sandals. Some were white, others black. Wide, narrow, large, small, expensive, cheap...

In her mind's eye, she saw a pair of black boots. The very boots that had walked up and down in the detention centre. Zhu Dachang's voice was ringing in her ear, saying, 'You take care of yourself.'

Gritting her teeth, she bent her head and, hauling those two great sandbags up, she stood. She trudged out of the ring of feet surrounding her and pushed her way down from the pedestrian bridge.

Then she faded into the crowds on the street.

AFTERWORD

Northern Girls was my debut novel published in 2004 and I am so pleased that it is the first of my books to be published in English.

I have a soft spot for this novel. Written when I was an inexperienced writer, it is a work that virtually erupted into being. It is primal, natural and vibrant and, at the same time, is heavily imbued with my personal style. Like many of my readers, I am drawn to Qian Xiaohong, the protagonist, and her genuine, charming approach to life.

Qian Xiaohong is a familiar figure to me. She is typical of the people from my home village. When I started her story, I planned simply to write about the village, but once I began, I felt the place to be too restrictive for such a character. I wanted to toss her out into the wider world and see what she was destined to experience. Through the eyes of Qian Xiaohong and her companions – as well as the testimony of their bodies – we feel the cruel realities of the times and the difficulty of surviving.

These are the women on the lowest rung of the social ladder, the real working class. A vulnerable group of marginalised people, they are almost never brought to the public's attention. This often neglected segment of society demonstrates an instinctive ability to survive, and this, I thought, was something worth treasuring. They make up a large proportion of the population and do much of the nation's dirty work, quietly enduring insult and injury. The hardships they encounter are actually more shocking than anything I've recorded, reaching well beyond the scope of what is represented in my novel.

Qian Xiaohong has character. She is a principled girl, unwilling to sell herself. She's frank and kind and has a sense of responsibility. Like many who make up the lowest strata of society, she possesses an impregnable vigour and vitality. In her honest way of living, she penetrates the duality of those around her and demonstrates a desire for self-respect. Her primary motive is to carry on surviving and this drives her ever forward, constantly moving along at an untiring pace. In the wider context of rural China, being on the move like this is very much a reality that many are forced to live through.

To have created a character with this sort of drive to keep on living has been, for me, a true joy.

I want to express my gratitude to Shelly Bryant for doing the difficult job of translating my work. After our correspondence and discussions, I am filled with confidence in the English translation of *Northern Girls* and highly anticipate its release.

I am especially grateful to Penguin's Jo Lusby for her appreciation of *Northern Girls*. She is as rigorous as she is lovable. My friend Eric Abrahamsen, who has translated my short stories, has also offered much enthusiastic assistance. And I must thank my editor, Mike Tsang. One can just imagine how important he has been in the development of this work.

I consider myself very fortunate.

Sheng Keyi
Beijing
January 2012

CHINA  LIBRARY

WANG XIAOFANG

THE CIVIL SERVANT'S NOTEBOOK

Dongzhou City needs a new mayor. Devious plots, seduction, blackmail and bribery are all on the table in a no-holds-barred scramble for prestige and personal gain as the city's two vice-mayors compete for the top honour. At the centre of it all is a humble witness to events, a notebook whose pages contain information they should not ...

Penned by a former insider, *The Civil Servant's Notebook* is a political page-turner that offers a glimpse into the complex psyches of those who roam the guarded halls of Chinese officialdom.

www.penguin.com.cn

HE JIAHONG

HANGING DEVILS
Hong Jun Investigates

Set in the mid-nineties, *Hanging Devils* is a true-to-life
story of cold-blooded murder and corruption from one
of China's foremost legal experts.

Hong Jun, a recently-returned lawyer from the US,
opens a practice in Beijing intent on helping ordinary
people defend their rights. His very first case leads him
to the hinterland of China's snowy northeast where
the brutal killing of a local beauty took place ten years
earlier. In his quest for justice, Hong Jun revisits the
buried secrets of the recent past, and delves deep into
the underbelly of the provincial police and court system
in a case that proves to be anything but ordinary.

www.penguin.com.cn

CHINA LIBRARY

DIVERSE STORIES
UNIQUE PERSPECTIVES

Comprising literature and narrative non-fiction,
twentieth-century classics and contemporary bestsellers,
the China Library brings together the best of writing on
and from China, all in one dedicated series.